ALSO W

Reviews of *Tremors of the Heart*

'The book was well-researched and the descriptive language draws you into the various scenes.' (Reader from Canada)

'Can't wait to see how the powerful prologue scene fits into the rest of the story!' (Reader from Canada)

'I loved this book and found it difficult to put it down. I am a New Zealander, so am familiar with the threat of earthquakes! (Reader from New Zealand)'

'I don't normally read romantic fiction but this was romance with a difference. Very well written.'

(Reader from the U.S.)

'Sweet and satisfying romance novel…lovely prose.' (Reader from the U.S.)

Review on 'Goodreads', posted by Emily Meadows of the Online Book Club:

'If you like romance novels, you will love *Tremors of the Heart*. This is a romance novel that delivers. The characters were perfectly imperfect, and the plot was suspenseful. The villain, Mother Nature, is as unpredictable as always.'

A NOTE TO MY READERS

I hope you have already enjoyed reading my first book, *Tremors of the Heart*.

Dancing in the Mist begins *The Butterfly Trilogy*, which is linked by the friendship of three women. The women are also connected by a butterfly and it's up to the reader to find that image.

I owe the idea for *Dancing* to my mother. We took a night ferry between Wales and Ireland years ago. When we sat in the waiting room in Wales, my mom looked at all the people around us and grinned. She turned to me, a fledgling author, and said, "You should write a book that starts in this waiting room."

And here it is.

ACKNOWLEDGMENTS

A middle of the night ferry sailing to Ireland inspired this novel. Thank you to the many people who have supported making an idea reality. My husband Colin. My mother Leta, who made that ferry trip to Ireland with me and sat with me in the waiting room, watching future characters for this book. My friend Laurie Morrison, who reads all of my manuscripts and cheers me on. Bill Paull, master of Gaelic, who helped me find the name for Dorcha Dhubh. Miles Fenton, artist, for help with stages in creating a painting. Allayne Greene, owner of Belcarra Stables, for checking my steeplechase coverage and introducing me to her horses. Niki Follows, ballet dancer, for ballet terms. Theresa Renico Noble, Major, U.S. Army Retired, helicopter pilot, for guidance in the use of helicopters in maritime rescues in fog situations. Laurent Desmarais, Search and Rescue, Canadian Coast Guard, for making the ferry sinking and rescue scenes accurate. The Irish National Stud staff in County Kildare, who arranged for my husband and I to tour the stables and meet some of Ireland's 'first star' thoroughbreds. Cousin Bob Jones, for his feedback and support. Diana Gabaldon, author of *Outlander,* who read Chapter 12 of *Dancing* and said it would make a good script. Frank Daley and Chyserr, for publishing assistance. June Hutton and Cathy Scrimshaw for guidance in industry standards. Cousin Dorn Beattie, who designed an amazing cover. Karen Hutchinson, friend and editor of the 'Bumper Guardian', who kept me writing. To my father, for giving me an Irish family tree. To my brother and sister-in-law John and Carole, for their support. To 'Queenie', a bicycle I pretended was a real horse when I was 10.

EXCERPT

If he could get some rest now, he'd be more alert when they got to shore. He'd be able to keep track of Ashley's movements and track her until she passed on the package.

Then he would either turn her in or let her go.

And never see her again.

His arms tightened, drawing her closer.

He drifted and woke up, drifted and woke up, half-listening to the chatter around him, half-listening to the crew on their portable radios, keeping tabs on the other boats.

Finally, he slept again and dreamed of satin pillows and blue pansies.

"DANCING IN THE MIST"
CHAPTERS

Chapter One

"Blood, Foghorns and Mist"

They'd set up this meeting in a dark lane in Harlesden, an area of London known for gun crime, and dangerous anyway, even in daylight. They were taking a monumental risk meeting their informant here at night. Detective Inspector Daemon O'Hare knew bullets were going to be flying.

He could feel it.

Just like he could feel the Glock 26 attached to the clip on the belt under his vest.

He looked over at his partner, Sam Matthews, and they both shook their heads and scanned the windows and rooftops around them.

They'd been waiting for almost an hour, checking for texts from the rest of their squad.

"I don't feel good about this," Daemon whispered, searching the dark corners in the cobbled alleyway.

He and Sam knew how to blend in. That was part of their training for undercover work as detectives with the Metropolitan Police out of Scotland Yard. They'd both let their hair grow shaggy and neither one had shaved for at least a week. Torn jeans. Ratty jackets.

Blending in.

They hadn't slept a whole night in a week either since they'd caught wind something big was happening. The whole squad was working on it, searching databases, decoding encrypted messages and interviewing informants like this one. Trying to figure out a massive, unexplained change of money and power in shady places. High places.

And suddenly, there he was.

Sliding around the corner of the building, the man's head turned left and then right, searching the darkness. He seemed to be twitching, either from drink or fear.

Or both.

"You got my money ready?" We agreed on £200. Right? I want it now."

Daemon could smell him before he could see the dirt on his grubby hands…held out for the cash. He didn't know his real name. Too dangerous. Just like the informant didn't know Daemon's last name, or his rank.

"You have to wait. I need something from you first."

Daemon hadn't even finished talking and the bullets were already pinging off the building behind him, spraying plaster and sounding like bees.

Daemon and Sam dove for cover, pulling out their guns and training them…ready.

Daemon grabbed his informant and rolled, tucking them both behind a dumpster.

But it was already too late.

***

She was all long legs and wild dark hair. And she was beautiful.

And the timing couldn't be worse.

Daemon leaned against the wall, dragging his gaze from the woman curled up on the bench seat in the corner of the ferry waiting room.

Things had moved fast since the shooting last night. It was just this morning that he'd had a debrief meeting at the Yard and a fast trip by police helicopter to the ferry port of Holyhead, Wales. Before he'd died, the informant had muttered "2:15. Night sailing."

Daemon straightened and checked his watch. A little while more to wait, so he thought back to last night.

To the blood.

There'd been lots of it.

Blood all over Daemon's fingers as he'd knelt beside the man, desperately trying to keep him from bleeding out. He'd died anyway, but as the police ambulance had wailed in the background, Daemon had managed to understand some of his last choking words…key among them:

Ferry

Package

Kidnapping… they finally had something.

Here, amongst this mass of nighttime travelers a package was going to be passed…to the next in a long line of couriers.

A kidnapping was being planned.

***

Daemon rested his shoulders against the wall again, steady green eyes assessing each person as they arrived to wait for the 2:15 a.m. ferry to Ireland.

He was watching. Watching for something out of the ordinary.

Or maybe something that just looked like ordinary.

His gaze drifted again to the woman. He'd noticed her earlier when she'd first come in.

There was something about her that kept pulling his attention and somehow making him want to hear her voice. See the expression on her face. Talk to her. Find out who she was.

She was small, slender and had a dancer's grace when she walked. She looked young, probably mid-twenties at the most.

But he looked away again to scan the crowd and watch the doorways and think wistfully about the soft bed at his Kensington apartment in London.

His apartment held his clothes and music and soccer gear and the mystery books he loved to read. But here he was, stuck at a Welsh ferry terminal in the middle of the night.

His cleaning lady had seen more of his apartment this year than he had. It seemed like his stakeout life was taking over his real life.

But he needed to stay awake until the ferry came, so he dragged himself upright and searched the room for a better spot to blend in. His lips lifted in a wry grin as he looked at the empty space on the bench beside the woman.

***

Ashley Gallagher was dreaming.

She wriggled, in her sleep…trying to find a more comfortable spot on the hard bench. In her dream she was dancing and it was years ago. She was twelve and in the barn with her beloved Arabian horse, Sirocco.

They had been practicing for a ballet audition.

In the dream, thunder rolled in the distance as over and over and over she followed the patterns and positions, scattering dust stars and horseflies as she danced.

Plié.

Here in the darkened barn, the pure notes of the Nutcracker echoed through the rafters. Three Arabian stallions watched Ashley intently as they listened from their stalls.

Glissade.

Outside, she heard the voices of her two brothers and her dad as they moved the mares down to the river. The family's Camelot Stud boasted some of southern California's best Arabian horses and Ashley's favorite stood four stalls down, ears twitching to Tchaikovsky.

***

She jolted awake, in present time, a fine sheen of perspiration on her forehead. It was always like this. She would never forget that day.

She could still remember Sirocco's satiny black coat and softly quivering nose. He'd once been a gawky little black foal with impossibly long legs and he had pulled her heart.

She'd named him herself and whispered it now...Sirocco. It meant a wind that comes in from the Sahara Desert and reaches hurricane speeds.

Perfect.

The little guy had pedigree bloodlines and had grown up to show them in speed and endurance. He had been destined to be one of the best stallions at Camelot.

Had been.

Enough…this dream had only bad places to go and it was a long time ago.

She wriggled again and tried to find another spot until, completely frustrated, she decided to just sit up and watch the growing crowd.

As an artist, she loved to watch people and this was the perfect place. Her fingers itched for her pencils and sketchpad.

People slept on the floor, in corners, on plastic seats and benches. There wasn't a sound except for the wheezing overhead fans as they whirled their way through the silence.

Then, someone rolled over and began to snore. Someone else coughed and a baby started to cry. A head shifted here on bent arms and a body stretched over there on a pile of rolled up coats. Along the far wall two Carmelite nuns dozed, wrapped in the dark folds of their habits. They still wore the robes many other orders had discarded after Vatican II in the '60s.

This was the last stop before miles and miles and miles of open Irish Sea. Years ago, the ferry trip would have been much longer, with slower Sealink Company ferries and a destination of Dún Laoghaire, south of Dublin. Dún Laoghaire had been a sea base for raids on Britain and France way back in the 5th Century and if she had time, she'd like to see it before she went home.

But the Stena Line had bought out Sealink and the routes had been changed. Tonight, she was headed straight to Dublin.

She could have been there already. Her trusted travel agent had suggested she take the much faster Irish Ferries Company or even flown Aer Lingus and been there in less than 2 hours. But Ashley had wanted the experience. She'd wanted to try this. And the English trains were a lot of fun so the trip that way from London to the ferry had been worth it.

Now, she just wanted a nap and a bath and maybe something to eat that was warm and not just junk food. Her stomach was empty except for the three chocolate bars she'd grabbed from the vending machine earlier. Maybe some fresh air for a second or two?

She yawned and lifted her arms over her head, stretching out the kinks in her shoulders. Then stood…leaning over for a minute to massage her knee. Limping, just a little, she rolled her suitcase over to the door.

***

Across the room, Daemon missed a breath when he saw her stretch. As her arms rose, they pulled her sweater tighter against her breasts. Her breasts were small, but with her coat off now, he could see that her fine-boned body had curves in all the right places.

He gripped his cellphone and checked again for an update text from Sam. They had been friends since childhood and boarding school and had entered detective training at the same time, starting as beat cops and putting in the time and experience to reach Chief Inspector rank and their current partnership. They'd even taken firearms training together, learning to use the Glock 26 issued to plainclothes officers of the CID (Criminal Investigation Department) when they were involved in surveillance.

Like now.

No text yet. He looked up…wondering where the woman had gone.

***

Once outside, Ashley could hear the waves and the foghorns. The fog had really rolled in since she'd arrived. It smelled out here. There was a distinct 'eau de fish' held in by the towering banks of mist.

The wind blew her hair, tugging at it and whipping it into her mouth and across her face. It felt glorious…blowing the cobwebs away from her brain. In the dim light, she could just make out the barnacles crusting the supports of the wharf. Between every echoing blast of the foghorns somewhere off in the distance, she could hear the unmistakable splash of small, silver fish.

When she came back in, she went over to the ticket counter to talk to the young girl on duty to see if the ferry was going to be on time.

"Will you be in Ireland long, Miss Gallagher?"

"I don't really know. I'm going over to paint a horse. I guess it depends a lot on how long he can stand still."

The girl giggled. "And where is this horse?"

"In County Kildare, on a stud farm."

"And have you been painting for a long time?" The girl was now showing more interest than Ashley could handle at this hour of the night and the seat in the corner was calling her name. She just wanted to curl up and sleep again until the ferry came.

"Yes, a long time." Ashley turned away before the girl had a chance to say anything more.

She walked back over to the bench and tried to get comfortable.

Her head cradled on one hand, she yawned and searched the room again for interesting faces. And she saw the stranger she'd noticed earlier. Her first impression had been one of height.

The stranger dominated the space around him with his lean, rangy build. He was tall but not heavy and there would be muscles under his leather coat. There had been a sense of powerful confidence about him as he'd come in earlier, bringing in swirling mist and night air when he'd opened the terminal door. He paused now, and seemed to search every corner and examine every unmoving figure.

She felt a strange tug as he hesitated a heartbeat to look her way.

Apparently satisfied, he started over towards the check-in desk. Overhead lights shone on blond, shaggy hair. He was too far away for her to see the color of his eyes, but possibly blue to match the light hair.

He only carried a small duffle bag over his shoulder and she thought maybe he was meeting someone instead of traveling himself?

At the counter, the man paused; once again searching the room with a gaze so intent Ashley was convinced that he was looking for someone. He leaned one hip against the wall as he waited and then dug a lean-fingered hand into the pocket of his coat. Ashley heard the distant growl of his voice as the clerk appeared and the sound reminded her of lions.

She watched, curious, as the man produced his cellphone and slid it across the counter. The clerk shook her head and handed it back.

"You're quite certain?"

"Yes, sir. Absolutely. Maybe later?"

Ashley didn't hear anything else. Exhausted, she squirmed against the unrelenting seat and adjusted her denim bag under her chin. Yawning again, she decided not to fight it any longer and put her head back, thinking about a comfortable bed. Warm sheets…she squirmed on the seat…satin pillows maybe. Resting her cheek against her bag, she drifted into an uneasy sleep.

***

It was Shaughnessy Ryan! The text from Sam had just come in with a picture. Team members in Daemon's squad had been working their computers, searching names the informant had struggled to get out.

Shaughnessy had been one of those names. The Specialist Crime Directorate at Scotland Yard had traced him this far and the confirmed report had him on the 2:15 a.m. Stena Line ferry to Ireland.

Curious? Yes. Circumstantial? Daemon didn't think so.

He raked his fingers through his hair and groaned, thinking of the hours they'd all just spent pouring over those names with Chief Superintendent McBride. Daemon had worked with the Directorate on special assignments for years. This branch of England's CID was the only one that was set up to chase criminals like Ryan across international borders.

Daemon could still hear McBride's voice, rough with too much coffee and not enough sleep. "You've got a jump on this case, Daemon. We've got our links ready in Ireland. The Irish police… the Garda… and their detectives are standing by if you have to go that far. And listen…every person on this list is dangerous. Watch your back."

Now he had a face.

No need to make an arrest. He just needed to see who Shaughnessy passed the package to next and follow them. If things got ugly, he had his Glock in his duffle and McBride had alerted Customs and the ferry company that he would be armed.

Now he needed that spot to blend in.

The woman was curled up asleep again in the corner of the bench seat and there would be just enough room for him to squeeze in. He couldn't see much of her now, even as he walked closer. A thick fall of long, dark, curly hair partly hid her face and he could only see a small chin, straight nose and the side of a smooth pale cheek. Her hair was so dark it almost looked black.

Intrigued, Daemon felt an unusual urge to push aside all that silky hair to get a better look.

He tried to accommodate his rangy 6'2" length on the seat without disturbing her, and sighed. No matter how many years ahead on the force he would never get used to lack of sleep and hard benches like this.

***

As the woman slept, he pulled out his cellphone, eyeing Shaughnessy's picture and pages of booking sheets. Everything from petty theft to breaking and entering to major crimes like the one he was part of now.

The curtain of hair beside him twitched slightly, catching Daemon's notice, though he'd been conscious of her anyway. There was something about the slender shape tucked up under the trench coat and the occasional drift of a light, tropical perfume that he couldn't quite identify.

He watched, transfixed, as a delicate hand emerged from under the coat. He felt unexpectedly pleased to see that the hand bore no rings. A muffled groan escaped and a tousled butterfly came crawling out of its cocoon.

Confused eyes still swam with the fuzziness of sleep. The depth of the blue stunned him. They were almost like the pansies in his mother's garden back home.

Feathery eyebrows drew together in a frown and her pale skin grew even paler. It was the suddenly ashen face that pulled Daemon's attention to her obvious distress.

"Are you alright?" Daemon watched as the confusion cleared and she seemed to try to wake up completely.

"Ow!"

"Are you alright? What's wrong?" he repeated. She winced in obvious pain.

"My knee. I'm sorry, but my knee is cramping. Ow!"

He watched as she uncoiled those long, long legs and reached forward to massage her knee and calf muscle. Her long hair drifted forward in a cloud and the soft, sweet scent of her perfume teased his nose again.

Had he just heard an American accent?

"Maybe I can help. My sister has a bad knee and this works for her." Daemon didn't give her a chance to say no; he just reached over to move her hands out of the way, sympathetic when he felt the strength of the knotted muscles around her knee.

***

Ashley jumped at the feel of his fingers on her skin. Their heat seemed to seep into the cramp and she forgot how to use words. She just watched him knead and rub and push into the pressure points until the knot started to loosen and give way.

She'd thought earlier that his voice reminded her of a lion. And he had that shaggy fair hair. Up close, his face was strong and compelling in a craggy sort of way and she had to fight to keep from touching the rough beard stubble on his jaw. His face was only a few inches away and she could almost feel the rasp of that stubble on her fingertips.

She sat on her hands.

His eyes weren't blue after all. They were green! As he looked up and saw that she was watching him, the green darkened to emerald.

"Better?"

"Hmm?

"Is the cramp going away?" The man leaned back on his heels and waited.

"Oh." Ashley experimented. She gingerly eased her leg off the bench and onto the floor, waiting for the screaming pain to start again. It didn't. She took one long, tentative breath and then another.

Then she smiled.

***

For a moment Daemon again forgot to breathe. The spontaneous smile lit up her face; a face filled with pure relief and delighted surprise. A soft, rosy blush had come back to her cheeks as the pain disappeared and she no longer looked like she might pass out.

"How on earth did you do that? I've never been able to make it go away that fast! Thank you so much. I think I overdid the walking today and my knee couldn't take it."

"Not a problem. That looked painful. Why don't you prop your leg up? Here…"

He lifted her leg and rested it on his own knee. It felt sort of right that it was there. She must have felt a connection too because he could see questions in her expression.

"All I can say is thank you. Did you say your sister hurt her knee? What happened?"

"Rugby."

"Pardon?"

"She was playing rugby and got kicked in the knee. Hard. With cleats."

"Ouch!"

"What about you?"

"I had an accident when I was twelve."

She visibly pulled away from something that seemed to bring her bad memories. Daemon had seen crooks clam up this quickly when they were being questioned. But there was something else here.

The animation in her intriguing voice stilled. Until this moment he'd been caught by the softness in that voice and wondered again if she might be American.

But he didn't really have time in his life for softness anyway. There was no place in his life for anything but long, lonely stakeouts in bleak places like this.

And he was on a job and a life was depending on what he was able to find out tonight.

He dragged his attention away from her with surprising effort and carefully checked the dark corners and huddled shapes again. No Shaughnessy. He slumped in his seat.

"Look," he said. "I'm going to go and get a coffee. Would you like one too?"

He watched as she turned to face him again and focused on her soft lips as they lifted in a smile.

***

"I would love a coffee. Thank you. Let me…"

Ashley looked in her pocket for some change but he was up and gone before she had a chance. His long-legged stride had already taken him halfway to the machines on the other side of the hall. She watched as his leather jacket strained across his shoulder when he reached into the back pocket of his jeans. He shifted his duffle to the side as he put coins into the machine.

Unable to look away, she shook her head at what was happening.

Okay. Nothing was happening except an outrageously good-looking stranger with amazing hands.

She suddenly felt warm.

Hunger! That's it. She was hungry.

She reached into her denim bag. The crackle of paper told her she'd found her one surviving chocolate bar. She unwrapped it and left half on the seat for the stranger.

She was just pulling a brush through her tangled hair when he came back. The strong smell of black coffee drifted her way and she looked up.

"What?"

He was staring.

"Nothing. You just have beautiful hair. I didn't know if you took milk or sugar so I haven't added anything. Sorry." He handed her one of the cups.

***

Daemon eased back onto the seat, smiling as she handed him part of her bar. He noticed a tiny speck of chocolate at the inside corner of her top lip and then pulled his suddenly unprofessional thoughts together and tried to remember why he was here. Instead, he found a million questions he wanted to ask. Maybe if he kept scanning, kept an eye on the room while he talked?

Blending in.

Right?

"Do you have a name?"

There, that was the first and most important of questions. Followed by an unspoken one. Was she married? Would she like to spend the rest of her life with him? Daemon shook himself away from that train of thought. Not now. Not in his line of work. Not ever.

She smiled again and without hesitation her answer came in that soft, accented voice.

"Ashley."

Daemon held out his hand. "Daemon."

Her much smaller hand met his in what should have been a friendly 'strangers in the night' kind of handshake.

Daemon half expected her to pull away. When she didn't, he found his gaze drawn again to her mouth. Would it be as soft as it looked? He had a mental image of running his fingers over the edge of her top lip...

The intercom blasted into the silence, its shrill whine jerking their hands apart and driving Daemon to his feet. He picked up his coffee and turned. "I have to stretch my legs. I'll be back." Thoughts raced through his head as he walked...he needed to find a dark corner...needed to watch for Shaughnessy...needed to have his head examined.

***

Ashley watched him walk away, her thoughts almost matching his...I don't know who he is and I'll never find out. He probably has a wife. He's probably even a crook the way he keeps searching this room. He's probably running from the police or something. I need my head examined.

***

Then another stranger arrived. This one stood in the doorway and seemed to grab at the door frame for support. Ashley watched him in fascination as he awkwardly tried to pass through the sleeping crowd on the floor. He bumped the leg of a small, red-haired boy, asleep clutching his battered suitcase. The case slid out from under the boy's chin and he woke up, fists ready. But the man growled and his size must have made the boy think twice. He was heavy as well as tall.

"Doesn't take much of a guess as to why he's late," chuckled the lady one bench over. "I saw him in the pub hours ago! He could hardly stand even then."

"Really?" Ashley followed the man's unsteady progress to the check-in counter. "He's huge," she whispered to the other woman.

She catalogued his features: Grey unkempt beard, greasy-looking hair. Dirty, badly fitting clothes. He looked a bit mean. He probably weighed over 250 pounds, and most of it was likely too much beer. Oh, she thought…it would be ale over here.

He was definitely drunk.

"Excuse me," she asked the other lady. "Could you please watch this spot? The man who was sitting here should be back in a minute. I just need to move around a bit." She flexed her knee; grateful the cramp was gone. She took a deep breath and rose carefully, grabbing her coat and denim bag.

More and more people were arriving now and the clock was ticking closer to boarding time. A quick walk around the waiting room and she thought she'd live. Turning to go back to her seat, she felt someone grab her shoulder.

"Pardon me, beautiful lady. How did I get lucky enough to travel on this boat with a sweet thing like yourself?"

The rough voice behind her was whiskey thick and the stench of it hung in the air. Without even looking, she knew who it was.

She shrugged off his hand and turned to get out of his way, coming face to face with him and getting a much closer look than she'd wanted. Far away he'd been disgusting. Up close he was even more disgusting.

She pulled away but he wouldn't let go.

"Leave me alone." Ashley tried to keep her voice calm and searched the room for Daemon. He made her feel uncomfortable too but in a completely different way.

The man suddenly staggered and knocked her bag to the floor. For a drunk, his movements were surprisingly smooth as he bent over, picked it up and handed it back to her. "My apologies young miss. I won't be botherin' you again this night."

Then he was gone, melting into the darkness beyond the Exit door.

***

Across the room, Daemon emerged from the shadows, his cynicism re-established; suddenly more tired than he had ever been. He remembered what McBride had said. "Shaughnessy will either be going across on the ferry or he'll pass the package on to someone else at the terminal." The words echoed in Daemon's head. "If he gets on the ferry, follow him. If he passes along the package, your backup outside will watch to see where he goes and they'll grab him. He's just a small fish but we'll sit on him. See what he has to say."

And then the rest…

"You need to stick to the package. We need to find out what it is and where it goes next."

Stick to the package. And guess who had the package now?

In the half-dark outside, as he'd stood fighting the urge to go back to ask Ashley more of those million questions, he'd seen Shaughnessy go in. He didn't need to pull out the picture on his cell. He'd never forget a face that ugly.

Daemon had slid in behind him and watched. Shaughnessy didn't really need to pretend to be drunk. Waves of whiskey followed him in the door. He'd looked over the crowd, much like Daemon had done earlier.

When Daemon had first spotted Ashley heading back to their seat, he'd cursed his job. He couldn't follow her. He couldn't leave his spot. And then he was ready to forget the job and be a bodyguard because he saw Shaughnessy cut her off and grab her. Daemon felt a surge of protectiveness he'd never felt before and had to stop himself from acting on it.

He couldn't blow his cover. He didn't know if Shaughnessy would recognize him. And then he felt something completely different and his eyebrows rose.

He could see that Ashley was angry. She'd pulled away. Her face was flushed and she didn't look happy. Too bad he wasn't close enough to hear what they'd been saying. It looked like she was telling him off.

And then it was even harder to stay in the shadows when Ashley was jolted and her bag fell to the floor.

An accident? A choreographed move?

And Daemon's heart sank.

Shaughnessy, faster than such a big man should be able, had scooped it up for her. But first he'd slipped a small brown package into the top opening.

The package Daemon now had to follow.

And he had a whole new set of questions he'd have to ask her…likely in the interview room of an Irish jail cell after she passed the package to the next courier.

The night suddenly stretched ahead of him interminably. He curled his aching shoulders forward and stared at the Exit door. Shaughnessy had left behind an oily darkness that made Daemon want to head back to his comfortable bed in London.

He knew Sam and the others would trail Shaughnessy and then scoop him up. He would be in his own jail cell in the morning. For crimes pending…lots of them.

He looked around for Ashley, this time with reluctance. She was back at the bench, watching the clock, one delicate foot balanced on her bag.

Daemon had wondered about the seeming fragility in this woman. He'd seen sadness when she'd withdrawn after his question about how she'd hurt her knee.

For a short while he'd almost wanted to….

"The ferry has now arrived. All foot passengers please proceed to the boarding area." The intercom's loud blare drove passengers to their feet.

Daemon shook his head as he moved out of the shadows. Now he had a reason for following her. Not exactly what he'd been thinking about though. Pushing his way through the milling crowd towards her, he kept seeing images of her smile and that sweetly innocent mouth. The images jarred with the ones of her with Shaughnessy.

Even that she would be breathing the same air. Who'd have thought? Who'd have thought she'd be the one? That she was part of this?

He took out his cellphone and sent off a request to run her name through the database. He'd checked for her name on the ferry list to see if she had a passport picture that had been scanned at Customs.

He almost didn't want to know what the squad found on her.

If Shaughnessy was a small fish, was Ashley another one? Or was she a shark? There was a high-level kidnapping in the wind. Something big. Scotland Yard didn't think the actual couriers knew the details. They usually didn't. If that were the case, maybe Ashley would only get a minimum sentence; probably in some American prison. She sounded American. He hadn't had a chance to ask where she was from.

One of those million questions that wouldn't matter now.

He saw her look up at him. Her face registered something. Was it gladness that he was coming back? Was it practiced or spontaneous? He took a deep breath.

Be detached. Controlled. Reserved.

He hated his job.

Maybe he'd just do this last assignment. Maybe then he'd get some nice desk job so he could go home to bed every night. Or maybe change jobs completely. The thoughts rattled around inside his head like some kind of promise.

***

Ashley watched as Daemon crossed the room, passing through the suddenly active crowd. Something was different. His eyes were chilly now; his lips set in a firm, straight line. Tired. That was it. He was as fed up with waiting as she was. With something edging on disappointment that she was about to see the last of him, Ashley shrugged into her coat and shouldered her tote bag. She'd already checked her suitcase. The one with the tubes of specialized paints she'd had to go through hoops with Customs about. She needed them for the commission in Ireland. Her brushes were in there too, and most of her clothes. All that was in the duffle was her overnight stuff. And something she didn't know about.

If she hadn't been wearing her coat, she'd have noticed the sharp edges of a package she'd never seen before. A package that nestled just inside the top of the bag.

She nodded to Daemon as he drew up beside her and felt something completely different from Shaughnessy's rough grab. When Daemon put his hand on the center of her back, it was just to gently guide her through the huge line heading out the doors onto the loading platform.

***

People had come out of their cars in the parking lot, streaming down the pier from the village, or up off the floor and benches of the waiting room. All wore the long wait on their exhausted faces. Faces that were wrinkled with sleep if they'd been lucky enough to grab a nap somewhere.

The line was gradually herded through Security and up the steep gangplank under the glare of the huge dock lights. The ferry was huge. It loomed above the crowd and its massive funnels seemed to climb up into the night sky. Lights blinked in the stateroom portholes and winked on and off in the mist.

As Ashley reached the ferry's deck, Daemon stepped away from her and nodded. All he said was a strangely terse "Have a good crossing. Look after that knee."

And then he was lost in the massive crowd.

Feeling strangely empty, she followed a steward down a hall to the stateroom decks, her ears ringing with the pounding of the engines. There wouldn't be a lot of time to actually sleep, but maybe she could grab a decent nap actually lying down on a real bed.

***

Daemon checked to make sure Ashley was out of sight before he flashed his badge and I.D. at the officials. He got them to look up her stateroom number. Not that she could go anywhere until they docked in just over three hours.

It was rotten luck this job hadn't ended at the terminal; rotten luck Ashley was the next link.

Rotten luck she was the first woman in years who had caught hold of something inside him.

He grimaced as he thought of the hours ahead. The staterooms were all booked. Even police connections couldn't get him a bed.

But he had ferry police taking a shift for him, stationed outside Ashley's stateroom. So, he could catch a nap for a few minutes.

The observation deck was already crowded with dozing figures…the other squirming, uncomfortable unfortunates who would have to make do. Daemon grumbled, adjusting his creaking body onto yet another bench. From time to time his head dropped heavily, only to jerk up again as he gazed into the murky darkness of the Irish Sea.

Unexpected angles and possibilities had teased him tonight. Possibilities of a connection with a woman like Ashley. They whirled in his brain and he rubbed the aching spot on his forehead.

As he struggled to find a more comfortable position he sighed under his breath, "I hope she gets seasick down there in her cozy bed." His stomach suddenly rolled as the ferry left the sheltered Welsh harbor and met the open ocean. With each surfing dip into the waves the ferry lurched and he cursed the fries and hamburger he'd grabbed at the pub earlier. He was beginning to feel green.

***

To the east, a figure stood huddled by a darkened car, murmuring into his cellphone.

"I found a link," he slurred. "An easy mark. The tag on her bag said 'Ashley Gallagher' and gave her Dublin hotel. Can you believe the luck?"

He stopped to take a drink from his bottle.

Liquid heat. It felt good.

"Bless us, this night went well. I've called Connor. The lad will be waiting in the lobby of her hotel and grabbing the bag from her when she checks in."

A moment's silence and a frown crossed his face.

"No, t'isn't risky at all. I know, I know. It's changing the plan. I know I was supposed to be on that ferry. Don't worry. We'll fix it on the other end. If we have to, the lad will just kill her and grab the package."

The misty night swallowed Shaughnessy as he stared out to where the sea should be. Shivering, he huddled into his shabby coat. He needed one more small drink before heading home.

He lifted the bottle again to his mouth, gulping and then spitting it out as he saw two uniformed officers materialize out of the fog.

"Shaughnessy, we need to have a conversation. You'll be coming with us," he heard one of them say. And before he could blink and start to run, his hands were behind his back.

Any thoughts he'd had about being a clever soul were suddenly gone. Now he just had to keep his mouth shut or there would be a bullet in his forehead instead of a pat on the back.

***

Shaughnessy's plan had been perfect. Except that the plan was about to change. Miles to the west, in the thickening fog, another ship rolled on the waves. A ghostly dark shape was chugging its way through the night, the freighter's steady journey edging it closer and closer into the same patch of ocean as the Stena ferry.

As Daemon restlessly tossed on the deck bench and Ashley lay in her stateroom (pillow over her ears to muffle the thumping of the ferry's engines), the freighter's skipper yawned.

Too many nights at sea fogged his tired brain. He missed the imperceptible shift of the compass. The freighter churned onward in the salty spray on a collision course with the ferry.

Still miles away, the Stena Lines emblem caught stray bits of mist-muffled starlight. Then it, too, disappeared into the mist.

Chapter Two

"Restless Dreams, Icy Waters"

Thunder rolled through Ashley's nightmare. Fine tremors shook her body and she pulled her blankets closer. She was back in her parents' barn and she was only twelve and everything was on fire. She pressed both hands against her ears to shut out the claps of thunder and the echoes reverberating everywhere around her.

"No. No," she moaned. Dark images of Sirocco filtered through her restless dream. She held out her arms, needing to reach out across the wall of flames. Then Sirocco was gone, the memory teasing her, taunting her. It was just on the other side of her tightly closed eyelids. Bunching the covers in clenched fingers, she could hear the running footsteps, the shouts and screams. They seemed so real and so much closer than they usually were.

The thunder was right on top of her and she could hear shouts. "Get out! Get out!"

Tears streamed down her hot cheeks as Ashley bunched the pillow against her chest, hugging it for support and comfort. In her dream she ran again to unlatch the stalls but her feet were so slow and her hands were so clumsy. The fire bell rang and rang and rang, right by her head. It filled her ears with its ringing. Her breath came in gasps and she reached up in her dream to brush the burning cinders as they landed on her face and legs.

"Wait! I'm coming! I'm coming!" She cried out in her sleep, her face contorted.

The deafening crack of the beam in the barn's roof always came at the end of her dream… that and Sirocco's scream. She heard the cracking and waited, heart stopped, for the scream. It came. But it merged this time with other screams. They seeped into Ashley's nightmare and they didn't belong.

Her brows drew together in confusion as she struggled to figure out what was different. There hadn't been knocking on a door before.

"Miss! Miss! The ferry's going down! Miss! Wake up!"

Ashley woke to a completely black world.

Black, except for the light coming from under her door. There were screams. The thunder was real. Except that it wasn't thunder at all.

Scrambling off the bed, Ashley searched for the lamp. She flicked the switch but nothing happened even when she tried over and over. Her dream was still fresh and the tears on her cheeks were wet and salty. Her throat felt scratchy from crying and her fingers shook as she fumbled for the door in the dark. She got it open at last, searching for the person who was shouting. It was the steward, pounding on the stateroom door next to her and whirling to head on to the next one. And there was a ferry policeman too. He was carrying a huge flashlight and the lights in the hall were flickering.

"What's happening?" She yelled to the policeman as she grabbed her shoes and coat, glad she hadn't bothered to get undressed before she'd crawled under the covers.

The floor lurched under her feet and the engines stuttered and then stopped altogether. The incessant throbbing had been awful but the sudden silence was terrifying.

"A freighter's run into us. There's a huge hole in the hull and we're going down. You need to get to your lifeboat station on Deck B! I'll get you there. Do you have your bag?"

Ashley was suddenly wide-awake, adrenalin rushing as she grabbed her tote bag and the lifejacket that hung on the back of the stateroom door. Seconds later she was following the policeman down the companionway.

Out in the open it wasn't silent at all. The night was alive with sound… metal rending apart below her with an almost-human screeching sound, echoing roars coming up through the ferry's funnels. Down below somewhere, she could hear cars crashing against each other on the car deck.

The floor tilted again and she stumbled, reaching out to steady herself and falling against a metal projection on the wall. Her head collided on something hard and when she reached up to test the spot, her fingers came away sticky.

She leaned against the heaving wall and then balanced enough to climb the narrow bucking stairs, with the policeman following close behind.

***

Ashley wove through the crowd surging through the corridor upstairs and stepped out of the way to avoid being swept off her feet. As she did, she saw the little red-haired boy from the waiting room. He was sitting on the floor, tears rolling down his cheeks, his arms hugging his cardboard suitcase. He was all alone, his face white in the glare of the emergency lights and her heart broke for him.

"Why aren't you with your mother?" Ashley exclaimed, bending down to get his attention. She reached out to touch a cut on his head. The blood had matted the boy's red hair, darkening it almost to black.

"She's in Dublin. She's waiting for me and she's going to be that upset, she is. I'm not going to be there because this boat is sinking and we'll have to swim all the way to Ireland." The boy's voice caught as he tried to talk, tried to be brave. He wiped at his nose with the backs of his fingers. Ashley's heart went out to him and she tugged at his arm. "Come with me then. We'll be just fine. We'll go outside and they'll look after us." Ashley put her arm around his shoulders and hugged him against her side as they cleared the crowded doorway and reached the promenade deck.

All down the side of the ship, people were being loaded into crazily swinging lifeboats. Far below them, a flotilla of boats was already tossing drunkenly on the waves, almost obscured by fog.

Chill wind blew Ashley's hair against her face and she was momentarily blinded. It was freezing out here and the cold bit right into her.

"Ashley! Quickly! There's room on this boat." And then Daemon was there. She had never been so glad in her life to see someone.

Daemon nodded his head at the policeman, and then carefully handed the little boy to the waiting arms of the deckhand below them and turned around for her. For a split second his eyes warmed, the green reflecting the lights of the ferry. "I couldn't get to you," he said. "I was cut off in the passageway."

He put one warm hand on her shoulder. How could he be so warm when it was so icy cold out here? Ashley wondered, her teeth chattering. Then the ferry lurched again, the deck slanting beneath them. A number of people screamed.

The crowds had cleared and almost everyone was now away on the bobbing boats. The ferry's horn still blasted into the fog, sounding a bit abandoned, somehow lonely.

"Hurry, we've got to get away before she starts going down!"

Shouts came up to them from the lifeboat and Daemon swung her up against his chest. She hung on as he stepped over the side.

It was just for a moment but Ashley's heart stuttered.

Then the lifeboat tilted as Daemon sat down and she felt cold wood against her legs. His arms held her tightly all the way as the boat was lowered, banging against the ferry's side.

Metal against wood.

Metal against water. Echoing into the fog.

The horn continued to send out long muffled blasts and a voice called over the public address system that the crew could now abandon ship.

Waves rocked them as they reached the water and Ashley's stomach churned. She turned her head into the warm leather of Daemon's coat, taking long, calming breaths.

She couldn't see his face but she could feel his arms around her. This was the second most terrifying experience of her life but this time she wasn't alone.

The ferry went down in a matter of minutes.

Fifteen shattering explosive minutes.

A freighter had hit them. A ghost ship no one had seen.

***

Lights continued to flicker through the swirling fog, visible one second and gone the next. A freak gust of wind cleared the "Stena Lines" emblem long enough for huddled passengers in the lifeboats to watch the funnel slide under, swallowed by tons of grasping, relentless waves. Silvery columns of spray climbed into the sky in its wake and settled into the night as the lifeboats raced to get away from the sucking undertow.

Pushing back her salt-tangled hair, Ashley also pushed away every flickering moment of every 'Titanic' movie she'd ever seen and concentrated on helping the others get settled. Frantic moments had passed with the regular clicks of oarlocks and splashing of the oars. Some passengers still sat, staring sightlessly into the darkness, but most found some way to help.

Sometime later, Daemon had let go of her to help with the rowing on an organized rotation. He sat ahead of her now, his shoulders straining at the oars. She dragged her attention again to the white patch she was putting on the little red-haired boy's forehead.

"Here, Kevin, hold this in place. What's your last name sweetheart?"

"It's Driscoll. Is my head still bleeding, Miss Gallagher?"

Ashley gave him a reassuring smile. “No, not now. You’re going to look like a pirate when you get home though. Do you think your friends will be impressed?”

His face white in the glare of the emergency lantern, Kevin shivered in one of the lifeboat’s rough, woolen blankets and managed a grin. “I think they will be, that’s for certain sure. Do you know we match now?”

Ashley followed the direction of his pointing finger and felt the small square of gauze on her own forehead. Daemon had done that for her earlier, his fingers gentle on the gash she’d almost forgotten about. She hadn’t been able to read his expression in the dark. But she’d thought there was concern. Then he’d been up and rowing with the rest.

***

Daemon stretched his aching muscles and coughed. The fog was gritty and he took great gulps of it every time he shouldered into the oars. He was beyond exhausted but then everyone else was too. Quirking his lips, he thought about that comfortable bed in his London apartment. His eyes widened for a second with images of Ashley in it beside him. Under him.

Where had that come from?

“Rowers, get ready to change over.” He’d never heard anything so welcome as that disembodied voice. It was a crew member somewhere at the back of the lifeboat.

“As long as we keep moving and keep the other boats in sight, we’ll be okay.”

“How long?” Another voice, this time from a lady at the front.

“It should be light in a couple of hours. The rescue helicopters and Irish Coast Guard boats were alerted and will be on their way. It’s the fog that makes this dangerous.”

Daemon ran his fingers through mist-wet hair and thought again about Ashley. His first concern when the collision had jolted him awake had been that he had to find her to keep track of the package. He wasn't going to let them be separated in the lifeboats and lose her.

And then he'd thought of really losing her.

As in her drowning.

He grimaced ruefully into the night. It could have happened.

There had been fatalities. People in the staterooms close to the point of impact, and on the car deck where some had stayed in spite of warnings.

The Irish rescue system had called in the Royal Navy. Now they just needed to keep moving, to follow the boats ahead. To stay together.

Except for the grinding exhaustion evident in every face that he could see in the flare of the lantern, he thought everyone on this lifeboat had escaped major injury although a lot of bandages had been handed out and there would be bruises and scrapes on everyone.

It was the bitter cold that would be their enemy tonight. He saw blue lips and chattering teeth all around him and knew some of the constant shuddering came from shock. Some of the passengers would be hypothermic by morning. The blankets weren't helping much because they didn't keep out the insidious fog and wind. The only lucky break was that it wasn't raining.

As Daemon crouched low in the lifeboat and crawled over the slatted benches to Ashley, he was caught by swirling contradictions. In the unworldly sheen of the emergency light, she looked as innocent as the little boy she held. As he watched her gather her coat close around her shoulders her body shook with cold but she was caring for someone else.

Her face too, reflected the strain and shock of the night. Dark smudges already stained the skin under her eyes. He wanted to reach out with the tips of his fingers and test the softness of the black lashes and eyebrows. The sooty black contrasted with the stark white of her skin.

His eyes narrowed. The first time in a long, long time that he'd felt that special pull from a woman he really wanted to see again and she turned out to be a crook.

Why should he be so surprised? The irony of it made his lip curl up at the corner. Why not someone like her? She wouldn't attract suspicion. She was a perfect choice.

"Daemon! Watch out!" Ashley called out in alarm as a sudden huge swell jolted the boat and threatened to roll him over the side. She held out her hand to steady him and frowned in concern as she saw him wince.

"Your muscles must be killing you," she murmured in sympathy. "If it wasn't so cold, I'd suggest you take off your coat and I could work out some of the soreness. Like you did with my knee."

***

As soon as she'd said it Ashley remembered his warm hands on her skin. How strong and steady they had been as they'd massaged out the knot in her muscles. She wondered how his bare skin would feel under her own hands.

"That sounds like heaven but you're right. It's too bloody cold. At least these life jackets help a bit." Daemon huddled into his own torn coat and she watched as he fingered the ripped sleeve and oil-stained pocket and gathered his duffle bag closer to keep out the wind a bit.

"How long, Daemon? Has anyone said?"

"The mate said we should be seeing helicopters as soon as it gets light. Not too long now. They had to call in the rescue crews and we're a long way out."

"Oh." Light seemed like such a long time to wait.

"Daemon?"

He looked over at her, his eyebrow lifted at the question in her voice.

"Daemon, do you think it would be okay if I fired my travel agent?"

Daemon's laugh came out as a bark and he actually smiled. It was the first time she'd seen him smile since she'd met him.

"Why? Because this hasn't been the perfect holiday you'd expected?"

She giggled. The giggle surprised her as much as his laugh. She guessed it must be shock.

"It wasn't her fault really. She did try to talk me into taking Aer Lingus. Or the fast ferry. I'd be over there in Dublin by now. In bed."

The thought of it hurt. Her fingers were raw with the cold and her teeth were sore from chattering. The 'being-cold-chattering'…not the 'too-much-talking-chattering.'

***

The unexpected absurdity of her question stunned Daemon and he didn't know what to say. He wanted to reach out and hug her. Spirit her away from all of this and get her a really good lawyer.

Waves splashed at the side of the boat, and seemed to hang, suspended, in the dark. An occasional swell would send sheets of spray over them all and Daemon had given up trying to stay dry.

"Oh no!"

"What?" Daemon jerked upright.

"My paints and brushes!" She pointed wordlessly to the bottom of the sea, and then stopped…thinking instead of the bodies down there now. She felt shocked and sick.

Daemon had a sudden, terrifying thought. Had she transferred the package to another suitcase? Was the mystery package now at the bottom with her other things?

"Did you have your other luggage in the room with you?"

"No. Just my tote bag. I checked in my suitcase when I first got to the terminal."

Thank God!

Daemon smiled. "Just wondered. Did you say brushes and paint?"

"Yes. I need them. I don't know what I'm going to do now. I have to be at my job tomorrow." Ashley moaned in frustration.

"So, you paint? What do you paint? Tell me about it." Anything to pass the time, Daemon thought. Maybe he could trip her up and find out something. She was too tired to think clearly. She had to be. He certainly was.

He moved closer.

The little boy, Kevin, was finally asleep. He'd crawled onto the bench at Ashley's side and was curled up against her. She'd given her own blanket to him and the double wrap had given Kevin enough warmth that he had been able to drop off into exhausted sleep.

One more contradiction about the lady crook. At least she liked kids.

Because Ashley was shaking with cold and he told himself he was worried about the blue in her lips, Daemon justified putting his arm around her to give her some of his own flagging body warmth. He could see the bandage on her forehead. It still seeped red.

"Does your forehead hurt?"

"It just aches. Everything aches. You know, when we were in the waiting room back in Wales, I was dreaming about satin pillows and smooth sheets."

***

Ashley couldn't help herself. Her head was disobeying her and leaning itself onto Daemon's shoulder. It felt so good.

"Satin pillows?"

She grinned when she saw Daemon's eyebrows rise in what she thought was probably a pretend leer.

Or maybe not?

Her cheeks felt warm.

Her brain was suddenly playing with erotic images of Daemon's fair, shaggy hair above her as she lay on white satin pillows. Him looking down at her. His arms…

She shook her head.

"You asked me about my painting?"

He nodded and tightened his arms around her.

"Horses. I paint horses for their owners. I'm going to a stud farm in County Kildare to paint a Grand National steeplechase winner. Have you heard of Dark Night? His Irish Gaelic name is Dorcha Dhubh?"

"Have I ever! Anybody who follows the pools knows about his history. His colt Black Cloud is the favorite to win this year." Daemon whistled. "You must be really good to be hired to paint the old boy. How did you manage something like this?"

"I've been painting for years now. My best friend Beth, who I've known since high school, specializes in portraits of people and seascapes." She smiled as she thought of Beth. They were each other's yin and yang…Ashley's long dark hair and Beth's long white-blond hair making a dramatic physical contrast, but as strikingly complimentary as their painting styles.

"And you?"

Ashley gave in to the urge to press her face against the warm leather of his jacket.

"I love horses and landscapes."

She yawned.

"Beth was the one who organized this commission. We co-own an art gallery in Carmel, California and do painting commissions too."

She felt the rumble of his voice in his chest against her cheek.

"I thought you sounded American!"

She smiled into the salty dark.

"I may have dark hair but I grew up knowing how to surf. Beth is the one who looks like a California surfer girl but I was right beside her on my little board."

She lifted her head and tilted it, wondering.

"Beth and I have been friends forever. We even got matching butterfly tattoos. Supported each other through heartbroken romantic disasters. Helped each other study for finals. Do you have a friend like that?"

Daemon laughed.

"I do. Not the tattoos. Although I'm wondering about yours."

She felt warm again.

"Yes, in answer to your question. I have a close friend. His name is Sam. We've been friends for a long time. We went to school together. He loves the ocean." Ironic grin now.

Ashley's teeth weren't chattering as hard now. She listened to the sounds of the waves slapping against the sides of the lifeboats and heard the muffled voices of the crews as they shouted back and forth to each other across the tops of the rough chop. The echoes of the voices floated across the hazy line between the water and the banks of fog and had an eerie quality that seemed to fit the otherworldly nature of this whole night.

"It'll be all right, Ashley. This is a nightmare right now but it's going to turn out just fine. By the way, what's your last name?"

"It's Gallagher," she murmured into his coat. "And yours? What's yours?"

***

Above her head, Daemon gritted his teeth against the cold and the unexpected emotion surging through him. He hadn't expected to feel so protective, so concerned. "Smith. Go to sleep."

Maybe he could use this to his advantage for a while; steal some time and still do his job. He could stay close to her. Just for the next few hours. He could watch her that way without her catching on. Maybe find out about the package before she handed it over.

He smiled at an old lady on the opposite side of the bench seat; her hair had long ago escaped from the tidy knot on the back of her head and she was all wrapped up in a huge paisley shawl. She had a standard issue Stena Line blanket tucked around her shoulders. She caught Daemon's big smile and smiled back, her face warming in gratitude as she said that he seemed to be such a compassionate young man.

Then, traitorously, not in the line of duty at all, his cheek dropped to rest against Ashley's hair. Even through the salt spray hanging over all of them, he could still smell her sweet fragrance. It eluded him. Peaches? Roses? He rubbed the tip of his nose against her satiny skin and breathed in the scent.

This seemed to be the best way to bear the night…at least until they got to shore. Daemon rested as he started to feel the warmth from Ashley's body and the blanket and their two coats. As he drifted off into the first peaceful doze he'd had in hours, he mulled over the possibilities of what other jobs he might like to do instead of stakeouts and chases. Anything that didn't have grime and blood involved.

***

Time wore on, ticking with the clicks of the oarlocks. The third shift of rowers took over and propelled the lifeboat through the never-ending night. Isolated in shifting mist, everyone held their own thoughts. Fear had numbed and ebbed. Lights bobbed ahead and there was comfort and safety in a large group. They weren't alone.

But their ears were strained to hear something else. An engine. A boat. A plane.

Ashley jerked as she felt someone shift behind her. She woke, disoriented and alone. Kevin had moved away a bit in his sleep and Daemon was gone. She searched the crowded boat and saw him up ahead, once more at the oars. Her heart ached at the thought of his straining muscles.

She lifted the lifejacket and sodden trench coat away from her shoulders a bit. It felt like wearing a cold, wet bathing suit and she cringed. Longing for a hot, steamy shower, she stared off into the dark, imagining huge fleets of rescue ships that weren't there.

People had died.

Countless numbers had gone down with the ferry.

She was so lucky.

"Ashley, you're shaking again." She looked up to see Daemon carefully moving over the tangled mass of legs and arms until he reached the spot beside her.

"Your lips are almost as blue as your eyes."

As she moved her head to look into his face, he realized he was literally only a whisker away. His lips were only a breath away from hers. There really were whiskers. He obviously hadn't shaved for a while.

Ashley reached up to gently lay her hand against the fledgling beard. The stubble felt rough and somehow... she liked it. She wondered what it would feel like against her bare skin.

"Your razor's probably at the bottom of the sea and you can't shave."

She saw the corners of his lips tilt into a grin and felt his arms around her again.

He rubbed his chin against her cheek. "Do you mind?"

"No. I think I'm glad. It makes you look human and vulnerable like all the rest of us in this boat."

***

Oh, he was human all right. He was having very human thoughts tonight.

Daemon lifted Ashley forward to give him the space to unbutton his coat. He wrapped them both in its folds and settled the blanket around the outside, tucking Kevin into the group too.

He felt his cellphone in his pocket and as soon as Ashley was asleep, he was going to check again to see if there was cell service out here. He needed to see if there was a text from Sam and McBride.

He needed to let them know he'd made it off the ferry. To see if they'd had a chance to run Ashley's name through all of their computers. If she was who she said she was.

To see if Shaughnessy Doyle had talked. To find out why he'd given Ashley the package.

He turned his thoughts away from the silk of her hair as it brushed against his collar. And then she lifted her head and....

And sneezed.

"Daemon, I think my brains have frozen." She huddled against him again and as she rested her head against his shoulder, he got a whiff of her perfume.

"Ashley?"

"Hmm?"

"Your perfume. What is it?"

"It's called 'Tresor'."

"I've heard of that. I think my sister uses it. It has peaches in it, doesn't it?"

"Hmm. Peaches and vanilla and roses."

He lifted her hair away from her neck moving his nose closer for a brief, brief moment. "Right. Peaches." He searched for a word to tell her how much he liked it. How much he wanted to breathe it in and forget salt and stakeouts and rolling lifeboats in the Irish Sea. Forget that she was a crook. He missed his bed in London and hot coffee. He thought about more than the perfume and cursed his benighted luck for the hundredth time tonight.

"Do you like it?" Ashley whispered, on the edge of sleep.

"I do."

***

For that brief, brief moment, Ashley didn't want the night, this horrific night, to ever end. She curled her frozen fingers into the grey mittens she'd remembered were in her pocket and tried to let the sound of Daemon's heart and Kevin's soft breathing lull her into sleep. She concentrated on the warm smoothness of Daemon's jacket against her cheek.

The lifeboat jerked on a sudden wave and Daemon's arm tightened around her again. They both sat, silent as the night wore on.

***

Gradually, Daemon could feel Ashley drift into sleep, her small frame snuggling against the heat that was building between their bodies. He was aware of that heat too, letting his aching body relax against hers. Kevin's face was still white and the bruise on his temple was now vividly purple. Daemon wondered how such a small child could be sent off traveling on his own and if some mother was going to be in hysterics right now thinking the worst.

As he sat, struggling to sleep a little, Daemon braced his feet for another wave swell. The boat hung on the edge of the breaking crest for a moment and then dropped into another trough, sending his stomach with it. Because of the fog, the sea was relatively calm but the swells still made it difficult to make any headway.

If he wasn't still dancing on the edges of seasickness, he could almost be hungry. His stomach rumbled a little and he wondered if the denim bag at Ashley's feet had another chocolate bar hidden in it.

Nestled in there with the package.

As if she knew, even in her sleep, that he was thinking about her, Ashley stirred a bit against him and her fingers tightened in the material of his jacket. They had gone there of their own accord and one hand was close to burrowing right into his pocket. Daemon tried to concentrate on the click and splash of the oars, the slap of the waves and the whistling of the wind.

Wind.

He looked up at the sky in sudden surprise. The wind had shifted and grown stronger without him realizing. He could actually see a star. Two stars. The fog was starting to lift and it was clearing whole sections of night sky. Off in the distance he could even make out part of the moon as the clouds scudded across its surface.

There would be help soon. If this fog lifted enough, it would make it easier for the rescue boats and copters to get to all of them and this would be over.

He shifted Ashley and Kevin enough to be able to reach for his cellphone. No service.

But he could connect on the rescue boat.

He yawned in spite of himself. It wasn't easy to hold Ashley like this. Even as his mind ticked off strategy and tried to figure out what to do when they did get to shore, his body betrayed him. Her soft curves were too easy to feel through the thin material of her coat.

Her head had gravitated to a spot just below his chin and her breath was gently blowing against his neck. One slender arm had somehow managed to slide around his waist, burning his already overheated skin right through his damp shirt.

***

Other people in the boat had started pointing to the stars and there was a general feeling of good humor and cheer in spite of the unforgiving cold. Complete strangers were sitting, huddled together for warmth, sharing life stories and telling jokes. Others were sleeping either sitting up and swaying with the boat or leaning against each other in companionable groups. The crew was getting ready to shift the rowers again and Daemon was glad that he'd done his share and could rest now.

The grinding fatigue of rowing had worn off now that he'd stopped and now, he was just plain sleepy.

If he could get some rest now, he'd be more alert when they got to shore. He'd be able to keep track of Ashley's movements and track her until she passed on the package.

Then he would either turn her in or let her go. And never see her again.

His arms tightened, drawing her closer. He drifted and woke up, drifted and woke up, half-listening to the chatter around him, half-listening to the crew on their portable radios, keeping tabs on the other boats.

Finally, he slept again and dreamed of satin pillows and blue pansies.

Chapter Three

"Rescue and Hot Water"

It was quiet in Ashley's dream. There was just the sound of droning flies, stamping hooves and far away thunder merged with the music coming from her iPod.

Then, suddenly, the thunder was not so far away. Several giant claps and telltale flashes of lightning drew nearer and nearer. Suddenly, the air was full of ozone and a strange hissing sound. A startling white sheet of brilliant lightning erased the darkness of the barn.

The winter supply of baled hay in the loft over Ashley's head came alive and fiery sparks showered down everywhere. Millions of tiny lethal firebombs rained on loose straw.

"Dad!" Ashley screamed, rooted in shock for a heartbeat. "Dad! Fire!"

***

"Ashley!"

A stranger's voice? Someone here in the barn with her? No. She was alone. There was no one here but her. There was no time to get help.

Ashley struggled against the weight of an arm around her. She pushed against it but it just tightened.

"Ashley, sweetheart, it's okay. You're dreaming!"

"No! There's lightning! There's a bright, bright light!" She felt a gentle hand on her cheek. On her hair. Smoothing, soothing.

"Ashley, wake up. It's the helicopter. Help is here."

She woke up in startled confusion, fighting the arm, fighting the constriction of blankets. She fought to get free, only to find her lips making contact with bare flesh.

"What?" She pushed away from what seemed like a solid wall and tore at the material around her.

"Whoa! Here, I'll help you. Just relax a minute."

A sleep-roughened voice hovered somewhere just above her ear.

Ashley felt the darkness of the blankets lifted away and looked up into Daemon's eyes. They were concerned. In fact, Ashley thought she'd disturbed something confusing in them before Daemon glanced away to follow the direction of all the excitement.

It was just light enough to see the markings on the Irish police Cósta helicopter that hovered above them. The blinding flashes of light in Ashley's dream had been the searchlights of the helicopter. Close behind it was the unmistakable shape of a rescue ship.

"What took them so long to come?" Ashley tried to tug her hand from beneath Daemon's partly unbuttoned shirt…her face flushing as she realized her fingers had done that, burrowing in.

"We passed another lifeboat an hour ago. Our crew radioed over and they said there was a really bad storm last night to the north of us. The rescue services have been scrambling to get to everyone at once with our ferry sinking and the fog and the other storm." Daemon looked out as the other lifeboats began to turn around and converge, ready to be taken out of the water.

"They've already picked up a lot of ferry passengers. We just drifted a bit further away from the main group. But they're here now."

Ashley watched as rope ladders were flung down towards the boats and people started the precarious clamber up. She thought about all the people in the waiting room; all the masses of huddled, sleepy people. All the people who hadn't made it to safety.

She looked into Daemon's face so close to her and saw extreme exhaustion. His lips, chapped by the salt water, curved in a tired smile as he scanned a grey ocean lit up by helicopter searchlights.

"There's an ambulance boat from the Red Cross coming too. I'm sure there are lots of injuries and the cold last night has probably taken a toll."

"What about the people who were killed, Daemon? What happens to them?"

She saw grimness and he shook his head.

"There will be divers. They'll pull up as many bodies as they can."

And then there was nothing more to say and she leaned into his hug.

***

Daemon looked around them at the blankets and lifejackets and wondered that they had been able to make do with so little.

"Some of these people are going to need treatment for hypothermia. How about you?" He gently touched the bandage on Ashley's forehead and his eyebrows wrinkled as she grimaced.

"You know, considering what we've just been through, I'm really okay. You probably have just as many aches and pains from all the rowing you did last night."

"I'm sore and tired, but I'll live."

Daemon searched for Kevin and spotted him a row or two away, with another small boy and an older lady. He seemed to be all right and had shed his blanket. He caught Daemon's glance and grinned, pointing at the helicopter, mouthing the words, "Do you see it?"

Daemon grinned back and gave him a thumbs-up signal.

With the fog lifting there was now a stiff wind coming off the waves and more of a chop, making Daemon's stomach lurch. He saw a lot of white faces and arms around stomachs and noticed the new tightness around Ashley's mouth every time the lifeboat tilted.

"What about the ship that hit us, Daemon?"

He squinted against the brilliant morning sun shining against the metal on the sides of the boats and could now clearly see the Irish harp logo on the side of the helicopters.

"It was evidently an accident. The skipper was so tired he missed a compass change and didn't know he was heading for the ferry until it was too late. He'd just left the wheelhouse to a junior crew member and gone to bed." Daemon shook his head.

"I guess it was so foggy that visual contact didn't work. The radar on their ship wasn't functioning properly either. They were onto us before they realized what was happening."

"But they just left us!"

"Our crew has the bare facts and not too much else yet. There'll be a major inquiry. Probably the ship sliced by without much damage to its own hull and couldn't turn around in time to find us in the fog. They did get in touch with the Coast Guard and it was the fog that held everything up."

"Then our own crew saved our lives. They did an amazing job."

***

Ashley watched those same exhausted crew members shout out to each other now that they were close enough to make contact without their radios.

She and Daemon sat in the lingering chill, wind blowing their hair. Murmuring voices and the splashing of waves against the hull mixed now with the pulsating, eggbeater noise of the helicopter overhead.

The sickening roll of the sea was a constant.

She didn't really want to pull away from the warmth of Daemon's body but her mind tried half-heartedly to find a subtle way to disentangle her fingers from his shirt. The chopper suddenly got close enough to blow whitecaps their way and the roar from the rotor blades was deafening, so she didn't hear Daemon's muffled intake of breath when her fingertips touched his skin.

"Hold on below!" The loudspeaker brought a disembodied voice through the air. "We'll have you on the boat and warm as fast as we can."

***

It had been all Daemon could stand earlier when he'd felt Ashley unbuttoning his shirt and burrowing her nose and cheek against his chest. Now she was attempting to undo the damage but she was creating even more havoc to his nerves and he could feel himself growing hard.

"That's all right. Here…let me help."

He firmly put her away from him, gritting his teeth as her fingers brushed against the hair on his chest. Hair and skin so suddenly sensitized that it almost hurt.

Ashley seemed to visibly pull her dignity around her again, concentrating on finger combing her tangled hair. He didn't know if her face was red because of the wind and the cold or from sheer embarrassment. He hoped it was the latter and it wasn't just a show from a hardened crook.

Daemon watched the approach of the rescue ship and maneuvered to help the small children and their mothers get organized. Shivering in the chill air, they all pulled the boat blankets around their shoulders. They were now sodden and crusted with crystals of salt from the spray but kept out some of the wind.

***

Ashley noticed that Kevin was neither as white or as shaken-looking as last night and called out to him. "Morning, Kevin. Are you feeling better?"

"Yes, thank you, miss. And how are you this wonderful morning? Thanks be to God that they've found us."

"You are so right. I think you and I will both have battle scars for a while but that means we can show off and tell great stories. You'll have to make sure you don't scare your poor mother though. You'll have to give her a big smile when you see her."

"I'll be doing just that, miss. My mum will be at the ferry building. She was going to be meeting me this morning."

And then the little boy choked on a sob. They all knew that there had been deaths. His mother wouldn't know he was alive.

Ashley realized she'd have to call her own parents and Beth as soon as she could get to a phone to let them know she was all right. Her cellphone battery had died hours ago.

She moved over and got close enough to engulf Kevin in a huge hug…one that he more than reciprocated.

"And will you and your husband be helping me to find her?"

Ashley watched Kevin as he scanned the boat for Daemon. "My husband? Oh, no, Kevin. This is just a very, very kind man who helped us both."

A very kind man who has popped into my life to confuse me no end, thought Ashley.

She put her hands on Kevin's shoulders to steady him as the boat rolled again. "But, yes. We'll make sure you find your mother."

Ashley carefully edged back to her seat to look for her tote bag. The denim was soaked on the outside but she hoped the flap and inner lining had kept everything dry inside. She hadn't opened the bag since she'd been in the waiting room because she'd been so tired, she'd just thrown it on the floor beside the bunk in her stateroom and collapsed onto the bed. And last night she'd had no reason to look inside.

She stuck her hand in now to check for her passport and papers and jolted in surprise. Her fingers had touched something unexpected.

Something cold and smooth.

What on earth? She opened the flap wider to have a better look and there, in the middle of her jumbled carry-on supplies, sat a small, rectangular package. It was wrapped in plain brown paper and looked and felt like a small book.

She drew it out, holding it up and turning its smooth sides this way and that. No address. No writing on it. What was it?

An edge of the paper had come undone a little, probably caught on something sharp in her bag. She tentatively touched the rough edges with her fingertip, thinking suddenly of letter bombs and packages deliberately planted in luggage.

Drugs?

She held the package in the palm of her hand, torn about what to do. She looked for Daemon, finding him ahead of her helping the crew.

She'd just have a quick peek, since it was open. If it looked suspicious, she'd just heave it over into the water. She slipped her forefinger under the ragged edge and lifted. The brown paper ripped apart to show the pale blue of a book cover. Ripping the paper even further, she saw the marbled edges of the pages.

Nothing exploded.

Ashley held the package up to her ear. Nothing ticked.

Completely perplexed, Ashley opened the book, checking for names or addresses inside the cover.

Nothing.

She searched for a letter inside or anything that would identify an owner. It had obviously been put in her bag by mistake. Maybe somebody who sat beside her while she was sleeping had a bag like hers? Before Daemon had come to sit by her.

Before…The drunk in the waiting room! He'd knocked her bag down. Suddenly frantic, thinking that he had been using drunkenness as a cover while all along he was looking for someone to rob, she dropped the book onto her lap and searched her bag for her passport. Her heart almost stopped when she couldn't find it right away. But there it was. And her papers all seemed to be there. Her wallet was intact and nothing else was missing.

Except all her clothes and paintbrushes. She sighed and then realized for the millionth time that she could also be at the bottom of the Irish Sea. Nothing else about this whole thing seemed quite so bad, considering.

Brows furrowed as she concentrated, Ashley turned the book in her hands. Nothing remarkable on the cover, just the embossed title, *Yeats—Poetry of the Irish Isles*.

Someone had good taste. But what would she do with it now?

She flipped past the flyleaf. Nothing. Muttering in frustration, Ashley missed the jolt of surprise as Daemon turned and looked her way.

***

She had the package in her hands. She was just sitting there, holding it in front of everyone. He waited, breath held, as she tore off the brown wrapper; waited as she held what looked like a book in her hands.

A book? Probably a paper inside, he thought. The plans had to be hidden inside.

The look of sheer confusion crossing Ashley's face stunned Daemon for a moment, but his informant…the dead one…had said the couriers weren't told what they were carrying.

So why had she opened the package? He watched as she flipped the pages of the book. Watched as her fingers traced the flyleaf and her eyebrows wrinkled. What was she doing? Daemon was going crazy. Then he watched in horror as she held the book over the side, arm outstretched as if to throw it away.

No! He had to see what it was! Don't throw it away! What are you doing? Daemon shouted it in his head and had to stop himself as he rose mid-way out of his seat to go to her.

Then he watched, as Ashley seemed to freeze, almost as if she'd heard his voice. She looked up and her expression riveted him. She looked almost bewildered.

He turned away, giving her time to do whatever she was going to do. He breathed a huge sigh of relief as she brought her arm back in, book intact, and put it on her lap.

Thank God! At least he wouldn't have to explain jumping in after it! Daemon's mind whirled with possible explanations for her behavior. But he was too tired, too sore, too spent to figure it out.

He needed to arrange to get a watch on her. The Garda would help with that and he could get things started with their own detective branch.

He needed to get in touch with Sam and see what he'd found out. McBride would be waiting for a report.

But first he needed to get off this bloody boat.

***

Ashley couldn't decipher the look she'd just caught on Daemon's face. It was something close to the expression on a deer when it was caught in a hunter's sights.

But about what?

Well, she thought, that's about how she felt. Life was just getting 'curiouser and curiouser' as Alice had said in *Alice in Wonderland* after she'd fallen down the rabbit hole.

She opened the book again, her gaze scanning past page one and then two and then flipping to the poem, "The Lake Isle of Innisfree". That's odd, she noticed…there were words underlined… lines underscoring certain words and phrases.

I will arise and go now, and go to Innisfree,

And a <u>small cabin</u> built there, of clay and wattles made.

Actually, she thought, it was probably not so curious. This was a new book. It was probably just someone's favorite poetry. They'd underlined the best parts. She did it all the time.

Sighing, she tucked the book back into her bag and closed the flap. She'd look at it again later. Maybe when she got to the hotel and was lying in a warm bath or curled up in bed.

Sudden thoughts came unbidden of her asleep in Daemon's arms, head resting on his chest. She glanced at him again, focusing on the tawny head, the way that the hair grew long and curled over the collar of his shirt. She forced herself to continue her train of thinking.

She'd worry about the book later. Later she'd be able to think of what to do. After she'd brushed her teeth. She jumped as Daemon sat down beside her.

"Are you all set? I think they're getting ready for our lifeboat next."

***

A launch picked up a group from their lifeboat and brought them over to the ladder that hung in place down the side of the rescue ship. The crew helped people, one by one, onto the swaying rungs. The passengers who were waiting to go reached out to hold the ladder steady and Ashley had to look away for a second, her stomach lurching with apprehension.

The children were handed up first. Kevin searching for Ashley before he started his climb, as if to say, "Watch me!" She nodded encouragingly for him to go ahead.

The launch emptied and came back to the lifeboat, again cutting its engines and taking on the second group.

Ashley turned her head to Daemon, surprised to find that he was watching her intently. He seemed…serious.

"I guess it's my turn in a minute, Daemon. You know, we spent all this time in the boat and I didn't even ask why you were in Ireland. We don't know anything about each other at all and now it's time to go."

He put his hand on her back to help steady her when it was almost her turn. The hand rested there, warmth seeping through the material of her coat and dress.

I don't want to go, she thought. I don't really want this to be over.

Ashley watched as he acknowledged her comment and tilted his head as if to think for a second. One eyebrow raised a little.

"I'm writing a book. Comparing the coast of Cornwall with the area around the Cliffs of Moher on the West Coast of Ireland. I've been thinking about it for a long time."

"So, you're a writer?"

"No, just a hobby. I have another job in London. Boring really."

Ashley found it hard to figure out his suddenly cryptic look. The lion's got something on his mind, she thought. Then, completely unplanned, Ashley surprised both of them by leaning over just to place a quick kiss on Daemon's cheek and then she carefully moved up the line to get ready to be handed over to the launch.

"I'll look for you on the rescue boat. But if I don't find you, thank you for everything. I couldn't have borne this without you." Ashley remembered that day so many years ago, when she'd had to face horror all alone. This time she'd had Daemon to keep her warm and help her feel that everything was going to be all right. She suddenly felt bereft. She was never going to see him again. Once she mixed in with the huge crowd from the ferry, she wouldn't be able to find him.

"How about having dinner with me tonight?"

As Daemon spoke, she looked up at him and her heart squeezed for just a second. For some wonderful reason she felt possibilities. Even just for the space of a dinner.

Her lips lifted into a giant smile. "I'd love to! Where and when?"

Dinner with a lion. Dangerous.

Appealing.

She wanted to find out what lay behind the strange tension she'd seen since the waiting room.

"But Daemon, you probably need to get some serious sleep."

"Once I make some phone calls and put my head down somewhere for a bit, I'll be ready to have a good meal. You can ask and I'll answer some of those questions before we go back to the real world."

***

Before I have to arrest you, Daemon thought ruefully. One of those phone calls was going to be to Scotland Yard to find out if they'd finished the search on her.

"Okay then," she said. "I have to call the stud farm and my parents and friend as soon as I can. I'll check in at my hotel and grab some sleep. Here..." She showed him the name of the hotel and they picked a time to meet in the restaurant on the hotel's first floor.

Daemon, worried that she was going to be out of his vision once she got to the rescue boat, saw her safely to the launch and watched as she hoisted the tote bag onto her shoulder. The wind blew in her hair, playing with the almost ebony highlights. It also blew at the flaps of the bag.

A piece of brown paper still stuck up between the layers of denim. It waved, like a flag...taunting him.

He reached up his hand to brace her as she stood on the wooden step placed to help passengers disembark and the lifeboat rocked with another swell.

***

Ashley looked down on the top of his head, watching the breeze lift shaggy strands of the wheat-colored hair.

Don't, she told herself. Don't go there.

Then her fingers reached out of their own accord and she leaned down to touch his hand, holding on to it on for a second before the rescue officer took her elbow to help her leave the boat.

"See you later," she murmured.

"Right, see you later."

Daemon looked up at her one more time and then she had to take that first step and she was up the ladder and on to the ship.

***

Her fingers had been feather-light, feeling familiar to him already. He shook his head and lost no time asking a crew member for a ship-to-ship radio. A badge and ID convinced the officer to turn it over and Daemon was through to the rescue ship to put someone on Ashley the minute she stepped on board.

Someone to trail her movements. Someone to see if she passed the brown package on to someone else.

***

Far away, outside a little pub in Wales, a man crouched over the receiver of a telephone in the red phone booth and whispered urgently. Sweat beaded on his forehead.

"We have a wee bit of a problem. It's the package. Now don't go on with yourself! It's just a small problem." He began to sweat in earnest.

"What is it? Well, it seems the ferry went down last night. No, no! She wasn't killed. No one was killed. Connor is still going to be waiting at her hotel. He'll get the package for certain sure. But the problem is that Shaughnessy himself got nabbed by the police."

He fidgeted, shuffling his feet and wrinkling his forehead. He nervously checked through the parking lot beside the pub. This wasn't the best of times and places to be talking to his boss.

"What's that? Yes, I know for certain how to deal with this. I'll be looking after Shaughnessy. Yes, of course I know he might talk."

He'd been set to meet up with Shaughnessy for a drink. But he'd seen the takedown. And Shaughnessy had already been drinking. It wouldn't take much for him to tell everything. He felt for the gun in his pocket. All he needed to do was get into the cellblock.

He grinned.

Easy.

"And the young lass? She won't be a problem. Connor will know what to do. He'll grab the package. She won't know what hit her."

He groaned, groggy from his night of drinking. He hadn't even made it home; he'd just crawled into his car and sagged back onto his seat. He was in big trouble talking to the boss.

He shouldn't have contacted him at all. He'd never even seen him and wasn't supposed to use this number. But he was in even bigger trouble if the package had sunk with the ferry. He hadn't told the boss that was a possibility.

He quickly made a list of all the saints and angels he could call upon to help him through.

The book had passed from courier to courier and was close to the end of its route. Each one had underlined something vital to the plan, all in code. A line here…a phrase there. They all added up to time, place, details. All of it added up to the final vital message and none of the in-between couriers was the wiser. No one could be a stoolie to the Metropolitan Police or anyone else if they got caught.

But Shaughnessy was going to be dead as soon as he could make it happen.

The boss had come up with a brilliant plan. But Shaughnessy had come up with his own brilliant plan. Plant the book with an unsuspecting tourist so he wouldn't have to be on the ferry himself. He'd wanted to drink instead. The problem was that in his drunken mind he hadn't counted on the fact that the tourist might just open up the book and throw it away.

Just now the boss had brought up that small detail. Now the package was in a stranger's hands. Such a small mistake Shaughnessy had made and such a permanent hole in his head there'd be as his punishment.

They had to get the book back.

***

The Shelbourne Hotel sat on one of Dublin's main streets and its Georgian elegance would have impressed Ashley if she'd been more awake when she stumbled out of the shuttle bus and dragged herself in the front door. She was even too out of it to think about how she looked or the curious stares she was attracting from guests and staff alike.

The desk clerk raised his eyebrows as he looked at her.

"Do I have seaweed in my hair?

"Pardon me miss? Seaweed?"

"Seaweed. I've just come off the ferry that sank. Or a lifeboat anyway." She yawned, unable to catch it in time. She couldn't miss the look of shocked amazement on the clerk's face.

"The ferry that sank! Of course, miss. You must be…" the man paused, much more sympathetic now.

"Gallagher. Ashley Gallagher. I have a reservation. I know I'm late but please don't say you've given away my room!" She watched, dismay all over her exhausted face.

"Here you are, miss. No problem. We heard the news and they phoned from the Red Cross to say some of our guests would be coming. I should have known it was you from …"

"The way I look?" Ashley grinned and pulled her fingers through her hair. It hung, listlessly, over her eyebrows and down the sides of her face.

"For certain sure, miss. Would you be thinking a hot shower and a cup of tea? We'll take care of that right away. And your luggage?"

"At the bottom of the Irish Sea." For the second time in the last long hours, Ashley thought of the poor passengers that were at the bottom of that same sea and she could feel her stomach muscles tighten.

"We'll find you anything you need, miss. Toothbrush, toothpaste. Anything. Just let the housekeeping staff know."

"Thank you. Just a bed for now." She signed the register and shifted her tote bag onto the counter. As soon as she noticed the green liquid leaking off the bottom seam of the denim, she grabbed it back and tucked it under her arm.

Ashley reached inside the still-dripping bag and looked at the clerk. "I wonder if you could tell me if there's a 'Lost and Found' for the ferry line? Someone made a mistake and put their package in my bag. There was a huge rush when the rescue boat got in and I didn't have a chance to ask anyone."

"There must be, for sure. Shall I be doing some checking for you?"

"Please. And could you please keep this for me at the check-in counter? I'd hate to lose it before I find out who it belongs to." She didn't hear the muffled curse that came from the corner of the room as she passed the book over to the clerk and watched him lock it in the cupboard.

***

Connor had waited so long for the woman to arrive. He'd hidden behind the racing form for hours, terrified that he'd raise suspicion. He wasn't dressed for this place either. The doorman had started sending him dark looks and he'd considered waiting outside. But it had just been too cold. Who would think it was almost April?

Now it was too late. Shaughnessy would kill him. Or the boss would. And before they did, he would kill Shaughnessy himself for coming up with such a stupid plan. As the woman followed the clerk's directions to the elevator, Connor slid out the door, checking the street for the nearest hidden spot to use his phone.

***

Three blocks away, Daemon sagged weary shoulders against a wooden chair, a cup of coffee and his charging cellphone in his hand. He was ready, but reluctant, to make that call. Afraid of what Sam would say about Ashley. He knew his friend hated injustice and wouldn't shield the truth.

"We have a cot in the back for you, Chief Inspector. Sorry we can't give you something more comfortable. We'll get you a bite to eat and let you get some sleep."

Daemon blinked eyes that felt like gritty sandpaper and rubbed his hand over an equally gritty chin. "Sounds good. Are you sure the hotel is well-covered?"

"We have a man at the front, one at the back and an extra person on your woman's floor at the hotel. She won't know they're watching her. But."

Daemon looked up at the officer in front of him. "But? I don't like buts."

"But it seems your package is safe for now."

Daemon raised his eyebrow and said, "You have my attention. Why?"

"She gave it to the clerk at the front desk and the doorman we hired said the package is locked up under the counter."

Profound relief hit Daemon in the stomach. As long as the doorman was watching the counter and there were Garda plainclothes people everywhere ready to take over, he might be able to rest for a few minutes. He'd learned to sleep sitting up and fall asleep fast.

He shrugged his aching shoulders and looked regretfully at the blisters on his hands. Hours of rowing and fighting salt spray had left their mark.

"Good news. I'll just check in with my partner and then I'll grab that cot for a while." Daemon stifled a huge yawn and sipped at the strong, hot coffee the officer handed him. He didn't know if he could last much longer. He hadn't been horizontal for so long he'd forgotten how to unbend his body.

As he watched the steam rise from the mug, he wondered what Ashley was doing. She'd talked about satin pillows and smooth sheets.

He put through the call.

It wasn't what he expected.

***

Daemon swayed slightly on the chair. Crazy visions of an innocently slumbering Ashley floated in his mind. She'd be curled up in a tangle of silky hair and some skimpy lacy thing. Or, wait…her suitcase was at the bottom of the Irish Sea. She'd likely be wearing nothing at all! Unless she had a nightgown in that bottomless pit of a denim bag her lacy negligee or whatever else she wore was down there with the fishes.

The coffee burned his throat. The doughnut he'd eaten when he first got to the station sat in his stomach in a great, gooey lump.

"What happened with the search on her? And yes, I'm happy that you're grateful I didn't go down with the ferry!"

He could hear the strain in Sam's voice. He knew everyone would have heard about the sinking. Would have been worried. He'd been worried!

There was a long silence that made him feel uneasy.

"Go ahead and tell me. Something's happened."

He could hear an indrawn breath.

"They shot Shaughnessy. Someone got through during a shift change. We were waiting for our guy to sober up and spit out whatever he knew. He's not dead. That's the good part of the bad."

Daemon's heart sank.

"And the bad?"

"Just no answer until he either recovers and spills or we can convince him his friends want him dead more than we do. And your girl…?"

Here it comes.

"She seems to be clear. She comes from a small town in California. Has a clean record…not even a traffic ticket. Artist. Runs a gallery and everyone wants her paintings.

That's the good part. But if she's clear, why did he pass her the package?"

The cot creaked under him as Daemon sagged. He didn't know the answer to that one but something was off. Way off.

What was she into? Or…could she be a pawn?

Was somebody using her?

"Let me know what happens with Shaughnessy. I'm going to play this one as it comes. Stay away from bullets, Sam." He knew his friend was as tired as he was. Heard it in his voice.

Daemon couldn't stay upright any longer. The cot bent in the middle and smelled of old cigarettes and damp. The woolen blanket scratched and the pillow was lumpy. Somewhere behind his head a tap dripped and a telephone rang. The work of the downtown Dublin police station went on without him.

But Daemon didn't notice. He flung one long, lean arm over his tortured, bloodshot eyes and played back the last few hours. Over on the small washbasin stand stood a replacement razor and a new toothbrush. On the hook behind the door was a fresh shirt and pair of grey pants. His own soaked clothes had gone home with the officer's wife.

His duffle with the Glock was beside him on the cot.

The officer's wife had brought him grilled eggs and toast and some hot soup and his stomach had finally settled. That and a hot shower and he felt like he could live. The lady had also brought him a fresh peach and the scent still clung to his fingers. He was remembering the smell of Ashley's hair and the perfume that floated up and lingered in the air when she turned her head.

Chapter Four

"Scampi and Dreams of Lions"

Warm afternoon sunlight trickled through the brocade hotel room curtains. A flickering ray of light danced on Ashley's face as each cool breeze puffed the drapes and then let them fall. With a sigh, she buried her nose under the pillow and tried to recapture the blissful darkness of sleep. Instead, her sleep became restless.

She dreamed of cinders, stinging, burning, fluttering and swirling around her head. She rolled over in the tangled blankets and groaned. The embers returned, brushing at her cheeks and sliding off her shoulders. She pushed them away and tossed in the bed, trapping herself even more in the mass of sheets.

The barn was on fire.

Smoke billowed from every corner. Ashley raced for the nearest stall, grasping in the sudden amber glow for Faisal's halter. The horse screamed in terror and shied away from her, slamming her slight body against the wall before she finally got him out and through the double barn doors. As she slapped him on the hindquarters to get him away to safety, she blindly headed next for Shali…guided through the smoky haze by the frantic stomping of his hooves.

Shali was easier to lead out and she could hear the fire bell and the ranch's alarm siren. Footsteps pounded her way and she knew someone would head the horses off if they tried to run back into the flames.

"Sirocco! Hold on! I'm coming!" The big Arabian had been there for her when hours and hours of dance lessons had kept her from human friends. He'd always been there. He was screaming now as the falling embers hit him and then a solid wall of flames rose between them. Ashley's eyes squinted against the heavy smoke, the intense heat and her tears. Sirocco was the farthest away, in the corner, at the end of the stalls.

“Why didn’t I get you out first?” Ashley was sobbing now and the frantic shouts from behind her only vaguely registered. She thought she heard her name and pushed it away. She had to find an opening in the fire. She had to get to her horse. She could hear his high-pitched whistle and heard the timbers smashing as he hammered at his stall with his huge hooves, desperately trying to break free.

Then help came and it was Daemon! He advanced arms outstretched. He’d never been in her dream before. Shaggy hair shimmered in the light from the fire. She reached out for him but his shape shifted and shifted until he turned into a lion.

She stepped back and the lion roared.

Ashley woke with a jerk. Her arms grasped at the air as she sat, stretching towards the end of the bed. She pushed back sleep-tousled hair with trembling fingers and they came away smelling of salt and fish. Shaky and drenched in sweat, she dropped her aching head down on her raised knees and willed daylight and sunbeams to drive away the nightmarish images.

She hadn’t had these nightmares for years. She thought she’d conquered them. She’d always be sad. She’d always remember. But she didn’t know where this was coming from.

Rubbing the clamminess from her cheekbones with the backs of her hands, she swung slender legs over the side of the four-poster bed and untangled the rest of her body from the sheets. She stretched her arms above her head and yawned, trying one more time to call back the one image she wanted to remember. Daemon…strong arms and reassuring body beside her in the lifeboat during a very scary night.

She didn’t even know who he was. She’d never see him beyond dinner tonight so why should she be dreaming about him?

She pulled off the oversized shirt she'd borrowed from one of the cleaning staff and briefly thought of her own sleep shirt at the bottom of the sea. Fish would be swimming through her suitcase now, wriggling tiny silver bodies around the piles of twisted steel and crumpled deck chairs.

And around the dead.

She took a breath and thought about the phone call she'd made to her mom. Her mother had started crying. Had probably been crying for hours. Her dad had been gruff but she could hear strain in his voice.

"I'm okay," she'd said. "It was awful but Daemon helped me get off the ferry in time…no…please don't start crying again. Who's Daemon? Um, he's a wonderful guy, but…can I tell you I met a great little Irish boy named Kevin? He was all alone on the ferry. And could you please tell Beth? She'll be scared for me too."

Distracting her nurturing mother with a tale of an abandoned little boy had been the only way to make her stop worrying about her only daughter at peril on the sea. Ashley's dad and brothers had been ready to come over on the next plane to bring her home. She'd had to make all sorts of promises to get them to calm down and relax.

She dug her toes into the plush carpet and sighed, more aware now of her surroundings after the few hours of deep sleep that had come before the nightmares. Thanks to the Dunvey Stud Farm, she had all this luxury to herself for two whole extra days if she wanted. Right now, she definitely wanted.

Lord Dunvey had been wonderful. He'd been worried and was grateful she was okay. He'd told her not to worry about her painting equipment. He would call his bank manager in Dublin and she could see him tomorrow about getting money to replace her brushes and paints.

Ashley turned on the taps in the shower and every worry disappeared under pounding, needle sharp spray. She stood suspended, eased by hot water and sweet-smelling soap, working lilac suds into her hair and body to massage away the salt and the headache that had lingered after the blow to her head. The aches floated away with the gauze bandage. The cut stung a little but it was already healing.

Lazy rivulets trickled and lingered here and there all down her spine and she arched her back. Her whole body had flushed from ivory to rose by the time she stretched out one foot to turn the knob off with her toes. She reached out for a thick towel, wiping her face and wrapping her chilling body in its folds.

She tucked another towel around her dripping hair and stepped out, grabbing the hair dryer.

Her knee was aching again and she sat on the edge of the rumpled bed and dug her fingers into the tense muscles. She kneaded her calf muscles and flexed, doing the exercises she'd been doing since the accident. When the beam in the barn ceiling had broken loose it had hit her across her legs, breaking her left leg and damaging the ligaments around her knee. Physio had helped. Walking was no longer a problem, although she limped a bit when she got tired.

Her perfect posture and ballerina gait had come back. Dancing hadn't though. Her feet could tap the beat of any piece of music and she could slow dance. She could hum her favorite pieces of music.

But her legs and knee couldn't hold her in a jeté or a plié.

Or on a horse.

She remembered other hands. Hands with lean fingers over hers. Daemon's fingers making the cramp go away.

Gradually, the ache eased and she sagged back onto the pillows for a minute, smiling and just resting.

"Ah, bliss!" she sighed. "Now for the big decision. What to wear? Wrinkled clothes or fishy clothes, also wrinkled?"

There really wasn't much choice. But she had her wallet and her Visa and some Irish pounds. She pulled a pair of wrinkled grey slacks and a navy silk blouse out of her tote bag and made a quick call to room service for tea and a scone.

She grabbed an iron from the closet in the room and grinned. It was going to be okay. An hour later, mindful of the speeding time and looking forward to seeing Daemon for dinner, Ashley stepped out into the sidewalk traffic on St. Stephen's Green.

And into the gun sights of Connor Donovan.

***

He'd been watching her. Watching to see if she'd picked up the package from the lobby. She had! She'd tucked it into her bag and the bag was over her shoulder as he'd watched her walk right out the door.

He'd caught up and was waiting for a spot where she'd be alone so he could grab her bag and put a bullet into her head. Just in case, mind you. Just in case she'd looked at the package. Just in case she was going to tell someone about it.

He needed it back.

But there was heavy foot traffic on the street and she kept vanishing into the crowds.

He had to wait.

He pushed his gun back into his shirt and hugged the sides of the buildings, trying to stay close to her.

***

Someone else was watching her. A rather rumpled Daemon O'Hare had been leaning against a pillar across the street from the hotel, just out of full sight. He'd moved into the shadows as he'd seen Ashley come out of the hotel. Fighting conflicting emotions, he'd watched her long hair lift in the slight breeze. She'd looked up into the sky and smiled, raising her face to the sunshine and basking in its welcome warmth.

The tangled mass of curly hair had been tamed, turned into a smooth fall of gleaming ebony.

She looked beautiful.

He'd never seen her in daylight; only in the glaring lights of the waiting room and in the dim yellow emergency lights on the ferry; then the flashlights and lantern on the lifeboat.

This morning his eyes had been so sore from all the salt he couldn't see much at all when they were finally rescued. He'd spotted glimpses of her on the Garda Cósta boat but not up close. He'd wanted to give her time and space to pass the package along. But she hadn't. Not on the rescue boat at least.

He rubbed against the grit again. Not as sore now that he'd had a sleep, but the sun was too bright. He should have borrowed sunglasses. His fingers traced the line of his jaw and he smiled, remembering that Ashley had liked his stubble. It was gone now. He wondered what she'd think. He'd have to grow another beard on his next job but for now…

Enough! He cautioned himself. You're on a case here.

But his gaze kept straying to the way the slim grey slacks followed the line of her legs and hugged her gentle curves. She was wearing a short jacket instead of her long trench coat. The coat was probably at the hotel, drying out.

For the next hour, he stayed to the shady side of the street, keeping a carefully paced distance behind Ashley. His mind followed orders. But he couldn't stop from following the lazy bounce of hair against Ashley's back.

Watching her walk, Daemon's police training catalogued details. Like the way she held herself. She carried herself like a dancer. He should recognize that. He'd dated Shelley long enough.

Tonight. He quickened his steps, expertly dodging the foot traffic, always half a block behind her, watching, waiting. The tote bag bobbed along on her shoulder. The doorman had called in as Ashley had left the hotel, reporting that she'd retrieved the book. A ragged piece of brown paper peeked out of the corner of the bag now, mocking him, tantalizing.

***

Half a block ahead, Ashley approached the tall, stately columns of the Maritime Building with a mixture of relief and awe. The relief came from being so close to getting rid of this package. The awe came from the building itself. It resounded with the echo of the thousands and thousands of footsteps that had walked its stone floors. The building made her fingers ache for paper and brushes. She could almost feel the frescoes over her head come alive beneath her fingers.

"Can I be helping you miss?"

She dragged her glance from the ceiling to the face of clerk and pulled out the package.

Two people in the shadows reacted…one with shock and one with fear.

"I was on the ferry that went down last night. I have a package that someone must have accidentally left in my bag at the terminal in Wales. I wasn't able to leave it with anyone at the dock this morning." She handed over the book, torn brown paper and all and looked hopefully into the man's face.

"There's no name on the parcel, miss. And it's been opened. We can't take this."

"But it doesn't belong to me! Someone's going to be looking for it."

"Rules. Terribly sorry I am. We have mountains of unclaimed bits here you see. Mountains. The rules are we can only accept intact packages or things that have names. Or maybe expensive things like jewelry." He handed the book back to her, shaking his head. "Maybe if you take it to the ferry terminal in Wales on your return journey?"

"But I won't be going back that way. I'm flying home from Ireland."

"Sorry, miss." The man put a 'This desk is now closed' sign on the counter.

Ashley sighed and put the book back in her bag.

***

Two pairs of feet followed her as she turned to leave the building.

Daemon hung back, keeping her in sight as the crowd milled around her at the door. He was just making up his mind about what to do next when a shape moved out the milling mass of people and shoved against Ashley, knocking her into a side corridor.

Daemon started to run, putting his hand on the gun tucked into his belt.

The man had pushed Ashley down and was grabbing at her bag…pulling it away from her shoulders.

"Ah, clever", Daemon sighed. "The old 'grab and run' swap. Wait…here's the switch." He prepared to say goodbye to the lady with the blue velvet eyes and follow a lowlife.

But the man had drawn a gun and was pointing it at her head. No one else was watching and this looked wrong. It looked even more wrong when Ashley started to fight back.

She whirled and kicked out at her attacker, knocking him off balance. As he surged forward and backhanded her in the face, she hit him again and his gun fell to the tiled floor. Then she used her hands to pull back at her bag. She took advantage of his shock and shoved him as he struggled to get up. He hit her again and then took one look at the attention he was getting from the crowd and made a dash for the side entrance before Daemon could get to her.

A security guard was already on the run after the mugger.

Well, I'll be damned! Daemon thought, as the crowd dispersed, some stopping to pat Ashley on the back, others pausing for a minute to chat with her. Then his feet moved him closer, until he stood near enough to hear what she was saying to the other security guards.

"I didn't want it in the first place. I can't even give it away. Now someone tries to steal it. I don't know what's going on!"

Daemon stopped as she pulled out the book again and waved it around before stuffing it back in her bag. As she gave the guards a description of the man, Daemon took out his cellphone and did one better. He texted the picture he'd just taken as he'd run to her. Now he sent it off to both McBride, Sam and the Garda detectives. They'd find him.

He needed to see if she was all right. She seemed angry, rather than scared or hurt but she'd been hit. He needed to get his own hands around the neck of the mugger.

And the investigative hairs on the back of his neck were standing straight up.

***

"Ashley!"

She would have recognized the voice anywhere.

Gruff. Growling. Like the lion in her dream.

"Daemon?"

He was right beside her, blond hair neatly combed, clean-shaven, and infinitely a sight she welcomed.

"Are you hurt?" He reached out his hands to run them over her shoulders and arms where the man had grabbed and shoved her. His fingers stroked the front of her neck, where the barrel of the gun had rested for those few seconds. And his palm comforted the place on her cheek the man had hit. The mugging had stopped Ashley's breath but this did too.

"I'm okay. But I think I hurt him. My bag has my passport and all my important papers. And the contact numbers for the Stud. I couldn't let him have it."

She took a giant breath as she felt Daemon put his forehead on hers. That brief contact warmed and steadied her and intensified as he put his arms around her and pulled her closer.

"I think you did hurt him. He was limping when he ran off."

In spite of the light words, Ashley noticed the concern in Daemon's voice and felt protected, even though it had been her own swift moves that had pulled her from danger. She pulled away a bit and leaned down to flex her knee. "Could we sit for a minute? My knee is aching."

She smiled ruefully. "Too much karate, I guess. I'm not a Superhero. They have muscles of iron."

For one tired moment, Ashley wanted to give in to another person made of iron. She wanted to put her head down on Daemon's very broad shoulders and cry. But they'd both been too wet lately and she still had things she needed to do.

As he led her to a nearby bench, her eyebrows narrowed. He looked exhausted. The lines of fatigue stood out even more noticeably this morning in spite of the crinkle of his smile. And something was different. She reached up to touch his jaw.

"You shaved."

Daemon rubbed his chin and his lips curved into a small smile. "Sorry. You liked my beard but my whiskers itched. Do you mind?"

"Mind what?' Oh, your whiskers. No." She wondered what his cheek would feel like against hers now.

And then she didn't have to wonder as he sat beside her and flung one arm around her shoulder, once more pulling her close and resting his cheek against hers for a moment.

"Who do you think he was Daemon?" She could feel a shudder ripple through her now that it was over.

"And he had a gun! He could have just grabbed my bag. Why would he need a gun?"

***

Daemon was wondering the same thing himself. This was more than an exchange. Whoever that was, and they'd find him, he wasn't just part of an exchange.

There had been visible anger and even fear on his face. He'd needed that bag.

And what was in it?

It felt so good to just sit here with Ashley. He could smell the peaches again. And she was warm and her skin was so smooth. Not a lot of makeup…just a trace of lipstick this morning. Her hair was shiny and hung down her back just past her shoulder blades and it felt silky.

"I don't know. He knew what he wanted though. He came out of nowhere and that's the only reason he got to you so fast."

Silence as Daemon replayed the image in his mind, cataloguing the man's features, the swollen drinker's nose, shambling gait and hunched shoulders. He'd work with the sketch artist this afternoon. He needed to do something to shut down the rage he'd felt and the overwhelming need to protect her.

He watched her body sagging as reaction wore off.

"Did you get any sleep?"

She looked up at him and yawned and then grinned.

"Not a lot. Nightmares. But the bed didn't go up and down and there were no foghorns and helicopters. So, yes, I guess a bit. How about you?"

She tucked her head in again against his shoulder.

***

"Oh, I got a bit of rest. I'm fine."

He thought about the precinct cot with its lumps and the pervasive smell of pee and mold. But she was right. It didn't bob up and down and he didn't have to keep getting up to row.

As he drew his fingertip along the curve of her jaw, Ashley tensed, but she didn't pull away. In fact, she turned her face into his palm like a sleepy kitten.

God! Daemon groaned…I want to keep on touching…. The thought warred with reason. She was under investigation. But she'd told the security guards about the package. She'd even pulled it out to show them. What was that about?

And the mugger hadn't just wanted to pick up the package. He'd wanted to hurt her.

Whys haunted him now.

"The last time I saw you there were salt crystals all over your hair. Here," he touched her hair. "And here." He touched her cheek.

"Anything more about what happened last night?"

He shook his head and shrugged his shoulders. "Not yet. Usually, these things take weeks to investigate. We'll read about it in the papers and the ferry company said they'd send us all a letter later on about lost luggage and damage claims."

"I don't really care. About the damage claims I mean. I do need to replace my paints and things, but I was traveling light anyway because I wanted to shop before I go home."

"Where's home?"

Daemon realized he didn't know anything about her. He'd had the trace started and she'd come out clear. But he wanted to hear this from her first. See if she was capable of telling the truth.

"I told you I was from California. I grew up on an Arabian stud farm near Ojai with my parents and my two older brothers and I live in Carmel. I told you my best friend Beth Duncan co-owns the Sirocco Gallery with me and we went to the University of California in Los Angeles and took design courses too. I'm usually there unless I'm on a commission somewhere like this one."

It had come easily enough and sounded plausible. Daemon hoped inside that it was true. That somehow, she wasn't involved in this at all. That this was a huge mistake.

"What about you?"

"Security," he said. "I freelance, helping companies set up new alarm systems. Like I said, boring. That's why I write on the side. Makes life more interesting."

Ashley frowned and looked at him more closely. "I don't see you in that kind of a job at all. You're too…"

Daemon cursed under his breath. Adlibbing was part of his job. She was getting to him. He couldn't even lie and he was totally blowing his cover, if he'd had any at all. He had to think, get her off this train of thought.

"How are all those things you said you had to do today? Have you called your parents?"

"I did. My mother couldn't stop crying and my brothers and my dad wanted to come and rescue me. I told them I'd already been rescued and they don't have to get on a plane. I told them about you and they said to say thank you."

She looked at him again. "Did you make your own calls? Is there someone to worry?"

Daemon shrugged.

The Yard knew. He and Sam were as close as brothers. Always had each other's backs.

He couldn't tell his parents and his sister and brother where he was. Undercover was like that. They wouldn't have known he was on the ferry. They knew he disappeared for weeks on end sometimes and knew he worked for the police. They did know he had a detective's rank.

But not knowing the details protected them from this kind of worry. And they had an emergency contact at the Yard they could call if they were in trouble. McBride would have contacted them if something had happened to him.

It was all taken care of. But it wasn't really. And he was fast growing tired of this kind of life.

Especially knowing that having someone warm and soft curled up against him like this wasn't in his immediate future, if ever.

"I did and everyone who needs to know is happy. I have a mom and dad and a brother and sister who would be relieved to know I didn't end up with your suitcase on the bottom of the Irish Sea."

He grinned and saw the blue deepen as he met her glance. He knew from the expression on her face that she wanted to know more. But he had to get her off this track. Kept reminding himself this was all a necessary act.

"Didn't you have to go search out paints and brushes?"

Ashley remembered, with dismay and she looked at her watch. She'd almost wanted to tell him about her frustration with the package but something held her back. She hoisted the tote bag back on her shoulder and stood up.

"I'll see you later."

"Be careful, Ashley. Keep vigilant about everything around you. The man who attacked you is probably still running. But we watchful." And then before he could stop himself, Daemon leaned over to kiss her on the cheek.

Or meant to.

She turned her head at the last minute and his kiss met her lips instead. And it was too late. He put his hand around the back of her head and pulled her closer to deepen the kiss and he was lost.

Her response, startled at first, warmed, and her lips opened to let him in, until he stepped away and cupped her chin.

"Go get those paints."

As soon as she turned her back to walk away Daemon simply melted into the shadows. He followed her, watching the windows and the alley entrances and the crowds ahead until he saw a plainclothes Irish Garda officer fall into place and take over. He'd alerted them to double up and watch for a possible sniper. The mugger wasn't necessarily gone and he'd obviously had an agenda.

Daemon quickly put in a call to bring himself up to speed on what was going on. Shaughnessy was still unconscious but hanging on. They were hoping they'd get something, anything from him. The situation board was filling up with suspects and possible suspects and Ashley's picture was up there beside a picture of the murdered informant and a close up of the ugly bullet hole in Shaughnessy's chest.

And the cryptic words the informant had choked out with his last breaths.

***

The reservation for Ashley's rental car was still on the computer at the rental office.

"Right hand drive. It's been a while. Hope I remember how to do this." But she could manage. She'd 'managed' life without dancing. Without being able to ride any more. She'd 'managed' missing Sirocco. She could 'manage' driving a car on the wrong side of the road.

In an hour she'd replaced her brushes and paper and most of the paints she'd need. The store had even offered to deliver it to her hotel. That left her arms free for everything else.

By store closing at 5 o'clock, Ashley had worn out three detectives and Daemon, who'd taken over.

She'd replaced everything she'd lost. She even had a new tote bag that didn't smell like fish. She had new lingerie, new perfume, new everything. She'd even had time to have another shower and a short nap. This time without dreams…restless or otherwise.

No lions this time.

She'd kept taking out the book and scanning the underlining to see if there was a pattern to it. Maybe it was just a student's book or something.

By eight o'clock she sat in the "Saddle Room", the hotel's ornate dining room. Her nose stuck in a menu she decided it wouldn't be hard to decide what to have.

"Ah, scampi!" The tip of her tongue reached out to run along the edge of her top lip.

"Do that again."

Startled, she looked up and then up some more, to see the grin on his face.

He'd shaved. Again. And she caught the fresh tang of aftershave as he leaned forward to touch the soft, moistened skin above her upper lip with his fingertip.

"Do what?"

"What you just did with your lips." His voice was gruff again.

She could feel the heat rise in her cheeks and remembered that kiss.

"I was thinking about hot, fat, buttery scampi. It's been so long since I've eaten something that even resembles proper food. Chocolate bars don't count." Involuntarily, the pink tip of her tongue did it again.

Daemon grinned as he muttered, "Lucky scampi."

Ashley just laughed. She handed him a menu and dipped her head back into the folds of the menu as he pulled out his chair.

He looked so different. The rumpled pants and salt-crusted leather jacket were gone. A navy sports jacket fit perfectly over his broad shoulders and under it he wore a neatly pressed white shirt and dark grey slacks. He'd had a shower himself and his shaggy hair was now tamed and picking up the light from the chandeliers on variations of wheat and blond.

He didn't look like a lion tonight…unless lions knew their way around a wine list.

How can I concentrate on food when he looks like this? Ashley thought, and then looked up as he asked twice what kind of wine she liked.

"Where were you?" He looked puzzled.

"Sorry, I think I'm still suffering from ferry sinking and jet-lag. I can't concentrate." Except on your face.

***

"I said would you like white or red?" And then Daemon thought, I'd like to ply you with wine and find out if you're always a cool and together lady or if you have a weak spot when your guard is down. I'd like to lay you down on a bed somewhere and find out if you're soft everywhere. Naked…everywhere. Mine…everywhere.

"White. Sparkling. Sweet."

They placed their orders and their glances suddenly connected over the flickering candlelight.

It was time for the questions to start. For Daemon to put what he'd learned at the Yard into action. Cool, detached. Always detached.

A logical line of questioning. Random.

But not.

"I saw you in the Marine Building today and wondered if you'd ever been a dancer. You have a dancer's walk. My sister took ballet when she was younger and there's a distinctive way a dancer holds their body."

Ashley looked down at her napkin. He could see that she didn't want to talk about this. But she couldn't avoid his question altogether.

Daemon sat, wondering what was going through her mind and if she was thinking up a story to tell him. But the expression on her face wasn't a cover. He'd hit on something with his casual remark…something that had hit a nerve. There was something to this.

"I haven't danced for a long time. Not any real kind of dancing. I started ballet really young and was practicing for an audition to the youth corps in New York when I had my accident."

He watched a little wrinkle crease the skin between her brows. He wanted to put his finger out and smooth the crease away. She wasn't faking this.

"I guess dragging my toe-shoes to ballet lessons for years taught my body how to walk a certain way. We were trained for years to have a straight back, to keep our heads up, our hips in position. You never forget. It's part of your bones." She took a sip of the wine that had just arrived, letting the coolness slide down her tight throat.

She didn't really smile but the edges of her lips tilted up just a fraction.

"I love music. But I haven't seriously danced since I was twelve. The audition didn't happen." Her voice trailed off.

"You had said you had an accident. What happened?" Daemon's brows lifted in question. He tried to give her time. Tried to be gentle. Not to push. She looked up and he could see that she was struggling.

"I can't talk about all of it because it's too hard and I still have nightmares. All I can say is that a barn roof fell on me. My leg was broken and my other leg and knee were badly bruised. I've had physiotherapy and it doesn't hurt all the time anymore."

"A barn roof fell on you?" Daemon's heart jerked at the image of her under rubble.

She nodded.

"It only hurts now during ferry sinkings and when I've walked too much."

Daemon could hear loss in her voice and even in the glow of the candles he could tell that her normally ivory skin had paled. But there was humor there too and he admired that.

He wished now that he could take the question back. Could chase some life back into eyes that had lost their sparkle. There was an interest creeping inside him, curling around the edges of his heart and his professional guardedness.

"Is that why you paint?"

***

"What do you mean?"

"Painting is like dancing. It makes beautiful images. Did it help to take up any of the emptiness?"

How could he know that? How could a stranger see into her heart like that?

"It tore me apart to give up dancing. I grew up with ballet and horses. And I lost them both. At first, I couldn't ride because it hurt too much. And then when my leg healed, I couldn't bear the thought of climbing on a horse again."

"So, when did you start painting?"

"I was going crazy." Ashley's mouth curved in a wry smile. "Someone handed me a sketchbook while I was recovering and told me to draw. Then he put a brush in my hand and told me to paint. I wasn't very good at first but then I discovered my fingers loved a brush almost as much as my toes loved to beat out the steps of a dance."

She took another sip.

"And then one day I was limping out to the paddock and there was a tiny colt and I grabbed some paper and started to sketch him. Horses, even little ones, have such clean lines and Arabians have that distinctive arched head."

And then her unvoiced thought…painting made a horse live forever. Not like in real life.

***

Daemon pulled himself back into undercover mode again while they waited for their meals to come. He kept reminding himself that she hadn't passed on the package yet. He still had to treat her as a suspect as long as she had the book. But the pain had been real. Something bad had happened to her. Not just the accident. She had retreated from whatever it was that she hadn't shared.

He still couldn't figure her out. Every time he looked at her, she looked less and less like a part of this. His intuition was in overdrive. Checklist then. Observations.

She didn't fit the group of suspects they'd been given by his former, dead informant.

From head to toe she was elegance and grace. Her long raspberry silk dress skimmed her slender body from its halter neck top to the calf length that teased at her long legs. New high heels and nylon stockings had replaced her ruined clothes of the night before.

When she turned her head, her long fall of ebony-dark hair swung to one side. He could see the shimmer of pearl earrings that matched the single pearl on her right finger and the pearl necklace at her throat. The pearls covered part but not all of the bruises the mugger had put on her skin.

Daemon forced himself to be detached. His feeling of rage about her attack was getting in the way. He had to shed the image of her being hit and just concentrate on facts.

Then he'd maybe think about the fact that there was no ring on her left hand.

For some reason that made him smile.

***

The waiter arrived before he could ask anything else but Ashley could feel Daemon watch her all the way through the first course. She was more and more aware of the warm, heady heat his gaze triggered and her own attention kept straying to his mouth. His lips.

The ones that had…

She couldn't figure him out.

Inside her own powers of observation as a painter, there was something off. He wasn't just a casual writer or a day-job security planner. He was something or someone else.

He seemed so guarded one minute, so closed and serious.

And then he would say or do something so human. She hoped he wouldn't ask anything more. She didn't want to share the pain she'd tried so hard to leave behind. Keeping it inside would make it all go away some day if only the nightmares would stop.

***

Across the table, Daemon's attention kept straying to the tip of Ashley's slender fingers as they traced the rim of her wineglass. He could see them in the air in some ballerina pose, graceful, fluttering. He could see her at twelve in a pink tutu. He wondered if she'd been just an innocent child then and how she'd gotten mixed up in all of this.

His heart and mind surprised him with all the contradictions piling up to shout at him that she might just be innocent after all.

Could Shaughnessy have planted that package in her bag?

He followed her hands as they picked up a fork and started to eat the scampi. And he wondered how those hands would look holding a paintbrush; and remembered how they'd felt resting on his arm and on his face like they'd done in the lifeboat. Stretched out around his waist and under his shirt.

He jerked to attention and almost choked, grabbing his water glass and taking a gulp to stop coughing.

"Are you okay? What happened?"

"Wasn't paying attention." Lie.

Great heaping lie. He'd been paying attention to her instead of his food. He tore his gaze away from her and concentrated on his steak. The best meal he'd had in weeks and he didn't care if it was sawdust.

When Ashley spoke again, about traveling and hobbies and inconsequential things, he was forced to look at her. He saw her mouth move, that soft mouth that now glistened with the butter from the scampi and tiny effervescent drops of wine.

And he saw the tip of that pink tongue again as it touched the side of her lips. And he couldn't tear his attention away.

He wondered again what there was about her accident that had made her skin grow so pale and her expression so sad. It was more than just a derailed career and a bad leg.

***

The next few minutes they both kept to the edges and tiptoed around anything personal. Daemon fought to invent bits and pieces of his life and was able to give her some of the truth. About his brother and sister and his growing up years in Cornwall.

That he loved reading mysteries and loved the sea, even though he got seasick and couldn't stand being on the sea in a boat.

Ashley told him more about Beth and her loyalty and support over the years. He didn't know about the hours and hours she'd spent crying on Beth's shoulder in high school, when the nightmares were at their worst. And how Beth had held her and understood.

He listened to her chat about Carmel and about her university years and relaxed his guard enough to tell her that he had gone to boarding school and then Oxford.

"Wow! Oxford is a dream university. And it's a beautiful town. I've only seen pictures but I'd love to go there some day. Maybe if I have time before I go home."

I wish I could take you, he thought. He could hold her hand and walk with her through the quadrangles and show her where he'd studied.

"Do you do much reading Ashley? Like poetry?"

Here we go, thought Daemon, I'm sticking my neck out but I have to see what happens. She'll clam up or look guilty and I'll know.

"What do you mean?"

"I just noticed the book you carry in your bag. You had it out in the lifeboat. It looked like a special edition. Is it something important?"

He held his breath.

Ashley took a sip of her wine and swallowed, the wine's liquid path imperceptibly shivering the pearls at her throat. Daemon watched, fascinated.

"Actually, I do read quite a bit. But that book isn't mine."

Daemon choked again as a mouthful of steak collided with her answer. Ashley got up to pat him on the back, patting and rubbing in circles and handing him his water glass.

He wanted her to keep rubbing in those gentle circles. Maybe on his bare skin.

In a bed. On the silk sheets she'd talked about…driving him crazy.

"Are you alright? Can you breathe?"

Daemon coughed one last time and had more water, tears and more coughs coming as he nodded.

"I'm fine. Go on. You were saying about the book?"

"I have to get rid of it before I leave Dublin. Someone else needs it. You know, you don't look very well."

"I think I have a headache." Daemon pressed his fingers to a truly aching forehead. No sleep for two whole nights, too much coffee and one perplexing, blue-eyed woman.

"I'm sorry." Ashley put her hand up and motioned for the waiter and the bill. "Let's forget dessert and coffee."

"No, it's okay."

Daemon swallowed carefully until his breath returned to normal. He decided to let the subject drop but he had an uneasy feeling that either Ashley was crazy or he was.

***

The rest of dinner was disjointed, each of them retreating to their own thoughts, toying with their coffee and thinking about what was next.

Ashley wondered why Daemon had suddenly clammed up.

Daemon was busy trying to figure out how to keep Ashley and the book in sight tomorrow when she headed off on her painting job. If that was really where she was going.

It had been hard enough to get through today with only three hours of sleep. At this

point, he was damned if he was going to let someone else handle the night watch.

"Are you sure you're okay?"

Daemon looked up into Ashley's face. It was full of obvious concern.

And then it hit him.

He knew what he had to do.

Chapter Five

"Satin Pillows and Clark Gable"

Daemon needed to talk to McBride and he needed to do it now.

He scraped back his chair and told Ashley he had to check for a message from his office. She was leaving in the morning and he had to do something now. Something fast.

He grabbed a private corner and called McBride.

"There's something wrong. I don't think she knows what the book is. She's been waving it around and doesn't seem to care who sees it. I think Shaughnessy slipped it in her bag as a diversion. I know you've put someone on him until he wakes up. As soon as he does, I need to know who was really supposed to get it next if it wasn't her."

He rubbed at the pain in his forehead and rolled his shoulders to loosen the tightness.

"She was attacked today. I thought it was just for show but the man was rough and had a gun to her head. She didn't want to give him her bag and fought him off. The guards lost him in the crowd."

Daemon listened to McBride and nodded his head.

"I sent you a picture…you got it? Good. It was clear so I didn't need to work with the Garda sketch artist. They're searching their own data banks for known felons in Dublin who might match. My guess is he's going to go after her again."

Daemon described the book he'd seen Ashley looking at on the ferry and told McBride she'd openly admitted she had it but it belonged to someone else.

McBride filled him in with more of their check on Ashley and what he heard made Daemon's stomach clench. She'd been telling the truth. Now they needed Shaughnessy to spill his insides and clear her.

Daemon's gut already knew. It terrified him that if she was just a bystander she was now in terrible danger. If there'd been a sniper, she'd already be dead and someone else would be on the run with the book.

He couldn't let her go anywhere alone.

They had to find out who the mugger was. Who the next courier had been. How Shaughnessy had screwed up.

More and more it wasn't about following the book. Now it was about keeping her safe.

He clicked off and called his Irish contact. The officer in charge agreed to keep someone on the front and back doors of the hotel tonight and call in their squad detectives.

In London at headquarters Sam had a map of the whole area up on the computer screens and his squad was working with every informant they could find. Daemon had a running list going here in Dublin with his Irish counterparts.

***

By the time Daemon got back to the table, the check was waiting and Ashley had finished her coffee. Even with the extra caffeine she was drooping and Daemon knew exactly how she felt. It was time to put his plan into action.

To let him stick as close to her tonight as he could.

He let his forehead wrinkle in pain. Only part of his act was for Ashley's benefit. The rest of it was real.

"Got my messages and I can put everything on hold for a couple of days."

He rubbed his forehead and looked as miserable as he could without overdoing it. He hoped he looked pale and suffering.

"You need to call it quits and head back to your hotel then." Ashley gathered up her tote bag and started to look for her credit card.

Daemon gave a strangled laugh, remembering the lumpy cot at headquarters. "Sleep's going to be a problem. They gave my room away when I was late checking in and put me in a room over the pub. Lumpy bed, noisy bar."

He rubbed his forehead again. "Listen," he said, giving the waiter his Visa. He ignored Ashley's protest.

"I'm going to head back to the pub before I fall asleep on the sofa in your lobby. It looks more comfortable here. I'll look for something else tomorrow."

***

Ashley remembered how warm she'd been tucked up against him in the lifeboat. About how strong he'd been, without even knowing her history, in guiding her through her second disaster and giving her the strength to deal with it.

He'd given her comfort and she'd been a total stranger.

She shook her head.

"Daemon, there's a really simple option." She stood and turned towards the check in desk.

"I'll go find out if there's another room free here for tonight. The Dunvey Stud is paying for a suite and my original room is probably still good. I'll see if they can give you that one. I don't think the hotel is full."

She was gone before she could hear Daemon's soft curse.

***

"Damn! This is NOT what I wanted!"

He watched her leave the room and then looked at her empty chair. Her bag was on the floor beside it and the book peeked out from the corner.

If she really was a courier…and it was now a really big if…she was sloppy. Keep this up and she was dead. The thought made Daemon feel cold. He saw images of Ashley, ebony hair flung in the dirt, empty blue staring up at him lifelessly; a bullet in her forehead. It hit him in the stomach like a fist.

Even if she was innocent and she'd just been in the right place at the wrong time with Shaughnessy, she was in danger. She could end up lying in the same dirt, with the same bullet in her head. Today's incident proved that.

And even if she turned the book in, the person who'd tried to kill her had seen her with it and she already knew too much.

His head pounded.

He had to regain objectivity somehow. He knew she was in danger but the whole point of this was searching for clues and heading off a potential kidnapping. Someone else was in danger too.

They had the informant's list. They had a general area now…not in England or Wales but in Ireland. They just had to follow the book.

And why was it a book?

Why hadn't they used encrypted phones or Internet sites? Everything was done on-line now. Bombings and terrorist attacks. Why a book? Paper was so yesterday.

But maybe that's why it was clever. No one would have expected this.

His fingers itched to grab hold of the book. He'd had courses in code breaking. This was the first time anyone had seen what was being passed along.

Saving lives and catching criminals had been everything since he'd been 16. He'd gone into university with the intention of becoming a lawyer. Had always wanted to. His parents had been proud. And then, inexplicably, halfway through, he'd shifted paths and he and Sam had signed up with the Metropolitan Police. They grew up in privileged homes in the countryside, shared a love of sports and swimming, rowed together and ridden horses on equestrian teams in university. No one understood their choice about police work.

His explanation to himself and everyone else was that he wanted to see for himself what was happening on the streets.

He'd told his shocked family that he couldn't be a good lawyer unless he understood how criminals thought.

And the best place to do that was at their level, in their territory. He'd never intended to stay in the forces this long.

But he'd worked his way up the ranks, from being posted to the streets to detective training and then attachment duty. He was now a well-respected crime specialist. But now, at 34, it was time to get out and finish that law degree.

He'd learned to deal with people in all walks of life and he'd seen all kinds. But he'd never seen anyone like Ashley. She didn't fit any of the profiles.

He looked up to see her coming back into the room and suddenly it was too late to grab the book for a quick look.

"No luck. Someone else booked it."

Thank God!

"I have another idea."

Daemon knit his forehead again, puzzlement mixed with pain.

"You can sleep with me."

Her simple, five-word solution almost knocked Daemon off his chair. His brain was stunned, his body suddenly hard in spots that made it difficult to sit. He waited for her to finish.

"Look…the Dunveys upgraded me to a suite. It's way too big for just me. There's a locking interior door and when it's closed it makes two separate rooms. It would be really stupid for one night to have you go back to a lumpy bed when both of us are beyond exhausted and need to sleep."

She stood by his chair, looking down at him. Her expression was so earnest Daemon was without words.

His brilliant plan had been to sleep on the sofa in the hall outside her door. He'd asked the manager, after showing him his badge, if that was a possibility. He was cleared and the officer on duty was going to be his backup if exhaustion caught him off-guard and caused him to sleep in and miss her when she left.

***

Ashley watched Daemon's apparent surprise and could almost see the wheels turning in his head. She could imagine what was going on behind those suddenly guarded green lion eyes and they were lit with a curious fire. A fire that matched the heat she was feeling inside.

Was it want? Did she want this to go somewhere?

Did he?

"I'm leaving in the morning, Daemon, and you can find something else then. And I could lock the door."

"Like Clark Gable?"

Ashley cocked her eyebrow when he grinned.

"I know who Clark Gable was" she said, "But what does that have to do with doors?"

"My parents were great Clark Gable fans. We saw all his movies at film festivals when I was growing up. In that famous old movie, *It Happened One Night*, he was a reporter assigned to follow a runaway heiress. They ended up in a hotel for the night and there was only one room available. They shared the room but had to hang up a blanket to separate their beds."

Ashley laughed. "I do remember!" Then she caught a huge yawn with her hand. It had snuck up without warning. "Come. They gave me three toothbrushes and this will give you a chance to grow that stubble again." She held out her hand.

***

Daemon stood, taking her hand in his and putting his other arm around her as they walked to the elevator. He watched Ashley yawn again and she staggered as the elevator jerked to a start.

It was seemed natural for him to pull her in close to steady her. A surge of heat ran down his side as she tucked her arm around his waist. He caught that tantalizing scent of peaches again as it lingered on her skin.

He took a deep breath. This was going to be a long night. What he really wanted was to find out what was beneath the soft silk of her dress. To find out if her nipples would harden and peak when he kissed them. To lift her up into his arms and then put her down on what was likely to be silky sheets and big pillows. To strip away everything until they were skin to skin and he could be inside her.

But this was a job.

She was a job.

He didn't want her to be a job.

But until she was officially cleared, he couldn't sleep with her.

***

Ashley was so tired she didn't know if she could stay on her feet long enough to get to her room. Delayed reaction to the ferry sinking and the attack and the long sleepless night was coming in waves and the cut on her forehead and her bruises made her feel battered.

All she wanted was for Daemon to pick her up and carry her into the bedroom. Carry her to her bed. Lie down beside her and let her find out what was underneath his shirt. To take off his belt and feel his skin and rub her cheek against the stubble already showing up on his jaw.

To lie beside him and under him.

Daemon's arm helped her stay upright until they got to the right door and she fumbled in her purse for the key. She heard his whistle when he saw the suite. It was huge.

She smiled when she saw his reaction to the sheets and pillows. Were his thoughts going where hers were?

She slid out from under his arm and went into the bathroom, coming out with a pile of towels and soaps and a toothbrush and toothpaste.

"Here you are. This should be more comfortable than your lumpy bed. And I had an extra bottle of these in case my knee acted up…"

Ashley held out her hand to offer him a bottle of pain pills. "There's a glass of water poured in the bathroom. I'll be two minutes and you can have it to yourself."

***

Daemon took the pills and the towels and looked longingly at the bed. He wanted a long night with Ashley in her bed. But tonight, there were too many questions.

He stopped her before she turned to go, lifting his fingers to stroke the side of her cheek. Her skin was so soft. Warm.

"Ashley…"

She was suddenly trembling and leaning into his touch and before he could stop himself, he was putting his hand on the back of her neck and his lips on hers.

It started slowly.

And then she was kissing him back and he could hear the erratic catch of her breath. She went up on tiptoes to wrap her arms around his neck and he deepened the kiss, possessively holding her in place with one large hand on her bottom and the other on her breast, one finger teasing the nipple he felt through the silk of her dress.

Her breast was soft. Small. Firm. Perfect.

Like her.

He dragged his mouth and his hands away and just stood, holding her, catching his breath.

"I'll bring you an extra blanket," she whispered and stepped back, out of his arms.

Away from the immediate possibility of them taking that next step.

"Have a good night's sleep, Daemon. Thank you for everything. I'll see you tomorrow morning before I leave."

And then Daemon took a step forward, pulling her close to him again. He put his chin down on her hair and breathed in the scent of her perfume and felt the softness of her warm silk dress and the smooth coolness of her skin.

He dipped his head lower and looked into her face, saw her surprise, felt her heart beat faster. He threw all police training and caution and common sense away in a complete absence of any thought other than her lips were so close and they were all puffy from kissing him.

A lot had gone on between them in the past twenty-four hours.

She was no stranger now.

He raised one hand to her chin, lifting it slightly, and lowered his mouth to hers. His lips belonged there.

He wasn't made of ice and she sure wasn't either. This time it was a kiss built of shared experience and yet more than that.

Daemon had felt pulled by her from the minute he'd spotted her asleep in the waiting room in Wales. He'd felt it the minute the ferry had been hit and he couldn't get to her in the crowded companionway. He'd thought she was going to drown. He had gone beyond just trailing the package. And now they were both drowning.

When they came up for air it was Daemon who stepped back this time. He rested one hand lightly on her hair and then traced one fingertip along the arch of her eyebrow, watching her intently.

She put her own hand up to rest on the side of his cheek and leaned forward to whisper "Thank you. Sleep well," in his ear.

"I'll miss you," she said.

And then she turned and went into her room, closing the door softly behind her.

Daemon waited, thinking about Clark Gable.

She wouldn't. It was too 1940s.

The lock clicked shut.

His breath exhaled as he let a chuckle escape. Suddenly, tomorrow held possibilities. And tonight, there were satin pillows on his bed.

But in the morning Ashley was gone.

***

Sunlight streamed in through the windows and there was an insistent knocking at the door that dragged Daemon from the deepest sleep he'd had in months. He leaped to his feet, pulling on his jeans and a shirt and picking up his ringing cellphone.

He pulled open the door to the waiting Garda.

"She's gone, Chief Inspector. She just went down the hall with her suitcase and bag. I waited until she got into the elevator. Our man in the lobby will take over and we've got a GPS on her rental car."

Daemon felt as empty as the room. He'd allowed for falling asleep though...that's why he'd planned for backup.

But he needed to be trailing her.

With his gun and a team.

He ran into her room and checked everywhere for something, anything she might have left that would help them.

He'd already found out the location of the Stud. He knew the direction she'd be driving. But there'd be someone else after her too. Waiting for a good spot. A lonely spot. To grab the book and kill her.

Trained for speed, he grabbed his leather jacket and duffle and dragged impatient fingers through his hair as he ran for the door. There was no sign of Ashley in the street outside. She'd obviously done a pre-check-out because the officer said she hadn't stopped at the front desk. She wasn't just going somewhere in town because she'd taken everything with her.

Daemon waited for the Garda to check in with the officer who'd been given clearance last night to follow Ashley if she left the hotel. It took a few minutes to get him on his car radio.

"She's just picked up her rental car, Inspector. I had to go back for my own car but I've got her in sight. We're on the main road heading southwest out of Dublin."

Daemon looked at his watch and calculated time. He needed a police car and backup fast. He pulled out his cellphone and called Sam.

"She's gone. But the backup plan worked and she's being tailed. Do you have the…."

There was silence as Daemon listened, his face grim, to the update.

"Shaughnessy just woke up. He's scared and started spilling."

The pause was killing him. He couldn't wait to know. "Ashley?"

"Is free and clear. Shaughnessy told us everything about what he keeps calling 'his brilliant plan' to avoid the night ferry. He had a friend, Connor Donovan, waiting for her in Dublin."

So, his name was Donovan. Now the police had a name to go with the picture he'd taken of Ashley's attacker. And Ashley was clear. He couldn't think yet about what that meant to him.

He listened to Sam as he waited for the car, pacing the sidewalk and looking at his watch.

"None of the couriers know anything except their own little bit. Anything that came before they get the book wouldn't make any sense. They have only one bit of information they are told to add in the form of a word or two they are supposed to underline. Then they wrap the package up again and pass it along. Only the last person knows all the details."

Sam's voice grew gruff.

"You're getting involved with her, aren't you? I'm picking up on something. Do you want me to come over and help you keep her safe?"

Daemon couldn't mask the panic in his voice.

"I want her to be safe. Now that I know she's not part of this I just have to keep her alive and then we'll see if something can happen. I'll let you know. Do what you can from there."

"Right. There's a new problem though."

Daemon's heart couldn't take much more. The problems kept gnawing and eating him alive.

"Shaughnessy is terrified for his life. The man who got to him told him he's dead. He's compromised the plan. Shaughnessy confirmed it's a kidnapping but he doesn't know who or when. Just that it's soon and in Ireland. And it's big."

"And Ashley."

"Shaughnessy said they have to find her. The next few couriers have been given her description and Shaughnessy's buddy in Dublin has been following her. By now he'll have found out where she's going and passed it on to the next link in the chain. And Daemon…"

Daemon waited, his heart and body tense with strain. And worry.

"Daemon, she was dealing with a lower-level crook when she was attacked yesterday."

Daemon waited for the next part. The ugly part.

"The next link is closer to the top and he won't be fooling around when he goes after her. You need to find her but we can't lose the chain. Somehow, we need to keep the book in the open so you can find out who it goes to next."

His imagination in overdrive, Daemon clicked off, looking at his watch and the front door, cursing the flying minutes. Finally, the flashing red light of an unmarked police car pulled up in front of the hotel, an officer rushing in to meet Daemon.

"I'll drive you, Chief Inspector. I know where she's headed. The car ahead is keeping in touch with us."

Daemon ran to the police car and they were off, dodging in and out of morning rush hour traffic, their siren blaring until they hit the city limits and out into the outlying districts of Dublin. And then the car radio suddenly lost contact with the first car. Nothing.

Daemon sat, frozen, as the police tried over and over to get his partner on the car phone. While he changed frequencies and sped through the countryside, he checked routes and figured they were still on track. Daemon had told him Ashley was probably headed in the direction of the stud farm and it was well known enough that the officer knew the way she'd have gone.

Likely unfamiliar with the rental car, she probably wouldn't have been driving fast. Daemon reached into the back seat for his jacket, searching for the small map of the area he'd picked up from the chief yesterday. He'd been expecting to follow someone, if not Ashley then the next link in the couriers.

There was more than a map. He pulled out a folded piece of paper in what must be Ashley's handwriting. It held the faint scent of her perfume and he concentrated just for a brief second on sweet peaches.

It meant she hadn't been so completely immune to what had happened last night that she'd been able to just walk out this morning without even saying goodbye.

In the next second his heart almost stopped because if he hadn't taken out the wallet with his badge and police ID in it and put it under his pillow, she would have found it and known that he was a police officer.

She'd obviously put the paper in his jacket this morning on her way out the door. The thought of her walking by him as he'd slept made Daemon feel odd.

He'd been the one who had been watched.

"Dear Daemon,

I wanted to say goodbye but you were sound asleep and I didn't have the heart to wake you. You must be exhausted. I hope you feel better today and your headache is gone. Help yourself to the shower and stay in the room as long as you want.

I said last night I'd miss you. I will.

Thank you so much for everything that you did to keep me safe.

I'll remember you.

Ashley"

She'd drawn a small lion at the bottom of the page and darned if it didn't look like him! He looked up at the highway ahead of them, anxiously scanning the sides of the road.

"Keep me safe. Keep me safe."

Her words became an intonation in his head. How could he keep her safe if he didn't know where she was? He sat, cursing his brain. All along she'd been innocent. All along, even when he'd thought she was guilty, his brain had been fighting with the inconsistencies and doubts. Something was wrong, something was wrong.

"Damn!" He shouldn't have fallen so deeply asleep. Deep sleep was not regulation for a police officer on a case. Even with backup. But exhaustion had chased him into immediate oblivion, only disturbed by haunting dreams of Ashley on the other side of the connecting door.

Ashley asleep on the same satin pillows, her hair scattered across the smooth ivory surface.

They'd lost contact with the police officer trailing her.

Were they both dead?

***

Hours earlier, Ashley had woken to sunlight and silence. It was early enough that she'd had time for a quick shower and then she'd needed to get on the road. Lord Dunvey had told her she could have an extra day to rest but she wanted to get back to normal and start her job. A horse was waiting and she smiled, thinking about her new brushes and blank watercolor papers.

She'd rolled over in the bed, hugging her pillow until she sat up with a jolt.

Daemon! He'd been right there…on the other side of the connecting door! Ashley put her fingertips on her lips, remembering the way his mouth had felt on hers, the easy slide of his arms around her. It had been so natural. But it wasn't.

Today was the first day of her job. She was going to be living on the stud farm until the painting was done and then she was going home. To California. Home to steady routine and commissions and her gallery.

Daemon lived half a world away and meeting on a sinking ferry was not exactly a normal way to start any kind of relationship with anyone.

This had nowhere to go.

Except out the door and into her rental car and on the road.

But God, she'd miss him. Her heart felt stripped and empty.

She'd checked in the outer room and noticed Daemon's leather jacket on the end of the chair where he'd dropped it last night. She'd focused on his closed bedroom door, she'd imagined him, asleep inside, his lean body stretched out on the white sheets, exhausted and completely asleep.

If they'd known each other longer or in different circumstances, she might have opened that door. She might have gone in on bare feet, dropped her robe to the floor and climbed in with him.

She might have nestled in beside his warm body and used her fingertips to trace the line of his jaw and his neck to find out if the golden stubble on his cheeks repeated itself in longer hair on his chest. And maybe those feathers of golden hair on his chest would taper off into a silky line leading to…

She'd shaken her head wistfully and gone back into her room to shower and pack. By the time she was ready, Daemon's jacket had still been untouched and there was only silence. He was beyond tired and she hadn't wanted to knock on the door and wake him up. So, she'd torn a piece of paper from the hotel stationary pad and left him a note. It wasn't enough. Not after everything they'd been through.

But she'd had to leave and just put the note in the pocket of the jacket. She'd rested her hand on its shoulder for a minute, remembering how it had looked when she'd first seen him, the way it had hugged his rugged frame perfectly. The way the warm leather and his arms had kept her from freezing on the ferry. She picked up the coat and nestled her nose in it for just a moment. Long enough to memorize the scent of the leather and Daemon.

She'd stepped back and collected her new suitcase and tote and the trench coat that had just come back from dry cleaning. She turned her head, looked once more at his door, and left.

A taxi had taken her to the rental company and she'd been in her car in minutes. She'd rented right-hand drive cars on other trips to the UK but it was always a challenge to get going.

Luckily this was an automatic and she didn't have to worry about shifting with her opposite hand. But driving in any new city was a challenge.

Now that she was out on the open road she was frustrated. Traffic was horrendous and road signs were tucked away in unusual places. She'd had to go around and around to get clear of the one-way streets and thought she'd never figure it out.

So, she didn't notice the other two cars shadowing her and following every turn she made.

***

Miles of whitewashed cottages lay beyond the Georgian houses of downtown Dublin. The main road into County Kildare opened up into vast rolling fields of lush green.

Ashley finally relaxed enough to start thinking more about the horse she was going to be painting and less about the way that Daemon's hair grew over his collar.

More about the past of this Grand National steeplechase winner than about the way that it had felt to lie against Daemon's shoulder in the lifeboat.

Dark Night had won two Grand Nationals in a row. The Irish thoroughbred had a long, unbroken line of wins to his credit and was now retired to stud. He'd had several colts in the past few years and they were scattered all over Ireland and the rest of Europe, some of them doing extremely well themselves, especially the colt Black Cloud.

A peal of thunder suddenly cracked overhead and the sunlight disappeared. Rain sheeted down and forced the car's windshield wipers into overdrive. Ashley quickly pulled off onto the verge of the road, locked the doors and waited out the dark skies and torrents of water.

The traffic was still heavy enough that the two cars following her just blended in with the rain.

She checked her GPS again and with one finger she touched the smooth cover of the book. She hadn't looked at it since yesterday at the Marine Building and she was curious about the underlining. Opening the front cover, she flipped through to the first poem and looked at it closely. For the first time she noticed the underlining seemed odd.

It wasn't just descriptive phrases or passages. Sometimes it was single words, out of context. Or someone had underlined groups of words that didn't seem especially unique without the words around them making them significantly beautiful or special. "For instance," she wondered out loud, "what about this one?" Her finger traced a line from "The Fiddler of Dooney."

"My cousin is a priest in Kilvarnet"

And then she flipped pages and spotted "An Irish Airman Foresees His Death". She'd always found this one really sad, but the underlined words sounded almost angry:

"Those that I guard I do not love."

Another poem, "The Wild Swans of Coole" only had one thing underlined. It was a number:

"Upon the brimming water among the stones
Are nine-and-fifty swans."

Ashley leaned her head back to rest for a minute and saw again the drunk in the waiting room, knocking her tote bag off her shoulder and then reaching down to pick it up. She felt again the moment of adrenalin when the man at the Maritime Building had grabbed her tote bag and hit her.

There really was something weird about what was happening to her and somehow, she didn't think this was just someone's favorite poetry.

The underlining was too random.

Something was going on.

The magic of Ireland reappeared then in the warm sunlight that seemed to have come out of nowhere to break through the dark clouds. The rain had stopped and a whole flock of ducks had flown in to land on the huge pond beside her car.

Ashley stowed the book in her bag and grabbed her sketchpad and a pencil. She couldn't capture the furious quacking but she wanted to have impressions of exploding spray as new ducks landed in the dense clumps of lily pads. One huge drake plunged his head into the water and came up with his beak dripping, trailing soggy green strands of grass and pond muck.

One of the biggest ducks came in for a landing on Ashley's windshield, startling both her and the duck. The feathered fellow web-flapped all over her windshield wipers. He left juicy, clinging bits of lily pad behind at each step and Ashley stared, transfixed, as he reached out his yellow, waxy beak and pecked at a choice piece of green. Raising one tiny, beady eye, he stared right in her direction and must have realized he wasn't alone. He flew off to join his flock.

By the time the ducks had taken flight to go and forage somewhere else, Ashley had two pages that held startlingly vivid drawings…maybe never to become part of a painting but part of a serendipitous moment in time.

She headed back out onto the road and passed a grouping of stores that hadn't closed yet for the long Irish lunchtime. When she spotted a sign advertising photocopying, some strange sense of premonition made the hair on her neck prickle. The book was just creepy.

She climbed out of the little car and grabbed her bag, pulling it close to her until she got inside the store, where she quickly opened up the book and ran the pages over the glass of the photocopier. She grabbed a chocolate bar from the display at the front of the store and was outside again in minutes.

Inside her car, she had a sudden urge to be a spy. Just in case this was something tied to a crime. She bent her head and studied the lines again, dragging out her pencil to underline some new passages on the pages of the original book. Then she lifted the seat covers and tucked the photocopied pages underneath the thick sheepskin mat.

She patted the spot and smoothed it until there were no telltale lumps. "I'm paranoid," she murmured to herself. "Stark-raving paranoid. But something doesn't feel right."

Her stomach growled suddenly and she realized she hadn't stopped anywhere for breakfast. She checked her watch and started the car, pulling back onto the main road. A sign several miles along advertised a pub and even though they usually closed for the main part of the day, she thought maybe she could get something to take away.

Heavily wet green fields slid by beside the car until she reached the turnout into a large parking lot and pulled up in front of 'The Four Shamrocks'. Passing several weather-stained Guinness signs at the front, Ashley swung the huge oak doors open and plunged into velvet darkness, heady with the smell of ale and stout. A wiry old man with a long white beard and an apron stained with age popped out from the back and brought her a menu chalked on a slate board.

"A pint for yourself, young lady?"

"No, thanks, but a coffee maybe and a pastry or something for the miles ahead?"

"We do a cut lunch if you'd rather, or the wife made scones not an hour ago."

Ashley pointed to the scones. The pub was filled with a hazy silence and the smell of smoke from over a century of customers, mostly locals coming in to talk about their sheep or the price of vegetables.

There was a television screen over the bar and a scattering of people watched a local rugby game.

Some of them were busy texting. Today it was computers and technology that competed with farming to lure young people away into the cities.

She looked up through the dimness and could see dusty rafters that tilted away from the ceiling in places, threatening to collapse but held in place by cobwebs and cooking oil and time. Years of elbows and sliding mugs had worn the bar counter smooth.

But the place was warm and dry and quiet. As other teatime customers trickled in, there was a feeling of comradeship, friendly banter back and forth amongst those who knew each other and polite nods to Ashley.

When her coffee came, Ashley dropped several Irish pound notes on the counter and said thanks, taking her coffee and scone over to a table. She was aware of passing time and didn't trust the weather so it was a hurried lunch.

When she was done, she stood up, smoothing the creases out of her long tan skirt and gathering her purse and tote. It took a few minutes to adjust to the bright sunbeams after the pub gloom.

Her car sat, peacefully waiting in the still air, just as Ashley had left it.

Almost.

She nearly missed the open door because it was on the driver's side. It hung, gently swinging with the breeze.

Off its hinges.

Heart suddenly clutching in her chest, Ashley's steps slowed and she had to force herself to walk the last few yards. A cautious glance showed that the inside of the car was empty. But the vacancy was black with malice.

Innocent sunshine filtered in to light the front seat and Ashley was stunned. The car had been trashed. Violently. The glove compartment and side pockets had been turned inside out.

Her suitcase was in the trunk but the trunk had been pried open and the case had been dumped…clothes she'd bought in Dublin lay spilling over the floorboards in an obscene splash of patterns. Her paints and brushes seemed unhurt but they were scattered everywhere. Her precious papers had been handled roughly and just tossed into the gravel.

Hands shaking, Ashley reached out to gather them and put them away from harm.

Extending her hand toward the swinging door, Ashley pushed the useless metal out of her way. Mouth dry and breath short, she leaned into the car, searching for something, anything, to give her an idea of what could have happened. She drew back, startled. An unmistakable, very familiar smell hung in the humid air of the car, mingling with her perfume and the 'new car' odor of the rental.

It was a frightening smell because it could only have come from one sort of place and it didn't belong here in her car. It merged with the imminent threat involved in the violence in front of her.

And then a stranger came; stalking her from behind with the cat feet that such people are born with. Out of the shadows a large, rough arm reached out into the sunshine to circle her throat. He had a gun. And once more it was jammed into her throat.

She was going to die.

All she could think of was that this had been a terrible trip and she wanted to go home. But then she heard a 'click'. And then another 'click.'

And a curse and she felt the gun lift away.

Why?

But the arm was back and it began a deadly crush. She tried to kick out again the way she'd done before. He was too close. He was too close.

In some disjointed part of her mind, she noticed a tattoo almost hidden by the dark hairs on the man's arm.

And how familiar that smell was.

And how much she missed Daemon.

And wanted him here.

Then she could only think about the fact that her breath was no longer coming at all and things were getting dark.

She didn't like the dark.

Chapter Six

"Lies and Sweetened Tea"

Something cool and soft drifted through Ashley's fingers. She clenched and unclenched her hands, trying to identify the shivering substance. For some reason, she was incredibly glad that she could feel anything at all. Gradually, other sensations sorted themselves out in her numbed brain.

She was having a terrible time trying to breathe.

She floated, disconnected, her head whirling with scattered visions that both frightened and puzzled her. Noises assaulted her ears. It sounded like…gunshots?

The skidding of car tyres on gravel, a siren. More shots.

And then she stopped breathing and everything was quiet again.

***

"Ashley! God!"

It was Daemon's nightmare. He'd found her by her car. But it was the image that had haunted him.

She lay, sprawled on the gravel, her long hair tangled and covered with dust. She was so still.

There wasn't a bullet hole in her head. But there was a gun in the gravel beside her. Had she been shot? Frantically, he checked her. She wasn't breathing and his heart threatened to stop.

He put his mouth over hers and started CPR. He breathed for her and breathed for her and his tears welled up and spilled.

He'd only just found out she was innocent and he'd lost her before they'd had a chance to even start.

He wasn't going to give up but her beautiful lips were turning blue and her skin was getting cold.

He pushed, desperately, on her chest and pushed again and suddenly she coughed.

Blessed, blessed cough.

He watched her eyelids flicker and grabbed her hand while he opened her coat and looked everywhere for blood or a dark, ugly entrance wound.

Nothing.

"Ashley, sweetheart. Open your eyes. Please!"

***

There was a voice.

It sounded like it might be right beside her but all of the sounds were muffled.

Ashley thought she could feel fingers on her cheeks and an arm under her shoulders, lifting and pulling her onto something softer.

It must be raining again because something wet was dripping on her face. She tried to wipe it away but she couldn't move her arms.

"Is she all right, Chief Inspector? She's not looking good, she's not."

"Ashley, can you hear me? You're going to be all right. The publican is calling the doctor in the village. He's coming right now."

The voice sounded hoarse and rough. Richly sensual in a way she should be recognizing. But her ears were ringing. The fingers kept touching her face, stroking her eyebrows and cupping her chin. Someone had put something very cold on her forehead and she started to shiver.

She could hear voices again, above her head, and she could make out words but they didn't make any sense.

"Am I dead?"

She thought she'd said it out loud but it was a croaking whisper and it startled her. The words had started in her mind but it wasn't her voice. It couldn't be her voice. She didn't talk like that. But it was her thought.

"No, Ashley, sweetheart. You're not dead." The voice had a crack in it. It sounded like somebody was upset. "But the person who did this to you would be dead if we'd been here sooner. Hang on. Help is coming."

Seductive that voice.

Seductive and dearly familiar.

There was a definite pull to it.

"It hurts." This time the voice that came from deep inside her head had a whimper in it. She never whimpered. Never. Not since that day so long ago when the ceiling of the barn had fallen on her. No whimpers ever since. She didn't allow herself to whimper.

Except in her nightmares.

"Try, Ashley. I know it hurts. But try."

Her brain wasn't working but the voice was gently commanding and she struggled. Fragmentary slits opened and then she closed them against the brilliant sunshine.

Too bright.

She squinted and tried again.

Then they opened fractionally wider and all she could see was an immense sky with giant puffy clouds.

Milcs and miles of blue softened by the Irish mist.

And the searing pain of the sunlight.

Then a hand gently covered her eyelids and it was darker. She was aware of another hand, feather light, touching the skin of her neck and her forehead, smoothing back her hair.

Ashley rested a minute and then took a tentative breath, remembering that it had been impossible to breathe.

She started to shake and warm arms wrapped themselves around her. Something that felt like a blanket was draped over her.

"Oh, my God!"

She tried to make herself get up but something was holding her down.

"Ashley, don't move. I've got you. You're okay. Stay still. It's me. It's Daemon."

Daemon!

How?

Memories came flooding back. An arm choking her. An attempt to kick out at someone. A gun and a click and another click and expecting a bullet in her head.

And then a curse and she'd been choked and choked and choked.

And it had been so dark.

She couldn't stop shaking.

This time she looked straight into the keenly searching emerald green gaze of her own private lion. The look on his face could only be the look of a lion. Tension and fury. His eyes were flashing with it. But there was fear there too. And there were tears.

Her lion was going to growl and roar any minute. But he whispered instead. He bent his head to her ear. "It's okay. It's okay."

Ashley's mind whirled with kaleidoscope images. Pages of underlining, a strange smell, scones and coffee, old beams and cobwebs, webbed feet and lily pads, a rough hairy arm.

A hairy arm?

"Daemon, his arm was hairy."

"What was that? Here, whisper in my ear, it won't hurt so much." The shaggy blond head came close to her and she repeated what she had said.

"His arm. The man who wrecked my car. His arm was hairy. It tickled my nose when he was choking me." Her shaking intensified.

"He had a gun. But it clicked. And it clicked. I think it was out of bullets."

It was getting easier to focus. She looked around and started to notice things. A police car, its light whirling. Someone in uniform standing next to the publican. Noises as people around her talked.

Garda. She remembered now…they were the Irish police.

"What is it doing here?"

"What do you mean, Ashley?"

"The police car. What is it doing here? What are you doing here?"

"We were looking for you. We were worried. I'll tell you all about it after the doctor comes."

Ashley sighed and dropped her head against Daemon's chest. She could feel the thudding of his heart under her cheek. The heartbeats were racing. Then he shifted and she realized she was cradled in his lap and he was sitting on the ground, gently rocking her.

"Daemon, it's cold."

"I know. We'll get you up in a minute."

Ashley rested against the feel of leather and hard muscles and felt tiny fingers of unease jiggle in her stomach.

"Daemon?"

He bent his head to her again.

"Daemon, why are you here? I'm so glad you're here. But why?"

Her question was answered with one shattering sentence from the Garda officer. "Chief Inspector O'Hare, sir. The doctor is here."

***

Inspector? O'Hare? Was Daemon with the police?

"What?" Ashley croaked.

"I'll explain it all later. Here, let the doctor look at you."

It was too much of an effort to think and she looked away, until she felt the cold of something metal against her skin. She stared straight into the kindest face she'd ever seen and the first real sense of safety she'd felt.

"Top of the morning to you lass. Although, to be true, it's not been a good one for you, has it? No, don't shake your head. It must hurt terrible bad for sure."

The man must be the doctor. He was doing doctor things, listening in her ears and and using utterly gentle fingertips to check her pulse and listen to her heart. He tested her ribs and carefully examined the tender spots on her neck. He took the cold metal away and Ashley could see that it was a stethoscope.

"Well, Miss Gallagher. I think you'll be living to see another day. To be sure, you'll be hoping it will be a better one. You'll be having some monstrous bruises on that poor neck but ice will help. I can't find anything broken and Chief Inspector O'Hare says he couldn't find a bullet wound."

Over the top of her head, she could hear the strangest conversation and it filtered down to her ringing ears in spasmodic bursts that she was only now beginning to understand.

"Chief Inspector, on my first glance she seems not to be badly hurt. I was worried about her hyoid bone. It's the bone in the neck that's often crushed and causes death in this kind of assault. But I'd feel better if she could be taken in to the next village. There's a proper examining room there and an x-ray machine. We'll check her throat and ribs and make certain sure there's nothing damaged."

The word 'Chief Inspector' once more.

That didn't make sense. Nothing made sense.

"You're a lucky young lady, you are." It was the doctor, down to her eye level and speaking softly. He had whiskers and the biggest eyebrows. They twitched when he talked.

"I'll ask the two officers here to get you into my examining room and they'll look after your poor car as well. It's a shame this has happened to you."

Officers.

Two of them.

Ashley could only see two men. And one of them was Daemon. The publican moved into her line of sight and smiled down at her.

"We had a fright we did, when we saw that big hairy blaggart with his arm around your neck. If your young man hadn't come when he did, we'd be burying you for sure. The siren scared him into the woods and he got away before we could see his face, more's the pity. But you're alive and that's the beautiful thing."

Ashley's sore lips lifted in a half-smile and she tried to thank him for his concern.

Daemon's arms were around her and she wanted to see his face. She wanted to ask him what was going on. To explain what she had heard. Her fingers held onto his hand tightly as the world spun around for a crazy, tilting second. The other hand reached down to search for the cool something she'd felt earlier.

Soil. Smooth, peaty earth mixed with the gravel in the parking lot. She stared at her fingernails. They were dirty. She'd have to have to deal with that later. A manicure. And a pedicure.

Maybe a massage.

That would be good.

***

Above her head, Daemon's heart jerked as he watched tears spill over. Reaction? He wasn't really surprised. He dipped his head to rest his chin gently on the dark hair now freckled with bits of grass and peat bark.

"Did you see what he looked like, sweetheart? Don't talk or nod your head if it hurts but it would help us if we knew."

Daemon couldn't remember the last time he'd used the word 'sweetheart' with anyone but Ashley. Or the last time his heart had been beating so fast against his ribs.

"I saw bits of him," she whispered. "When I tried to kick him. He was standing with his back to the sun and it made him all shadowed. But there were bits."

Daemon felt agony again on what he had seen when they'd driven up. Ashley, crumpled on her back in the sunlight, golden beams glittering in her long, tumbled hair and her limp fingers flung out against the wet dirt. The only color at all had been the trickle of blood coming from the corner of her mouth. He'd dabbed at it with his handkerchief to wipe it away.

***

Daemon had seen too much blood today. But the blood on Ashley had done him in.

The first Garda to follow Ashley was dead. It had looked like his car had been cut off and run onto the verge of the road. He'd had his hand on his gun. If he hadn't been a detective, he'd have been unarmed. But specialist detectives over here, like Daemon's detective squad with the Metropolitan Police were authorized to carry a gun.

The dead officer had been reaching for a Sig Sauer P226. He hadn't been able to get off a shot.

Daemon had had better luck.

There had been a brief shoot-out with Connor. His partner had apparently dropped him off to deal with the policeman and driven ahead to kill Ashley.

When they'd spotted Connor running from the car, Connor had opened fire on them. Daemon had been grazed by one of the bullets and Connor had put a bullet into the other detective's shoulder.

There hadn't been any way to disarm him. They'd both been hit.

When Connor raised his gun again, Daemon's Glock had ended the carnage.

Connor might have been able to add more to the investigation. But he hadn't given them a chance.

***

"You tried to kick him?" Daemon had seen Ashley in action once before and smiled a little, wondering if she'd connected and if she'd done any damage. He hoped so. "Who taught you self- defense?"

"My brothers. They thought it was their duty as older brothers to look after their little sister."

"Remind me some day to thank them."

Some day? Daemon stopped on the thought…It was appealing.

"Daemon?"

He put his ear to her lips.

"I think I could draw a picture of him. His arms were hairy. And there was a tattoo. And something in my car smelled funny."

"Okay. Rest your voice. We'll ask the doctor if you could have something for your throat and then we'll take you to his surgery office." The doctor nodded his head and turned to the publican.

"Tea. Sweet…not too hot. And Chief Inspector, you and the other officer are bleeding."

He could feel Ashley's fingers grip his arm and she tried to say something. He just gently put his palm over her mouth and said "Rest your throat."

Daemon lifted Ashley sideways enough to get his injured arm out of his jacket. The bullet had just grazed the leather but it had somehow penetrated the seam and his skin had been nicked.

"Just a quick cleanup I think, sir. You'll be fine."

***

Ashley felt herself slipping away again and tried to hold on. There were voices and things happening all around her.

She heard something about a Garda being killed.

They thought the killers had been following her all the way from Dublin and spotted the police car behind her. They'd needed him out of the way so they could get to her.

Why was the police car following her?

Her brains hurt.

"Get me up!"

Ashley pushed against Daemon's arm and struggled to get up, to get her shaking legs working. She needed…she didn't know what she needed.

"I need tea so I can talk. I need my sketchpad and a pencil."

She turned her head toward Daemon, her heart icy and cracking…her thoughts dark and confused and hurt.

"You're not who you said you were, Daemon Smith. And you've been following me."

Her voice broke with emotion, her throat so tight that she could only get out a tiny, sandpapery whisper. She turned her head away, trying hard to get up.

Instead, Daemon leaned forward to get his feet under him and pulled Ashley up with arms that tightened around her. She had no choice but to hang on and lean her head against his chest to stop the spinning. She swallowed a wave of frustration, wincing at the pain in her throat. Her chest was filled with building anger and bitter disappointment.

***

Shock on shock today. It swirled all around her.

Shock and disbelief.

If Daemon was a policeman and not what he'd told her before, then why had he been sticking so close to her ever since the ferry? He'd lied. Why?

Just for one stolen moment, she melted into the warmth of his jacket, his body heat seeping through his shirt. She was so cold and he was so warm as he strode through the watery sunbeams into the pub, with her carried high up in his arms.

The sweet, heavy smell of ale hit her senses again once they got inside and her head swam with the combination of motion and alcohol. When Daemon put her down in an old padded armchair she clutched onto the scarred wood of its armrests and waited until the room stopped spinning.

The publican brought over a mug of sweetened tea and she took it with shaking hands, raising it to her lips and blowing on it a bit before she took a tentative sip, wincing as it stung.

She looked over the rim of the mug at Daemon, who stood talking to the other policeman over by the bar. They seemed deep in a four-way conversation, occasionally looking up and sharing what they were hearing on their cellphones.

Suddenly, she squeaked. “Why didn’t I ask before? My purse! My bag! The book!”

Daemon ran over, telling the person on the phone to hold on. “What’s wrong?”

“The tote-bag! Did he take it? Daemon, you haven’t told me why you were following me. Tell me now. I think I know what’s happening.”

He scraped a chair over beside her and told the person on the phone he’d call back.

A moment of reckoning. Explanations and questions.

“Daemon, I need answers.”

He sighed. “I was more worried about you. But there was an initial search and your bag and purse were thrown into the bushes by the road. We were hoping to find the book but it wasn’t there.”

Ashley reached out her hand but couldn’t bear to touch him yet. Her heart was hurting. She could feel its disjointed squeezing and the pain was ripping her apart. “Daemon, you lied about who you are. You’re a policeman?”

He nodded his head. “Metropolitan Police. You know it as New Scotland Yard.”

“You’re on a case?

He looked at her and then away, his jaw rigid, expression shuttered.

“Is it about the book?”

Daemon swung his head back to her, his face tense, waiting.

“Daemon, I don’t know what that book is, but there’s something really strange about it. Ever since I left that waiting room, things have been happening to me. I can’t blame the ferry sinking on it but I’ve been mugged twice now. I need to know why.”

She took another sip of tea, its sweet warmth running down her tortured throat.

"I can't tell you everything but I was in the waiting room to witness a transfer. We didn't know what the package was going to be but we knew the man who was going to pass it."

"That drunk who bumped into me?"

Daemon watched Ashley's face as she obviously replayed troubling memories.

"Shaughnessy Ryan. He's lower-level scum working for a syndicate in England. He has contacts over here and both the Yard and the Garda know him for petty crimes. We didn't expect him to be involved in this because he's not the smartest crook."

"He put the package with the book in my bag?"

Daemon watched her as dawning realization crossed her face. The next questions were going to be hard to answer. He waited for them.

"And you thought I was a crook? You thought I could do something against the law? Something important enough for Scotland Yard to be involved?" She could hear her own voice and it held more pain than the kind that was coming from her throat and bruised skin. She felt such betrayal that she felt sick.

"You were following me because you thought I would pass the package on to someone else?"

She watched his face.

And she knew. No explaining this away.

Daemon waved the officer off when the other officer came over to ask him a question. "In a minute. Give me a minute."

***

His heart was breaking. Daemon had heard the expression so many times and thought it was overdone. Deaths in the family. Good friends shot in the line of duty. Crushing grief. Yes.

But this was different.

"Ashley, when I saw you in the waiting room, I didn't know who you were. I saw an incredibly beautiful woman who stood out in a room full of people. I chose to sit beside you because I was intrigued and I wanted to talk to you."

She looked at him, not saying anything, willing him to go on.

"When you went outside, I was searching the room, waiting to see if Shaughnessy would show up. That's why I was there. The only reason I was there. I need to see who he would pass it on to next."

"He passed it on to me."

A pause, laden with unease, regret and understanding.

"He passed it on to you. Remember, I said that I didn't know you or anything about you. When I saw him put the package in your bag I was on a job. I had to keep track of you until you passed it on to someone else."

"It was your job." Ashley's voice was without expression. Deadened. "All those hours in the lifeboat, Daemon. My head on your shoulder."

A tear ran down her bruised cheek. "Thc dinner in Dublin. You kissed me. I was just a job?"

Silence.

"In my room. Would you have slept with me?" Another tear.

"Am I still your job?"

Daemon put his hands on her shoulders and waited until she looked at him again.

"No."

He shook his head, serious green connecting with blue.

"No, you are not my job. I know you now. I also know Scotland Yard checked you out. Shaughnessy was shot by someone in the chain but he lived. He told us that you are completely innocent."

He traced another tear with his fingertip and wiped it away.

"Can you believe that I needed to be sure? That I've been working to be sure? Hoping?"

The tears spilled over then and ran down Ashley's face, no stopping them now. She dipped her head, resting it on Daemon's sleeve and sobbed.

She nodded her head.

"I was following a woman I didn't know. But even before we got off the lifeboat, I knew there was something wrong. I knew you couldn't be that person I thought you might be."

"And the book?"

Daemon dragged tense fingers through his hair and let out an exasperated, angry breath.

"I'm going to get fired for telling you this but after everything you've gone through, I can share part of it. The damned book has something to do with a kidnapping that's about to happen."

She lifted her head in astonishment.

"So, you think the book is important? Part of the plan?"

"We don't know who or what or where but it's going to happen here in Ireland. We knew that the package had to have something in it that was being shuttled from person to person instead of through the Internet. For the past few years, a lot of criminals have gone back to the old-fashioned way of doing things because technology is getting easier to hack into."

Ashley put her hand up to Daemon's mouth to still his words. He stopped, looking intently at her, waiting for any reaction other than contempt.

"Daemon. Did you know at the start that it was a book? Because if you didn't then I think I know why they're using a book."

Daemon called over the Garda and told him to listen. Notepads came out and both men waited for her to tell them more.

"Daemon, is the book still in my tote bag?"

"No, it's gone. And we don't have a lead yet on who took it. Why?"

"I felt strange about the book even when I first saw it. I thought it was just somebody's poetry book. It was a collection of Yeats."

"Yeats? Appropriate since he's one of Ireland's most famous poets."

"I noticed when I found it on the lifeboat that it had underlining in it. All sorts of phrases and some single words. I thought it was that someone liked those parts. I love Yeats and the way he used words."

"But?"

"But the way things were chosen didn't make sense. Single words, parts that weren't unique or especially beautiful or profound or anything. It made my skin crawl."

Daemon looked at the other officer, who had been briefed on the case.

"Code, sir?"

All three of them looked at each other and said, "Yes!"

Daemon reached for his cellphone, ready to call Sam to tell him they needed to grill Shaughnessy again. Shaughnessy hadn't spilled this part and hadn't told them this was what they'd been doing with the package. Hadn't even told them it was a book.

Then he stopped.

"You know, I don't think Shaughnessy knew it was a book. He's too slow and too much of a drunk to have been trusted to do any of the coded part at all. I think he was just supposed to pass on a brown paper package."

Ashley smiled ruefully. "And he was immensely stupid to pass on such an important part of the operation to a complete idiot. Daemon, I was going to throw it overboard! I thought it might be a letter bomb."

Daemon smiled back. "I know. I saw you. I was almost ready to jump overboard to get it back. So, next step we see if anyone was a witness to your attack. We get fingerprints from your car and hope the book doesn't get passed on again until we can get to it. We need some of that underlining."

Ashley went completely still, holding onto her mug for warmth and just staring at him. “That’s not necessary. I copied it. You can have it now.”

“What!” Two male heads swung in her direction, intently focused on her face.

“I told you I didn’t feel good about what I was seeing, so I went into a store along the road and had it copied. I hid the copies under the sheepskin seat cover in the car. Could someone go and check?”

The officer was off and running and Daemon leaned forward and kissed her on the forehead, not surprised that she stiffened and pulled away from him.

“Daemon. I did something else. I don’t know if it was a stupid thing or a smart thing.”

He watched her, urging her without words to tell him the rest.

“Before I copied it, I added my own underlining. I don’t know why. I just thought if there was something bad about the book and that if the man who tried to take my bag in Dublin and the man in the waiting room were both involved with it, that I needed to add a roadblock.”

Daemon didn’t know what to say.

His heart wrenched when he thought about the danger she was in now. The one certainty about this case was that Scotland Yard knew this was big-time. But she was also bloody brilliant and having a copy of the book was invaluable.

The Garda officer ran back into the pub, the papers clutched in his hands. Three heads bent over the pages, pouring over the choices of words, intent on what they might mean. At the same time, loose gravel sprayed against the side of the building and a car door thudded shut.

***

Two more officers brought with them a shaft of sunlight that splintered the pub’s gloom.

"Detective Inspector James, you called in for the forensics team. They've started on the car already. What else would you have us doing for you?"

"This is Chief Inspector O'Hare from Scotland Yard and the young lady who was hurt by the suspect. We need to be getting her to the doctor's surgery in the village. She's had a bad time of it. So, if the team could just free up her purse and suitcase and bring it to the doctor's I'm sure she'd be grateful."

One of the men knelt by Ashley's chair and she dragged in as deep a breath as she could through her raw throat and felt Daemon's fingers tighten on hers.

"Miss, we'd take a statement from you now but you've got two officers who'll be going with you to the doctor's so we'll leave it for them. We'll be careful with your things. We'll bring them to the surgery."

Ashley croaked as she started to run on empty. "My car! If I can't use my car, how am I going to get to the stud farm?"

She looked at Daemon, panic showing as she thought about Lord Dunvey's reaction to the whole chain of events that was interrupting the start of her commission.

Daemon stood up, turning to James Rafferty, the Garda officer. They stuck their heads together for a few minutes, taking out cellphones and making calls.

When Daemon came back, he rubbed his hand on Ashley's back and nodded to the crime scene team to get started.

"It's okay. We're getting another rental car brought to the doctor's office in about an hour. The crime scene team will go over the first rental and collect whatever they need and bring what they've cleared over to the surgery too. You'll get the rest in a day or two."

"My paints and brushes and papers. I'll need them more than anything. And my pencil and sketchbook. I should do a sketch of the man who attacked me before I forget the details."

"Done."

"And Lord Dunvey?"

"We've already contacted him. He'll have your room ready and you have the night off. He can't believe you've had this happen."

"Perils of Pauline."

"What?"

"You talked about old movies. This was a very old silent film. A girl who had nothing but bad things happen to her, one after another. I'm thinking I should have stayed home and painted the Grand Canyon donkeys instead."

Then Ashley swayed, her face growing pale, and she leaned her aching head on the padded backing of the chair. Daemon took one look and scooped her up into his arms, nodding to James to follow. They crunched their way over the gravel outside and Daemon opened the back seat of the police car, making sure Ashley was belted in before he went to check on the forensics team.

They'd been called in because this wasn't a simple mugging or robbery but part of an international conspiracy. And there was now a murder. The murder of a police officer.

Hard at work putting evidence in plastic bags and dusting for fingerprints, they had already collected Ashley's prints to eliminate them from others on the car. They cleared Ashley's purse and passport but weren't finished with her bag.

***

Ashley looked up as Daemon put the purse in her lap and then he climbed into the front seat beside James and they pulled out onto the main road again. For the few miles into the village there was blessed silence in the car. No sirens, no radio, no talking. Ashley's voice had disappeared along with her energy so she was grateful she didn't have to talk.

Her adrenalin had trickled away and she felt completely drained.

So, she just sat, staring at the back of Daemon's head, sick at heart that everything she'd known about him was a lie. That he could have ever thought she was the kind of person who could be involved in a kidnapping.

Suddenly he was no longer someone she could trust.

She remembered something she'd read long ago about lions. "Beware the lion's stretch and yawn. It hides teeth and claws." She couldn't remember who'd written it, but she thought it was ironic that she hadn't realized how much her own lion, gold and shaggy, had hidden from her.

She turned her head to watch as they began passing children on bicycles and she thought about the little boy Kevin for the first time since they'd left the rescue ship. He'd been so brave on the lifeboat. He'd even grinned at her and chatted away with the other children. But he'd taken one look at the contorted, tear-stained faces of his mother and father at the dock and had broken down himself, sobbing in their arms.

He'd been able to stop just long enough to break away from them to run to Ashley, throwing himself at her and holding on ferociously, as if he would never let go.

"She saved my life, she did. I'd have gone to the bottom of the sea if she hadn't made me come with her. She's a grand lady, she is."

Then Ashley had been hugged and cried on by all three and made to promise she would stay in touch with them for the rest of her sainted life.

Ashley thought that at least part of all of this had been honest emotion with no lies. Her fingers shook a little as she checked her purse. Passport and papers were inside. And lipstick. Nothing like the sight of lipstick to make life feel normal.

She poked at the corner of her lip, feeling the dried blood. And the smallest of cuts on her arms and legs from collapsing on the gravel.

Her throat was the worst.

But being strangled would do that, wouldn't it?

An hour later and the doctor himself confirmed that she was going to be all right. He'd poked and prodded and x-rayed and examined and sent her out the door with pain killers and orders not to talk at all for the rest of the day.

"Even to the police," he'd said, looking seriously at Daemon and James. "If she needs to give you a statement it can be in writing. She said that she wants to do a sketch of the man who attacked her. That doesn't take talking." He turned to Ashley, making her promise to do what he'd asked. She nodded, not able to talk above a whisper now anyway.

"Aside from the very real bruising of the cartilage in your throat and the bruising and cuts, I would say that what you're suffering from most is shock."

Ashley smiled grimly.

She knew all about shock.

Chapter Seven

"A Handful of Southerly Wind"

The rental car had been delivered to the doctor's door and a police car arrived about the same time with her painting supplies and the contents of her tote bag but not the bag itself.

"Sorry, but there are too many fingerprints on the bag. We'll need it as evidence. And the car we'll impound because our attacker was brilliantly stupid and wasn't wearing gloves. He's left prints everywhere; especially on the door he pried open. Thanks be, for such intelligent criminals."

Ashley gratefully accepted the policeman's best wishes for her recovery and more gratefully accepted her pile of belongings. Except for the tote bag, which she never wanted to see again, she had everything she needed for now. She turned to wave goodbye to Detective Inspector James, who smiled and waved back.

Daemon pocketed Ashley's new keys and put a gentle hand on her back, ushering her out the door and stowing her things in the trunk of yet another small rental car. She didn't protest because she didn't have anything left inside. She didn't want to talk. Couldn't talk. Wasn't allowed to talk.

She tensed against a sudden, aching urge to walk right up to Daemon and either slap his face or put her arms around him and never let him go. She wasn't sure what her choice would be so she just got in the passenger side of the car and buckled her seatbelt.

When Daemon got in, he passed her the victim statement sheet and a pen. "Fill this out later if you can. If you need to rest and let that pain pill work you can do that too. I know where the stud farm is. Just relax and I'll get you there."

Drawing a long, cleansing breath, Ashley kept her thoughts neutral as the car left the whitewashed cottages of the village behind and passed miles of sheep-dotted hillsides and stone fences. She filled in as much as she could of the statement, juggling it on her lap between bits of bumpy road, trying to stay calm when the questions brought back memories she wanted to blot out. And the sketch was next.

The man at her car. His hairy arms.

Hairy arms? Ashley thought. He must have had his sleeves shoved back when she was fighting with him and when he had his arm around her neck, she'd felt the hair against her face.

She made a list first, in words, cataloguing sounds and sensations; especially the smell in her car; somehow familiar. "A black sweatshirt, Daemon! It was softer than a regular shirt. He was big, probably taller than you and you are tall. Muscles. For sure he lifts weights. I couldn't push him away."

She started a rough sketch and a phantom took shape on the page. Not much good without a face but the body had a distinctive outline. "A tattoo! I remember a dragon on his arm. It was on his right arm. The one around my neck!"

All this talking was frustrating and exhausting and hurt her throat. Ashley finally put the sketch on top of the victim statement and clipped the pages together, tucking them into the file folder James had given her. She handed Daemon back his pen and put her sketchpad and pencil in the side pocket of the car.

The pain pill was working and a haze of medicated sleepiness clouded her vision and made her arms and legs heavy. Deep, dreamless sleep was all she wanted in the world. A sleep without lions or hairy arms or sinking ferries.

Or fires.

***

Ashley didn't wake up until she heard the sound of the intercom at the front gate of The Dunvey Stud. Daemon had pulled onto the long, winding entry road and followed what seemed like miles of white fences and startling green meadows. Manicured lawns surrounded the Stud and she could see horses everywhere.

The main house and stables were tucked in behind a grove of ancient oak trees and when the car passed out into the open Ashley and Daemon simultaneously took a deep breath of amazement. The stud was quiet elegance in the traditional Georgian mansion ideal. Sandstone and pillars and white cornices everywhere. Giant windows caught the late afternoon sunlight and shone with a pale golden luster.

Early spring flowers were starting with a profusion of crocuses and daffodils and an arrangement of trellises showed where there would soon be rose gardens and climbing vines. The stable ran on forever. A rambling, one story building, there were green stall doors on both sides of a well-swept corridor and grooms led horses to and from the nearby paddocks.

Lord Dunvey met them at the front door. His rather fatherly welcome was enough to make Ashley feel like melting in a puddle on the floor but she kept her aching shoulders back and mimed a ‘thank you’ as he asked them to come in. Lady Dunvey, sophisticated but warm and gracious, met them inside.

They sat in the huge oak-lined library, sipping small glasses of sherry, except for Ashley, who got lemonade because of her pain pills. Daemon gave Lord and Lady Dunvey a sanitized version of the attack. “But even though her attacker got away and we don’t think he had a reason other than robbery for targeting her, I think it would be a good idea for her not to be alone for the next few days. I’ve heard you have tight security.”

“Not a problem at all,” agreed Lord Dunvey. “We’ll put a groom at her disposal. He’ll be her guide around the stables anyway. Young lady, we are so pleased that you are finally here. Your reputation precedes you and I’ve seen some of your work of course. I would be quite happy for you to take more time to rest after this scare.”

***

Daemon excused himself to go and unload her supplies and a maid led him to Ashley's room on the main floor at the back of the house, close to an outer door that led onto a patio and the stables.

The room was all Queen Anne furniture with clean curved lines and cherry-hued wood. Blue carpet and light blue walls trimmed in gold filigree accented the huge bed with its white duvet and white cotton lace pillowslips.

"Wow!" Daemon whistled. "She's going to love this."

He went back to get one more load and then into the library to say goodbye.

Ashley stood on spaghetti legs to walk with him to the front door.

"I'm going to get a room in the bed and breakfast down the road for tonight. I'll bring the car back tomorrow. The local Garda will be waiting for your victim statement and I'll drop that off now too and grab a late supper."

He stood, looking down into Ashley's face. Into eyes blurred tonight with pain and medication. She swayed a bit on her feet and he reached out to steady her.

"Oh, what the…" he groaned, pulling her into his arms. He could feel her stiffen and begin to resist and he groaned again, this time with regret. He dropped his arms and gently touched the livid purpling bruises on her neck and the cut on her lip. And thought about the ironic good fortune that the gun they'd found beside her had been out of bullets.

"You take care of yourself tonight, Ashley Gallagher. My name is Daemon O'Hare, Chief Inspector, Special Crimes Department at New Scotland Yard."

He rubbed a fingertip against the tip of her nose.

"My job is not quite as romantic as Sherlock Holmes and not quite as dramatic at most times as the television shows like Morse and Dalgliesh."

He took a breath and a risk and kissed her cheek.

"I really was born in Cornwall. I did go to Oxford and studied law but I wanted to see crime up close before finishing. I do have a brother and a sister and my parents love me because I'm a good person and I have a good heart."

He kissed her other cheek.

"I played soccer in school and I get seasick in boats. And my best friend, like your friend Beth, has been my friend since we were toddlers. His name is Sam Matthews and you would really like him. He's tall and has a crazy, tilted smile that makes me laugh.'

Ashley's body relaxed almost imperceptibly, although Daemon could feel it instantly.

"And, Miss Gallagher. Although we got off to a terrible start, I would like to try again. Say tomorrow."

He felt her head shaking from side to side.

He ignored it. "I say this because…."

He lifted her chin, which was now stubbornly tucked into his chest.

"Because you are a gutsy woman. You are a brave woman. You are a brilliant woman who has put herself into danger to stop a bad thing."

He bent his head to kiss her nose again.

"And because…" He took another breath.

"Because you would be very easy for me to love."

He kissed her lips this time, avoiding the cut and the bruises. And then he dropped his arms to his sides, turned and walked out the door.

***

Ashley stood, watching him go, hot tears coursing down her cheeks. Her heart though, seemed to lighten a little when she whispered Daemon's words.

"Because you would be very easy for me to love."

She let the maid show her to her room and pamper her with hot washcloths and a bathtub full of sweetly scented suds. By the time she'd been given a light supper of soup that wouldn't hurt her throat, all she could do was crawl into her sleep shirt and collapse into bed.

She was so completely relaxed that sleep came almost immediately. There were dreams, but they were populated by horses, happily free and running, tails in the air, over vast green meadows full of wildflowers. She lay on her back, surrounded by butterflies and stared at a bright blue sky.

***

Miles away, two angry figures bent over the poetry book, foul and ugly language staining the air in the back room of an inn.

"This makes no sense! The last in the chain before me was Connor. And he's dead. He didn't have time to add anything to the book. And before him was Shaughnessy, blast his dark heart and stupidity. The man is too daft to have been trusted with adding anything. He was just to pass the package."

The man laughed in his ale. A brutal laugh full of fury. He wiped beads of liquid off his mouth with the back of his tattooed arm.

"He thought he'd be safe behind bars but one of ours got to him. I hear he's still unconscious. But we'll try to end him before he wakes up."

The other man turned a page and looked baffled.

"But what do you make of this? We're the last ones before the boss. There's supposed to be a plan in this. Any pieces we add now need to give the boss what he needs to set the plan going. But this is gibberish."

A fist hit the dirty table and the book jerked sideways. Coffee spilled close to the open page and one of the men slid it away, swearing when he was burned.

They stared again at the book, sweating profusely, imaginations in overdrive thinking about what their unseen boss would set in motion if they failed to give him what he needed to make this all work.

These last two men were different from the rest. Not at all like Shaughnessy and those who'd come before. The others had been pawns. They hadn't known anything about the plan.

By design.

The less the others knew the better the chance this would go off without a hitch.

But these two knew what was going to be happening. They knew the bits they had to add to the jigsaw puzzle that was the codebook. They just didn't know what had gone before. Each person in the link had done their own research, their own fact-finding. But unrelated. So, no one could spill a perfect plan to the coppers if they got caught.

And Shaughnessy had been caught.

Expressions grim, the two bent their heads, scratched their foreheads, drank coffee and then whiskey, sharing very real worry.

Long hours later, still stymied, there was a break in their thinking. A break borne of desperation and shared memory.

"The woman!"

***

Ashley woke to a rain-washed sky and lay in the huge bed, gazing out the big French doors. Not a cloud in that sky. Just brilliant blue. A perfect day to get out and meet her painting subject. She put one tentative hand up to her throat, testing the bruising, testing the deep-seated pain of the cartilage that had been so traumatized. The pain pills had taken the edge away but she was unbearably sore and ached everywhere.

"Okay, this is a drill. I am speaking in a whisper. What does it feel like?"

Still raspy. Still hurt.

"All right. Another day to be a mime. I'll have to be a horse whisperer."

She smiled, aware of the unintended pun. "A 'hoarse' whisperer". Funny.

After a shower to wash the peat and dirt out of her hair and the aches from her muscles, Ashley dressed in the change of clothes that the forensics team had cleared for her to take. They'd let her scoop up some of the overnight things she needed, so she had at least one day to feel like an almost new person.

A person someone had wanted to kill.

Might still want to kill when they found out what she'd done to their book.

Coffee, which burned when it went down and was hard to swallow, followed by porridge, which was surprisingly soothing, and she was ready to start her day. A sketchbook and her digital camera in hand, she wandered out to the paddocks, past a stable full of horses keenly interested in her passage.

They whinnied as she walked by and she offered her hand, palm up, for several to sniff. Then she talked to each horse in turn, rubbing the velvety noses that hung over the half-doors all down the corridor.

She breathed in the heady aroma of horse and hay and leather and loved it.

No Dorcha Dhubh in sight.

She liked his Gaelic name almost as much as the English version, Dark Night. But then she found him in a paddock near the house and leaned into the firm support of the white split-rail fence to watch him. The morning was cold and she was glad she'd pulled on a pair of jeans and a cream Aran sweater today. The field was wet and her boots were already covered in clinging grass. She pulled her heavy jacket closed and retied the soft scarf she'd wrapped around her bruised throat.

In the field beyond the fence, Dark Night erupted into a powerful, ground- thumping canter. Long, thin thoroughbred legs extended themselves and then tucked back under in a continuous windmill of speed.

Ashley reached into her pocket for her camera and caught a whole series of action shots. Then she switched to her pencil and sketchbook to do some movement drawings to set her mood. Some of her supplies still hadn't arrived from the police station but she had to do a lot of preparatory work before she'd be able to start anyway.

Sunlight flashed on the smooth black hooves pounding past her and Ashley's gaze followed, mesmerized, as the ebony mane and tail puffed out behind the stallion with each lap around the paddock.

"It's like smoke," she whispered into the wind. "I can see him dancing over flames somewhere. He'd sail right over because he hardly touches the ground."

"He certainly flies above the earth, he does."

Ashley swung around at the voice and then let her still-ragged nerves relax on a sigh.

"Lord Dunvey! Good morning."

"Morning, young colleen. Your poor voice sounds very sore it does. Did you manage to sleep well last night after your scare yesterday?"

"I did, thank you. Not a bad dream at all. In fact, no dreams for most of the night."

"And your young man, will he be coming over today with the rest of your things?"

"My young man, sir?" She swallowed, trying for more than a whisper.

"To be sure. If he's not your young man then he certainly wants to be. My wife has an eye for these things and she's never wrong. She can see sparks in this one."

"Oh, Daemon's just involved because we met on the ferry before it went down and he's been rescuing me ever since. Just coincidence."

"Hmmm. We'll see."

Both heads turned towards the stallion and both sets of elbows rested on the fence. Lord Dunvey whistled and

Dorcha pivoted mid-gait and broke into a smooth trot in their direction.

"He's been showing off for you. He loves to run but he loves even more to show his paces for a young lady. Ah, here he is then." Lord Dunvey put out his hand, mysteriously producing a lump of sugar from his cavernous Barbour coat pocket. The horse snuffled, breathing out wispy clouds of hot air and bending his head to work huge lips and giant yellow teeth to gently pick up the sugar.

"Do you like this horse of mine, Ashley? Do you like the looks of him?"

Ashley nodded, smoothing her hand over the soft black muzzle as Dorcha Dhubh reached his nose over the fence to push at Lord Dunvey's chest, as if to ask for more sugar.

"Not today, young fellow. We don't want you to be too wild now for your poses, do we? Do you know, Ashley, that he's still sowing those wild oats? The fire that led him to two Grand National wins has made him one of our best stud stallions and he has a lot of promising colts to his name. I'll tell you later about the one they think will win this year."

Ashley rested her chin on folded hands on the rail, letting her keen appraisal follow the dark mane as it lifted gently in the wind. The stallion's tail flicked sideways back and forth, tangling in his back legs until the wind and tail muscles straightened it out again. A nervous shudder rippled the silky black skin and he moved his hooves continuously, like a sparring boxer or a shadow dancer.

"He's like something out of an Arabian Night's book, isn't he? He reminds me of a bit of poetry I read once from a Bedouin legend."

"I think I know the one indeed."

Lord Dunvey tucked some tobacco into his briar pipe and tapped it down with his finger. A match flared in the cool wind and the flame blew outward. He didn't see Ashley's instinctive recoil at the flame and continued.

"And God took a handful..."

"That's the one!" Ashley's delighted gaze sought the old man's and her lips curved in a broad smile as she whispered the words with him.

"And God took a handful of southerly wind, blew His breath over it and created the horse."

"It's perfect, isn't it?" she said, not needing an answer. She watched as the stallion, giving up on more sugar, wheeled around and danced back out into the paddock, his feet not quite tied to the ground.

"As soon as my papers and paints come, I can get started," she said, "But I always do a lot of sketches first and then prepare a watercolor. If it meets with your approval, I'll ship it to California and do the oil version there over the next month. As soon as the oil dries, I'll crate it up and ship it back. I'll send you digital pictures by e-mail as I progress. Is that satisfactory to you?"

"Perfectly."

Lord Dunvey then reached out to take Ashley's hand, holding it in a warm, firm grasp.

"You know that I understand you've gone through a lot this past terrible, few days. I would be very happy to have you work a little, rest a lot and take your time with this. How is your poor throat this morning?"

Ashley reassured him that she was surviving in spite of everything and the pain pills were helping. The bruises were already changing color.

"I've been talking too much though, and it's getting harder to do anything but squeak. I'll have to go back to just whispering I guess." She looked at him then, taking in the well-worn Wellington boots, the khaki jeans, the grey cable-knit turtleneck sweater and the Irish cap.

He was a perfect match for this place. Refined. Old World. Sophisticated. Incredibly well bred and gracious. And so fatherly that she felt a pang, missing her own dad, so many miles away.

"You know, you remind me of my dad. I miss him a lot whenever I'm away, and I feel safe here. I appreciate that after this week. I'll be just fine and I hope you'll be happy with my work."

He nodded, told her to call him Michael and his wife Sarah, and spent the next few minutes puffing on his pipe. "You know, young lady, I couldn't think of calling you anything but Ashley now. Although I'd feel more comfortable calling you Megan or Kathleen with all that black Irish hair and your Celtic pale skin. With a fine name like Gallagher there must be Irish in your family?"

"My grandfather. He came from Cork years ago and I didn't get to know him very well before he died. He was a lovely man."

Michael puffed a bit more on his pipe, patted her on the back and wandered off to check on the stables before morning tea.

Ashley was left to continue her sketches and photography until she had enough to start a preliminary roughing out of the painting. When that was done, she would present it to Michael for approval. Lord Dunvey wanted a formal portrait with the main house as background, so Ashley would be superimposing Dark Night onto a sketch of the Georgian mansion with Michael holding his halter and standing with him on the curved parking circle.

***

An hour later a young boy came out with a message for her to come in for a cup of tea and she packed up to take a break. She took one more look at the stallion. He had stopped running and stood, ears pricked in her direction, his body perfectly still, huge dilated nostrils flaring as he tested the wind. He tossed his head and bent to grab a mouthful of grass.

Her breath caught a little at his pose.

Sirocco had once stood just like that.

On her way in, she turned at the sound of wheels on gravel and looked up to see her rental car coming down the long driveway. Her heart started to beat a little faster.

Daemon.

When he stopped the car in front of her, she waited for him. He climbed out, well-scrubbed and rested and leaned against the fence.

"Are you still angry?"

His gaze was direct and unwavering as he watched her face and Ashley had to listen to the heart that was racing trip-hammer fast in her chest as well as to the mind that was cautioning her to remember who he really was.

"Not angry today," she whispered, her voice straining with the effort to talk.

"Still upset though and I have to say hurt." Daemon winced, listening to the sound of her voice. "I can imagine. Here you are minding your own business and a crook tricks you, your ferry sinks, this great-looking guy chats you up in the lifeboat, takes you to dinner and keeps kissing you and obviously wants to sleep with you. Then you get mugged and strangled and the wonderful guy turns out to be a policeman who's been following you all along thinking you were the bad guy. Or woman."

He took a breath. "I'd be angry and hurt too."

***

Daemon looked down at the ground and then walked over to open the trunk of the car. He felt a hand on his shoulder and turned to find Ashley right behind him.

She was deadly serious as she met his gaze and swallowed, wincing, before starting to whisper again.

"My name is Ashley Gallagher. I was born in California, near Ojai and I grew up on an Arabian horse stud farm, a lot like this but not so grand. My best friend's name is Beth and I have two brothers I love to pieces but they tease me a lot. I'm 5'6 and weigh about 120 pounds if I've been binge-eating chocolate. Sometimes less if I'm stressed. I went to university in Los Angeles and majored in Art and Business. I run an art gallery with Beth in Carmel and I love pizza and peanut butter and Bach and the Moody Blues. And scampi."

She took a breath.

"And I hate my hair when it gets misty outside because it gets all curly and wild and I can't do anything with it." She held out her hand.

"And I have a tattoo of a butterfly on my ankle." She took another breath.

"And I'm happy to meet you too."

And the sunshine came out again when she smiled.

Daemon's breath exhaled and he hadn't realized he'd been holding it so long. His chest hurt with the tension. He looked at her hand and then into her eyes. The darkness had lightened to a pansy blue again and there was warmth there.

He held her hand in both of hers. Then he pulled her into his arms, pressing her head gently against his chest and rubbing her back with his hand.

"Did you get any sleep last night?"

He stepped back to search her face, watching for furrowed eyebrows and white skin. She did look better this morning. Except for the horrible purple bruising on her neck and the raspy, whispery voice.

"I took enough pain pills to get to sleep and then I slept all night. No foghorns, no waves splashing at the boat, no alarm clocks to worry about. It was wonderful. You?"

"The local Garda officer has an aunt who runs a great bed and breakfast about ten minutes down the road. She has a perfect loft above her garage she's letting me use and I think she wants to adopt me."

Ashley smiled and then he saw her face light up as she saw all the stuff he started taking out of the trunk of the little car. "You've got everything! This is great! Thank you so much!"

She reached up to kiss his cheek and he turned his head at the last minute to intercept her lips with his mouth.

Momentarily startled, her body relaxed against his. For a long, long moment they stood there, his arms full of stacks of papers and boxes of paintbrushes and his heart full of Ashley.

She finally backed away, her flushed face showing him that yesterday's emotion and anger and vast disappointment had eased. They would need to talk, but not yet.

"Here, you take this batch and I'll bring in the rest." Daemon handed her the first lot and turned to retrieve a large shopping bag full of clothes. The forensics team had kept her suitcase because it had been ripped open by the attacker and they needed to check for fingerprints.

He grinned as he remembered folding her clothes into the bag. In had gone delicate wisps of nothing…dangling from his finger. A lacy looking bra. Very brief, silky bikini underpants and a matching camisole.

Colors swam in his memory. He'd folded the raspberry silk dress she'd had on for dinner. Dove grey cashmere sweaters and ivory slacks. Peacock-hued neck scarves.

Sinfully sheer nylons.

He sighed, also remembering the ebony splash of her long hair, spread out in the dirt of the pub parking lot, her white face and the red of the blood that had flowed from her mouth. The memory woke him up to the danger she was in right now until they solved this case. It made him frantic but he had to be the cool copper and stay focused. He looked up as Ashley came back out for another load.

"Where do you want the rest of this?" he said as she took an armful.

"In my room if you can get it that far without collapsing under that mountain of stuff. I hadn't realized there was so much!"

He followed her into the house, remembering the way from the day before, and lay everything down on the bench seat inside her room. It seemed different today. He looked around, trying to figure out what it was. And then his nose picked it up.

Peaches.

There was an almost imperceptible hint of peaches in the room. Not heavy. Not too strong. Just a hint. Ashley had slept here. Then he thought, allowing himself just a second to think, about how that ebony silk would look spread out on one of those lacy white pillows.

How it would look spilling over his arm. How she would look beside him or under him.

He groaned, turning around to take the last load from Ashley's arms. She grinned at him and he followed the direction of her gaze. A pair of her nylons had tumbled off the top of the pile in the shopping bag and now lay over his elbow.

"They suit you. Very charming."

She started to laugh but coughed instead and put her hands around her neck to ease the pain. "I'm sorry," she whispered. "That was fate getting me back for teasing you."

"Any time. It's good to see you even try to laugh. But I'm sorry you're still hurting. Hurt anywhere else? He pushed you down. You must be sore other places too."

She nodded her head, carefully.

"All over. But heat helps and I need another pain pill. Let's go and have tea. Lord and Lady Dunvey apparently think you're my young man, so they'll be happy to see you."

***

Ashley caught an expression on Daemon's face that had never been there before and thought it looked like the one in her brother's when he'd been falling in love with her sister-in-law. She still didn't know where this could go but somehow the gleam made her heart a lot lighter.

Tea was hot, served with buttery raisin scones and clotted cream. A huge bowl of fruit sat beside the china teapot and there was a tray loaded with silver teaspoons and teacups and white linen napkins. No one had changed because everyone had work waiting as soon as they'd finished.

Lord Dunvey was heading off to a steeplechase meeting, Lady Dunvey to one of the charities she supported, Ashley to work with her sketches once she drove Daemon back to the Garda office. He needed to pick up an unmarked patrol car and do a conference call with McBride and the Garda National Bureau detectives.

Ashley walked Daemon to the rental car and as she drove them down the long gravel driveway, she had questions. Wanting to finally be in the loop.

"What's happening? I know you said the Stud Farm was safe last night because Lord Dunvey has such a tight security system. But why should I have to be careful now? Don't they already have the book?"

Daemon nodded, looking out the window, pretending to admire the grassy meadows and the galloping mares beyond the fence. "They do. But can you remember what you did to the book before they mugged you and took it?"

Silence.

"Of course," she squeaked. She swallowed and started sucking again on the medicated lozenge the doctor had given her to ease her throat. "I put in some extra underlining. That would make them really upset, wouldn't it? But how will they even know where I am? Didn't the man who attacked me get chased away? Wouldn't he have been hiding somewhere in the woods without a car?"

Daemon shook his head. "Ashley, think cellphones. He'd have just called backup. We were at the pub for a long time waiting for the doctor and the crime team. There's a good chance he had an opportunity to see what you'd done and had someone else come to follow you."

Ashley drove, panic making her calm somehow. How soon would they find her and kill her this time?

"These are seriously bad people, aren't they? No, don't answer that. If Scotland Yard and the Irish Garda are on this and you said it was kidnapping, then I guess I'm in trouble."

She glanced at Daemon and then quickly concentrated on the road, narrowly missing a herd of sheep coming around the corner. It took ten minutes for the shepherd to get the straggling woollies off the road and back onto the verge so traffic could move again. While they waited, Ashley's fingers turned white on the steering wheel, imagining snipers behind every tree.

"Daemon, do you have a gun?"

"I do."

"With you right now?"

"Yes."

Silence.

Was that comforting or did it just outline the trouble she was in.

"You're relatively safe at the Stud. But to make sure, we've arranged for one of the Garda officers to come and work at the stable. Lord Dunvey has a strict rule about screening new staff but we've cleared it with his stable manager. Luckily their man knows one end of a horse from another so he won't look out of place."

"Clever," Ashley agreed, afraid to nod her head and jar her neck. "So, should I be driving this car back on my own once I've dropped you off?"

"No. I'll grab my car and shadow you until you get back onto Stud property. Just promise me you'll stay there."

"Are you kidding? I'm not going to forget what happened yesterday. I'm not going anywhere. But you have to promise me something."

"What?"

"You have to treat me as part of your team. You have to keep me up to speed on what's happening. I gave you those photocopies. Has anything come up yet?

***

Daemon wished he could go back to the waiting room and have Shaughnessy pick someone else.

Anyone but Ashley. And then he realized that in an odd, ironic way, he had Shaughnessy to thank for being the reason he'd been able to spend the night with her in the lifeboat. That he'd been able to get to know her.

He looked out the window at the shepherd's dog and watched the way it danced and nipped and maneuvered the sheep, fast on its feet and gentle at the same time.

And at the same time, he had his hand on his gun and he was checking the surroundings on all sides, watching.

Was he falling in love with her? He wondered how this could play out. Where their lives would lead them after this case.

In the meantime, all he had to do was keep her alive. He noticed the tension in her jaw, the increasing pallor of her skin.

"Did you take that pain pill? You're beginning to look peaky."

"I did. It just takes a while. Strangling is not a big deal though. I'll get over it."

Daemon laughed in spite of himself. The mugger hadn't choked her sense of humor out of her.

"We haven't heard anything on the book yet. The pages are being looked at by a team of the best code-breakers at the Yard. All I know is that they agreed with you. This is not an ordinary pattern of underlining. They've identified it as a legitimate code."

"So, I wasn't crazy being uncomfortable with what I saw?"

"No, you were brilliant. A budding inspector. But I don't think you'd like a job with the Yard. Too many guys like Shaughnessy and your attacker with the tattoo."

"What about my sketch?"

"Your sketch made my skin crawl. It's so real the creep could walk right off the page. They're running it and the tattoo through records today and they'll let me know as soon as they find out. Sam thinks we're down to the last people on the courier chain because your attacker was serious and way beyond Shaughnessy's league. They've killed two people now and tried to kill Shaughnessy. They're serious."

Daemon checked his cellphone for messages and then looked out the window again. No traffic, nothing either side of the road that looked suspicious. Just sheep.

He patted his pocket, feeling the shape of the Glock. He didn't want to tell Ashley that they had already found out who her attacker was. The tattoo had been the clincher but her general sketch had been eerily accurate.

Owen Murphy was one of the worst. Ashley was lucky, very lucky, that the police car's sirens had interrupted him.

Because he had killed before.

Whoever was heading this operation was really anxious to find and control that book.

And the police were really anxious to find Murphy.

The shepherd turned in their direction and waved them on. The village was tiny and the Garda office served a number of other surrounding villages. This place was just a cluster of whitewashed houses, several small shops and a few bed-and-breakfasts catering to tourists in the summer. A petrol station stood on the corner and the pub stood a half-block from the far edge of the woods.

Daemon's unmarked car sat outside the Garda station waiting for him and he got out, keys in hand, and kept his attention on Ashley. He'd directed her to drive ahead of him and not stop for any reason at all.

***

By the time they got back to the Stud, Ashley was exhausted. She pulled into the parking spot at the end of the stable block and sat in the car until Daemon drove up beside her.

He got out and opened her door. "Can you grab a nap before you go back to work?"

Ashley shook her head and then regretted the move. "No, if I do, I won't wake up until tomorrow morning. I have too much to do. Will I see you tomorrow?"

He smiled, the warmth reaching the green and giving them a sunlit glitter. "I think we should go over those photocopied sheets. We have a copy here as well as in London."

Ashley grinned. She wanted this over but if she had a job to do that meant she'd be working with Daemon on something, then she'd get to see him before she went home.

Home.

It was so far away.

"Does this mean I'm part of your team then?"

Daemon leaned over to leave a warm, lingering kiss on her forehead. She wished for more, but there were grooms all around them.

"You're a part of my team."

Chapter Eight

"Men That Ride Upon Horses"

Dark Night loved to run. Even more, he loved to jump.

Anything.

But especially steeplechase jumps or anything that presented a challenge.

Or was in his way.

The next morning, Lord Dunvey took Ashley to the covered arena where an indoor jump course had been set out for the trainers. Three youngsters were being put through a set of regulation size fences and he was giving her some background on the Grand National Steeplechase.

"Our lad, Dorcha Dhubh, has the distinction of being one of the few Irish thoroughbreds to win the English Grand National more than once. He brought home a whole room full of Irish Grand National awards too, he did. He's a grand boyo."

Ashley watched as one of the Stud's beautiful bay colts bunched his front legs under him and flew into the air over a simulated water jump. "How has he done since he's been put to stud, Michael?"

"He's done us proud with a whole raft of sweet little fillies and about a dozen colts. Among them, the best is Scamall Dhubh. Scamall in Gaelic means cloud and Dhubh is black, or dark. So, we call him Black Cloud. Black is rare for a thoroughbred and he's inherited his dad's coat. Sometimes they call him Neal Dhubh. Neal means black in Gaelic too but it can also mean passionate or champion and both fit."

"I've heard of him! Isn't he the favorite to win the Grand National?"

"He is for sure. His owner is that proud of him for his first few years of racing. You knew, didn't you, that a horse has to be seven years old before he can enter the Grand National?"

“I did. It has to do with endurance and maturity, doesn’t it?”

“It does that. Steeplechase is a beautiful but grueling thing. I like the country jumping more, out in the fields. But the big money is in the steeplechase and flat racing.”

“How much is big money?”

“It can be millions. The bets are going totally daft this year.”

The bay pulled up at the tallest fence and the trainer patted his neck and they circled around again, taking the fence in stride the second time. Ashley and Lord Dunvey clapped.

“In fact, there’s so much money involved in the award purses that crime has crept into our sport, like many other sports. The police are onto some of the big syndicates that own some of the horses now.”

“I think I told you my family owns an Arabian Stud farm back home? Dad has talked a lot about corporations owning horses. It’s a shame that so many family-run ranches and stud farms can’t stay in business anymore.”

Michael nodded his head in agreement and then looked at his watch. “It’s time to meet with my manager. I’ll see you tomorrow morning.” He patted her hand and winked at her. “I understand you’re off to dinner with your young Daemon tonight?”

Ashley felt her skin flush and she looked away for a second. “He’s not really my young man you know. I’m going home at the end of this job and there’s a whole ocean and continent between London and Carmel.”

“You look a bit sad when you say that, you do. I’m thinking you wouldn’t be sad if you didn’t care. We think, Sarah and I, that he’s a good lad and we’ve watched the two of you. There’s something there. Think about it.”

And then he was off, shouting out to the trainer to try a reverse cycle of jumps.

"Think about it," Ashley murmured. "Oh, I'm thinking about it." She spent the rest of the day planning, putting some time into sketches of the main house, which would be in the background. And while she sketched, she chased a niggling little thought around her head.

A lot of the words from the book of Yeats that had been underlined had been about horses, one of them '<u>men that ride upon horses</u>.' Another one had been, '<u>shadowy horses, their long manes a-shake</u>.'

She stopped sketching and turned a piece of paper to the back, writing down the lines she remembered, writing down the things that were fluttering like snowflakes through her mind, melting as fast as she thought of them.

Lord Dunvey said there was a lot of money in steeplechase. Daemon said the kidnapping was going to be happening soon. And the Grand National was in a few days!

She sat down on a bench close to the front door and scribbled furiously.

Every idea that she could think of.

Little lines linking ideas.

Circles and question marks.

She had to see those pages. Maybe she and Daemon could find something. But he wasn't coming for two hours. She sighed and went back over to watch Dark Night. He was getting used to seeing her by the fence and she had an apple in her pocket today. He walked over, curious, and stuck his huge head over the fence, snuffling at her coat.

"Can you help me sort out my thoughts, old fellow? I think this is all about a hoofed crime somehow. Any ideas?"

The stallion seemed to ponder the question. He crunched the apple and nodded his head up and down, switching his tail and breathing hard.

Ashley's fingers scratched and massaged all down his neck as she whispered in his ear.

And then another horse made a whickering sound somewhere in the next paddock and he was off, great clods of turf flying up under his hooves.

Smoke and fire, Ashley thought again. Smoke and fire.

By early afternoon, she was done for the day. She had enough preliminary sketches to start the compilation. She needed to do a close up without fences and popped under the rail to go and sit in the middle of the paddock.

Since she'd grown up with horses she knew how to walk and how to move to avoid being trampled. She sat down on the ground, hands and feet still and just waited.

Dark Night showed his interest in her by dancing a little over at the stable wall and then moved, just as slowly, in her direction. He stopped, then started, then stopped again, making an ever-narrowing circle around her.

"What a clever boy, you are. You know just what to do. I'm going to sit here and watch and if you stand still, I have another apple. But you have to be good and let me sketch you standing there."

Murmuring softly, Ashley waited.

And waited some more.

She thought she heard the sound of wheels on the gravel but there were so many people coming and going all the time that she didn't pay attention. And she'd been assured someone from the Garda was keeping watch.

But she still felt the hairs on her neck quiver as she kept her gaze firmly on the big black horse in the paddock with her.

***

Daemon considered having a heart attack.

He stood by his car and watched, afraid to make any sudden movements. He liked horses. He'd taken riding lessons with the rest of his friends when he was in school. His parents had always kept horses on their Cornwall estate.

He and Sam had even taken 'eventing' courses together during school breaks and the Matthews had their own stable.

But the sight of Ashley's small body in the field, dwarfed by the size of the stallion, easily 16 hands tall, made him feel like he couldn't breathe. He moved carefully over to the rail and watched what she was doing. Her sketchpad was on the grass beside her and she was just sitting quietly, concentration fixed on the horse. He could hear the sound of her soft voice carrying on the wind.

He couldn't hear what she was saying, but the stallion was paying attention. He kept getting closer, nervously edging away as the breeze caught his mane or his tail and distracted him. Daemon could see the flaring nose and dancing hooves.

The breeze caught Ashley's hair too, and its shining darkness lifted in the wind and mimicked the tail and mane of the horse. Again, Daemon noticed the ballerina posture, the perfect straightness of her back and the way that she held her head.

He just stood, transfixed, at the rail. He could see her fingers quietly move to pick up the sketchpad and she rested it on her crossed legs. Her gaze seldom left the horse but her fingers flew on the paper.

Daemon saw her bag and small camera by the rail. He reached for the camera and trained it on Ashley and the horse. She brought something small out of her pocket but he was too far away to see what it was.

She held out her hand, her palm flat and the moment fixed itself in time as the horse gently bent his huge head to nuzzle. Daemon snapped the picture then another and another as she continued to sketch and then took another as she very carefully came to her feet.

Again, he wondered at her graceful dancer's movements. She had uncurled as if she was in some act from

"Swan Lake." In spite of her knee problems, she was still a dancer.

When she turned to come back to the fence, Dark Night walked behind her, his neck arched and his nose hanging over her shoulder. Daemon clicked the camera again. Two old buddies. They looked as if they had been friends for life.

***

Ashley spotted him and was intensely happy he'd seen this. It was a first bonding moment with the horse and she'd needed to feel connected to him for this painting to have meaning for her. She wanted it to feel real.

When she got close to the paddock fence, she turned to rub her hands along the sleek black flanks and put her hand up to stroke Dark Night's ears. Such velvety softness for such a huge horse. So gentle, inquisitive, so dainty.

She stroked the side of his face and his nose and then ducked to slide under the fence.

Dark Night nudged the fence rail and then turned to wander away in search of the perfect blade of grass.

"Oh, my God!" Daemon's voice was hardly above a whisper but she could hear the awe. He handed Ashley her camera and watched as she looked at the pictures.

"Daemon, these are beautiful. Have you ever considered going into photography?

And I don't mean pictures of dead people or crooks!"

He grinned for a minute before answering.

"Not really, but remember that book I lied to you about? The one comparing the seacoast of Western Ireland with the seacoast off Cornwall?"

She nodded her head.

"Well, it wasn't completely a lie. I have thought about it. Illustrating it has been on my mind too. Some day."

He reached out his hand to take her sketchpad and carefully flipped the pages, his eyebrows rising as he saw the incredible talent in this series. He'd seen a lot of horse paintings but these, like the sketch she'd done of her attacker, were so real the horse could have started prancing and whinnying and he wouldn't have been surprised. He whistled between his teeth as he handed the sketchpad back to her.

"He is beautiful," Daemon said. "He's done a lot for Irish bloodlines. I saw the race he won in England and he was far superior to anything else on the field that day. No wonder Lord Dunvey is so proud of him."

Ashley looked at her watch, horrified that it was so late in the day. If she was going to be ready to go and check the pages with Daemon she needed to fly.

"Lord Dunvey said you should come into the study while I get ready. It's just off the main entrance. Can you find your own way while I gather up this stuff and run?"

Daemon had obviously already showered. He was dressed today in jeans and a heavy black sweater and she smiled as she saw that the stubble was back on that chiseled chin.

Somehow, she didn't mind. As she watched him go into the house, she thought that she didn't have a lot longer until she would never see him again. It was a sobering thought. So, they'd just have to make the most of what time they had.

In half an hour she was ready to go. Showered, dressed in a simple sleeveless blue dress with her pearl necklace and a cashmere shawl to ward off the wind and the mist, she walked back to the car with Daemon.

He rested one hand on her back as they crunched across the driveway and opened the car door for her. A fine, silvery mist had gathered in the last half an hour and Daemon pulled the collar of his jacket up around his neck. He looked over at the broad expanse of lawn and the paddocks rich with emerald green grass and shook his head.

"You know, they say this is a country with a shade of green found nowhere else in the world. But I'll bet it's only green because it rains all the time or it's all this mist!" He shivered to make his point and considered the peat fire waiting at the pub. He couldn't get there fast enough. He'd been cold ever since he'd left London.

Ashley watched out the window as they saw signs pointing the way to the Irish National Stud, only about twenty miles away. "I didn't know that there were so many stud farms here. Lord Dunvey said they settle here because the Curragh region has so much chalk in the soil that it's famous for building strong bones in thoroughbreds."

Then Ashley remembered what had bothered her about the underlining in the poetry book.

"Daemon!"

He looked over, concern evident. "What is it? Is something wrong?"

"No. But I thought about the underlining today. There's a strange repeating of a theme that I hadn't noticed before. I'm really anxious to see those pages tonight so I can show you. I have a feeling your case has something to do with horses."

Daemon raised his eyebrows as he considered the possibility. "We'll have an early dinner and then we'll go and look at them. I've got them hidden away in the loft."

***

Dinner was at the "Rafferty's Rest" pub in the village. Not a huge building but warm and cozy and better lit than the first one Ashley had been in. She smiled as she walked in the big oak door. She'd never been strangled here either. The place had a lot going for it.

There was a golden glow from the fire and soft, diffused lighting overhead. People were already lined up at the dartboard and pints of ale were spread out on several tables. A local fiddler was scheduled to play later but Daemon and Ashley had other plans that included huddling over the pages.

Daemon didn't notice or question her request to sit away from the fire. The whole place was warm enough so nothing was said. She didn't want to explain. Not tonight.

"Would you like wine or do you want to try a Guinness?"

They stood at the bar counter looking up at the chalked menu on the wall. There were lots of grilled things on the list but there were salads and soups too. Ashley grinned when she saw steak and kidney pie, but there was also a scampi and scallop plate and that won. "I think wine please. White?"

***

Later, sitting with their glasses, knees touching under the small wooden table, Daemon asked her about her gallery, his eyes constantly moving to watch new people coming in, other guests sitting in the shadows. He had his Glock tucked into his belt beneath his jacket and kept one hand close.

"What kind of sales do you have? Is it a walk-in crowd in mostly tourist season or do you do mainly commission work?"

Ashley sipped her wine thoughtfully and considered.

"Beth and I have similar painting styles and preferences. We show other people's work as well as our own and we do get a lot of tourists in Carmel all summer. Beth handles most of that and I help. I've been away a lot this year on commissions and she gets them too. We try not to overlap because we don't want the gallery closed for too many days."

"And the name Sirocco?"

Ashley was prepared for him to ask because a lot of people wondered about the big painted sign with the horse and its tail flowing in the wind. She had a pat answer for everybody that didn't hurt her heart.

"It's the name of a unique wind in Saudi Arabia and the north of Africa. My family raises Arabian horses so it was a natural choice because they can run like the wind."

Then she laughed. "It's the horses that run like the wind. Not my family. Although my brother Daniel loved track in high school."

Daemon chuckled and smiled.

He reached out a finger and touched the dimple in her cheek. "I like the way that dimple shows up when you're happy.

But even as he watched, a shadow crossed her face and she looked down at her glass for a second. When she raised her head again, she was deadly serious.

"Daemon, I'm really sorry."

"What are you sorry about?"

"That I did all that underlining," she whispered, looking around to see if anyone was close enough to hear. "I thought if the book was part of something bad that maybe adding my own underlining might throw a wrench in things; buy the person who's in danger a little more time."

She ran her fingertip around the icy dampness on her glass. "But all I've done is put myself in danger, interrupt your case and mess everything up." She looked away again, studying the front door and the bar counter and the dartboard.

She was looking everywhere but at his face now.

And he noticed that she avoided looking at the flames in the fire.

She looked up when he closed his fingers on hers and she bit her lip.

"Ashley, remember I said you were a member of my team now? What you did by copying the pages gave our code department the break it needed. We may still be missing big pieces but we have more now that we did. By underlining extra bits of the book, you definitely have put yourself in danger. But…"

He tightened his fingers.

"But you've given me extra reasons to be with you. You've scared me to death and I have to admit I'm worried for you but you've bought some time for us to ask those questions."

Daemon watched as Ashley fought to keep the shimmer of tears that suddenly welled from spilling over onto her cheeks.

He leaned forward, wiping the tears away. "Is that such a bad thing?"

She looked up again and shook her head. "No and yes. It's a good thing because I want with my whole heart to be with you now that everything is out in the open. But it's a bad thing because even if I've bought us more time…"

She bit her lip again and took a breath. "Even if we have more time, there's still not enough of it."

Her words echoed in Daemon's heart. He'd been thinking those same thoughts. Not too long from now she was going to be climbing on a plane and heading home to California and her business and her family and her normal life. He, on the other hand, would be heading back to his flat in London and his job. He hadn't told her about his family and friends and history yet. She didn't know more than the bare bones about him.

He sighed. Maybe it was time to make some decisions about the rest of his career. His current life had long since worn thin.

"You know, I think we should get back to the pages," he said, looking up. "I had a thought this morning about how clever they were to make the package a book and not something else."

"Why? Obviously, a book wouldn't attract suspicion?"

"Right. But it also got through all those security checks on the ferry, even the body searches, because it would only have shown up as a book. Really innocent."

Their meals arrived to two appetites that had disappeared in their eagerness to get back to Daemon's. They made it through food that would have been delicious under other circumstances and then finally the check came. Daemon got up to pay and the trip back took only minutes.

***

The house was a cottage set back from the main road and surrounded by trees. It would be cool in the short Irish summer and protected from winter winds. There was a separate loft on the top floor of an old barn that was now used as a garage. Daemon took Ashley's hand as they climbed up the narrow stairway and she waited beside him at the top as he unlocked the door.

It was a huge room as barn lofts went. A large four-poster bed stood beside the window at one end and two old wing-backed upholstered chairs sat companionably in front of a gas fireplace.

"Sorry it's just gas and not an original peat fire. Mrs. Kelly said she's modernized the loft and the house this past year and gas fireplaces are safer. Not as many chimney fires."

Ashley sent out a mental 'thank you' for small miracles. She didn't want to be in an enclosed place with a raging wood or peat fire. Even simulated or gas flames made her nervous and the smell of real smoke could still trigger nightmares.

"I don't mind at all," she said, turning in all directions to study the cozy spot.

She watched Daemon go over to the huge closet and open it, disappearing inside for a second. He came out, photocopies in his hands and a conspiratorial grin on his face. "Found a good hiding spot for these. Don't think our courier knows you made copies but if he does, he wouldn't likely look in here."

"Daemon, you told me not to set foot off the Stud because these people will be looking for me. What makes me safe here?"

Daemon came closer to press a finger on the bridge of her nose.

"Relax, sweetheart, you're safe here. Remember, this is a Garda relative I'm staying with. There are several shifts of patrol cars watching this house and they'll be close behind you until this case is solved. You're what we call a 'material witness' and you have information the couriers need. We're not about to let them have it."

"And you're here too," Ashley whispered, "I guess I can feel safe with a Scotland Yard inspector, right?"

"Make that Chief Inspector, Miss Gallagher. The 'chief' part came with hard work, a lot of sleuthing, doing stake-outs and tackling mountains of exams."

Ashley smiled, as she thought of Daemon sweating over test papers. Then she grew serious again as she thought of the stakeouts and how dangerous his job was. This time it was her turn to raise her hand to his face. She rested it against his cheek and when he put his own hand on top of hers her heart stilled.

She took a breath again and let the warmth of his hand seep into her sensitized skin. Daemon's other hand lifted to her nape and his fingers gently stroked the back of her neck. It was an easy step for Daemon to pull her closer and when she came willingly, he bent his head to meet her lips.

"You taste like wine and the strawberries we had for dessert," he whispered, his voice husky. He ran his tongue gently over the rim of her upper lip and then across the straight edge of her bottom teeth.

The air in the room seemed electric. Daemon's lips met hers again and she felt as if his hands were melting through the thin material of her dress. Her body leaned towards his, magnetized, pulled. Time suspended for long moments as his thumbs stroked her cheekbones, trailing heat behind.

Butterfly touches, casting a firefly trail.

"Daemon." Gasping for air, Ashley took a step back. Pain must have cast shadows because Daemon loosened his arms and looked down at her face.

"Is your throat hurting?"

"No. Not that. Just that we can't do this." Her voice trembled and she searched for the right words. "I want to be here. I want to be exactly here. With you."

"But?" Daemon's voice was serious, his body tense. He watched her closely, waiting.

"But this can't go anywhere. Because I'm going home and you're going back to your job when this is over. And someone could kill me tomorrow, or tonight…" Her voice trailed off… serious thought jumbled as she followed the deepening emerald of Daemon's eyes. She could see, for the first time, that he was thinking similar thoughts, having similar battles with fate and attraction and…caring?

It was the caring that made her take that half step back into his arms. This time she was the one to meet his lips. She raised herself up on tiptoes to press her mouth against his. She made one more attempt to recapture reason and retreated just a heartbeat to meet his gaze.

"But..."

"But?"

"But if someone kills me tomorrow, I want to spend tonight with you."

And she kissed him again.

***

There was no more chance to regain sane, orderly thought. Daemon bent to lift her up against his chest. Her fingers clenched in the material of his jacket as he walked with her over to the big bed, letting her body slide down against his as he stretched one arm over to pull back the duvet and sheet. Then he stepped away to trace the outline of her swollen lips. He touched one corner and followed the flutter of her closed eyelashes with his warm breath as he kissed first one eye and then the other.

He felt the racketing of his heart in his ears and wondered if she could hear it too. And then his mouth found its way to the side of her neck and she groaned.

Just a small sound.

A small, small sound.

But that small groan had done him in.

A gusting wind rose through the trees outside the window, buffeting the panes and rattling the sashes. Neither of them paid attention. They were making a storm of their own.

***

Ashley's hands lifted to curl in Daemon's shaggy hair. She pulled his head closer and pressed a kiss on his chin and then in the hollow of his neck just below the open collar of his shirt. It was a natural progression to find her fingers acting on their own to unbutton the top few buttons and work their way down to his belt.

She stopped, face flushed and her breath catching, to look up at him again, watching, waiting. It took a fraction of a heartbeat for Daemon's own hands to drop from her shoulders to his belt. He undid the buckle, watching her closely.

"Okay?"

She nodded, unable to speak.

"Okay then." He took off his belt and turned her around to pull down the zipper of her dress and then slipped his hands under the open back to slide the material off onto the floor to lie in a neon blue puddle at their feet. The feel of his hands on her bare skin was driving her insane.

She wore only a blue camisole now, nylons, a black lacy bra and one of the very tiny bikini pants he had helped to pack for her. He reached over to turn off the room's main light, leaving only the lamp by the bed to cast the room in a warm glow.

A breath of outside wind ruffled the curtains over the window and the faint breeze wafted over Ashley's bare skin. She shivered slightly, both with the cold and nerves.

She watched Daemon strip off his jacket and shirt and soon the rest of his clothes and hers lay in a pile on the floor. When he took a second to put his Glock where he could reach it, she felt a cold shudder and she was plunged right back into the danger they were in.

But he must have felt it because he put his warm palm over her mouth and said "Shh. It's okay. I've got you. You're safe tonight."

And then she was in his arms again, bare skin against bare skin, the feel of the tawny hair on his chest against her sensitized breasts. Everywhere their skin touched she was warm.

They were both gasping when he broke a long, blistering kiss and nestled his forehead against her rumpled hair. He breathed deeply and smiled as he caught the scent of peaches.

"You know," he said as he raised his head to look at her, "I will never be able to smell peaches again without thinking of you."

"And will you?" Ashley asked.

"Will I?"

"Will you think of me?"

He nodded gravely, his gaze steady on hers. "I will. Maybe there's something we can do about oceans and continents. Let's mark that place and remember where we put it. Later." He bent his head to kiss her again.

Ashley lost all coherent thought as Daemon's mouth lowered to the spot between her breasts. Her heartbeats raced with each movement as his lips nuzzled each breast and circled each nipple. His hands traced the shape of her back and her behind and down to the softness of her mound.

Sheets of electric fire tingled wherever he touched and she cried out when he put first one finger and then another inside, making her whole body clench and tighten.

She hid her cry against his neck and then groaned again.

And then he put his arms behind her knees and she was in the air, her arms hanging on to his shoulders until she felt the cool of the sheet against her burning skin. Daemon pulled the duvet over them both for a moment to bury them in a soft cocoon and she felt his hand explore the soft skin of her ears and her belly.

It was suddenly hot and he threw off the duvet and reached over to his pants to grab a condom. He left it by the bed and raised himself on one elbow to continue exploring.

"Sweetheart…where is this famous tattoo?"

She caught her breath on his latest foray with his finger deep inside her.

"Ankle."

"Butterfly?"

"Butterfly."

She felt him kiss it and then begin tracing his way back to her belly button with his tongue.

***

Daemon raised himself on one elbow to take handfuls of her silky hair in his fingers, letting the cool satin run over his skin. His mind was crowded with feelings both unique and terrifying. There was a sudden rush of protectiveness that was completely new.

He pressed her head against his shoulder and wanted to keep her wrapped in him until she was safe and this was all over.

But then he felt her gentle fingertips blindly tracing the hair on his chest that led in a tapered line to his waist and when she touched his erection, he couldn't think of anything else. His turn to groan. And cry her name.

When her mouth kissed the spot on his shoulder that was dimpled with a small ugly scar, he caught his breath.

She would obviously know it had been made by something hurtful and he could see her pain.

"Daemon, is this a…?"

"My first year. I didn't know how to jump out of the way of bullets then. I'm better at it now." He stopped her horrified gasp with his next kiss and made all thoughts disappear when he put on the condom and slid his body into hers.

Breathing became only a remembered thing as he only concentrated on feeling. Rising and falling with the drapes at the window, that feeling surged and fell, only to surge and fall again.

He used his mouth and his hands and his body to drive her up and catch her when she fell. When she cried out, he swallowed her cries with kisses and thrust into her again. And again.

There was no part of her he wasn't touching, memorizing, learning to love. He knew the gentle indentation of her knees and her delicate waist and the curve of her breasts…those sweetly formed breasts he'd noticed in the waiting room when she'd stretched out her arms above her head.

Her body was small but firm and toned and feminine and he loved each part he touched. And he touched her everywhere until they both orgasmed and then orgasmed again.

Finally, exhausted, he rolled onto his side, pulling Ashley with him. He kissed her forehead and smiled gently into the tendrils of hair that were curling at her temples. The crazy hair that she said she hated when it got damp. But it was exotically beautiful.

He wouldn't mention it now.

Not now.

Their breaths easing, he felt her tuck her chin into his shoulder and watched as she slid into sleep.

***

Ashley felt his hand as it lay against her back between her shoulder blades and she felt utterly, utterly safe. She breathed in the heightened scent of Daemon's clean, soapy skin and memorized it, keeping it in her mind for the days to come when he would be so far away.

She had never felt like this before. She had known others in university, had a boyfriend or two since. She wasn't a virgin. But this had been spectacular and that everything to do with the fact that it was with Daemon.

No matter what happened, she was falling in love with him. Fast.

***

It was much after that thunder started and its rumbling shook the windows. Ashley shivered in her sleep and nestled closer to Daemon's warm body. A few moments later, a sudden blinding flash of lightning lit up the sky outside the window and Ashley cried out, sitting up straight in the bed. "No! No! Sirocco!"

Daemon, years of training deep in his consciousness, reached for the gun he'd put in the drawer beside the bed. He sat up, kneeling on the tumbled sheets, and searched the room, scanning for dark shapes that shouldn't be there. Another sheet of lightning and a thunder clap right overhead and Daemon's skin chilled as he saw its effect on the slender, shaking woman in the bed beside him.

The sudden light had shown no one else was in the room but Daemon got up quickly to make sure.

Nothing. No one.

Just a shivering, shuddering Ashley.

He turned on the gas fireplace for heat and gathered her up in his arms, holding her, whispering in her ear until she stopped shaking. He watched the tears as they ran down her white cheeks to tremble on her chin before they fell to the duvet. Her eyes were closed tight and her fingers clenched on his arms but he didn't feel the pain.

He watched and listened as she came out of a disoriented daze.

"Oh, my God! Oh, my God!" She leaned her head against Daemon's chest and took huge breaths as she fought for control. "Well," she finally croaked, her voice strained and raspy. "That was an interesting way to wake up after what we just did together."

Daemon put one gentle fingertip under her chin and made her look at him. "Okay. Put it down to me being a detective but there's been something there since the first time we talked in that waiting room."

He put a hand on each side of her head and she had nowhere to hide.

It was time.

Chapter Nine

"Butterflies and Paint"

Ashley choked on the remnants of her tears and Daemon winced as he saw the tension in her bruised throat. She tried, coughed and tried again. He went over to the table by the door and poured a glass of water for her from the bottle their hostess had provided and she took a few sips before she tried again.

"It's so hard to talk about this. But for some strange reason the nightmares I used to have all the time are back and I don't know why."

She took another sip and he could see her try to focus on his face. He nodded to encourage her to go on.

"I told you that I had an accident when I was twelve?" She watched him as he nodded again.

"I was training for an audition to join a ballet school in New York."

"At just twelve? Isn't that too young?" Daemon whistled in surprise.

"No. A ballerina starts really young. If you show promise, they want you to be properly trained by special teachers. I wanted that so badly nothing else mattered."

She grew very still and Daemon could feel the shivering start again. He tightened his arms and drew the duvet up around them both. "Go on."

"I was on the stud farm my parents owned and it was summer. It was too hot outside or in the house to practice. So, I was in the barn where it was a bit cooler. I could smell the hay while I danced. There were two horses in their stalls and my own horse, Sirocco was furthest down the row in his own stall."

"Sirocco. The name of your gallery, right?"

"Yes. He was the most beautiful black stallion I'd ever seen. He was perfect, with his scooped Arabian nose and his arched head and long, long tail and mane. Right out of the Arabian Nights. His bloodline made him an Aislin."

"Aislin?"

"Pure Arab line with no outside blood. We grew up together and I started riding him when I was eight."

Daemon could hear the past tense in her words and his heart hurt, guessing what was coming. But it was worse.

"I was dancing. Tchaikovsky. There was thunder all of a sudden. Far away, and then closer. The air was full of ozone and the horses were nervous. They were shuffling in their stalls and tossing their heads. Then lightning hit the barn."

Daemon sucked in his breath at her words.

"The barn was on fire right away. I grabbed the horse closest to me and led him out by his halter. I went back for the next one and got him out too. But…"

"Sirocco?"

She nodded, the tears coming again.

"Sirocco was way in the back. There was a wall of fire between us. He…oh, Daemon. He was screaming. I can still hear it. He was screaming and I couldn't get to him."

Silence except for the breathing in the room.

"Then the main beam on the roof fell. It hit me and knocked me down. One of my legs was broken and the other one was badly bruised and the ligaments and tendons on my knee were damaged."

Daemon just held her, willing her to finish, his heart and his mind in agony, his stomach clenching.

"And Sirocco. He…Daemon...he died." Ashley's voice broke and she sobbed against Daemon's bare shoulder and he just held her, tears running down his own cheeks as he listened to her cry. When she finally stopped, her sobs turning into hiccups, he left her to get another glass of water. She took it in trembling hands and sipped until the hiccups stopped.

"Oh, Daemon. I'm so sorry."

"My God, why? Oh, sweetheart, why would you be sorry? No wonder you hate fire and storms so much. I'm sorry you had that to carry around for so long. I'm sorry you had to see your friend die. Did anyone help you with all this?"

Daemon gave her time to settle and then scooped her up, dragging the duvet off the bed and wrapping her in it. He sat with her in one of the big armchairs, rocking her in his lap.

He had angled the chair so they could get the heat from the gas fire without her having to look at it. But he was worried about getting her to stop shaking. Soon, the combination of his own body warmth and the fire helped her to relax and she finally sighed and rested her head against his chest.

"My parents arranged for a counselor and he was wonderful. He worked with me for over a year and both he and my physiotherapist were lifesavers. My sleeping nightmares grew farther apart but my waking ones didn't get better until I started to paint. Horses make me feel normal. But it was never the same."

"Why?"

"I could watch horses and paint them and admire them but I could never ride one again. At first it hurt my leg and knee. And then it hurt my heart because the horse wasn't Sirocco."

Daemon smoothed her hair and ran his hands over her back, stroking and stroking.

"Daemon? Could we talk about something else? Maybe how to solve this case so I can avoid being murdered?"

"That would be a good thing!"

***

Ashley smiled as she felt his arms tighten fiercely around her. Her heart had lightened with the sharing of this most painful part of herself. Maybe working as a team, they could piece together what was going on with the codebook.

Maybe together they could figure out how to solve the geographical problems too.

Maybe.

Later, with one of Daemon's shirts to wear as a nightshirt, Ashley was finally warm. She sat, one foot tucked up under her, the other stretched out to rest her knee and studied her half of the copied pages. Daemon, in the chair beside her, tried to concentrate. He kept looking at her and when she'd asked why he'd just said he liked what she was wearing and winked.

She watched as he studied the pages again and then saw his excitement as he seemed to see the same patterns that had startled Ashley.

"Look!" he said. "In "Galway Races", the line that's underlined is 'men that ride upon horses.' Then the next bit is 'riding upon the galloping horses.' I see the pattern now."

As Ashley leaned forward her face was lit by reflected firelight. "Daemon, in this one, Yeats is talking about his lover. It's called "He Bids His Beloved at Peace" and it's all about 'shadowy horses, their long manes a-shake.' Further down in the poem someone has underlined 'hiding their tossing manes and their tumultuous feet.' But they've double-underlined the word 'hiding.'"

She watched Daemon shove restless fingers through his hair and sit up straighter to stretch his shoulders and rotate his neck. Without saying a word, she got up and walked over to the fireplace to warm her hands before moving over to stand behind him. She could see the knots of tension on the sides of his neck and gently started to massage the strained muscles to ease away the ache.

***

Daemon had watched the way the firelight shone on her bare legs and tousled hair. He could understand now what she'd meant about her hair. It really had become a mass of curls down her back and around her temples. It emphasized the fragility of the bone structure in her face and shoulders and made her look incredibly young. As he'd traced the faint scars from the surgery on her knee his heart had ached at what she'd lost at only twelve years old.

He hadn't been ready for the gentle touch of her fingers on the skin of his neck and when she increased the pressure, he could feel the tightness loosening. "Ahh," he sighed, dropping his head forward. "That feels so good. You've more than equaled what I did for your knee…"

"The first time we met?" Ashley's voice was husky too, both with emotion and the soreness in her throat. She needed more sleep because of everything their bodies had been through this evening.

"Daemon, do you think Lord Dunvey will be shocked if I don't get home tonight?"

He chuckled and answered with a wry grin.

"Your Lord Dunvey took me aside while you were changing and told me he'd be extremely disappointed in me if I brought you home any earlier than a fashionably late lunch tomorrow."

"Oh my." Ashley's fingers grew still as she took in what Daemon had just said. "I don't know whether to be embarrassed or relieved. What about the Garda officer out there? Won't he know what we've been doing?"

Daemon just laughed and said, "undercover work?"

Then he groaned as Ashley's hands started to work down his back. He was only dressed in his jeans. Period. And she was more than aware of that and made fast work on his zipper.

"Daemon, you know that thing we did before?"

"Uh, before?"

"Could we do it again?"

"As long as I get to see more of your butterfly."

And then he was up, with her in his arms again. Later, when they lay, sweaty and exhausted…legs twined together and her head on his shoulder, he asked, "Do you think you'd be able to take a risk?"

"A risk?" Ashley's voice was gentle and she paused, waiting for his answer.

"The risk, I guess, of giving yourself a chance to just leap off a cliff with me. I don't know where this is going either. I just know I don't want you to go anywhere."

Her answer was clear as she nodded.

This time they slept.

The storm outside had passed and the night sounds were peaceful, a cow mooing in the pasture, a bird twittering in a nearby tree, small animals settling down again after the rain.

Ashley woke up several times with a start, but each time she felt Daemon's arms holding her. She finally reached out and curled her fingers around his hand, tucking it under her chin. Then she went back to sleep, dreamlessly, for the rest of the night.

***

When Daemon woke up it was morning. One of those magical Irish mornings when the sun shone and there was green everywhere. He saw Ashley's hand in his and smiled, remembering how he'd once thought about having her sleep-tumbled hair spread out on his pillow. It was there now. Her sooty black lashes were closed and she slept deeply. There were still tear tracks on her cheeks but she seemed peaceful now.

He pulled himself as carefully as he could away from her and got dressed, grabbed his keys and went out to tell the Garda officer to go. He got a small bag from the car and let himself back into the loft.

Ashley lay…legs and arms sprawled across the bed. He stood watching her until she started to shiver. The fireplace had been off for hours and only their shared body heat had kept them warm.

"Ashley?" Daemon sat on the edge of the bed and whispered in her ear.

"Ashley?" A little louder this time as he lay down beside her, fully clothed, and pulled her into his arms. But she just turned into his body and purred. Her arms came up to rub his back and she kissed his ear, the tip of her tongue teasing his earlobe.

Daemon's resolve crumbled as she ran her teeth over the whisker stubble on his jaw.

"Enough!"

He sat up, bringing her with him, and carried her to the shower, turning on the water and letting her down onto her feet as he pulled off his jeans and shirt.

She jerked completely awake when the warm water hit her body and her eyes flew wide open when he started lathering her back. He felt her reach one soapy leg up to tangle with his and she giggled.

Daemon shampooed her hair and she did the same for him, pulling little peaks of the lather on his head into mini-spikes.

When she bent to lick the beads of water off his chest and lower, he turned her around to soap her breasts from behind. As soon as the water rinsed the soap off, he slipped on a condom and thrust into her, feeling her back arch as her muscles tightened on his erection.

When they sagged against each other, spent, Daemon wrapped Ashley in a huge towel and put another one around his waist, reaching out for her hand to pull her into the bedroom and over to the fireplace.

***

While Daemon got dressed, Ashley used the hair dryer and opened the small bag he'd left for her on the bed.

Her eyebrows rose as she took out fresh underwear, a pair of jeans and an ivory sweater.

"Daemon? How did this get here?"

He came over to kiss her forehead. "Lady Dunvey packed you an overnight bag. In case we had to work all night."

He grinned.

And she did too. Suddenly it felt a bit like she had a new family in the Dunveys and they were cheering for her.

***

After a quick breakfast they headed back out to the car and Daemon stowed the pages in a briefcase in the back.

"That's it then. We're ready to go. I'll take you back to the Stud and then I have to leave for London."

Ashley wasn't prepared for the jolt to her stomach.

"London?" Why?

He put his arm around her shoulders.

"I have to meet with my team in London this afternoon and the code squad wants to go over the book. I'll take what we've found. There were some really good leads, especially that bit about the 'priest in Kilvarnet.' That was thanks to your new detective skills."

He started the car and she looked back at the cottage. So much had happened there last night.

She tried to be neutral and keep emotion out of her voice when she asked questions about where he worked in London and if he'd be going over the pages with his friend Sam.

And how long he'd be gone.

When Daemon took one hand off the wheel and reached out for hers it felt as natural as breathing. It was much harder to stand by the open car door at the Stud and say goodbye, even though she knew now it would only be for two days. It just felt like an ominous foreshadowing of the day she'd be saying goodbye for good.

Ashley moved into his arms when it was time for him to leave and just let him hold her. When he finally stepped back and stood watching her, she could see seriousness.

"I've set up an alternating team of Garda officers to keep an eye on the Stud until I get back. The Garda man we have here on staff will watch during the day. Please, do not put even one ballerina toe out of this place without a Garda to take you. Promise?"

"I promise. I'll be more than busy here anyway. I'm ready to start the watercolor so I'll need massive concentration. And…"

"And?"

"And maybe…"

She stood on tiptoes to kiss his chin. "Maybe it's better that you won't be here to distract me."

Without another word, he smiled again, with a new tenderness. Then he drove away.

Ashley went into the main house and straight to her room. She pulled out her favorite painting shirt and got to work.

The Dunveys had set aside a huge sunroom for her and she placed the easel they'd provided by a large window that let in natural light. She had a stack of watercolor papers ready and spent a few minutes selecting the sketches she was going to use.

She knelt on the floor, laying the drawings out to look at each one with a studied eye. She rejected some and chose others, arranging and re-arranging until she came up with the final juxtaposition that she wanted. She set to work with overlaps of tracing paper and spent the morning transferring sections of her work onto the special paper. The paper had a 'tooth', or roughness to it, and she had already put a background wash on it to get it ready.

By noon she'd started to pencil in the faint details and lines and stood back, ready to have Lord Dunvey come in to okay the first step.

She cleaned up the mass of papers on the floor, carefully numbering them and putting them into a leather portfolio before she left for lunch.

***

"Ashley, colleen, a good day to you!" Lord Dunvey came into the dining room as she sat down at the long walnut table. "You had said you'd have an initial composition to show me today. I'm that excited about it."

The table was loaded with food. A steaming pot of orange and carrot soup sat in the center of the table and there were cut meats and cheeses and bread rolls.

But Ashley just took some fruit and cheese and poured a cup of tea.

Lord Dunvey shook his head.

"You know, young Ashley, you need to eat if you are going to have the strength to finish all this. And here in Ireland it's sacrilegious not to at least nibble on a bread roll with jam and try that soup."

Ashley grinned, grabbed a roll, smothered it with strawberry jam and changed the subject, bringing up the painting. "I do have my first sketch ready and if you like it, I can start the final watercolor this afternoon. I really appreciate the time you've given me to pose for your part of the painting. You're a very good subject."

Michael got up to pull out a chair for his wife. Lady Dunvey watched as Ashley started to get up too.

"No, Ashley, you don't have to do that. We're not formal at lunch. It's only at dinner that we wear our tiaras and furs."

Lady Dunvey smiled mischievously but Ashley thought she'd look as classy and elegant brushing her teeth in the morning in her pyjamas, as she did when she addressed the Board of Directors for the latest charity ball meetings she attended as Chair. She obviously had a sense of humor too.

"So, Ashley, my dear. Did you enjoy your dinner last night? It was good that you got away with your Daemon and had a night off to yourselves. What do you think of young O'Hare?"

Ashley watched Lady Dunvey's face for any sign that she disapproved of her night away. But instead, there was nothing but sweetness and sincere interest. Apart from being surprised enough to choke on her tea and having to swallow and cough again until the spasm passed, Ashley was able to come up with an answer that came from her heart.

"He's a kind, intelligent, brave man. I haven't known him for long and…" She looked down at her plate to play with a piece of fruit and gather her thoughts. "And I'll be going home soon and won't be able to see him again. It will…"

She had to stop to catch her breath and control the break in her voice.

"It will be very hard to say goodbye."

Both Dunveys had the grace to give Ashley a minute.

Lady Dunvey finally spoke.

"My dear, life is so uncertain. We never know what it will bring us, but sometimes, no matter where we are, if we meet someone or something important, we have to grab it and not let it go. If this is a holiday affection and no more, then the pain will pass."

She looked at her husband and Ashley wondered what private memory was making them smile tenderly at each other. "If it's something more and it certainly seems to be, you'll find a way to hold it close and make a new normal in your life that will let this work."

Michael looked at his watch and then outside at the weather. "I suggest we take a quick look through the stables to walk off lunch before it rains again. After that, we'll see this sketch of yours."

Lady Dunvey looked at Ashley as they all got up.

"We have something planned for tomorrow night that you may find interesting. We have a video of our boy Dark Night at his Grand National win. You'll also see some footage of his colt, Black Cloud. Possibly even some bits with that new English colt who's supposed to be the main competition this year."

Lady Dunvey stopped to speak a few words to the maid about her afternoon plans and then turned back to Ashley. "You know the race is less than a week away now. How time flies! We'll have to book our race seats today."

And then her face lit up. "Ashley, I have a wonderful idea! Would you like to see the race? Michael? What do you think?"

Lord Dunvey bent to light his pipe and then looked up at her, his eyebrows raised. "Ashley?"

"I'd love to. Would I be able to sit with you so you could explain everything? I've been to flat races before, lots of times, but not steeple chasing. Other, of course, than what I've seen in movies like *National Velvet* with Elizabeth Taylor."

"Of course, you must be with us. We have a DVD of *Velvet* here somewhere if you'd like to see it again."

***

A short walk through the barn helped Ashley get back a sense of her purpose at the Stud. She listened as Michael led her through the row of low, white buildings neatly spaced in a semi-circle around the vast lawn.

"We borrow some of the ideas of the Irish National Stud. We've installed skylights in the stallion barns. There's an Irish thought that the destiny of the horses in Ireland is guided by the stars. So, our lads get to have starlight shining down on them even inside."

He laughed. "Except of course when it's raining! Which happens a lot."

Ashley followed him down a pebbled path to the mares' barn and stopped to pat several velvety muzzles. "How long are the mares here?"

"Until they foal or until many tries with the stallions fail to produce a foal."

"Do the foals go home with the mares when they're old enough?" They were headed towards the foaling yard now and Ashley could hear baby whinnies nearby.

"It depends on the arrangements made when people bring us their mares. If we agree on just a cash fee, the foals go home. If the owners just want it to be known that their mare has foaled from an important bloodline, then they sometimes just take their mare and an official document home with them. We keep the foal instead of the cash and add the young one to our stable. The mare would stay with the foal until it's weaned though."

Ashley peeked over the open top of a stall's Dutch door and breathed in the heavily sweet smell of fresh hay and leather soap. Then she recoiled, putting her hand over her mouth. "The smell! That's the smell that was in my car!"

Lord Dunvey looked up in concern and stepped in her direction.

"It was the smell of the leather soap we use in our barns at home. Is it common or used only by the exclusive Studs?"

Lord Dunvey picked up a bar of the soap, sniffing it. "It is a pricey one for certain sure. I think only the big stables here use it and some of the big stables in England. It's getting hard to buy because the suppliers have raised their prices and we're looking for alternatives. Some of the smaller operations are using cheaper soaps now."

He considered her question. "Do you think the man who hurt you might have worked at a stable then? I think it's unlikely he'd smell of this soap otherwise. He'd be working at one of the big stables too."

"I'll have to let Daemon know when he gets home." Ashley tried to shake her sudden feeling of dread and leaned forward to look over the edge of the stall. The mare inside moved around to give Ashley her first view of the tiny foal beside her.

"Oh, he's just gorgeous!" Ashley whispered, afraid to startle him. The foal stood, eyes hugely round in his fragile little face. Only days old, he still wobbled on his spindly legs and stood braced in an awkward fighter's swagger. His mother crunched hay…long pieces of it dangling from the sides of her mouth. She seemed content enough to let the visitors check out her baby, but she was watchful and the rippling of her muscles showed that she wasn't as relaxed as she let on.

The foal was intrigued with his audience and moved in a cocky circle. He tried a clumsy little jump into the air and landed on shaky legs, trembling, ears pointed towards them, dipping his head and snorting. A miniature 'whicker' of triumph and he went back to his mother, searching for lunch.

***

Others were watchful today too. Beyond the white rail and the close-cropped lawn, the sun gleamed on metal. It flashed and silvery beams of light glinted off into the surrounding trees. The metal belonged to a set of binoculars. They were held in the grimly clenched fingers of Terence Malloy, friend and co-conspirator of Owen Murphy of the tattooed arm.

He had followed every step that Ashley Gallagher had made today. In and out of the barns. Kissing the man who had been spotted going into the Garda headquarters this morning. Terrance had followed him back to the village and had taken a picture of him, both with Ashley and with the Garda chief. Everything was more important as the days passed. The boss had given them only two days to get the girl. Two days. She was being guarded day and night at this place and always someone was with her. They had to catch a break.

Malloy tipped up a brown paper bag, which held a precious bottle of his preferred whiskey. "Ahh! Now that's sweet." He felt the slow, sharp burn of the alcohol as it seared his throat and he gasped at its pain.

***

Daemon tipped back his chair in the office he shared with Sam at New Scotland Yard.

The room was filled with computer files and pegboards with pictures of the people they'd been investigating since the first informant and then Shaughnessy had spilled names.

Shaughnessy was still in the hospital, under guard. He hadn't been able to give them anything more.

There were multiple coffee mugs in front of them now and if either of them had smoked there'd have been overflowing ashtrays.

The code team had spent hours with computer scans and tech programs, trying to take any geographical clues from the underlining and put them on a map. Nothing so far. They needed another illusive piece. Another set of names. Something.

"You're going to wear out your watch, Daemon."

Daemon ran his fingers through his hair again and looked up at Sam's grin and couldn't avoid the curiosity in his dark eyes.

"Somebody's gunning for her, Sam. I know the Garda's on it but I need to be there."

I need to be there, not here.

"Special, is she? Doesn't sound like it's just a case with her. Do I need to come over and check her out? You haven't had that look forever, not even with the last woman you dated."

Daemon threw a bunched-up piece of paper across the table and then caught the concern on his friend's face. Sam had always been able to read him. Sam, with the rangy, tall frame and that smile that tilted slightly to one side, had been by his side and his best friend for years.

Sam knew.

"Yeah. She's special."

***

Ashley spent the rest of the day finishing her first steps on the painting. Lord Dunvey had been shocked with the clarity and accuracy of the sketch and watched now in fascination as she laid on the beginnings of the fragile layers.

Her fingers were deft and the background details grew and blossomed over the paper. She added a sticky paper called 'frisket' over the outline of the horse and other bits that needed to be more detailed later. She could paint right over it and then peel it off when the rest of the painting was dry. Then she'd concentrate on making Dark Night come alive.

While she worked, she envisioned the final oil she would do at home. She preferred oils because of their vibrant tones and the fact that she could be so much more detailed with light and dark. But watercolor had its own beauty and the soft natural tints were perfect for this first step. She would give the Dunveys both the oil and the watercolor.

She worked until well after dinner, only stopping for short bites of bread and cheese and fortified by endless cups of tea. She looked up when the maid came in to give her the portable house phone.

"It's Mr. O'Hare for you, calling from London."

Ashley brushed her hands on the sides of her painting shirt and took the phone, her pulse beating faster at the sound of his name.

"Daemon?"

"Hi. I was worried. You weren't answering your cellphone."

"I'm so sorry! It must still be in the barn! I had it with me to take pictures of the foals. But yes, I'm okay. How about you? Anything?"

"My friend Sam wants to meet you. He says hi. We've been working on this all day and there's something missing. I'm going to leave him to it and come back. How's the painting coming? And please tell me you've been safely tucked up at the Stud all day!"

"I have. It's going really well. Another few days and I should have enough to…" She stopped, reality suddenly slamming her in the heart. In another few days she would be packing up and leaving.

Not good.

"Go home? I don't like the sound of that" he said.

Daemon's voice held its own grave understanding of the speeding hours.

"Anyway, I was calling to say that there is progress. Scotland Yard and the Garda special crimes department are looking at the horse possibility. They've been looking for the priest too. Turns out he's new to Kilvarnet and no one there knows his past. And he's missing."

"So, there really is a priest there? And he's missing? Where would he be?"

"Don't know."

The phone call lasted only a few more minutes and it was hard to hang up. The sound of Daemon's voice was now so dear and Ashley ached to see him in person, to be held, to just be with him. When she put the phone down it was impossible to go back to work. She pulled off her painting shirt and put on a jacket to wander out into the gathering mist. She tugged the collar around her neck and walked over to the stallion barn to be with Dark Night and find her cellphone.

She'd forgotten to tell Daemon about the smell of the leather soap. She'd tell him as soon as he got back. He already knew there was a horse connection now.

The stallion was happily munching his ration of oats and looked up as she walked down the row of stalls to stop in front of him. He turned around in the big box stall and edged over to be closer to her. He was so used to seeing her now that they'd struck up a friendship. His nose nudged her arm and he sniffed her hand to see if she had a carrot or an apple with her.

When he came up empty, he just shook his head, scattering oat dust and bits of hay around them both. Ashley laughed and brushed off her arms and picked out the flecks of straw that had caught in her hair.

She spent the next hour just sitting in the barn, breathing in the smell of leather and warm horse. Listening to the sounds of hooves on straw and the crunching of large teeth on hay.

She slept dreamlessly that night and got up early to start work, mind busy on what she was doing. She looked up occasionally at the large wall clock, counting the times that the hands had gone around and trying to figure out how many more until Daemon's plane brought him back.

***

She worked until her fingers started to cramp and then she finally quit for the day.

Dressing in a black silk halter-neck blouse and her long oatmeal woolen skirt and high heels, she wandered over to join the Dunveys for a formal dinner. A crystal chandelier hung with Waterford crystal sat high above the huge table and lit the room with a soft glow. The table was laid with fine china and silver and crisp white linen.

When dinner was over, Lord Dunvey led the way to the huge screening room and started up the DVD he'd promised. "DVDs are fine but technology is changing so fast I'm thinking down the line they'll even have the smell of the stables and the field as an extra bonus."

Ashley settled into the plush velvet seat and watched the first part with keen interest.

"This first bit shows our lad from foal to colt and then on through his training and the first steeplechases. Then we'll see his wins in Ireland and England." Lord Dunvey settled into his own seat and used the remote to start.

Sitting in the dark, Ashley soaked up both new knowledge and affection at the same time for this tall, dark horse. From his first gangly, uncertain steps to the tentative jumps as a youngster, he had shown the heart and stamina that made him a champion. He'd had several Irish Grand National ribbons and trophies to his credit by the time he ran in the English Grand National.

Ashley watched the footage of the English steeplechase with her hand over her mouth, tension playing on her face as the horses left the flagged start and ran the nearly two and a quarter mile length course that had them jumping over thirty fences. Sixteen of those were unique and included ones with names like The Chair and Becher's Brook. The jump course put the horses over inclines and water and up slopes.

"Did you know, colleen, that the most interesting story about this race is the one about the colt Moifaa. He was coming to the Grand National from New Zealand in 1904 and his ship went down. The horse had to swim fifty miles to an island. He was found and ended up winning the race that year."

"No! That would make quite a movie, wouldn't it? I'm surprised it hasn't happened yet!" Heart pounding, Ashley watched as Bobby Trehearne, Dark Night's jockey, took him over the jumps and guided him to a victory. She turned to Lord Dunvey and whispered into the flickering darkness. "It's like he flies. He's so buoyant in the air!"

"He is just that, young Ashley. We keep him happy at stud by putting him over the jumps in the far fields. They're beyond the smaller jumps in the indoor arena. More like the cross-field hedges and rails he loved."

"What keeps him in the paddock now? He could just bunch up his legs and sail over."

"He could at that. But he's a gentleman, he is. Happy here. He has his ladies and we keep him well exercised. Now, watch this next bit. This is his colt, called Scamall Dhubh, or Black Cloud. He's too old to be called a colt but it's an affectionate term we have for him."

"He's this year's favorite, isn't he?"

"For certain sure. Lots of money on this young lad. He has his dad's legs and heart."

Black Cloud? Ashley's memory suddenly began to jump. Flashes of words. Where?

"Black Cloud is the image of his dad. But he has crimson fire in his mane and tail."

Ashley's skin began to prickle. But it was when she saw footage of the starting line-up for this year's race, she sat up straight, heart beating faster, skin clammy. "Oh, my God!"

"What is it lass?"

"Could you tell me about the English horse. This year's competition. His name?"

"He's that good he is. His name is Sweet Dancer. He's owned by a huge syndicate. Honest by all accounts but you never know with all the stakes for these races. There's been Internet chat lately about this horse. Great legs, good lift but a will of his own. He seems to have a different rider every big race. And there's a lot of money on him."

Lord Dunvey shook his head. "It's almost like they're having trouble finding someone to get the best from him. He's a contender but he won't be a match for Black Cloud."

The air in the screening room was suddenly too close, too heavy and Ashley was having trouble breathing. Was this it? Was Black Cloud a threat?

Did someone need Sweet Dancer to win this race? Did someone want him to win badly enough to kill?

She saw the pages again. The underlining. The poem was called "Sweet Dancer".

'The girl goes dancing there…

Escaped out of her crowd,

Or out of her black cloud.

Ah, dancer, ah, sweet dancer.'

Chapter Ten

"Poems and Peril"

Ashley squirmed in her seat for the rest of the video, anxious to get to a computer, her mind tumbling with bits and pieces of information, with dark thoughts and suspicions.

Lord Dunvey had put a computer in her room so she could check her e-mails from Beth and keep up with the business of the gallery. Sirocco Gallery was doing well in her absence but needed constant back and forth partnership agreements.

Tonight, she had other plans. She said goodnight and rushed to do some research. The first article on Sweet Dancer was a favorable one. His history as a starter when he'd been privately owned screamed promise. He was a blood red bay with black mane and tail and he looked magnificent in video clips, as he'd soared over the fences.

Later, articles from all sources started to be sprinkled with surprised comments about freezing at jumps, nipping at bystanders, intractability. All since his sale to the Midas Syndicate.

Ashley plugged in the syndicate's name. She got little except the bare facts that a small business had grown by leaps and bounds over the past ten years with interests in racehorses, slot machines and casinos worldwide and was now huge and sometimes implicated in crime.

"Okay, this is weird and I'm worried," Ashley murmured out loud into the empty room.

She grabbed a pen and made a list from the underlining: Sweet Dancer, Dark Cloud. Crimson Fire. A priest in Kilvarnet. A cabin by the lake. Nine and fifty. Manes-a shaking."

She threw the pen down on her desk. "It's a horse. I will bet you anything that the kidnapping is not a person but a horse and it's connected to the Grand National. The syndicate wants Sweet Dancer to win and they're going to kidnap Dark Cloud to keep him out of it."

All those references to horses!

All those mysterious single words underlined. They had to be times and places.

She looked at her watch. Daemon would be back tomorrow afternoon. It was late. She'd call him in the morning. But the Irish colt was in danger. Or was it his jockey?

The book did have a line that read, 'men who ride upon horses.'

"No. If they kidnapped the jockey the owners would just put in a replacement who'd ridden Dark Cloud before. They do that all the time." Ashley talked out loud as she got up and paced.

It was the horse that threatened Sweet Dancer, not the jockey. If the Irish colt was out of the race, especially at the last minute, then the field was clear for the English horse to gallop to the win.

Thousands and thousands of Irish and English pounds are in the balance depending on the outcome of this year's race. Ashley could still hear Lord Dunvey's voice. She could see him puffing on his pipe, his eyebrows lifted as he thought about the cash purse this year.

But was a huge cash purse worth murder?

Ashley changed into her jeans and a turtleneck and boots. She'd go in and work on the painting. She'd try to push the sense of impending danger to the edges of her mind for a while. The watercolor was coming alive. The soft shades were giving a hint of the more vibrant oils she'd use in the final version when she got back to Carmel and her gallery studio.

Both horse and owner stood in front of the grand house with the paddocks and trees in the background in more muted tones. Dark Night's mane and tail lifted slightly in a suggested breeze and the stallion looked straight at the viewer.

It was so completely realistic you could reach into the painting and pat his nose.

"Stop-action!" Ashley smiled.

Smiled just for a moment though. She couldn't keep the images of this beautiful horse and his famous son from clouding her mind. Her gut was telling her Black Cloud was in danger.

She was so sure and it was eating at her. She couldn't wait until Daemon got back tomorrow. Her fingers held the brush and she painted and tried to think of what to do.

She paced and painted. Paced and painted until she was almost finished. A brush stroke or two more and she'd only have to let it dry.

She would be able to get Lord Dunvey to sign off on this first painting and then she could pack it up and fly home.

She didn't want to go home.

Images of Daemon, in the lifeboat, in the restaurant candlelight, holding her in the salty dark and then again in the exhausted aftermath of their night together in Mrs. Kelly's loft; the images all crowded against each other and Ashley couldn't make them stop.

She didn't want to make them stop.

She cleaned and dried her brushes and tidied up the room, stretching her aching shoulders and massaging her knee. Far away in the front hall the antique grandfather clock chimed the hours and Ashley's anxiety grew. She tried to sleep, just lying down on the top of the duvet and then under it and then on top of it again. Turning out the light didn't help. The sense of dread just grew.

The clock chimed again.

Five o'clock!

She couldn't stand it.

Peeling back the cover, she crawled off the bed, dragging her fingers through her hair and grabbing her cellphone to call Daemon.

But then she stopped. If the syndicate was this big, they might be hacking into calls in or out of the Stud. Any calls.

The Garda chief would know what to do. Maybe they had a secure line.

***

It didn't take long to grab a piece of paper and a pen and outline her theory and all the new information for Daemon, including the smell in the barn. Not for the first time did she feel he was millions of miles away. She stuffed it in an envelope and grabbed her coat.

Daemon wouldn't be leaving London until noon. If the Garda could get to him early enough, he could check this out with his team.

She scooped up her purse and left a message on the kitchen table for the Dunveys.

The Stud security officer was on duty and contacted the Garda patrol car to meet Ashley at the front door. She waited for the young Garda officer to open the back door of the car for her.

"I'm so sorry to ask you to do this so early in the morning. But Chief Inspector O'Hare told me not to leave the Stud by myself and I have to get a message to him before he leaves London. It's an emergency."

"Don't you be worryin' yourself young miss. I'll just deliver you safely into the village office. There'll be a squad on duty to send your man the message. They do have a secure line."

"My man," Ashley whispered to herself as she stared into the darkness of a very early morning. She raised her hand to wipe the condensation off the car window. Only darkness out there. Nothing threatening. No eerie shadows.

And she was with a policeman.

No worries, the officer had said. So why was her mind so full of worries?

***

Grey mist shrouded the hedgerows and covered up the world as they passed the landmarks into the village. Lights were starting to wink on here and there as farmers got up to tend to their animals. They were fairy lights, struggling to wink brightly as the mist turned into a heavy fog.

The headquarters of the Garda was easy to find and the lights were on inside. An officer at the desk yawned as he bent over a cup of coffee and a stack of papers. He looked up in surprise when he saw Ashley come in and he raised his eyebrows and straightened up, adjusting his tie.

"What is it I can be doing for you this early in the morning?"

Ashley pulled the envelope out of her pocket and handed it to him. "I have to get this information to Chief Inspector O'Hare. Do you have a direct secure line for him? It's really important that he get it this morning before he leaves London. It's an emergency."

"Our detective squad will be here at eight o'clock. I'll get them to do it for you. Can it wait?"

"No!'

Her heart sank. There was no other way to reach him and she couldn't alert the whole Garda based just on her own suspicions. But she was so sure.

Daemon would understand. He'd be sure too. "You don't have a way to notify Scotland Yard yourself before then?"

"I'm sorry, miss. I don't have the clearance for that, unless you're certain sure this is an emergency of an international level?"

He looked straight at her, somehow questioning her, wanting her assurance that this was an emergency like that. "I can try to wake the detectives for you if you think I should?"

Ashley looked at her watch. Time was racing. It was already almost six. "Look. I think this might be really important. If you could try them at seven? Just another hour? They'll probably be up anyway?"

"All right, then. I'll see what I can do."

Ashley thanked him, left the note and went back to the car. There was no sense waiting at the office. There was nothing she could do there. In a world of miracles maybe Daemon would call her at the Stud. The fog had rolled in more heavily than before and the road disappeared only feet ahead as they slowly started back.

***

The Garda officer had to drive with caution and was focused on the road, only checking his rear -view mirror when headlights suddenly materialized behind him. "That's a strange one. This car has come from nowhere, it has." The car continued to follow, emerging from the mist to reveal a dirt-covered Land Rover. It veered into the oncoming lane and raced ahead to cut off the patrol car, forcing it off the road into a hedge. Only the officer's driving skills kept the patrol car from turning over.

Three men came out of the gloom before the officer could react and Ashley didn't even have time to scream. She heard a muffled 'phfft' and shattering glass. The young officer slumped sideways, a stream of blood staining his forehead bright red. Another sound and blood flowed from his chest.

Ashley's door was yanked open and a gun shoved into her side.

"Well, if it isn't young Miss Gallagher herself."

The voice from the dark wasn't a familiar one but something else was.

It hung in the air, clinging to the man's clothing. It was the smell of saddle soap. The expensive kind.

The kind Lord Dunvey and others like him used on their riding and racing tack. He'd said only high-end stables used it.

The syndicate stable must use it too. And this man must work for them and she'd been right about this whole thing.

Two long arms reached into the car to unclick her seatbelt and pull her out of the car. Her purse fell to the floor and her reactions, slowed by shock, finally kicked in. Her foot shot out and connected with the man's stomach and she followed up with a sideways jab to his jaw. When he swore and reached out again, she tried to slide under his arm to get out and run.

But he came at her again and backhanded her in the face, making her head spin and blood spill from her split lip.

She bit the hand. Again, and again until she was lifted right out of the car and set on her feet. As soon as she felt the ground under her she kicked out again and connected with a shin. An outraged yell told her she'd done some damage and it gave her the strength to try again.

This time someone else grabbed her too and she was lifted up into the air and shoved into the back seat of a Land Rover and gagged and blindfolded before she could scream.

Someone pushed her down on the floor and the engine, which had not been turned off, roared into life and they moved forward.

Behind them there was silence.

***

Daemon had come in before six to finish in the London office and pick up the latest report from the code department.

Ashley had been amazingly astute with her ideas and there had been success with Shaughnessy too. The more time he spent in the hospital with guards surrounding him and in constant fear of someone getting in to kill him the more he realized his boss would make sure he was dead sooner or later.

The more he realized how dead he was going to be the more information he coughed up. He wasn't as far down the ladder as they'd been led to believe.

He knew there was a priest in Kilvarnet and that he wasn't a priest at all. Shaughnessy had connections to some very familiar names in the Scotland Yard files and there was now an alert out for the fake priest.

The special crimes department had already put a trace on Shaughnessy's cellphone but it was a burner and there was no record of the number at the other end. Shaughnessy had never personally met 'the boss'. Just phone calls. He told Daemon he'd recognize the voice.

There was now a clear tie-in to extra heavy early betting on the Grand National. The kidnapping of a wealthy stable owner was now a possibility the department was looking into. Everyone attached to the Grand National in Ireland and the upcoming one in England was now being added to the list of people being investigated and potentially warned.

***

Daemon grabbed his files and rushed out to a street that was clogged with London's morning traffic and into a police car ready to take him to the airport. A police helicopter would take him to Bristol where he was connected to a short hop to Dublin on a bigger plane.

He was hoping to get to Ashley sometime later today after he got the main Garda squad up to speed. He'd originally planned to leave at noon but he'd caught an earlier flight.

There were so many new leads opening up one after another and he needed to be on-site to coordinate. He looked at his watch. It was just after seven and he grabbed his cellphone. He wanted Ashley to know how much her intuition had helped. And he wanted to hear her voice.

Even though it was early, he punched in the numbers for the Stud, listening as Lord Dunvey himself picked up…and then the bottom of his world dropped away.

"She's not here, Daemon. She left a note that she was going into the village to give something to the Garda. She said she'd found something urgent and she needed them to call you right away on a secure line."

Daemon's fingers tightened on his phone. "Did she go alone? Please tell me she didn't go alone."

"No. Our security man said she left just after five this morning with the Garda officer on patrol. The young Garda lad was going to take her and bring her back. Wait. There's a patrol car pulling up outside right now. It might be her."

There was a moment of silence as Daemon's mind raced. What could have been so important that Ashley had gone out so early? That had made her leave the safety of the Stud?

Then Dunvey again. "Daemon, lad. I'm so sorry to tell you this. Oh, my God!"

Lord Dunvey's voice broke.

"Sir, tell me. What is it?" Daemon shouted into the phone.

"There's been a terrible thing. I'm going to pass the phone to the Garda man. He's right here." A pause as Lord Dunvey spoke to someone else. During that pause the panic Daemon had just heard in Lord Dunvey's voice made Daemon die inside.

Then he heard a new voice. "Chief Inspector. It's Inspector Burke here. There's been an incident on the road. Young Miss Gallagher has been taken."

Taken.

Taken.

The words echoed in Daemon's head. He tried to keep his voice steady. Tried to keep his heart from banging in his chest. Tried to keep the images of Ashley in his arms and in his bed from numbing the conscious part of his brain. He had to stay calm to help her.

If she was still alive.

"Give me more!" Daemon shouted to his driver to hurry, to put on the siren. "Go on!"

"She came into the station this morning and left a message for you. She said it was urgent. The duty sergeant told her he'd give it to the detectives as soon as they came in."

Daemon cursed.

"Why did he wait? Why didn't he call me right away?"

"The sergeant said he didn't have the secure number to contact you. He had to wait for the detectives you've been working with."

Daemon put his head in his hands and tried not to think of how much time they'd lost.

How lost Ashley would be with these people. He gritted his teeth and put his ear back to the phone.

"What happened after she left the office?"

"She went with the Garda officer just after six to go back to the Stud farm. She said she'd wait for you there. You'd told her to stay put."

Daemon's heart broke as he wished that she had, no matter how important the message had been.

"We got an emergency call from a driver going by about half an hour later. He said a patrol car was off in a hedge at the side of the road. Other cars must have passed it too but didn't stop because the fog this morning was that thick, they'd not have seen anything."

Inspector Burke paused and Daemon waited for the space of a breath. "What did the driver find? Did he stop to check the car?"

"He did that. He only found our Garda officer. He'd been shot."

Daemon's mind stopped functioning for a second and then went into overdrive. If the Garda was dead, they had nothing. No leads. No way to start searching for Ashley. No way to find her.

He took a breath and then another and waited. "Is he dead?"

"Two wounds. One to the head. One to the chest. Both would have been fatal."

Fatal.

He needed to know. Needed to know if there was anything to tell if she was still alive.

"There was just Miss Gallagher's purse on the floor of the car. Some blood. Signs of a struggle. She must have fought. She didn't go easily."

She'd fought.

And they'd hurt her. There was blood.

Daemon had a flash of her on the street in Dublin with the mugger. Of course, she'd have fought. They wouldn't have taken her without a struggle. Not without her trying to get away.

"Do you want me to open the envelope and tell you what was in the message your young lady left you?"

"An hour ago. I wanted to know an hour ago." Daemon's voice was rough with strain as he tried to keep from yelling. The lost, wasted time.

If they hadn't killed her yet they would soon. They'd taken her because she'd added underlining of her own. As soon as they forced that from her, they wouldn't have any reason not to kill her.

The thought of them torturing her…

As the inspector read the message out loud Daemon wrote frantically on the back of his notes from yesterday's meeting with McBride.

It was the horse!

Of course, it was. Everything they'd seen in the pages had led to this. The English horse and the Irish colt. The syndicate McBride was already investigating. The priest who wasn't a priest.

"Miss Gallagher said she thought something was pointing to Kilvarnet for some reason. She said there were numbers underlined? A nine and fifty? She wondered if it was an address?"

Daemon looked at his watch. It was over an hour since Ashley had been taken. Sixty minutes where they could have come up with a million ways to hurt her to get her to tell them what she had done.

The police car pulled up beside the helicopter, the copter's rotors already in motion. Daemon told Burke to put out an alert to the Stud farm that owned the Irish colt and then Burke said to hold up as he read something else from the message.

"Miss Gallagher said you'd want to know about the smell? She said she'd remembered. It's an expensive saddle soap used only by high-end stables…the kind that would be used at the stable in England where they have that English steeplechase horse. She said you'd know what she meant."

***

Daemon ran up the steps and into the helicopter, buckling in and waving to the pilot to take off. He hung up with Burke and called McBride.

"They've taken Ashley and killed the Garda patrol officer who was with her."

"My God! I'm sorry O'Hare. I know she's come to mean something to you. Did the officer tell you what the Garda are doing to find her?"

"Nothing. They've completely botched this. They've given us a wasted hour and have nothing. But there are new leads."

"Tell me!"

"She left a message for me this morning at the Garda headquarters.

She said she'd found out there's an English entrant owned by the syndicate we've been trailing. The Midas Group. We already talked yesterday about the heavy betting they've been putting on their entry. The only real competition for the Grand National race is an Irish horse. Ashley figures it's not a person who is going to be kidnapped."

"It's the Irish entry!" McBride shouted it out and swore. They'd been at this for days, trying to narrow down who was the potential victim. They'd never expected this.

"So, it's not an owner at all," he said.

"No. I told the Garda officer to contact the Irish horse's owner and warn him. But now I've got to get the detective squad over there moving."

"Good luck. And Daemon?"

"Sir?"

"Daemon, I hope you find your young lady."

Daemon fought to keep his voice professional. "Thank you, sir."

McBride then said they were going to tighten up surveillance on the syndicate and see if they could impound the English colt and not let it run.

***

Daemon was sweating by the time the copter was in the air.

The leads needed to come together now and fast. He hoped and prayed Ashley could hold on until he could find her. They needed her. She'd know that. She wouldn't tell them and because of that, they'd hurt her. And then they'd kill her.

***

Ashley had been sitting in the back seat of the Land Rover for miles and miles, defiant as they grilled her and grilled her about the book. They hadn't touched her again except for the blindfold. She had no idea where they were going, except that it seemed to be taking a long time. It was only when they'd slowed to a stop and taken off the blindfold that she knew she'd missed any chance to stay alive. Now that she knew what they looked like it was over.

"Well then, we'll just introduce ourselves, shall we? Since you won't be telling anyone about us now. It's Owen Murphy in the flesh, I am. If you'd just co-operated, we could have made this quicker for you. But..." There was a grim laugh.

"But, since you've decided not to help us, then there's no point in us being gentle."

And he hit her again.

Ashley's stomach did a sickening lurch as she saw his arm. It was tattooed. The tattoo with the same evil looking dragon she'd seen once before. On the arm of the man who'd tried to strangle her at the pub. She'd sketched it for Daemon and he'd sent it to Sam.

"They know about you," she said as she wiped away the blood on her cheek. "They'll find you because I drew a picture of your tattoo from before."

"Is that right then? Aren't you the talented one?" The man laughed again and this time the other two men with him did too. It wasn't a pleasant sound. "And will you be talented and clever enough to save your boyfriend's life?"

Ashley tried not to react but something must have betrayed her.

"Ah. So, you do care about this O'Hare fellow. Do you care that we all know he's Scotland Yard? That we know he's looking for us?"

Ashley made an effort not to show any surprise.

The man gave her a leering smile. "Do you care that we watched you kissing him? That we've been watching you with him for a while now? And we know you were with him…and you know what I mean by 'with him'."

The man laughed again, apparently finding this all really funny.

"It was so easy to find you. After I got the book away from you at that pub, I thought I could just kill you then and that would be it. But the police interrupted. We didn't know you'd tampered with our little plan."

He put his hand at the nape of her neck and squeezed.

"Want to know how easy it was to track you down in the first place?"

Ashley just stared at him, not daring to show any emotion at all.

"You had a tag on your bag. Typical stupid tourist mistake. Our friend Shaughnessy at the ferry saw it. We sent another of our friends to your hotel to ask where you'd gone. They were hospitable enough to almost draw us a map."

***

Her kidnappers had pulled out ammunition that would end Ashley's life even before they hurt her and then shot her. They were going to hurt Daemon.

She had an insane urge to laugh. Her mind was starting to tilt in crazy images. Her travel agent suggesting that she fly to Ireland. Thinking it would be okay now to sue the hotel for giving out information about her. Thinking she'd never look at a poetry book again.

Oh yeah. She wasn't going to see her agent again. Or live to see another poetry book.

Then her mind was racing on other paths. She had to do something to keep them away from Daemon. She couldn't let him be hurt. Not for anything.

"Shall we be telling you how we'll kill your lad? We know he's gone to London. We know he's coming back because he's on this case and he's a smart young lad." The man reached out to cup Ashley's chin. She tried to turn away but his fingers were too strong. He touched the blood on her lip with the back of his hand and made an apologetic 'tisk'.

Ashley felt repulsion. Everything before had been numbed by surprise and shock. But now her fear wasn't just for herself.

It was for Daemon.

She was in love with him. She'd felt it coming for quite a long time but hadn't realized how deeply she cared about him until now. Now that she was facing the real possibility that these men were quite capable of killing him. She knew she was out of time. But she could try to keep them from going after Daemon.

Dark Cloud was out of time too. Hopefully, her note would give Daemon a chance to stop the kidnapping.

When Murphy pulled out his cellphone her throat constricted.

"Seamus, it's me, Owen. She's not going to be helpful at all, she's not. So, we need to take out her copper friend. Wait at the airport. You have his picture. We're needing him to be dead."

"No!" Ashley yelled, her voice raspy from strain and fear.

"Seamus. Did you hear that?" Another ugly smile. "You did? It seems she doesn't want the boyfriend taken out. I'd like you to keep him in your sights though. For insurance, you understand?" Murphy hung up and his laugh was no longer leering. It was just plain mean.

And angry.

"You have no idea how much trouble you've been. How much danger you've put us in with our very temperamental boss. Our boss who's not happy that you almost ruined our plan."

Ashley tried to look away, tried to distance herself from what was happening.

"You're going to tell us now. You're going to tell us how you changed the book."

And she did.

***

The worst part, after their threat about Daemon, was knowing another horse was going to suffer because of her. Another black, beautiful, innocent horse. She couldn't stop the tears, hot and salty, that flooded her cheeks after the three men left her alone and pulled the car back on the road.

She spent the rest of the harrowing trip just staring out the window. There hadn't been anyone else on the road but the man sitting beside her had been ready to shove her head down anyway to keep her from making any eye contact with passing cars or people walking by.

Somehow, now that she'd stopped trying to defy the men in the car, she had a feeling of calm and she started to plan. Her brothers would be proud of her and she was determined to tell them all about this in person.

The car had gone by vast fields of intense green, bathed in muted sunshine and fragile light. They passed whitewashed stone cottages built in the old square, squat style; some thatched, some not. The houses hugged the narrow lanes through the tiny villages along the road. The rolling hills gradually edged into the more rugged landscape of Sligo and it started to rain, making the roads slick.

The lazy smoke of peat fires rose from chimneys all around her and made Ashley feel even more alone. There were people close by who could help her if they only knew she was in such big trouble. But there was no one near the road and the tiny churchyards with their Celtic crosses were empty. There were no breaks in the driving and Ashley knew Murphy would order a hit on Daemon if she tried to escape. He might do it anyway and she couldn't breathe with the fear.

Her gaze sharpened as they passed the outskirts of Kilvarnet. Down the main road she could see the soaring spires of the village's Gothic church and the Land Rover passed a sign pointing to a local pub. The carved logo had the name of the pub and was decorated with a figure that had a lion body and the head of a man.

"This is where you've been meeting isn't it? This pub. And Kilvarnet has a priest. Is he real?"

"Now aren't you the quick one. The priest isn't a priest at all is he? He's my brother and has done a grand job of pulling the wool over everyone he has." Murphy's grin was almost proud.

"And my young colleen who is so smart. The part of the plan that you didn't ruin was the wording for the bit that told my brother how to take the Irish colt. He loaded him onto a truck this morning. The pretty young horse is on his way to meet us, he is. And so sad it is that he isn't going to be racing anymore."

***

Ashley knew the 'nine and fifty' had to be an address. So, she wasn't surprised to see the number 950 on the address sign at the end of a lane that led to a small lake. Nor was she surprised to see a small cabin there. It had a barn built behind it.

She could hear the waves lapping against the shore as the Land Rover stopped in front of the building and Murphy opened her door. This time she left the car under her own steam and looked around her, trying to memorize the landscape before they went inside.

It was a tiny lake, surrounded by trees and brush. The main road, backcountry as it was, would have traffic on it because it led to Kilvarnet. The view across the lake was discouraging. Rugged tree-covered hills rose up, forming a barricade to freedom.

Her only chance was the woods behind the barn.

There was a roaring peat fire going in the cabin and a series of rough-looking chairs and a small table. A rustic kitchen and even more rustic bathroom were built just off the main room. There was no bedroom, just a couple of old double beds that smelled musty.

Ashley sucked in her breath, making an effort not to look at the fire and thought she was never going to be able to get the smell out of her clothes and hair. If she lived, that is.

The poetry book lay on the table and Ashley was given a highlighter pen and told to get busy highlighting the lines she'd added herself. It was no problem because she'd spent so much time with Daemon going over the original pages that she'd memorized them.

The smoke was choking her with its acrid, intense odor and she started to cough.

"Could I have some water? I can't finish this if I choke to death before you do it for me."

"Oh! A sense of humor! Nice that you can have fun with this."

She did get her water though and once she was finished, they all waited.

Murphy picked up his cellphone and called someone, sharing the proper underlining and nodding his head. He wore a satisfied smile when he hung up.

"The boss thanks you and says you can stay alive until the colt gets here. You can get all close and personal with him since you love horses so much."

***

The day grew darker and rain pelted on the roof and blew against the windows. Ashley was left alone now that she'd done what they wanted. She was infrequently allowed to get up to use the tiny bathroom. There were no windows to crawl out, but at least she had a few minutes of privacy. She pulled carefully on the rope tying her wrists but gave up because the ropes were always retied after her bathroom breaks.

A loud crunch of gravel broke the tedious banter of the three men, deep in their card game and pints of Guinness. Ashley heard the unmistakable whinny of a frantic horse and she felt sick. Her fingers shook and her skin grew clammy.

Another horse in harm's way.

This time she wasn't going to let it happen.

Chapter Eleven

"On Her Own"

"Well, my colleen, would you be wanting to see your friend now?"

Murphy came over to drag Ashley to her feet and led her outside where the air was at least fresh and smoke-free. She stood in the rain and felt the cold drops fall on her head and run down her cheeks.

She shivered as she watched the men join someone dressed in a priest's collar and dark shirt unload a horse from an old red van. Black Cloud was a stunningly beautiful stallion. He stood half a hand taller than his father and had, as Lord Dunvey said, the 'crimson fire' in his mane and tail that came from his mother.

He was nervous. His hooves beat a dancing pattern in the dirt outside the van and he kept shaking his head from side to side to try to get away from the firm hand on his halter rope. He pawed the ground and whinnied constantly.

Murphy carefully approached the restless colt and reached up to put a piece of cloth over his head. There was a fractional settling of the anxious movements but the colt's skin still twitched and he was breathing heavily.

Ashley ached with sorrow as she watched. Her fingers clenched on the ropes and she longed to help him. "Hey!" Four faces swiveled around to stare at her.

"Untie my hands. I know you work with horses but you obviously don't know how to handle this colt. Let me try. You know I can't go anywhere."

Murphy and the others put their heads together, arguing. Finally, Murphy undid her ties. Ashley rubbed her wrists and stretched the ache out of her back. Her knee was starting to hurt from sitting so long in one spot and she limped a little as she walked over to Black Cloud.

"You're such a good boy, aren't you? This is a scary thing for you to go through. Do you understand that I'm scared too? Let's help each other."

She stopped just in front of the colt and watched as his ears pricked up and followed her voice.

He snorted and tossed his head again but seemed to be listening to her calm, focused tone.

"It's really going to be all right you know. We just have to be strong right now and patient. If you come with me quietly, they won't hurt you."

The stallion pressed his nose against her hand, breathing her scent and nodding his head up and down. But he started to settle and stopped prancing. Ashley reached up slowly and took the halter rope from the pretend priest. She glared at him and shook her head in dismay that someone like him would have the nerve to try to pass himself off as a person who made their life one of charity and leadership.

"You are scum you know." That was all she said. And she said it in such a sweet tone that the man didn't even react until she'd walked toward the barn with the horse pacing along peacefully behind her.

The other men opened the door and turned on the overhead light, which spluttered and then went dim. The electrical wiring in the barn seemed to be in the same state of disrepair as the main cabin. Murphy went over to an old dusty kerosene lantern and struck a match to light it. The lantern smoked and hissed as it caught and flared.

Ashley stared at all the straw and old bedding surrounding the lantern and couldn't stop memories of that type of tinder catching on fire and what had happened after. But the horse was her main concern now and he recoiled at the sounds of the lantern, pulling his head up and trying to jerk the rope out of her hands.

"Shhh! It's okay. I'm going to stay with you. It's all right." She stroked the black nose and watched as the nostrils puffed in and out and then calmed. "I want to stay here with him," she told the men. "You can lock the barn door and I can't go anywhere. I can look after him."

Murphy's face took on a cross between pure evil and sweet agreement and he led the other men to the door, closing it behind them with the rusty old hinge and padlock.

Once they'd gone Ashley dropped the halter rope and sank to the floor, putting her head between her knees and trying to keep a sudden wave of dizziness and nausea from overwhelming her.

"Oh, horse. Oh, horse we are in big trouble. But Daemon will come and get us. I'll come with the Dunveys and watch you win that race. Everyone knows you're the best. They'll keep Sweet Dancer out of it and you'll win fair and square."

The dizziness started to ease and Ashley took great breaths to calm the nausea but it got the best of her and she emptied what little there was in her stomach and just retched and retched. After she stopped shaking, she got to her feet and leaned against the wall.

"But. And this is a 'but' I have to be honest. Maybe Daemon didn't get my message."

Her head swam with the possibility that the Garda had somehow messed up.

"In that case, old boy. In that case I'm on my own."

***

Daemon's helicopter had landed at Bristol's airport and the police transport plane was waiting for him on the tarmac. Curious stares followed him as he spoke to the police at the plane's stairs and then climbed aboard and took a seat.

He'd had a frightening update. The Irish horse had disappeared. The call to the Stud farm that owned him was too late. Someone with knowledge of the colt's daily movements had cut the security wires and disabled the cameras. A powerful handsaw had cut through the fencing and two pairs of footprints led through the crushed grass in the paddock to where the ground was torn up with signs of a powerful struggle.

Black Cloud was gone.

There was no ransom note. No phone call to warn the owner of the colt's fate. He was just simply gone. No witnesses to the type of vehicle. Only a set of tire tracks at the side of the road.

Daemon was waiting to hear from the Garda investigative team in County Kildare about what kind of tyres had been used and what weight of vehicle might have been sitting in that spot. He picked up the secure phone from the plane and called Lord Dunvey.

"Is there any news?"

Lord Dunvey had nothing to add to what he'd been told earlier. No signs of Ashley anywhere. No news from the Garda. He'd been waiting by the phone, too anxious to do anything but pace. His wife had cancelled all of her meetings and was pouring endless cups of tea.

Daemon promised he was doing everything he could to find her. His heart felt leaden when they asked if Ashley's parents should be called.

"I don't think just yet. There isn't anything they can do from so far away except worry. And the police are keeping this from the news so they won't see something before we talk to them."

So far away.

The three words echoed in his ears and in his brain and heart. Ashley was so far away. In the moment and in the future, no matter what happened.

Daemon thought about his own future and it looked bleak. He was tired of the life he was living. He rubbed the ache in his forehead and thought about the way his own parents had reacted when he'd told them he was going to put a hold on his law degree program and go into police work instead. They'd told him they understood but he'd never been sure. He'd hated the look on his mother's face whenever he'd come home on leave or holidays that first year.

It had been especially hard on his family when he'd been shot.

He would never forget the pain on his parents' faces. Not a word. They'd never said a word except to support him. But his sister had cried and cried and told him he should never get married and put a wife through that.

Maybe it was time to finish that degree. If he ever had a chance of a future with Ashley, he didn't want to see pain and constant fear on her face. The expression he'd seen when she'd noticed the puckered scar from the bullet had been bad enough. There were law schools everywhere, weren't there?

Even in California.

He straightened up and put away his phone, walking back to take his seat for landing.

Interesting that a plane could travel from Bristol to Dublin in less than an hour and they'd been in the lifeboat for over three. So much had happened since that night.

***

Tucked away in the barn by the lake, Ashley thought for about two seconds that she would tell Murphy she had copied the book and the police knew what was going on. Then she thought better of it. Bad plan. If they figured she'd told and the police were on their way she would lose all possibility of rescue. They'd just simply kill her and get rid of the colt instead of waiting.

She looked up at the stallion, hoping he would have a better idea of how to get out of their present situation. He just shook his head and munched hay.

"You know, Black Cloud. If I stay in Ireland…if I live through this that is…I might just try to learn some Irish. I know that 'dhubh' means 'black'. And Lord Dunvey said 'scammal' is the word for 'cloud. I wonder what the words for 'I love Daemon' would be?"

Then she got up and paced again, looking at her watch for the zillionth time. Murphy's answer to her question earlier about what was going to happen next was still clear in her memory.

“There are thousands of pounds being bet on this race. If we hide the colt until the race is over and the English colt wins, we’ll get our cut of the money from the purse and be long gone. We just have to lay low for another couple of days. That gives you two days of eating hay with him and then it’s all over for the both of you.”

And then he’d laughed.

So, they didn’t even plan on a ransom note. That way the Stud would have no way of tracing them or helping the police to know where to look. Murphy and his boss had no intention of returning the stallion. Or letting her go.

She had to act. She had to do this all by herself.

***

Ashley found a bale of aged hay and pulled it closer to Black Cloud. She grabbed a handful and sniffed, making a face. “This isn’t exactly what you’re used to but my nose tells me it’s just old, not full of mold. It should be safe for you to eat.” She offered up a sheaf and the horse snuffled at it, shaking his head and stepping back.

“That’s what I think of it too. Not impressed? Well, I’m not either.”

Ashley looked at her watch; then at the small window. It was too high up for her to reach, even if she stacked everything in the small barn in a giant pile. She paced, rubbing her blistered wrists absentmindedly and tried to think.

“It’s now four o’clock. It’s going to be dark soon. I think it’s still raining.”

She shivered and huddled into her jacket.

“And it’s cold.” Horses radiated heat so standing beside Black Cloud was not only comforting but also kept her warm while she thought.

***

Miles away, Daemon's plane had landed in Dublin and a Garda car was waiting for him, its engine running and the officer ready to go.

"Chief Inspector, where do you want to go first? We can be at headquarters here in no time."

'No time' depended on Dublin's traffic, which ate time that was precious. Daemon kept checking his watch and thinking about where to start looking. They'd pulled in the owner of the English horse and were now trying to find the mysterious 'boss'.

The Garda Chief Inspector was anxious to help.

"Sir, I'm so sorry the young colleen is in trouble. The car must have come out of the mist this morning and our young fellow didn't see until they were on top of him. He didn't even have a chance to put a hand on his gun. But..."

Daemon jumped on the word, ready for any kind of hope.

"But we have a witness to a car matching the type that had the tire treads we found at the scene. Someone on the road this morning saw a Land Rover moving in a suspicious way, no headlights, driver looking over his shoulder all the time. They got the car's plate number."

Miracles.

Daemon grabbed his cell phone and got the Kildare headquarters on the line. He looked at the Dublin inspector. "Have you called this in already to your aerial surveillance?"

"Yes, sir. It's only been in the last half an hour that we found our witness and traced the plates. It was a grey Land Rover. Older model, very dirty and the plates were hard to read."

Daemon called McBride with the new information, praying they could get a name. It came within minutes. It was a sign of the level of non-brilliance in this group that they hadn't even bothered to use a rental car. The Land Rover was registered to Terrance Malloy.

And he was a known associate of Owen Murphy. Owen Murphy of the tattooed arm. Owen Murphy who had already hurt Ashley once.

He was extremely dangerous.

And he had Ashley.

Daemon remembered the police at the scene of the Garda's murder had said Ashley must have fought the people who'd taken her. There were several sets of footprints so even with her unbelievable courage she hadn't had a chance.

But Malloy and Murphy would remember that and would be rough.

***

At headquarters he'd spread out all the copied papers on a large table with maps and laptops ready to go. Daemon and the head of the Garda detective squad hunched over the table, searching the areas around the small village of Kilvarnet.

It was just after one o'clock now and over six hours since she'd been taken.

He couldn't think about it but he couldn't think about anything else.

In the meantime, they had to hope for the smallest of miracles that one of the suspects would show up. Information on all of them, including the priest, had been sent out to all of the area Garda offices.

Daemon put Ashley's letter and his copy of the pages in front of him and rubbed his forehead. Her handwriting had the same clean, flowing lines as her sketches. His heart constricted as he noticed the faint scent of peaches that drifted off the paper.

"Kilvarnet and the area around it has a number of small lakes," she had written. "The poem talks about a 'small cabin by a lake'."

Daemon leaned over the map of County Sligo. "We need to send a weather services helicopter over these lakes and it can't be a Garda one. We can't do anything that looks suspicious because we don't want to tip them off. We're looking for a grey Land Rover with dirt all over it."

"Sir, we're also looking for something like a van with a horse trailer. We just got the results of the tyre tracks left at the Irish stud. The tyres were standard issue for heavy vehicles of mid-size.

"There were also tracks behind them from a heavy trailer."

Daemon felt a surge of hope. Things were happening. They were getting somewhere at last. "That's great! If they've taken the colt into Sligo we just have to wait until one of the names on our list needs to go into a village or shows up at a traffic blockade."

Daemon needed to move. Being here wasn't making him feel like he was doing enough. But suddenly there was a break.

"Chief Inspector! We've got the priest!" One of the Garda had run into the room with a cellphone in his hand. "They're holding him in an office just south of the village. If you come with me right now there's a helicopter waiting to take us there."

Daemon didn't need more than a minute to gather up all the papers and run out the door behind the officer. Now he could take action. It was just taking so damned long to get to her.

***

In the barn by the lake, Ashley paced, trying to think. Black Cloud stood peacefully now, munching some of the old straw and occasionally stomping his hooves, making the metal rings on his halter clang. Ashley came back to him, running her chilled hands along the sleek black flank. She stroked his long neck and velvety nose.

"You are a handsome fellow you know. I had a horse like you once. Can I tell you about him?" Black Cloud pressed his nose against her chest and nudged her.

"Okay then. His name was Sirocco and he would have loved to jump fences like you do. But he got to race in the fields and we spent a lot of time together riding in the hills above our own stud farm. You don't get to meet many Arabians in your stable but they're special, just like you."

She rubbed the spot between the stallion's eyebrows and breathed gently into his nostrils, letting him get close and feel more secure. "I let him down, you know. I don't think he would have been mad at me but I was mad at myself and I can't seem to forget what happened to him because I couldn't save him."

Black Cloud tossed his head again, spraying bits of hay all over her.

"I have to let it go, I think, if I'm ever going to stop having nightmares."

"Daemon said that I keep forgetting that I got the other two horses out of that barn. He said Sirocco would have been proud of me." She raised her arms up to wind themselves around the colt's warm neck and pressed her face into the long red-black mane.

"The poem talked about 'crimson fire'. You do have that red in your hair," she murmured. "A gift from your mother; something to make you unique. I got this silly hair from my mother. She has hair just like mine, long and black and straight most of the time. But whenever it gets the least bit damp outside my hair goes crazy and curls."

Ashley jumped when she heard steps outside the door and the sound of the padlock being unlocked. Murphy came through with a plate of beans and a slab of bread and put it on the floor beside the lantern.

"Since you've done such a grand job of helping our lad and you were such a clever woman to save your copper boyfriend, we decided to feed you. It's not the kind of meal you're probably used to but you can't be choosy."

"No thanks. I've lost my appetite. I'd rather eat hay with this colt than eat your food."

"Not as smart as I thought. But suit yourself," he growled. "We're waiting for the boss to tell us what to do with you and the horse. He'll call soon. The race is day after tomorrow and then we won't want to be wasting good hay and beans on the two of you."

His smile was just plain cruel now. Frightening. Brutal.

When the barn door shut again Ashley stared at it, her skin cold. "All we can do is wait for someone to find us. If that doesn't happen, I need to get us out of here myself. And there is something I need to try first."

Ashley sat on the bale of hay and thought about the last time she'd been on a horse. It had been the morning of the accident. She remembered the way Sirocco had danced in anticipation of their ride. He had whickered softly in her ear as she'd put on his halter and saddle and they had both been excited about the freedom of an early morning gallop.

Ashley reached out one of her arms now to stroke the strong muscles of Black Cloud's broad back. Muscles that bunched and gathered to lift him over the hurdles in the Irish Grand National to lead him to victory. She fervently prayed those same muscles would lead him to victory in the English Grand National just two days away.

"We need miracles my friend."

***

In the Garda office in Kilvarnet, Daemon sat staring out the window. The weather helicopters had made a wide sweep over the forests and lakes within an hour's driving distance of the village. They'd searched the landscape for cabins and trailers and so far, hadn't found anything.

It wasn't usually dark until almost 7 o'clock this time of the year but it was a cloudy day and they were running out of good light.

They'd have to talk to the 'priest' and find out what he would tell them.

He was slouched in a wooden chair at the big table in the interview room. He didn't look much like a religious man now and he'd refused to co-operate.

"You've got the wrong man. You're right. I'm not a priest. Probably didn't take you long to find that out. But all I've done is rifle the local collection box on Sundays. That's not a big enough crime to be grilling me like this. I don't know anything about a horse or a woman."

***

Owen Murphy's brother Daniel sat staring at the wall and closed his mouth. His brother and the boss would kill him if he spilled anything. He'd been stupid to come back to Kilvarnet but they needed supplies at the cabin. He'd thought if he came in his collar no one would think he was out of place. He hadn't expected to be grabbed the minute he drove into town.

The new fellow, he wasn't a Garda. His accent was English. And they kept calling him Chief Inspector O'Hare. He suddenly jerked back in his seat. This was the boyfriend! He was Scotland Yard. He was a detective!

And Murphy started to sweat.

"We know you're not Father Macklin. We know you're Daniel Murphy."

He was done for.

It was O'Hare talking now. He was angry. Daniel looked away and tried to concentrate on the fly walking up the wall.

"And we know the Land Rover you've got outside is registered to the scum who tried to kill Miss Gallagher before. All we have to do is dust the car for fingerprints and I'm sure we'll find his as well as yours."

Daniel gulped, his sweating increased, small droplets gathering along his hairline, his priest's collar growing hot around his neck. He didn't have any answers.

"So, you have two choices here."

He finally looked up, impelled by the authority in the Chief Inspector's voice. "Yeah? And what would those choices be?"

The English detective smiled grimly. "Well, the first one is that you keep clamming up and don't tell us what we need to know. You'd like that one, wouldn't you?"

Daniel didn't have anything to say.

"And I'd really love the second one. You already know I care about Miss Gallagher. I understand the Garda found a camera in the Rover with a picture of me with her. That's really sick you know?"

Daniel was really sweating now.

"So, you'll understand how I'll feel if something happens to her. Or if you've already been a part of hurting her."

***

Daemon couldn't stop himself from grabbing the man's arm. "So. If you don't tell us where she is and where you're keeping that colt..."

The man attempted a shaky grin, showing even, white teeth. The beautiful teeth that had helped him in his disguise as a respected member of the community.

"Yeah? What are you going to do?"

Daemon proceeded to give the man a long list of things that could happen to him in prison. A list that started with a trial for kidnapping. The horse would have been bad enough but the gang now was on record as kidnapping a person. The list grew with what he would face if Ashley had been harmed or even, God forbid, killed.

A Garda officer came into the room with a report in his hands. "Fingerprint results, sir."

Daemon took the paper and looked at it, the corners of his mouth lifting into a surprised smile. "Well, well, I think we've got you."

And they had. They could tell by the whitening of Daniel's face, the clenching of his fingers on the wooden table edge.

"So, now we have some other options for you. If you confess and help us to find Miss Gallagher and the colt, we'll go easy on you. We might even agree to help you during the trial for kidnapping. Maybe we can convince the judge to have mercy on you and give you solitary confinement for the rest of your sorry life instead of throwing you in with the other prisoners, who might want to kill you themselves for harming an Irish Grand National hopeful."

Silence. Then a muffled growl. "What promise could you give me that I'd be safe?"

"The only promise I can give you is that if Miss Gallagher has been hurt you won't be safe from me."

Daemon knew then that he'd struck gold. He looked into a face that was frightened. That showed Murphy knew he was hearing the truth. His face fell and the obstinate sneering facade dropped away. "I'll talk."

***

Daemon looked away. He looked at the wall, out the window, at the hand that was clenched on the papers he held. He wanted to hurt this man for what he'd done. But he was a professional. His job made him stay calm. It didn't keep him from wanting to know the most important thing first.

"Is Miss Gallagher still alive?" He held his breath, hoping for miracles, dreading the worst.

"She is that. But not for much longer. My brother and his friends will be eliminating both her and the colt after the race. Or before. They're waiting for a call from the boss. If he says kill them now…"

Daemon didn't need to hear more. He leaned forward and glared in Daniel Murphy's face. "You will tell us where she is and tell us now." It was a quiet request. But Daemon's tone held malice and steel.

***

Sirocco's muscles had tightened on that long ago day and he'd stretched out in an effortless canter as they'd checked out the new grass in the far paddock. It had been planted in the spring and was irrigated to keep it green and lush during the hot summer months. Ashley's long hair had mixed with Sirocco's flying mane as she'd leaned forward in her saddle to aim her gaze between his ears.

She'd loved to talk to him, telling him about her plans and her dreams and those ears had turned and focused on her voice.

Ashley brought her thoughts back to the present, rubbing her knee, massaging it and flexing the muscles around it experimentally. The physiotherapist had told her the knee might be permanently weak because of the tendon and ligament damage. Riding would be hard, but not impossible. Ashley just hadn't wanted to ride again. Hadn't wanted to ride another horse that wasn't Sirocco. The memory of that last ride was too painful.

But this was different.

She stood up and scanned the barn. Black Cloud was tall. Ashley could, once, have been able to swing her foot up into the stirrups and then into the saddle. But Black Cloud didn't have a saddle and there wasn't one in the barn. There wasn't anything but hay bales and broken tools. There wasn't going to be a stirrup to help her get up on his back.

"That's okay. I'll just have to improvise. And I've ridden bareback before so we'll have to make do." She looked at her watch. It was crowding five already and even though it was April, the misty gloom was chasing the end of the day to see which could make the sky the darkest.

Daemon would already be in Ireland. It helped to know he'd have heard she was gone. If only the Garda had given him her note. It was too late to keep the horse from being taken but he'd know what was up at least.

She looked for the nearest bale of hay and dragged it over to another one farther away. She panted, trying to figure out how to pull it up high enough to get one on top of the other. She jumped when a mouse skittered out from under the pile of loose hay she'd just dislodged.

She caught herself before she yelled. She couldn't afford to call attention to herself now.

"All right. Let's see if this would work. You're going to have to help me."

She led the colt over to the two bales and held the halter rope in one hand, taking a deep breath and willing her knee to behave. It felt rusty and complained but held steady under her as she climbed up her improvised ladder. She took a rest, leaning against the warm body so close to her and waited a moment, running her hand along his back, remembering how it had felt to make this next move. Once it had been so effortless.

Her heart banged in her chest and she started to hyperventilate so she concentrated on just breathing. Finally, she felt calm enough to give it a try.

"Here goes. You'll have to stand still for me." She took a handful of his dark mane in her fingers and rested her other hand on the colt's neck. When she swung her leg over Black Cloud's back and stepped off the bale of hay, she felt like she was flying. The exhilaration took everything else away.

She was hopeful for the first time that she could somehow pull off that miracle and get away. She hadn't expected this crowding of sensations, this return of everything she'd thought she'd lost. The ballet…yes. It was gone forever. But if her knee held, maybe she could work on it and do gentle rides.

If she lived that is.

Her heart squeezed and she leaned forward to rest her cheek on Black Cloud's mane. The feel of his steady, sturdy back gave her a confidence she hadn't felt for years. The horse hadn't moved, just occasionally flicking his ears and turning his head to look at her.

"You are a wonderful boy. I think I love you. I really do."

"I love Daemon too. I have to talk to him. I have to see him again." She put her head down on Black Cloud's neck and her sudden tears mixed in with the coarse hairs of his mane. They stayed that way together for long moments, dark hair blending in with dark as the tears flowed and then ebbed.

"Enough." She sat up and wiped away the salty wetness with the back of her hand and slid down onto the hay bale. "Now I just need to figure out how to open the barn door."

***

They had to wait until it was dark.

They knew now which lake. It was about half an hour away and surrounded by open meadows and dense woods. They could use the woods as shelter and do a commando raid but darkness was better. If they spooked the kidnappers, they'd kill Ashley. They'd already be nervous because Daniel hadn't come back with their supplies. They'd have to figure he'd been caught.

Daemon and his Garda team had dressed in black, their hair covered by dark military watch caps. They were armed and wore bulletproof vests because this was a hostage situation.

They'd start off now in the direction of the lake and wait by the road that led into the cabin. The last helicopter sweep had reported a faint spiral of smoke coming up through the trees about a mile away. They hadn't been able to see the cabin but they knew it was there.

They'd start walking in as soon as it was completely dark.

***

Ashley started to gather tools. The latch at the front door wouldn't budge, but the door at the back would let a horse through. The hinges could be pried off with something sharp.

She had found a broken screwdriver and was prying bits of wood from around the edges of the hinges. It was tricky and she was frustrated but making progress. She had to keep stopping though, every time Murphy or one of the others crunched up the path to check on her.

She managed to look suitably distressed and downcast when they'd come in to find her sitting on the single bale of hay she'd pulled over into the middle of the barn.

"Have you heard from your big boss yet?"

"Wouldn't you just love to know?" It was Malloy this time. He laughed at her, lounging by the door, looking her up and down. He was the creepiest of the four and Ashley's skin crawled.

"Yes, actually, I would like to know what it is you're going to do to me and this poor colt."

Ashley looked over at Black Cloud and watched as the reflection from the kerosene lantern shone on his glossy coat. His calm spread out in waves and enveloped her.

She waited until the crunching of steps on the path died away and then she went back to work.

Chapter Twelve

"The Trophy Is Freedom"

Ashley's fingers were raw. The screwdriver slipped repeatedly, taking bits out of her skin, leaving red welts down her fingers and on the heel of her hand. She'd stopped even bothering to say 'ouch'.

Black Cloud had wandered over to check out what she was doing and she chatted away with him, both to still her increasing nerves and to distract him. She hadn't been enclosed in a small space with a horse for this long since the accident.

"I remember I used to take my homework into the barn. Especially the English literature we had to study. I'd memorize lines of Shakespeare and read it to Sirocco. He was probably the most well-educated horse in Southern California."

Her laughter was subdued and a bit nervous because of her task and the fact that she had to somehow hide the damage to her hands the next time the goons came in to check on her.

"To be or not to be," she chanted to the walls and the cobwebs. "Achoo!" The dust was becoming annoying. Every time Black Cloud danced, he would kick up dust bunnies and stray bits of straw. Not good for the itchy lungs.

"How about…'to be free or not to be free?'" "Does that have a good sound to it?"

"Ouch!" She dropped the screwdriver and sucked her finger, licking at the oozing blood. "It would be ridiculous if I got us out of here and I couldn't paint anymore because I've chopped off my fingers!"

She had all but one hinge free and the door was propped closed by gravity. She wanted it to look closed for the next security round and she'd just have to hide her hands.

The check came, as feared and this time it was Murphy. Ashley scrambled to sit on the bale of hay.

"Here's the thing. Too bad you didn't eat your beans, because my brother isn't back yet from the village with our supper. He's turned off his cellphone and I'm worried that he's done a foolish thing and gone and been arrested."

Murphy paced back and forth in front of the door. "This we can't blame on you but we'd have been done and almost finished and not suspected if it hadn't been for Shaughnessy giving you the book. Without your interference we'd be rich by now and away from this cold and bleak little island to somewhere else and we'd be rich and famous and warm. A place where we wouldn't have to smell sheep and see green fields ever again."

He punched the front door of the barn, loudly enough to startle the horse and make Ashley jump. "So, my impulsive colleen. It's a grand thing that you've calmed down the horse here. If you manage to keep him quiet tonight, we'll make your deaths all the more painless tomorrow."

Ashley's heart dropped. "Tomorrow? I thought you said the race was two days away?"

"Well, you see it's this way. We just spoke to the boss. He's a bit angry, he is. In fact, he's a lot angry. There've been too many delays; too many times the coppers have almost got us. And he's dodging Scotland Yard now as we speak."

Ashley looked at him, her heart in her mouth. "What do you mean?"

"Apparently, they've got our man Shaughnessy eating out of their hands. He's spilled the names of all the couriers he knows. Not us but the ones they used before him in England. Blessed be, he doesn't know the name of the boss."

Murphy kicked the wall, sending splinters flying. "And you see, they've also taken the English colt. They won't let him run at all, at all. They know the jig's up."

Ashley couldn't help but smile. She looked at Black Cloud and patted his flank. "At least the wrong horse is out of the running now."

Murphy grew quiet and grim. "That may be, but the boss is angry and he's ordered us to get rid of you both and sooner than we were planning."

"Why?"

"It's simple. You're evidence. If we have you when and if the coppers catch up with us, we're dead men. There's no death penalty in Ireland any more but the boss will have us killed. He's on a rampage and can't show his own head. But he has a grand large organization and others to do his dirty deeds for him."

Ashley looked straight at him and sat as quietly as she could on the edge of the hay bale. It was hard to see him from this distance and in just the lantern light.

"So, if tonight is my last night, I guess you won't let me call my parents and my brothers to say good-bye?"

"Sorry, that's not going to happen."

Ashley knew that before she even asked. And she wouldn't have wanted to upset her parents anyway. Not when she was still planning her escape. "How about no one comes in to check me tonight then. Just a peaceful night's sleep so I can forget about what's going to happen tomorrow. The horse and I can sit here and hold hooves together."

"We'll see. Can't even give you a blessed plate of beans until my brother gets back, more's the pity. Condemned always get that last meal." This time a smile with almost human good humor in it. But the smile disappeared in an ugly line.

"If our boss is as angry as we think he is, tomorrow will not be a pleasant one at all." He left his words behind him to echo among the flickering firelight and the dust motes dancing around the lantern.

Ashley dragged her aching knee back off the hay bale and got to work on the hinge. It was almost ready to take off. If they got out of this place, she'd have a whole new list of skills to show her brothers.

Carpentry, massage, code-breaking. It went on and on.

She thought about the Dunveys and how sad they would be not to get their finished painting. Maybe they'd hang the watercolor instead. She'd finished it last night. Record time. Maybe she'd known she wouldn't get a chance after all to get it done.

She worked and worked, chipping and grooving and slicing her fingers. A pile of wood shavings and blood grew at her feet and she stopped several times to pick them up and hide them.

Her stomach growled and she placed a hand on her flat abdomen to hush it. "Stop that! We don't get fed tonight. I'm too busy and those guys don't have beans tonight anyway. To tell you the truth I hope they starve."

Maybe the reason the fake priest hadn't come back was that Daemon had caught him?

But she wasn't counting on miracles tonight.

All she could count on was herself.

The first miracle was the final hinge was free and the doors were not heavy. They were easy enough to prop up to look like they were still solidly closed.

Ashley looked around the barn again, searching for anything out of place, suspicious.

Nothing.

"Okay my boy. I'm all packed and you're all packed and I think we might just be ready to go." She looked at her watch again. It was now almost 6 o'clock. Daemon wouldn't be able to see in the dark unless he was coming with a lot of helicopters and big trucks with heavy headlight action. This was a dark little lake and there were only dim lamps inside the cabin too.

"You know, I heard helicopters come over here earlier today. I wonder what they were doing? I think they'd need lots of light at night to see, wouldn't they?'

A frightening thought had just entered Ashley's head.

Fire.

"I think a barn on fire would attract attention, wouldn't it? But I don't know if I can do that. I don't know if I have the courage to do that." Her heart was sinking fast and she needed it to wake up and be strong. Her brain was being strong for her and flying with ideas now.

"Okay, first we have to limber up here. You've been standing too long my boyo. Let's walk." She grabbed his halter and rope and began to lead the colt around in loose-limbed strides, one step at a time clockwise and then back around the other direction. There wasn't enough room to put him at a lunge pace but a quick walk would have to do.

She wished she'd had some ice to freeze her knee before she did this. But a quick massage and set of exercises would have to do.

She was interrupted by the crunching on the gravel of someone coming close. Oh, God! Murphy said he'd think about leaving her alone tonight. What was this? Had they heard from their boss again that they needed to kill her now?

She looked at Black Cloud and watched as he followed her every movement. How could anyone hurt such a beautiful horse? The only reason they hated him is that he was so fast.

The barn door opened and just in time Ashley reached her perch on the hay bale.

Opened to admit someone she didn't want to see.

It was the third man. The one with no name. He hadn't said much of anything to her and he didn't seem as rough or crude or mean as the others. He wasn't carrying anything. At least she didn't see any bulges that might be a gun.

"What do you want?" she asked.

"Nothing miss…just checking to make sure you don't need the bathroom or something? And that you're not planning anything. Doesn't look like it. It's pretty peaceful in here."

"Thanks. But no thanks. I don't want to go back into that house. Sorry."

"Fine. Be back later. Just shout if you need anything."

Ashley put her head down on her knees for one brief, 'sorry for herself' moment. Just brief. She needed fewer and fewer of those now. She let the tears roll down her cheeks and then she leaped up look at her watch.

"Okay, I'm ready." This time Ashley whispered.

***

They were almost in position.

Daemon was in a Garda patrol car, flanked by two other vehicles full of Garda officers. They'd pulled up on the verge of the main road. Daniel Murphy was in the back, his hands tied, his feet manacled. An officer sat beside him and one of the detectives sat in the front with Daemon. Backup from the nearest Garda police helicopter base had been set up and dispatched to fly a circle grid around the area when they gave the signal.

A squad member had gone to bring the owner of the Irish horse. If they were able to get the horse out of this alive there would need to be a vet and transport ready.

And there was another, very welcome, very unexpected bit of backup in place.

Sam Matthews had just arrived from London.

He hadn't told Daemon he was coming. Hadn't told him he had been on the way since just after Daemon had talked to McBride. Hadn't told him a partner is always there in a crunch.

So, Daemon got out of the car and checked his Glock and his ammunition and stretched out his exhausted body to get ready for whatever was going to happen. He was relieved for the millionth time that they were authorized and trained to carry. He hadn't realized all those years ago that he'd need a gun tonight to rescue someone he….

Loved?

He breathed the word to himself, full of wonder. I love her. I love Ashley.

He looked up at the sky. The light was finally gone and his men were putting on night vision glasses and one team was starting up the lane aiming for the cover of the trees.

They were going to flank the cabin and barn and come in quietly and fast once they cleared this open meadow.

***

Ashley stood beside Black Cloud with her ears trained on the path by the front door of the barn. There were no sounds. She walked right up to it and put her ear to the door. Nothing.

She could hear the far-off sound of bottles clinking and men laughing. Maybe they were playing cards and drinking themselves into a coma.

Her brain was seriously hurting with all the things that could go wrong.

"I could open the back door and just tip-toe us out and we could creep away into the woods and get away that way," she whispered into the guttering light of the lantern.

She shook her head. "No. Someone will be coming in another hour and I don't know where I'm going. I could get lost in that forest and they'd just follow me and find me. They probably have flashlights." She'd looked for one in here but there was no sign of anything even remotely helpful.

If Daemon got her message and somehow figured out where she was, he'd be almost here by now. And with lots of company to protect him.

She could make a break for it and they couldn't hurt him now.

So, the only other thing was that if Daemon was looking for her, he wouldn't be able to see. He wouldn't know which cabin unless he saw the sign with the 950 on it.

She stared at the lantern. "I need to start a fire."

She looked at Black Cloud. "I know. I know. I'm the one who's so afraid of birthday candles or gas fireplaces. But Daemon needs this."

She paced, limping. "If I start it too big it might flare and cut us off. Fire is tricky that way. And the guys will come rushing over and burst in or find the back way I've dismantled and they'll still just catch us." She paced some more.

"A little fire. That's what I need. I'll start it small and then we can still tiptoe out of here…." She looked over at Black Cloud. "Do horses tiptoe?"

She stopped pacing and considered. "They won't know until the fire really takes off and they can see it from the cottage. By that time, it will be big enough for the helicopters to see or people on the rest of the lake. Someone will come and Murphy won't be able to bring us back here. They'll be too busy running away."

Ashley's lips tilted up into a grim ghost of a smile as she remembered all those years ago in the counsellor's office talking about her fear of fire.

"It's not the fire itself that you're afraid of Ashley," the lady had said. "I know you think it is. It's just that the fire hurt you and killed your horse. It's what that particular fire did. Fire can be a beautiful thing. It can warm you when you're cold. It can cook your food. It can be a beautiful decorating tool in a huge fireplace in a mansion. Think about that."

Ashley WAS thinking.

Fire, in this case, tonight, was going to be a beautiful thing. It was going to help her get out of here.

She gave Black Cloud another huge hug and then led him over to the hay bales where her makeshift steps were.

She found some old rags and ripped them up into strips to fashion a rough blindfold for the colt.

That way he wouldn't see the fire. She couldn't afford to have him scream.

Some of the other rags she tore extra thin. She poured a tiny bit of kerosene lamp fuel onto the cloth, put the lantern in front of the main door of the barn and spread straw all around it in small piles, listening all the while for anyone who might be coming.

Once she had her tinder ready, she ran over to the back where the doors were propped up to look sturdy. She lifted first one and then the other away and leaned them against the wall of the barn. The fresh air blew in, ruffling her hair and smelling of peat smoke.

She ran back to the lantern and checked to see if there was a way of lighting the cloth without burning her hands. She took the glass chimney off the lantern and dipped one end of the cloth into the flame, holding her breath until it caught.

"I can't believe I'm doing this," she thought, cringing at the sight of the ugly little flames inching their way up the rag.

Once the starter cloths started creeping towards the bigger hay piles and then the bales themselves, she looked at Black Cloud. He was watching her, watching the fire, shuffling nervously.

"It's okay. I have something for you here." She walked quickly over to her makeshift ladder and climbed up, leaning forward to put the blindfold in place. He tossed his head, almost pushing her off her perch, but her soft voice calmed him.

"The fire over there is to help us. It has to help us. I want to get away before they know we're gone." She slid onto the horse's back and tried to calm her frantic breaths.

She was desperate to get out the door and away before the sight of the flames reached the cabin and alerted the men. Maybe they'd been drinking too much and wouldn't know the barn was on fire before it was too late and she was already deep in the woods.

The flames were rising and her heart trip-hammered at the sight. She had to pull her head away and not look. There wasn't a lot of smoke yet so that was a good thing.

Black Cloud moved forward at the slight nudge of her good knee and headed eagerly for the open door. Ashley wasn't able to close the door after her because she wouldn't be able to get back on the horse if she slid down. She reached down to remove the blindfold.

There were trees close to the barn and Ashley turned Black Cloud into them first. "You're doing just fine, my big boyo. Just keep walking on."

The Robert Frost poem she'd had to memorize in high school ran through her head as a mantra as she rode.

'The woods are lovely, dark and deep…
But I have things to do before I sleep.'

***

In the cabin the three men were deep in a game of cards and one too many bottles of Guinness. They were in the kitchen and didn't have a good view of the barn from there. And it wasn't time for them to go and check the woman anyway.

"Besides," grumbled Malloy, whose turn it was to check her again in an hour, "She's probably in there, crying and wailing her heart out. Doesn't need checking."

It was only when they stopped laughing and turned down the Gaelic radio station that they heard a loud roar. Curious, Murphy got up to look outside.

"God! It's the barn! It's on fire!" Drunk, stumbling, they fell over themselves grabbing their guns and chasing off to the barn. They stopped at the front door in shock, their mouths open, to see how involved the fire was already. Huge plumes of smoke lifted into the night sky.

They didn't know how long it had been burning, just that they couldn't get near it.

"I don't hear any screaming. Women always scream when they're scared. And horses do too. No screaming. Did they get out? Check the whole barn! See if there's another way out."

Malloy and Murphy had murder on their minds as they raced with the third man around the back of the barn and found the missing door and loosened hinges.

"Damn, the bloody woman got away and she's taken the horse with her. We have to find her."

***

The squad on the ground and the helicopter in the air had both spotted the flames. The team with Daemon picked up their pace and ran, crouched low to the ground and using a zigzag pattern.

The helicopter pilot, fitted with night vision goggles, flew over the cabin. As he circled, he spotted the red van with the horse trailer, half-hidden in the trees by the flaming building. He had his co-pilot radio Daemon.

"It's on the other side of the meadow. Just follow the smoke and the flames. It's a huge fire!"

The helicopter hovered, shining strobe lights down on the scene as the co-pilot took night-vision photos for the crime squad. A few minutes later there was an enormous explosion and the van beside the barn blew up and added to the heat and fury of the fire.

Daemon couldn't breathe. How could he run if he couldn't breathe? If he was already dead?

He'd heard the noise. If Ashley had been in that barn, or the van, maybe that's how they had just killed her.

To get rid of evidence.

They must know, with the helicopter overhead, that they'd been made. The fire had just taken away any chance of surprise.

He shook his head and forced away the images of how Ashley might just have died. He couldn't think that way.

They turned onto a diversionary road that linked the two closest lakes. When they reached the turnoff into the second lake, Daemon reached out his hand and pointed, "The address! It's 950 Coole Drive. Nine and fifty…like the poem!"

When they reached the end of the road and saw the cabin the barn was so engulfed, they couldn't get anywhere near it. Daemon's heart was sick.

And that's when a bullet broke the branch over their heads and another one hit Sam in the shoulder. His vest helped to deflect the bullet but he'd be checked by emergency services later for bruising to his shoulder bone.

Daemon and Sam both managed to get off shots and heard a shout of pain but the bullets kept coming. Daemon motioned to crawl around a nearby tree and come at the man from behind. Distracted by frontal fire from Daemon, Sam was able to tackle him and finally brought him to the ground.

Daemon slid to his knees beside the struggling man and shook him until he could focus enough to get his rage under control.

"Where is she? Is she alive? Where are your other men?"

Daemon knew he was going to have to answer charges at Scotland Yard for this but he hit the man and broke his nose.

All the man told him was that the others had taken off after Ashley. That she'd gotten away with the horse and was somewhere in the forest.

"They have their guns loaded and they're going to kill her. Damned woman. She's wrecked everything!"

And Daemon hit him again.

***

She'd gotten away with the horse.

Daemon felt hope leap up from the dark place it had been hidden in ever since he'd heard Ashley had been taken.

He could hear gunshots from another part of the woods.

They had their guns loaded and they were going to kill her.

Another Garda took over shackling the kidnapper and then he and Sam were running again. The bullet had just creased Sam's shoulder and his vest had taken the worst of it.

They followed the sound of the shots and shouts from the other Garda team. Huge flames were shooting up into the sky through the collapsing roof of the barn and images of Ashley's nightmares haunted him. One barn fire and collapse and dead horse was enough in her lifetime. How could she have just survived another one and stayed sane? And now she was running blind through the forest with two killers in pursuit, death on their minds.

And then they got a break.

Daemon grabbed his communicator when it beeped and crackled and gave a signal to his team to follow the lights from the copter. The pilot had spotted two men on foot coming out of the trees ahead of them and was training his lights on them.

When they broke out into the open Daemon and his team were waiting for them. Mulloy and Murphy stopped dead and raised their guns, firing off a volley of shots. Sam dove out of a crouch and tackled Mulloy before he could reload and was on top of him, wrestling the gun out of his hands.

And Murphy was Daemon's.

When Daemon rushed him there was a dangerous moment when both of them had a good shot. But Murphy's went wild.

And Daemon's didn't.

His bullet had hit Murphy in the shoulder and the next hit him in the knee. When Daemon reached him, Murphy was already on the ground, bleeding and cursing.

When Daemon knelt at his side and grabbed his wrists to put on restraints, he looked at the man who'd hurt Ashley.

Who'd had his arm around her neck. Who'd put bruises on her.

Who'd terrorized her for days.

And she was out there somewhere, still afraid. Still on the run.

They stopped to reload their guns and breathe, watching their backs and every movement from the trees in case there'd been a fourth man they hadn't known about.

Ashley had gone out the back of the barn and would have only gone one way. She'd have ridden into the meadow and out towards the main road. But there were big ditches and high fences that way. And she'd still be running. She'd have heard the gunshots and think they were still coming after her.

Sam put his hand on Daemon's shoulder and gripped it tightly. "Black Cloud is a steeplechaser and you've said Ashley knows horses. They'll make it. And don't forget the lights from the copter."

Daemon sent some of the team back to the cars, to wait in case they needed to cut off anyone who got that far. To aim to wound. They needed everyone alive to give up their boss.

***

As soon as Ashley had been safely away from the burning barn, she'd urged Black Cloud into a steady pace. His gait was so even she'd only needed her knees for holding on.

She'd leaned forward and whispered into his ear.

"My knee hurts, boyo. Not as much as I thought, but it does. I hope I can stay on until we get to the road."

Behind her she'd heard crashing footsteps, shouted curses, gunshots and a huge explosion from the barn. Towering plumes of flame and acrid smoke had towered above the trees. Black Cloud had danced nervously from side to side, almost unseating her. Tears of pain had cascaded down her cheeks from the jolt to her knee and she'd fought the urge to just fall off and crawl somewhere to hide, her arms over her head to shut it all out.

***

Now she was almost out of the trees. Out into the open and the unknown. She'd shut out the memories of Sirocco's scream and the flames that had ended his life and now she was going to make sure this horse didn't die too. It was up to her.

"It's all right. I promise. Do you see that space in the trees? It leads to the main road and help might be there." Then she looked up as she heard the unmistakable whop, whop of copter rotors. It must be the Garda…it had to be them.

Exhilarated, she felt a rush of sheer joy, but she'd heard crashing behind her and shots. If she was caught, she was dead, so she urged Black Cloud on. But when they reached the opening her heart sank when she saw what was next.

Hedges. Ditches. Darkness. Black Cloud would break a leg in this.

Then the helicopter came back and shone huge spotlights over the field. It was like an indoor arena and she could see safety ahead but no way around the obstacles.

They had to go over them. And try to outrun the bullets she knew would come next.

She hadn't jumped a horse for years. She just had to hang on and let Black Cloud do the work. She took a huge breath and rode out into the field, sure there would be a bullet in her back any second.

The horse took over. He gathered himself and cleared a low hedge.

The next one was a water jump with hedges all around and he hesitated at the shadows, whickering nervously, shudders rolling through his body.

She bent forward, as close to his ears as she could get, cajoling and praising. "You can do this." Throwing her arms around his neck, tears running down her cheeks, she shouted, "I love you Black Cloud. I love you. Sirocco is watching over us. And Daemon is waiting… I know he is."

They flew over the water jump and raced on to the next one, a double hedge with loose leaves flickering in the downdraft of the helicopter. Not a problem. Aced it.

Another hedge…another water jump…another massive ditch…

She had the easiest job of all. She wrapped her fingers in his mane and breathed in the scent of horses and memories. She gave him her own courage as they thundered toward freedom and towards a man that she loved with all her heart.

***

Daemon stood at the edge of the field and watched an apparition come out of the forest. At first it was just a huge, dark shape and he was reminded of the legendary Irish banshees. They were gnarled old women who would fill the sky with wailing if someone was about to die.

There were no wails, even if this figure did fly. As the apparition got closer, Daemon's heart and breath caught and he didn't try to stop the tears.

Ashley's long hair tangled with the streaming black mane of the colt. She was glued to his bare back and floating over the hedges and ditches as if she'd been born to do this. She'd been able to get away all by herself. She was coming straight to him and bringing the colt with her. She'd saved them both.

***

Ashley couldn't see now. The colt's mane was flying into her face and she was riding blind.

Black Cloud was magnificent. This was the ride of a lifetime and the trophy was freedom. He soared, bunching up his forelegs and stretching out his back legs and he wasn't afraid. He took every jump on the field, taking them both out of danger and home to Daemon.

There were no bullets whining past their ears. Ashley could only hear the colt's heavy breathing and the hoof beats that matched her pounding heart. The road was just ahead. She lifted her head slightly to see if they were clear or if Murphy and his gang had gone around on the road and were waiting for her with guns.

That would be too cruel.

But there were police cars. Lots of them! They had whirling lights on top and looked like the best ice cream sundaes with cherries on top she'd ever seen. She let out a joyous whoop and pulled back on Black Cloud's mane, using her heels to signal him to slow. His excitement was high and he didn't want to stop, but the road was full of strange shapes and he gradually pulled up.

Ashley just sagged against him, not able to think. Not able to feel, not able to hear. She just wanted to empty her mind of all the fear and worry and tension and mystery. And that horrible poetry book.

No tears. Not now.

Her head lifted at a shout from beside her, off to the edge of the field. It sounded familiar. She raised her head and searched in the glare of the helicopter light.

Daemon!

But he shouldn't be here! Murphy was out there and he had a gun and she needed Daemon to hide. She didn't want to be responsible for yet another ugly bullet mark on his beautiful body.

But no…she looked behind her when she heard shouting. Murphy and Mulloy were being dragged out of the trees, struggling with the Garda. They were handcuffed and swearing.

And Daemon was suddenly standing right beside her, his arms lifted up for her and his heart there for her to see.

It was over.

Chapter Thirteen

"Daemon in The Mist"

Daemon stood beside Ashley's horse and just looked up at her, memorizing all the familiar angles of her body and noting all the changes since he'd seen her last. He had no words right now. His heart was too full.

She was bruised and bloody and dirty everywhere. She had hay in her wild, riotous hair and something that looked like soot on her nose. Her jeans were torn and the grey turtleneck sweater had seen better days. She had a split lip and blood on her cheek and her eye was swollen.

She was beautiful. And she was alive.

She was speaking to him but he could barely hear her because of the helicopter rotors. She leaned down and he reached up and took her hand.

Her voice was soft, full of something different. It sounded a little like wholeness. Complete faith and serenity. She was a bit like a superhero up there on that incredible horse.

"Daemon?"

"Ashley?"

His voice was strained and hoarse and tense with remembered terror for her.

"Daemon, would you catch me if I fall?"

A Garda took the reins and Daemon held out his arms. Ashley pressed her cheek against Black Cloud's neck. She kissed him and thanked him for his courage and steady ride.

Then she took her hands off his mane, swung her leg over his back and slid off into Daemon's arms, with trust that he would catch her and keep her safe all the way to the ground.

But he didn't let her put her feet down. He kept her in his arms and just held on.

***

Daemon put his head against her head and breathed in the peaches and the peat smoke and the kerosene and the acrid smell of burning wood.

When he was done with his hugging and holding, he pressed his lips to hers and kissed her. Then he lifted his head away to search her face and he kissed her forehead and her nose and her chin and both ears. Then he kissed her lips again. And Ashley met every single kiss and kissed him back. If she stayed like this forever it was fine with her.

Only the noise of the helicopter lifting up from the field and startling Black Cloud brought them back to their senses.

"Daemon, we have to stop for a minute and see if Black Cloud is all right. He went over every jump but I don't know if he's hurt himself. Can we check?"

"This colt helped you get away. He can have anything he likes."

Daemon let Ashley down with the utmost of care, steadying her with his arm while she made sure her knee would hold.

"It's sore but, oh Daemon." She leaned against him for just a second and murmured against his shoulder.

"It was terrifying and I was so scared but it was wonderful! I haven't been on a horse since the accident and it was like flying!"

"You were flying all right. You melted together and cleared every ditch and hedge. I don't think I took a single breath the whole time. Where did you learn to ride like that?"

Ashley grin was a little watery now. "I started riding Sirocco when I was eight. An eight-year-old riding a stallion has to learn to hang on."

The three of them carefully walked out to the road, Daemon's arm around her, Black Cloud resting his head against Ashley.

A man who looked a bit like the friend Daemon had spoken of with such affection, was waiting at the cars and

Daemon waved him over as he whispered in Ashley's ear…Look who came to help. This is Sam."

***

So, this was Sam.

Ashley watched a huge smile light up the face of the man walking toward them. Sam was tall and lean with dark brown hair that curled over the collar of his police vest. When he got closer, she could see that
his smile held real tenderness and care.

She smiled back, a flood of gratitude rushing through her that Daemon hadn't been alone during this horrible night. That Sam was not just a partner but his life-long friend. A friend who'd flown all this way to be with him.

She held out her hand but Sam kissed her on the cheek and when Daemon took the horse's reins, Sam put his arms around Ashley and pulled her into a gentle hug.

"You took the breath away from all of us, Ashley. I don't think any of us will ever forget what you just did."

***

There was a police medical team standing by and a horse trailer and local vet. Ashley was put on a gurney inside the ambulance and her cuts and scrapes treated. She was bruised, hurting and shaken but not badly injured. Black Cloud was pretty much unscathed but still twitching after his experience. Being able to run in the Grand National would be up to his owner, who had hired his own helicopter and was on his way. Ashley and Daemon sat in the back of one of the patrol cars drinking coffee out of a thermos while they waited for him.

Wrapped in a thick blanket and with Daemon's arms around her, Ashley was warm for the first time since she'd been taken.

They got out of the car when a man who could have been the twin of Lord Dunvey stood in front of her and held out both arms. Ashley walked straight into them and hugged him. She could feel the old man's heart beating fast and could understand what he'd been through. Maybe better than anyone here could. She had lost a horse. She knew what that was like.

She rubbed the man's back until he finally let go.

When she stepped away, she could see his tears and she led him over to his colt. He ran his arms over Black Cloud's shiny hide and patted his nose and head and then put his arms around his neck and held on and cried.

Ashley walked back to Daemon and leaned against his side.

"Daemon, this has been awful. Just awful. But it's been the best night I've had in years."

Daemon looked at her, his eyebrows lifted in surprise. Here she was, a hair away from being murdered, caught in a burning barn by killers and she was saying she'd had a great time.

He put a hand on her forehead.

She grinned at him. "I know you think I'm crazy. But I got both of us out alone. I didn't want this horse to die too. I set the fire and burned the barn down."

"You set the fire?"

"I was told that they were going to kill me tomorrow. I didn't have time to wait for the police. I knew you were coming but I didn't want you to get here and just find my body."

***

Daemon put his arms around her again, shaking with reaction and so proud of her he was without words. It was going to take a long time for the image of her being dead to fade.

"Do you have any idea how scared I was today, Miss Gallagher?" he whispered into her hair. "Do you know how helpless I felt when they said you were gone and I didn't know how to find you?"

"But, Daemon, you did find me! I got away myself but if you hadn't been here with the helicopters and the police,

I think Black Cloud would have fallen in that field. He wouldn't have been able to see. Murphy and Malloy would have caught up to me and they would have killed me right there and rolled my body into one of those ditches."

"Did they hurt you?"

"Not really. They shoved me around and they threatened me. But Daemon. They killed that poor young Garda. I can still see the blood on his face and I'll never forget him."

"I'm sorry too, sweetheart. They'll get a murder charge for that. You were a witness and we can pin several other murders on them, plus the attempted murder of Shaughnessy."

"Was that the man who put the book in my bag? I'd try to kill him too, but I have to thank him. In a skewed, strange way I met you because of him."

Daemon could hear the first crack in Ashley's voice. He needed to get her home.

Home.

He swallowed hard because he didn't know where that was.

"Back to the Stud? The Dunveys are waiting to pamper you royally. Sam just called them and Lady Dunvey couldn't stop crying."

"Daemon, I need to call my parents and my brothers and Beth too. I don't know if this will get into the news. And I do need to talk to the Dunveys. But…"

She went still in his arms, resting her head against his chest. "But not tonight."

"So, where do you want to go?" Daemon's heart was tight with anticipation and he watched as she lifted her head and looked at him.

"I want to go back to the bed and breakfast. Right now."

Right now. Right now.

The urgency in both of them became next to impossible to keep under control and it was only saying goodbye to the colt that pulled them somewhere else.

Ashley walked hand in hand with Daemon over to where Black Cloud was waiting to be loaded into the trailer. Ashley dropped his hand to run her fingers over the spot between the colt's dark eyebrows. She purred to him, whispered in his ears, breathed in his nostrils.

Then reached out her arms and hugged him.

"Thank you, my sweet colt. My Scammall Dhubh. My Black Cloud. Tonight, you saved my life. And I saved yours. We belong to each other now."

And then Daemon heard tears choke in her throat.

"You gave me back Sirocco tonight. You didn't know you were doing it but you brought back my joy in being on a horse. You made me feel like I was flying again."

She kissed the black nose and Black Cloud nudged his head against her chest. She rubbed his forehead once more and whispered 'goodbye'.

She and Daemon both shook the owner's hand, wishing him luck at the race and telling him they'd be there with the Dunveys.

"Young lady, you will be more than just there to watch. I would like you and your young man to be with us in the winner's circle if the colt rides as well as he did tonight. I understand he was like black smoke and fire going over the hedges and ditches in that field."

***

Ashley lasted as far as the patrol car and then sagged against Daemon's side, falling asleep in his arms even before the car started. She woke up briefly at the Garda headquarters, where she filled in a statement and struggled to stay awake.

Her purse had been retrieved and she got it back, collecting her passport and her return ticket to California. She checked that everything was there and wished it had all been stolen so that she wouldn't be able to go anywhere else but with Daemon forever.

She'd think about it later.

Tonight, she needed to sleep. Well, maybe she'd brush her teeth first.

And let Daemon wrap his body around hers and make her feel safe again.

***

The Garda put Murphy and Malloy and the third man into the backs of three patrol cars. Daniel Murphy, still sitting in his own patrol car, would be joining the others on a police plane to Dublin for lockup in the prison there.

They were all talking. Afraid for their own lives. Talking about who was involved and who was guiltier than they were. They were all complicit in multiple murders.

And Owen Murphy finally told them the name of the boss. It was the owner of the English syndicate after all. He and his English colt would be sitting out this Grand National and, with the kidnapping and murder charges, many more after this.

***

Daemon was going to borrow another patrol car and start the long drive back from Kilvarnet. But it had been a long night and Ashley was beyond exhausted. Daemon hadn't realized how tired he was too. So, they booked in at a local hotel and barely made it into the room before both of them collapsed on the bed.

They tore off their shoes and dragged the blankets over themselves.

Ashley was asleep in seconds, sprawled on top of Daemon and he wasn't far behind. His arms were tight around her and he swore just before falling asleep that he would never let her out of his sight again. They slept right through the night and didn't wake up until the birds started singing outside their window.

"Good morning," Ashley murmured against his chest.

And then both of their stomachs growled

Ashley groaned and laughed.

"Daemon, I haven't eaten since night before last at dinner! How about you?"

"Hmmm? I don't know. I can't remember. I was too scared for you to think about food."

"How about we shower and have breakfast and come back and make love for hours?"

Daemon growled his pleasure and started to nibble on her hand. Then he rolled over towards her and pulled her up against him, tucking her head in the hollow beneath his shoulder. He could hear her heart thudding against his ear.

"Daemon, they threatened to kill you if I didn't tell them about the underlining. I had to tell them."

"I'm glad you did, sweetheart. If you hadn't, they might have hurt you even more. But it's nice to know you cared about me."

"I care."

He backed away and met her gaze. "You care?"

"I do."

"How much?"

***

They didn't make it to the shower. Instead, they rolled all over each other kissing every spot they could reach, frantically running their hands over every memorized part they'd been so afraid they would never see again…the stubble on Daemon's jaw, Ashley's feathery dark eyelashes.

This time their lovemaking was urgent instead of passionate. It was the kind of urgent that comes from desperation and fear. Fear that this was the last time. Or could have been. It was frantic and frightened them both. Daemon was still gentle but he was more possessive than before. Ashley was anxious to explore and make sure he was still there, still alive and all right.

They slept again for a while; still exhausted, still hurting from the emotional roller coaster they'd been on. Still afraid they would wake up and find the other person not there.

Maybe that was why Daemon hung on so tightly while they slept, winding his legs with hers and keeping his hand on her shoulder.

Maybe that was why Ashley slept so closely tucked against him that a straw couldn't pass between their bodies and her breath blew with his on the pillow.

When they woke again the birds were still singing and the sky outside the window was sunlit and bright blue. There was no wind and the room felt warm.

"A shower?" Daemon rose up on one elbow and played with Ashley's tangled hair, making a production out of picking up the bits of hay that still stuck in her curls.

Ashley groaned. "I must look terrible. I smell like peat smoke and God knows what else."

"I don't know about that. I still smell peaches."

Daemon playfully sniffed her hair. Then he made a face and agreed about the smoke and kerosene. "You really burned down a barn?"

Ashley's face lit up with pride and she straightened her shoulders. "I did."

"Good girl. Brave girl. Don't ever do that again."

The shower was bliss.

Lots of lather, lots of scrubbing, lots of shampoo and hot water and rinsing off. Lots of kissing and nibbling…and other things.

They shared the hair dryer and comb and then Ashley realized she had nothing to wear back to the Stud. She had to see the Dunveys today and call her parents.

"Daemon, what do I do? I can't go back like this. I don't want to ever see these clothes again." She was standing by the bed dressed in the robe provided by the bed and breakfast and at least it was clean and fresh.

Daemon pulled out his Visa card and smiled at her.

"You stay here for about half an hour and try to get some more sleep. I'll go shopping for you. This village must have at least one clothing shop."

Ashley's face lit up with glee. "Diamonds and furs and a tiara? And food!"

Daemon just grinned and left the room. Then he turned around at the door, his face serious again.

"Lock the door behind me. We don't know if any of this gang is still around. We don't know how many there were. So, no walking around on your own for a day or two. Okay? Promise?"

Ashley stood, a gentle smile on her face, and remembered the last time she'd left, in spite of Daemon's warning. She hadn't even been safe with a Garda beside her.

"Promise."

***

Lying down on the bed was a mistake. Ashley just meant to rest for a minute but she fell soundly asleep again and in a matter of seconds was dreaming. But her dreams had shifted this time. Instead of burning barns and falling beams and screaming horses she saw Daemon. He was surrounded by mist, walking away from her. Daemon in the mist and shifting each time the wind blew at him.

"Daemon!" Ashley called out to him in her dream.

He turned around, stretching his arms in that lazy, leonine stretch of his and then he smiled, his lion's teeth glinting. "You don't want me in your life, Ashley. You want to go home. You'll say goodbye and you won't see me again." The swirling mist blew again and covered up his face. She couldn't see him anymore.

And then he walked away, swallowed up entirely.

"Daemon!" Ashley woke up, sweating and teary and stared at the empty room, her heart pounding. Daemon's jacket was still where he'd left it, thrown over the chair by the television set.

He'd gone shopping. Yes. That was it.

He was coming back.

But the dream had been so real. The only thing that was real was she was going home. She was the one who was leaving. She'd be here for the Grand National and then she needed to climb on her plane and go home.

Ashley fell back onto the pillows and reaction hit. She was sobbing when Daemon came back into the room. He took one look at her and dropped his packages.

"What is it?" He sat by the side of the bed and grabbed one of her hands, pulling it away from her face. Her eyes were puffy and rimmed with red and the blue velvet was a pale, washed-out powder blue.

She sat up and rubbed her face. Then she hiccupped and turned to Daemon, smiling. "Just reaction. I'll be fine."

She refocused with nothing but willpower and pretended to be excited because Daemon had gone out to buy clothes for her.

She sat on the edge of the bed and watched as Daemon handed her a bag. When she pulled out a gorgeous lavender silk blouse and black slacks her jaw dropped.

"How did you know what size? This is perfect!"

"Remember I've packed and unpacked suitcases of your clothes before."

The last bag was a mystery and she took it with a frown.

When she looked inside and saw a small box her heart thudded and she couldn't breathe. It looked like a jewelry box.

She looked up at him, questions on questions ready for answers.

"You asked for a tiara and furs. It's hard to paint in furs and a tiara would look silly when you're riding a horse from now on. But this will be a reminder of the best part of these past few days."

She held the box in her hand for a minute more and then opened it slowly. It was a gold shamrock necklace on a fine gold chain. The shamrock was inlaid with diamonds and sparkled in the morning sunshine. It was the most beautiful thing she had ever seen and her heart welled up and tears spilled again.

"Woman, you cry more than anyone I've ever met. Even my sister doesn't cry as much as you do. I can take it back."

"No. I love it so much my heart is squeezing. I can't breathe and I want you to put it on right now. It is completely, absolutely perfect because it's always going to remind me of you."

"Even when you're in your gallery in Carmel thousands of miles away?"

Thousands of miles away.

Ashley flung her arms around Daemon and kissed the hollow at the base of his neck. She breathed in the fresh scent of his shaving cream and his skin. "Anywhere I am. Forever."

Daemon brushed aside Ashley's hair and put the necklace around her neck, feeling the gold warm to her skin almost as soon as it settled into place.

"All right then," he said. "Let's get dressed and go for breakfast."

The spell was broken.

The tears dried up.

The day began.

***

Bacon and eggs and soda bread and fruit and everything else that could be piled on a plate was piled on a plate and Daemon tucked in with enthusiasm. Ashley sat at her seat in the restaurant and watched in fascination, picking at her own breakfast.

"How can such a lean guy like yourself eat like this and still stay in such good shape?"

Daemon looked at the small pile of fruit and eggs on Ashley's plate. "How can such a tiny person like yourself eat so little and not blow away with the next strong breeze? I love your shape. But I worry."

"When I'm not being kidnapped or on a sinking ferry, I actually have a totally normal appetite. But do you really worry about me?"

"I do." Daemon leaned across the table to take her hand and kiss it.

"Not just when I'm on a sinking ferry or being threatened by killers in the woods?" Ashley curled her fingers around his.

"Especially then. But other times too."

"I worry about you too. You already have a bullet hole in your shoulder. I'll bet your parents worry about you all the time!"

"They do. But I didn't tell them about the ferry sinking and being threatened by poetry-book-carrying killers. They'd just worry."

"Right".

Daemon's cellphone rang then and he had to pick it up because it was McBride.

Ashley looked up, a piece of fruit on her fork.

"She's just fine this morning, sir. A bit peaky, some serious purple bruises. And she still smells a bit like smoke from burning down a barn all by herself…yes, sir, she burned down a barn."

***

Ashley could only listen to one half of the conversation. Daemon seemed to be teasing but there was such affection in his voice that she knew he was proud of her.

When he hung up, he smiled.

"McBride is giving me three days off and thinking about hiring you. Want to stay and be an Inspector with Scotland Yard? Code-breaking department?" He grinned.

Ashley looked up and her heart echoed the rush of happiness she saw in Daemon's face.

Three whole days. More time. He didn't have to go back to London today!

"So. What do we do?"

Her question hung in the air for about a minute. And then Daemon chuckled. "I can think of one thing I'd like to do right now. And then several things I'd like to do later on."

***

The first thing they needed to do was to go back to their hotel room and take advantage of the big bed before they had to check out. The minute they locked the door Daemon's hands were all over her and in seconds her clothes were on the floor.

She quickly pulled off his shirt and her fingers were on his zipper, pulling it down and peeling his jeans down around his ankles, kissing the backs of his knees.

For seconds more they stood, holding each other, and then Daemon picked her up and placed her on the bed, climbing on top of her and tracing the contours of her breasts with his hands.

Ashley had learned so much about his body. The shape of his ribs and shoulders and abdomen were so familiar under her fingertips and lips and she knew where to kiss and where to touch to hear him gasp.

She'd learned that his feet were ticklish and that he hated to be tickled. But the backs of his knees were fair game and he would arch his back when she kissed him there.

He learned that Ashley would shiver with tension and her skin would heat when he kissed her in the hollow of her shoulder or at the bottom of her neck in the little hollow there. He memorized the sound of her breath catching when he slid into her. And her whimper when they both climaxed.

There were no Garda patrols outside today. No thunderstorm and lightning threatening. No alarm clocks or landladies or kidnappers to steal their time. They weren't due back at the Dunvey Stud until late afternoon.

They had all the time they wanted to tangle their legs together and wrap their arms around each other and join sweat-slicked bodies together again and again until their panting breaths matched each thrust and each withdrawal and each new slide in and out.

They didn't share their love in words in that room but they did in actions. They did over and over again.

“Daemon?”

“Hmmm?”

“Daemon, I don’t think I ever want to get out of this bed.”

“Me either.”

“Okay.”

***

The drive back to Kildare was a new experience for Ashley, who had made the trip out to Sligo on the floor of a dirty car. This time she got to see miles of surf and white beaches in Galway. She got to see green fields and flocks of white sheep with spring lambs.

She and Daemon stopped once for scones and clotted cream and chatted amiably with the publican about the price of Guinness.

It was a different world.

When they pulled into the long driveway up to the main house of the Dunvey Stud, Ashley looked for Dark Night.

He stood, almost as if he’d been watching for her.

He leaned, almost nonchalantly, against the white fence rail and swished his tail in greeting, nodding his head up and down.

She opened her door and ran out to meet him, throwing her arms up and hugging his neck. She rubbed his nose and talked to him about his son’s adventure and told him how proud he would be.

Then the Dunveys appeared at the front door and called for her and she had to go. Daemon walked with her and shook Lord Dunvey’s hand, only to be engulfed in a fierce hug himself. Lady Dunvey patted his back in circles and then she cried all over his shoulder.

They both cried when they saw Ashley. Lady Dunvey clucked over the bruises on the sides of her jaw and the purple smudges everywhere.

They would be devastated to hear that she was going back to the bed and breakfast tonight. But she knew they would understand.

"Will you be coming in for tea young Daemon?"

"No, I'm sorry. I have to do a report for my boss. I'll leave Ashley to fill you in. I'll see you later."

He came over to kiss Ashley on the cheek before he left and when he drove away the life was sucked out of her. A preview of what would come.

***

Ashley walked, hand in hand with both Dunveys as they took her inside to have a cup of tea and fill them in on every harrowing detail. She told them about the shooting of the young Garda and her sorrow about his death. And the threats and the old barn and how wonderful the colt had been.

"And," she said. "And I rode him. I jumped him over hedges and ditches when we were trying to get away."

The Dunveys were awestruck; Mrs. Dunvey fighting emotional tears.

"But, colleen, you said you hadn't ridden for years because of your accident. How did you manage?"

"My knee was stiff but it held. The colt was steady and he seemed to know I needed his help. I think if I'm careful now, I might be able to ride once in a while. Dancing is gone, but maybe I can ride again."

***

When Daemon came that evening to pick her up a fine grey curtain hung over the roads and the fields. It was both eerie and strangely romantic at the same time. The mist shut out the world. It made everything intimate and close.

Instead of taking Ashley back to the bed and breakfast loft he pulled the car into a lay-by at the end of a small viewpoint over a rolling valley. There was a large meadow with dots of sheep here and there and around the lay-by there were ghostly trees. Ashley grinned as she thought she saw an equally ghostly Black Cloud trotting along between those trees.

Daemon didn't say a word as he took out an ancient-looking portable disc player and smoothed a large spot on the most level part of the viewpoint.

"What are you doing?" Ashley asked, her face full of puzzlement.

"You said that you have the possibility of riding again if you're careful."

"Yes. I hope so."

"You said you've lost dancing?"

"Ballet, yes. I don't have the flexibility or strength any more. But I love music. I love the feeling of movement. I can slow dance. Do you want to dance with me?"

"I do." He put on a CD of music familiar to her heart...pieces of dance movements from ballets she had once loved.

Daemon, standing in the mist, did a strange thing.

Instead of taking her hand and leading her into a dance, he swung her high up in the air against his chest and tightened his arms around her. Ashley, surprised, pulled back her head and stared at him.

"Daemon?"

"Shh. Don't talk. Just feel." And he danced, his arms around her, her head nestled on his shoulder.

He moved with the music of the ballet, back and forth in the slow steps of the minuet, danced to the flowing strains of "Swan Lake" and the romantic love songs of "Romeo and Juliet".

The mist and the music shut away the world. And he danced with her.

Chapter Fourteen

"The Girl with the Blue Velvet Eyes"

The box seats the Dunveys had booked sat high over the flag start of the Grand National course in Aintree, England.

The owner of the Irish colt had sent his private jet to pick them up and Sam had caught a ride with them.

Walking in through the gates, Ashley didn't know where to look first. All around her were the perfectly dressed…high-fashion women and men straight out of the pages of England's *Tatler* magazine…the *Town and Country* of Britain's upper classes. This wasn't just a horse race but a chance for people to be seen in beautiful hats and dresses and tailored waistcoats.

Her own group didn't look half-bad either. She looked at the Dunveys and smiled. Lady Dunvey's perfectly-cut, short layered hair gleamed silver under her Philip Somerville hat and she and Ashley had both chosen similar grey coat-dresses to wear and high-heeled black boots.

Ashley hooked her arm through Daemon's and they walked over to the rail to check the field. They could see some of the most interesting jumps in front of the stands and would be able to see the horses cross the finish line.

"Daemon, we only had two hours this morning to shop for something to wear. How did you get such a fabulous suit so fast?"

"I have connections," was all Daemon would say.

But he put his arm around her shoulder and pulled her closer. His golden lion hair was tamed today and lay just above the collar of his white shirt. He wore a three-piece navy suit and a burgundy pin-striped tie and looked so unlike the frantic detective in the muddy field three nights days ago that she kept shaking her head to sort out the reality and the fantasy of what had happened to them.

***

He didn't tell her he had racks of clothes like these in his apartment in London and at his parent's estate.

That he'd grown up being part of a world that called for dressing like this and if he left Scotland Yard and went back to school, his future as a lawyer would call for a return to suits and ties and away from jeans and stakeout gear.

But for today he pushed away decisions about the future and looked down on Ashley's silky hair under her burgundy Ascot hat. Her hair was now smooth and there wasn't a curl in sight.

"I can't believe the change three days can make. When you came riding out of that forest into the field and stopped in front of me you looked like a wild banshee, hair all over, dirt on that little nose of yours and fire flashing."

He saw her shudder, knowing she was remembering how she'd looked in the mirror that night. "I'm so embarrassed that anybody saw me like that, especially you."

Daemon stopped to turn her to face him and kissed her. He didn't care what all the people around them thought.

"You were the most beautiful woman I'd ever seen. I'd been terrified for hours that you were dead. And you were so alive up there on that horse."

***

They followed the signs to the stable area and had no trouble getting through the intense security. They had been mentioned in the nightly news. Now, jockeys and other owners shouted out at them as they passed.

Ashley was profoundly grateful she'd had a chance to talk to her family and Beth before all of this broke. Before her photograph and all the grisly details had been published in the papers and on the air.

Black Cloud was in the corridor of the barn area, brushed to gleaming perfection, his mane and tail braided and his tack shiny and clean. His jockey was already dressed in racing silks and talking to some of the other jockeys and he turned and waved at them.

"Chief Inspector, Miss Gallagher! Kerry O'Rourke here. I'm pleased to be meeting you. You did a brave thing you did, saving this colt. We'll do our best for you out there." He shook their hands and left them with the colt.

"He's dressed up today too," Ashley said. "He looks ready to win, doesn't he?"

Daemon put his hand up to stroke Black Cloud's nose. "I have a big thanks to give you today. You saved this young lady the other night and I don't think you realize how much that means to me."

Ashley's heart was filled with sudden emotion as she watched Daemon with the horse.

She rested her head against Black Cloud's neck for a minute before the trumpets sounded the beginning of the advance to the starting line.

"We have to go to our seats my boyo. You flew the other night. You'll fly again today."

The horse nudged her shoulder with his big head and then it was time to go.

***

The screaming over the next few hours had nothing to do with fear and everything to do with mad, crazy excitement. Horses did fly. They flew over hedges and fences and water jumps and brush. They galloped as a huge mass and then separated into obvious frontrunners.

But ahead of all the rest of them was the big black colt with the crimson fire in his mane and tail. He flew like a banshee in a windstorm and he won.

Ashley's voice was completely gone and Daemon had done his own fair share of jumping up and yelling. Faces wreathed with smiles, the Dunveys followed the crowd down to the rail to cheer on the rest of the field.

The owner of the Irish colt was good to his word and they were all invited into the Winner's Circle to celebrate. Then, with glasses of champagne and roses for the ladies and uncounted kisses and hugs, the day was over.

Both the horror and the joy were over. Only cold, bitter reality was left.

***

Daemon watched Ashley as she sat quietly in his car on the way to Heathrow airport in London. She'd had two days with him at a fancy hotel as guests of the colt's owner and Daemon had shown her the sites and they'd had dinner one night with Sam, who was looking distracted.

Later, Daemon said Sam's on-again, off-again relationship with girlfriend Miranda was off again and although it was time to move on, it was hard. It just hadn't progressed beyond friendship though. No spark.

But Ashley had to go back to Ireland to finish boxing up the watercolor and to spend a few days at the Stud and her mind was on the rapidly flipping calendar and just feeling so sad.

"So, my young lady," he said, as they waited for her Aer Lingus flight back to Dublin.

Ashley looked up at him, tears flowing openly.

"I'll be waiting for you when you come back to London next week," he said gruffly. "I'll pick you up and we'll have a weekend together before…"

He didn't need to finish. It was out there in the air between them.

Daemon just pulled her closer and let her rest her head on his shoulder as they sat in the waiting room.

"I guess you do have to go back to California, don't you? You have to convince your parents and those brothers of yours that you're still in one piece. And your friend Beth sounded really shocked when I talked to her last night."

"I'm glad you got to at least talk to her on the phone. We've been friends a long time. I hope you can meet her someday. And I'm so glad I got to meet Sam."

Beth had known Ashley for a long time.

Time Daemon wasn't going to have.

Unless.

Her flight was finally announced and she stood, clutching her new burgundy hat with the plumed feather and the small black bag that had replaced the famous tote bag.

"My stomach has butterflies. I don't think I've ever hated getting on a plane so much."

She couldn't finish and he watched as she just bit her lip and tried to smile. This had to be quick. He wouldn't be able to let her go at all if she kept standing here beside him.

"I'll see you in a week, Daemon…"

He didn't let her finish. He just grabbed her and pressed his mouth against hers and then he turned around and walked out of the boarding area and didn't look back.

***

Daemon got into his car and fought traffic back to his empty flat in Kensington and then got ready for work.

He tossed and turned all night, getting up to look out at the dark streets and wondering what he was going to do with his life.

When he woke up in the morning, he looked at the empty space beside him in the bed and put his hand on the pillow. Then he jumped out of bed and into a shower and went into the office to talk to McBride.

He had a lot he wanted to say.

***

At the end of the week Daemon got into his other car…an MGTC sports car he only got to use on non-work days. He loved this car and it had been part of his life since university.

It cleared his brain and breathed fresh air into his heart and gave him strength as he headed out of London and onto the main highway that crossed the southern part of England on the way to Cornwall.

He didn't stop until he got home. He turned into the long, winding driveway of his parents' estate and thought about the conversation he'd had last night with his mother. She'd been dignified and calm as usual but he'd heard a crack in her voice that had never shown before.

"Mother, I'm so sorry the press got that story about the Irish colt and what happened in Ireland. Getting my picture in the paper was the last thing that works for my job too. This is exactly why I've never shared my cases with you and Dad. I don't want you worrying all the time and I know this must have really upset you."

He'd listened to her tell him about the neighbors who'd called her when they'd turned on the television to watch the Grand National. The neighbors who'd gasped at the news that he'd helped to thwart a huge kidnapping and crime ring.

"There were guns, Daemon! And those people killed an Irish policeman and hurt that young lady, Miss…what is her name?"

"Her name is Ashley, Mother. Listen, I have some things to tell you. Are you home this weekend? I'm going to come home."

Silence.

"Home? Could you really? Oh, Daemon!"

So, here he was, in his cherished little car. He sat outside the stone walls of the place he'd called home his whole life and looked up at the window below the top gable and grinned. It was still his room. It held all his childhood memories.

Now he'd finally tell his parents about the new memories that he'd forged these past few days. He'd tell them about the changes he was about to make in his life.

And he had a feeling they'd be over the moon.

He had a three-day weekend off next week before he started his next case and he hoped to squeeze in that promised day with Ashley before she…

"I'm here!" He shouted into the echoing front hall and up the winding staircase past all the paintings of his relatives going back several centuries. He threw his leather jacket on the brocade chaise in the drawing room and walked out to the garden.

He smiled when he saw his mother in her Wellington boots and her Barbour coat, all decked out for early spring gardening in the muddy beds. She had a shovel in her gloved hands and was working away splitting some plants.

"Mother?"

She looked up at his call and dropped the shovel. She was running up the path towards him and throwing her arms around his neck before he had a chance to catch his breath.

***

Across the Irish Sea, Ashley had only needed two days to completely finish and was spending the last day testing her knee on the back of a small brown mare that belonged to Lady Dunvey. The mare was a sweetheart and seemed to realize that even without the fear of being threatened with impending death and destruction, Ashley was now nervous.

"I don't know if I can do this again little girl. I was scared to death that night. I didn't have a choice. I had to ride. But this is different. Today I'm only thinking about how I can't do this."

She stood, patting the mare's flanks and neck and willing herself to take a chance. It was a leap of faith but it was also something she'd needed to do for Sirocco.

"Okay. This is it."

She led the mare to a small mounting step used by jockeys when they had to mount a tall horse. It was perfect.

Once Ashley settled in the saddle she just sat for a minute, getting used to the feel of the leather beneath her and the curve of the horse's sides. She had on a pair of Lady Dunvey's riding pants with padded knees, which helped. Her riding posture felt natural and in all this time she hadn't forgotten the proper way to sit. Her shoulders straight and held back a little, she held the reins in a gentle grip.

She pressed her knees just a bit into the mare's sides and did figure eights in the indoor arena, then a trot. The Western saddle the Dunveys had found for her was easier on her knee than if she'd had to use an English saddle. The ride ended after just a few minutes but Ashley felt some of the same sense of exhilaration that had flooded through her the night of the escape.

She slid off carefully, putting her weight on her good knee, handed the mare over to a groom and went to her room to shower and pack.

She looked around the beautiful Georgian bedroom with the four-poster that had been her refuge for so many anxious, worried nights. She'd been in here with bits of the poetry book chasing themselves around in her mind, teasing her, taunting her.

Now it was all over.

She walked to the big paddock by the driveway and said her good-byes to Dark Night and pressed her head into his neck, holding him with outstretched arms. One last apple and she had to turn around and leave.

It was hard to say good-bye to the Dunveys. After her kidnapping they had almost adopted her. She poured her heart out to Lady Dunvey about how far away she was going to be from Daemon and how frightened she was to know about the danger he faced all the time in his job. How afraid she'd been when the kidnappers had threatened to kill him.

"I'm going to be a whole continent away. His job is here. My gallery and my parents and my friend Beth are thousands of miles away. Daemon and I can call and we can visit but that will be torture. I don't know what to do."

Lady Dunvey just held her; fingers crossed behind her back, and hoped miracles could happen. That something would happen to make this work somehow.

And then there was a phone call.

"Daemon!"

"Ashley, I have bad news. The worst! McBride is sending me to Scotland. I have another assignment and of course I can't tell you about it. The worst is that I have to go right now. I can't meet your plane. I can't see you before you go home."

Ashley was stunned. "Oh, no! I understand but I'm so sorry. I was hoping…"

"And I was hoping. Damned bad luck. Look…"

"It's okay. Really it is. Just…"

"Just?"

"Just please, be careful. I don't want your bullet hole to have company. I think I hate your job."

"I think I hate my job too. Ashley…?"

A pause.

"I was going to take you to Covent Garden. There's a great ballet season starting soon."

Silence.

"You would do that?"

"I would do a lot of things. Ashley, I will miss you more than I can say. I'll call you in California when I'm finished this case. You gave me your number."

"I'll be waiting. Be safe. I'll miss you too."

***

Daemon was in the estate's cozy family room, surrounded by tapestries and family photos on all the little side tables. He sat by the fireplace now and remembered his talk with McBride. It had been tense, but his boss had understood. Daemon had been tired of his job even before he'd met Ashley but seeing her in constant danger because of a case he was involved in had made it clear he couldn't have a relationship with her if it could get her killed.

He'd wanted to see his parents and tell them what he'd decided before he had to leave for his last case in Scotland.

They finally admitted it had been horrific for them to know he was in a dangerous job. Every time they'd heard on the news about a policeman being hurt or even worse, they'd died a little inside.

"And Miss Gallagher?" his mother asked now. "You haven't talked about her but we know she was involved in this case. We saw photos and interviews with her on the news. She's beautiful and she seems very brave and intelligent. What about her?"

"I'm in love her. Plain and simple. But it's not plain and simple what to do about it."

Daemon put his head in his hands and when he looked up his mother saw his anguish. She'd met his girlfriends through school and then college and had never seen this look before. Her face softened and she suddenly had hopes for grandchildren again.

"I think your father and I would like to meet her some day. Is that possible, son?"

Daemon could see the love she had for him. He'd seen the way she had always looked at his father and knew it was real.

It was time.

"Okay, then," he said. "I have something I need to tell you about."

***

Ashley was able to change her flight and go home to California earlier. She didn't want to be in London without Daemon.

When she sat at her window seat in the plane from Dublin to New York she looked down on the grey waters of the Atlantic and thought about the harrowing night in the lifeboat. The cold, the salt spray, the wet clothes and the warm shoulder she'd slept on.

She finally fell asleep and dreamed about tawny hair and the sound of Daemon's husky growl when he'd woken her up after a night of making love. He had been tender. Loving. Funny.

She thought, with a sinking heart, that he would be somewhere in Scotland by now, on a new case that would put him in harm's way again.

Some new stakeout.

Some new group of criminals who could hurt him.

She flipped through the onboard book on England and found a page on the cliffs and beaches of Cornwall and thought about the book Daemon had said he wanted to write some day. She thought about him growing up there and was surprised to find out how much it reminded her of the Big Sur with its huge waves and rugged shoreline.

There would be a lot to paint there. And she'd heard about the tiny, wiry ponies of the Moors in Cornwall and Devon. There were Andalusian stallions close by in Spain. They were stunning.

And maybe there were Arabian studs in England too?

With black colts for sale?

By the time she changed planes in New York and flew the last leg into Los Angeles airport she was ready to turn around and go back to England.

***

The first thing she did when she got home was start to make plans. She'd needed to talk both to her parents and to Beth.

"Beth, I have to move."

She sat in a beanbag chair at the Carmel gallery and watched the play of emotions cross her partner's expressive face.

"Ashley, you're my best friend. I almost lost you when your ferry sank. I almost lost you again when that man tried to strangle you. And then I almost went crazy when we heard in the news that you had been kidnapped! Now you're finally back here where we can eat pizza together and be under the same gallery roof and laugh and…."

Beth had run all the words together, her slender body slumped into the bean bag chair in shock, her dark brown eyes wide and huge and filling with tears.

"Now you're telling me you're leaving? For good? What am I going to do without you?"

"Would you consider moving too? To England? To start a gallery there with me?"

"What?"

The complete, undisguised dismay on Beth's face was too funny and Ashley would have laughed but she never laughed when her friend was upset. She walked over to sit in the next chair and held Beth's newly manicured fingers. They looked a bit bare without the engagement ring she'd given back to her fiancé Brad a month ago.

"I love Daemon. He doesn't know it yet but I do. And I'm pretty sure he loves me too."

"So? What's keeping you from being with him?"

Ashley's laugh had an ironic tone to it. "How about several thousand miles and an ocean, whether you go east or west from this gallery?"

"So, what are you going to do?" Beth sat up and shook her long blond hair away from her face. Ashley noticed a flare of interest that hadn't been there since things had started going wrong with Brad.

"My plan, my oldest and best friend, is to finish the oil painting for the Dunveys and either sell my interest in this gallery to you or have both of us put the gallery up for sale and move to England together."

She looked at Beth with her heart showing. "The night I had to get the colt out of the barn or get shot I thought about what I would do if miracles happened and I got out alive."

"Daemon?"

"I wanted more time with him. I want to figure out a way to be in the same country."

"What will your family say?"

"I've already told them everything. My brothers couldn't believe how well their karate lessons had worked. They were beaming. Dad has promised me a colt and he would send it to England as soon as I find out if having me around is what Daemon wants."

"What if it isn't, Ashley? What if this was just a fear and terror thing? Now that it's over and everything's back to normal, what if there's no more passion or love?"

"Then I finally get to be in the same country as Covent Garden. I can't dance but I can go to ballets all the time. And I could start an English extension of the family's Camelot Stud in the country that had the real Camelot. Dad said he'd love that and he'd come over to help me set it up."

"Then here's the thing."

Ashley watched as Beth thought seriously and hard. For about five seconds.

"The thing is I think you're crazy. But I think it's crazy in love. And you should go back and see what Daemon says. I will take the gallery from you. I've got enough saved to buy you out. For now."

"For now?"

"As insurance. I'll hold on to it until you and Daemon get yourselves settled. Or you find out that you'll be starting a gallery or a Stud farm on your own somewhere over there. If you end up coming home to Carmel, I'll sell you back your share and we'll carry on."

"And if I decide to stay in England?"

"If you are deliriously in love and stay in England with Daemon and start a new gallery and need a business partner and friend you can send for me and I'll be on the next plane. I've always loved adventures. Just not sinking in ferries. I don't like ferries."

Ashley jumped up and pulled Beth out of her chair and hugged her ferociously. Then she ran into the studio and pulled out her oils and got her canvasses ready and the final painting began.

***

It only took her two weeks because she worked day and night. She worked nights because she couldn't sleep. She watched the clock, wondering where Daemon might be. She wondered if he was all right. If he'd been shot. Or worse. When the phone rang and Beth said it was an international call her heart stopped.

She looked at the phone in Beth's hands and the look on Beth's face and felt a long few seconds of dread. Daemon was dead. He had been killed on the job. She'd never see him again.

"Hello? Ashley Gallagher here."

Silence for a tick of the clock, a beat of the heart.

"My lady with the wild dark hair who stole my heart?"

Her heart started to beat again. "Are you okay? Are you finished your case?"

"I am definitely finished. I've also had a chance to visit my parents in Cornwall. They said to say hello, as did Sam."

Ashley's lips curved into a smile, thinking about the handsome, kind young officer and her thoughts suddenly flew to Beth. She knew Sam was single. Hmm.

"You've never told me about your parents, Daemon. You said you had a sister and a younger brother? Do they live at home too?"

It wasn't really what Ashley wanted to talk about. She wanted to tell Daemon how much she loved him. She wanted to tell him she wanted to be in a bed with satin pillows with him right now, making love to him.

Without oceans in between them.

"No, they're both at college, living in residence. How's the painting going? The Dunveys called me and said they were really pleased with the watercolor. Are you all done with the oil?"

"Finished. It takes a bit to dry and then in a couple of weeks I can pack it up and ship it."

Or bring it over myself, she thought.

"I want to see it. Listen. I have to go because I'm at work tonight and I have to meet with McBride to debrief the case. I have some things to tell you but it has to wait until next week. I'll call you again."

A brief pause.

"Ashley?"

Ashley had trouble speaking over the lump in her throat. In two seconds, she was going to have to say 'good-bye' again. She was so tired of saying that word. She hoped fervently that the plan she was about to put into action would work out.

"Yes?"

"Ashley, we have to stop saying 'good-bye'."

But Daemon hung up before she could ask him what he meant.

She stood, holding the phone, staring into the studio and then jerked when Beth took the receiver from her and hung it up.

"Well?"

"He said we had to stop saying 'good-bye'. What could he have meant by that? At least this last case in Scotland didn't kill him. I don't know if I can handle knowing each next case could do just that."

"But?"

Ashley looked into Beth's sympathetic face and felt her lips start to tremble.

"But I can't stand to never see him again. I don't know enough about him and it's only been a few weeks since the night the ferry sank. Can you count sitting in a lifeboat a first date?"

Beth dissolved in giggles.

"So. You have to be with him," Beth said. "You have to go on dates. You have to meet his parents and find out if you even like living in England…and Ashley?"

"Beth?"

"Can I help you pack?"

"Have I ever told you what a wonderful friend you are? Can I tell you that our phone bills are going to be enormous?"

***

The oil was fantastic. The hues did so much more justice to Dark Night's gleaming coat and the lush Irish green of the paddock grass. Even Lord Dunvey's whiskers looked real enough to touch and Ashley put one fingertip to his warm smile and felt nostalgic about her time with him.

The painting was completely dry and ready to go in the special crate that would protect it and the watercolor on the way to Ireland. Ashley had decided not to take it in person because she had something more important to do.

She hadn't told Daemon she was coming.

She just wanted to come. She'd be able to tell right away if he'd decided oceans and continents were impossible to breach and if his job was just too dangerous and unstable for her to have a part in any kind of life with him. It made the flight back over that same gray, stormy ocean a bit harder in an anxious way. Not sad this time but anxious.

***

London, Heathrow airport was as vast as she'd remembered. The familiar black taxis were waiting in rows outside the terminal and she was soon tucked up inside, and on her way downtown.

She hadn't seen Daemon's flat when they'd been here weeks ago. Their time had been rushed. But she knew the address because she'd done her own sleuthing.

It was in an area she'd have thought a policeman couldn't afford and she was surprised when the taxi pulled up in front of an elegant, Georgian townhouse complex. She looked again at the address on the paper in her lap and then up at the address plate on the stone wall.

"Is this the right place miss?"

"I guess so. Yes, it must be." She stood, alone on the sidewalk, until the taxi was out of sight, and then she picked up her bags. She knocked on the front door and the building's uniformed doorman answered.

"Miss?"

"I'm here to see a Mr. Daemon O'Hare. Does he live here?"

"Is he expecting you?"

"No, but I can wait."

"It might be a long time. I think he went out quite a while ago."

Ashley, jet-lagged and exhausted, didn't think she could stand up much longer. She was endlessly relieved when the doorman let her sit on a chair outside Daemon's apartment. She sat for an hour and then got up to stretch the kinks out of her legs before the cramp in her knee could start.

Then she just sagged to the floor and rested her head on Daemon's door. She was fast asleep before she could hear the sound of the elevator coming up from the lobby.

***

Daemon watched the buttons on the inside of the elevator as they lit up the floors. The doorman had said he had a visitor but not who it was. He'd been expecting his sister to drop by but he thought he'd given her a key. When the doors slid open his heart skipped a beat.

She sat on the landing, the girl with the blue velvet eyes.

Her dark hair had curled and soft tendrils drifted across her temples and teased her closed eyelids. She was fast asleep. Daemon stood, looking at her, memorizing every pale, delicate feature. He watched as she breathed; watched the way her breasts rose and fell beneath the familiar, long trench coat. His feet finally moved and he knelt down to look in her face, willing her to wake up and once more be the butterfly that had crawled out of a cocoon in the waiting room in Wales.

"Ashley," he whispered. "Ashley, sweetheart; wake up."

***

The sound of Daemon's voice was tangled up in dreams. Wonderful dreams. He was in the mist again. But this time he was walking towards her and not away.

"Ashley?"

She forced herself to wake up and there he was. And he was smiling, his golden lion's hair shaggy again and his teeth showing in his wide grin.

"Daemon. Do you want me to be here? I can go back to California if you don't, but I have to see Covent Garden first. You promised me a ballet!"

Daemon just put his arms under her legs and lifted her up, high up, against his chest. He captured her lips in a kiss that held all the answers she needed. No words. Just heart.

"Ashley Gallagher, I don't know where you've come from but now you can't leave. I can't ever let you leave again. I don't care what I have to do to keep you here."

Daemon reached into his pocket and pulled out his door key and turned the lock. Kicking the door open with his foot, he let her slide down his body until her feet touched the floor and then he leaned her up against the wall and went out to get her things from the hall. When he came back, she had sagged down the wall and he scooped her up again to take her into his bedroom and put her down on his bed.

"Daemon! This is not the tiny flat you told me about. This is really, really nice. This whole building is nice."

Suddenly suspicious, Ashley looked at him again before her gaze went back to take in the very good taste he had in paintings and furniture.

"Daemon, you can't have done this on a policeman's budget. What haven't you told me?"

Daemon bent over to pull off her long leather boots for her and his own shoes and put their coats on the back of a Queen Anne chair.

"I told you I was a policeman and that's true. You know that. But I grew up on an estate in Cornwall. My family has always had money and they taught me about paintings and music and the ballet and literature and sports and everything else. I played soccer in school, just like my sister and I learned to ride horses when I was in boarding school."

"We have to go on dates."

Daemon watched the tired drooping of her eyelids and smiled gently as she sagged against his arm.

"Dates?"

"My friend Beth is very wise. She said I've just met you. It's true. Now that we don't have awful people chasing us, we don't have danger bonding us anymore. We have to find out about each other. We have to date."

Daemon's head bent to whisper in her ear and his breath tickled.

Ashley pulled away and looked right at him. She thought he looked less like a lion today and more like a lover. "What did you just say?"

"I said, if we have to date does that mean you have to leave and find a hotel and sleep by yourself tonight? Do we have to wait before we can…?"

Ashley's smile matched his own. "No."

"Thank, God!" Daemon pulled her into his arms and lowered his mouth to hers.

***

Daemon smoothed her hair and cupped her face with both hands as he studied her sweet smile, her fine-boned cheeks, the feathery lashes and brows.

An ocean and continent had just disappeared. She was back where she belonged. And then he sat back. He had things to say. "This trip to Scotland was my last case."

"What do you mean?"

"I've resigned. I've talked to McBride. I've talked to my parents, who are unbelievably happy about this decision, and I've given notice to the Commissioner. I'm on two weeks paid leave and then, since I don't have a case pending, I'm on my own."

"What are you going to do?"

"I'm going back to university."

"To finish your law degree? Oh Daemon!"

"In California."

"What?"

"Do you know, Miss Gallagher, that you look rather endearing with your mouth open?" He leaned forward to kiss it closed. "While you've been painting, I've been clearing up loose ends here. I've been looking into the University of Oakland in San Francisco. They have an exchange program with Oxford and I can apply to finish my degree program there. I can see you on weekends until you think we've finished dating and then…"

Ashley stopped him with a kiss. It went on and on and led to hands smoothing over curves and sharp angles and ribcages and breasts and then more kissing.

"I sold my gallery."

Daemon looked at her intently.

"Why?" It was a quiet word.

"Because my gallery was too far away from you. I love you so much my heart aches without you and I can't say goodbye any more. I want to set up a gallery here. If you don't want me, I'll go home and buy my half of the gallery back. But Daemon…."

"Ashley?"

"I don't want to go home."

"I love you too. When we've finished dating, I want you to be my wife."

Ashley wound her arms around him until there was no space, never mind oceans, between them.

"Yes.'

Epilogue

"Full Circle"

Ashley wore blue pansies in her hair on her wedding day.

They nestled in her wild curls and were a 'something borrowed, something blue' gift from Daemon's mother. From the garden she tended so lovingly. Ashley had spent hours in that garden with the gracious lady who had become like a second mother to her. They'd had endless cups of tea and worked together with the flowers that grew riotously and splendidly both in real life and in the water colors Ashley had done for her new family.

Daemon's mother and father sat now with Ashley's mother…in the front pew of a centuries-old stone church just outside the village in Cornwall where Daemon had grown up. Ashley had smiled when she found out he'd been an altar boy in this same church.

As Ashley started down the long aisle behind Daemon's sister and Beth, she tucked her arm through her father's. Her whole family and her best friend had come to England for the wedding. She and Daemon had decided to get married almost right away. They'd figured that their harrowing time in Ireland had been worth a year of getting to know each other.

Her brothers waited by the altar, standing beside Daemon and his own brother and Sam, all of them gallant in their tuxes, their grins matching and so full of love for her.

Daemon was so outrageously handsome he took her breath away.

***

Daemon watched his tousled butterfly walk toward him through the prism cast by the stained-glass windows. Tousled no longer, she was stunningly beautiful in a long, white satin wedding dress that was a perfect contrast to the vivid burgundy gowns of the bridesmaids. She wore only two pieces of jewelry…her engagement ring and the shamrock necklace Daemon had given her. Her bouquet was made of white roses and burgundy orchids…paired with ivy that was almost, not quite…the green of Ireland.

There was something else in the bouquet, tucked in with the flowers…a tiny gold and diamond butterfly Beth had brought from California…a perfect reminder of the delicate butterfly tattoos she and Ashley wore on their ankles…a reminder of their long friendship.

Daemon had liked Beth on sight.

And so had Sam. Ashley had seen sparks flying and crossed her fingers behind her back.

Daemon saw Ashley turn her head and smile at Lord and Lady Dunvey, who had arrived yesterday to a flurry of joyous hugs and happy tears.

Everyone who loved them was here…even little Kevin from the ferry, who sat with his parents and grinned at her as she passed by and gave her a wink.

***

"Three Years Later…Cornwall"

Batting away the blond pigtails currently coming undone, Rhianna O'Hare pushed the button on her Disneyland player and took a deep breath, stretched her little shoulders and started again. Over and over, she followed the patterns, scattering butterflies in the garden as she did a 'just-over-two years-old' imitation of the dance steps she'd watched.

Plié. (well kind of a plié)

She tried to bend her pudgy little knees but she couldn't quite keep her balance and kept on falling down.

But every time she fell down, she giggled.

It was hot outside but there was a mist coming in off the ocean and it was pleasant here among all the flowers. Rhianna could hear the horses in the barn and knew her mother would be in there checking on the new foal.

Glissade. (a little girl version.)

The sliding steps frustrated her beyond belief and she was ready to have a tantrum.

But then a butterfly flew by her nose and she collapsed in a tangled, giggling heap. She looked up to see her mother leaning against the door watching her, a tray of glasses in her hands and a huge smile on her face.

***

Ashley O'Hare was a joyous woman.

Her heart was full as she stood watching her daughter and then out at her new home. Their property on the rugged Cornwall coast was gorgeous beyond belief and reminded her of Carmel's pounding surf. She already had a million ideas for new paintings.

Daemon had come to California after all and completed his degree at Stanford School of Law. Now he was working with a law firm in St. Ives and he and Ashley had bought enough land for a barn and paddock for her father's gift, an Arabian colt named Morgan.

Their two other Arabian horses and the new foal were the beginnings of the Cornwall version of the Camelot Stud.

Rhianna had come within that first year and was now taking to their new life in England as easily as to her interest in watching the "Ballet for Tots" program in Penzance. She wouldn't be old enough for a long time to join in but she loved to move to the music.

"Mommy, butterflies tickle!"

"Do they sweetheart? And do you tickle them back?" The little girl burst out in a chorus of delighted giggles again and plopped herself down beside Ashley's paint easel.

Ashley and Beth had opened a new gallery in St. Ives this year.

They'd won the hearts of the locals with their landscapes, seascapes and paintings of the moor ponies of Devon and Cornwall. Beth had settled in to a small cottage not far from the gallery.

Daemon's friend Sam had been interested in Beth ever since he'd met her at the wedding. But until Beth had moved to England this year, they hadn't had a chance to really get to spend any time together.

And Sam was always away on a case with Scotland Yard. They knew he'd been investigating a move though, so Ashley held out hope.

***

The rumble of Daemon's sports car announced his arrival home. Rhianna leaped up to do shaky pirouettes all around him.

"See, Daddy?"

Daemon met Ashley's gaze over the top of their little girl's blond head and grinned. He grinned a lot these days. No more stakeouts. No more nights sitting up in cars waiting for crooks to show up. There was very little traveling and he could be with his family. He put his arms around his girls and hugged. His nose picked up the scent of peaches in Ashley's hair and he leaned his head forward to nuzzle her neck.

Ashley slept through the night now. She hadn't had a nightmare in a long time. All the members of the syndicate and their couriers had been brought to trial and faced long prison terms because of the kidnapping and several other murders that had been uncovered.

She could stand the lightning and thunderstorms along the coast without flinching and she loved the wild ocean seacoast of Cornwall.

Daemon and Ashley made frequent trips to California to visit her brothers and her mom and dad. Rhianna, after all, had to grow up knowing her whole family and loved both sets of grandparents and her Aunt Beth. Daemon's family had immediately scooped Ashley into their arms and blessed her for helping Daemon to leave the job that had scared them all.

Daemon's lion growl sounded in her ear and he brushed her cheek with his. "I have a suggestion. It's supposed to be really misty tonight. If we can get a babysitter, how would you like to take the car down to the beach this time and go dancing on the sand?"

Ashley's memories carried her back to that night dancing in his arms under the misty trees in Ireland and she smiled. Daemon had taken her to Covent Garden and brought her back the gift of ballet. And Black Cloud had helped her to make peace with that night of fire and grief so many years ago. Her life had finally come full circle, to the things that had brought her joy.

She watched as her green-eyed lion raised his eyebrow, waiting to hear her say yes.

"Yes."

Watch for Beth and Sam's story next in *A Perfect Star-Gazing Night*, and the final book of the Butterfly Trilogy in *Castles Under Siege*, with Gabrielle and Riley.

WATCH FOR *A PERFECT STAR-GAZING NIGHT*

Book 2 of the <u>Butterfly Trilogy</u>

COMING FOR CHRISTMAS 2023

WHILE YOU WAIT, HERE IS A TEASER…CHAPTER ONE

Prologue

"Blood Red Manolos'

Beth Duncan hadn't expected to find a body in her closet.

It lay crumpled on top of her favorite Manolo Blahnik shoes and blood had seeped all over them. She stood, shock chilling her skin, her mind numb, her breath coming in shaky gasps. The bright red seemed to have spread everywhere. It had oozed out in a sticky, congealing mass and she couldn't seem to drag her terrified gaze away. She backed up to keep from stepping in it and then forced herself to look at the man's face.

She didn't need to be an expert to know that he was dead.

Very dead.

His face was strangely blank but his eyes were wide open and staring at her. There was something almost pleading in them, something that was trying to connect with her. Not that he looked afraid. It was only that he seemed to be asking for help.

His body was limp and contorted, his bald head quite ordinary except for the hole above his right ear. It was a tiny hole, but grimly black and obviously the source of all that blood.

Horror hit as she realized whoever had stashed the man's body might still be around. Maybe they had hidden somewhere when they'd seen her come down her driveway.

"Think!' She whispered the word, expecting someone to leap out at her. She could either run or call the police.

Or both.

She needed to get out of the bedroom. She needed to get away from this thing that had torn into her blissful new life. Her cellphone was in the kitchen. There was no body in the kitchen.

She picked up the phone and called the local police, her fingers drumming on the table, her ears listening for anything that might be different from the usual noises on the roadway outside.

Her cottage was isolated. She'd chosen it for that reason. She'd wanted a quiet place to paint.

Where she could come home after work and hear the sounds of the sea birds and the crash of the ocean.

She'd been here long enough to fall in love with Cornwall, England and especially the town of St. Ives. She loved the wild ocean beaches and the rock cliffs and the fact that you could see the stars at night.

She'd been quite happy helping her best friend Ashley Gallagher run their art gallery in Carmel, California. But then Ashley went to Ireland on a painting commission and fell straight into the middle of a kidnapping. She had also fallen head over heels in love with a Scotland Yard detective named Daemon O'Hare.

She'd come home to California with plans that would shake Beth's life.

Plans to sell Ashley's half share of the gallery.

Plans that involved Ashley getting married and moving to Cornwall.

Plans that involved asking Beth to relocate with her and start a new gallery in St. Ives.

A new life. A new adventure.

Beth had always loved adventures.

Until about five minutes ago.

Chapter One

"If You Save Someone's Life, They Belong to You"

The sight of a white coroner's van and three local police cars with their lights flashing was strangely overwhelming and comforting all at the same time.

Beth looked out the window, one hand on her cell, the other holding her list of emergency contacts. She watched as the man's body was carted out of her cottage and into the van. The forensics team in their white coats and boots still huddled over the puddle of blood in her closet, taking samples, putting things in plastic bags and tracking the sticky red mess all over her bedroom.

Fingers shaking, Beth tried one more time to call Ashley's number but there was no answer. Her brain still in a fog, she finally remembered that Ashley wasn't even home. She and Daemon had taken their three-year old daughter Rhianna to see her grandparents in Oxford. They weren't due back until the end of the week.

Beth put down the phone. She'd have to deal with this alone.

She was okay doing it alone. Really, she was. She only thought when you dealt with dead bodies it would be helpful to have somebody with you. To make cups of tea and tell you it was all right to have someone murdered in your bedroom.

"Miss Duncan, I'm ready to go over your statement and ask you a few more questions. Are you sure there isn't anyone else you can call to come and be with you? This must have been a shock."

The constable in charge came into her tiny living room and stepped over the charts and slide rules and photographs that Beth had organized on the floor this morning to discuss with her architect.

"You doing some building?"

Beth's gaze somehow registered that the sketches were in the way and she wondered if she should be picking them up before they got walked on. Before they got blood on them. Then she wondered how to get blood out of the shoes in her closet. What should she do first?

"Miss Duncan?"

"Sorry."

She tried to focus on the constable. He'd been very professional. The police had come right away. Something about murders tended to get that kind of response.

It was hard to think about ordinary things. About life before the murder. This morning she'd been so excited about the architect coming tonight.

She dragged her thoughts back to the constable's question.

"I'm going to be adding on a new room. It's for a painting studio. I need more light. This cottage is really dark and I need bigger windows if the heritage council will let me."

She'd never noticed before how many dark corners there really were in the cottage. It was all on one floor and fairly open, but she had stood, waiting for the police to come, imagining squeaks and rattles everywhere.

Imagining footsteps.

"Right," the constable agreed. "It's a lovely cottage; very traditional like most of the places around here. But I agree it does seem dark."

He made more notes on his clipboard while Beth thought about dark places and things hiding in them. She started to shiver and the constable draped a blanket over her and patted her on the shoulder. Another officer had made her a cup of tea and she held it in freezing fingers.

"I know what a big job it is to remodel, Miss Duncan. Sometimes it's a huge step simply to get everything passed by the Council. They're sticky about rules."

He shook his head sympathetically and then got back to business.

“Listen, here’s the statement. We’ve got most of it. You will need to give me a few more details.”

Beth took the clipboard and dragged over a chair to sit at the small table, scanning the hard, bare facts, nodding her head as she checked through the pages.

How could someone’s death be so black and white? Shouldn’t someone care who he’d been?

He had BEEN. That was the whole point.

Before that tiny hole in his head.

She tucked her hair behind her ear and tried to concentrate.

“Constable, I have no idea who this man was. I just know when I came home early from the gallery, I needed a sweater and I opened my closet and found him crumpled up inside.”

She took a deep breath, trying to stay focused, wishing her fingers would stop shaking.

She looked over at the cellphone sitting on her counter and thought about Sam. Maybe she should call him. His name repeated over and over in her head, mixed in with the shock.

He’d said he was going to be coming over later anyway. Papers or briefs…oh right, her building permits. He’d picked them up from Daemon for her. Daemon was a lawyer now.

Sam was down from London. He was on leave from his job with Scotland Yard and checking on his apartment here…they called them ‘flats’ in England. Every chance he got he spent time in St. Ives. He loved the ocean and wanted out of the big city.

Sam would know what to do. She always felt safe around him. He was a detective, like Daemon had been. His image blinked into her mind.

Sam Matthews.

Tall, rangy, capable Sam with the beautiful dark eyes and the wonderful smile.

Sam with his girlfriend, Miranda, who kept popping in and out of his life.

Beth looked down at the clipboard and noticed her fingers had turned white, they were gripping the board so hard. She forced herself to relax and smoothed out the paper she'd rumpled.

"Constable, you asked me to look around. I've checked everything and I don't see anything else out of place or missing, except all the plants at the back door have been knocked over. It's such a mess somebody must have been in a hurry."

The officer took his pen and the clipboard and scanned over the lined paper, making sure he had added the plants. He looked up, obviously curious about this, his forehead wrinkled in concentration. His forensic crew had already taken samples of some of the footprints in the plant soil.

"Anything else?"

"The chairs in the dining room were pushed over and the back door was open. I came in the front door this afternoon and I'm sure I closed the back one this morning when I went to work."

"Were your doors locked?"

Beth smiled, a grim one, but it lifted the corners of her mouth.

"The first thing my friend Ashley told me when I moved here was no one in Cornwall locks their door. These small villages are such tight communities everyone looks after each other. It's not the same in California, where people have security systems and guard dogs."

A huge guard dog was suddenly looking appealing and Beth made a mental note to look into a Doberman. She looked over at her new goldfish, Winston, doing laps in his fish tank, and figured he wouldn't be much help if someone waltzed into her house again with murder on their mind. She vaguely wondered what Winston would look like sitting up on the stand in the courtroom as an eye witness. Or a fish witness?

She giggled and then put her hand over her mouth.

She never giggled. Must be shock.

"Oh my God!"

Beth's naturally pale skin lost whatever color it usually had. She suddenly thought about the possibilities.

"Do you think whoever did this will come back? That I interrupted them by coming home?"

The constable scratched his head and looked at the crowd in Beth's bedroom before he answered.

"Don't really know at the moment. We need to do a fingerprint check. See if we can come up with anything. I think I recognize your dead man. We'll try to figure out who might have wanted him dead. In the meantime, we'll post a watch on your house for the next couple of nights and you might want to lock all the windows and doors. Although..."

Beth's eyes narrowed as she waited for the rest of the sentence, her mind already mulling over the words your dead man. She didn't want a dead man. A live one would be good.

"Although?"

"Although if someone wanted this man dead, a closed door, even locked, wouldn't have stopped him."

"Wonderful! I feel safer now."

There was so much going on in the house Beth didn't pay attention to the crunch of gravel on the long driveway down from the main road.

***

Sam Matthews slowed to take his car into the final turn down to Beth's house and suddenly put on his brakes. He was smiling, anticipating a cup of tea and a chat with Beth. He had been thinking a lot about her lately. Had been thinking about her ever since they'd met.

But the scene in front of him made his heart stop.

Beth!

A body bag was being loaded into a coroner's van and all Sam could think of now was that something had happened to her. Something brutal had happened to end the life of the sweet, fragile blonde who had caught his attention the second she had walked into the law office in St. Ives where he had been visiting with their mutual friend Daemon O'Hare.

Sam had been friends with Daemon ever since they'd met in boarding school all those years ago. They'd bonded over rugby matches and cricket pitches and being lonely as little boys missing their moms. They'd shared the same dorm and engaged in food fights in the dining hall.

And when they'd hidden a frog in their teacher's desk drawer, they'd shared the same punishment.

Their friendship had extended into university and then to Scotland Yard.

Sam was still on active duty with the CID, or Criminal Investigation Department, but was now attached to a branch that gave assistance to police in other parts of England on difficult cases. He maintained his apartment here in Cornwall to breathe the sea air and stay close to Daemon and Ashley when he had time between those cases.

And to check in on this ethereal lady who at this moment might be…he couldn't say it. Couldn't think it. His fingers gripped the steering wheel and it took long seconds for him to realize the bag was much too long and too big for it to be Beth. But something bad had happened here and Sam jumped out of the car and ran for the door of the cottage, ignoring the police officer who tried to stop him.

***

Beth looked up from the table and the minute she saw Sam she felt tears that seemed to come from nowhere.

She hadn't realized how much it was him, and only him she needed.

She took a huge breath and stood, coming over to take his hand and reach up to kiss him on the cheek as he wrapped his arms around her and pulled her closer.

"Sam! Oh, God…I'm SO glad to see you."

She turned back to the constable. "This is my friend, Sam Matthews. He's a detective with the CID in London. Could you please share what's happening with him too?"

Sam ran his fingers through his hair and dropped his jacket onto the back of a chair. He put his hand on Beth's shoulder and looked at her closely. No blood, no scratches. But only something horrific would make her dark brown eyes look this haunted.

He'd never once seen her cry. Not in the three years since he'd first met her at Daemon and Ashley's wedding. She had been a solid source of support for Ashley and tackled a brand-new life over here with charm and an adventurous spirit.

"Beth, what's going on? Are you hurt?"

He settled her on a small sofa, tucking the blanket in and sitting beside her, putting his arm around her again. He could see strain in her fine-boned face and in the rigid way she was holding her shoulders. She started to shake.

Reaction?

But to what?

She looked straight at him and blinked fiercely, finally letting a tear fall, and then took a deep breath.

"I came home from work this afternoon and found a body in my closet."

Sam swore and drew her closer. He listened, intent, as she filled him in and then showed the constable his Metropolitan Police London ID before getting more details from him.

He held onto Beth's hand until it didn't feel as chilled and then watched as she reached out for a pen to sign the statement.

***

Beth felt somehow that her cottage seemed even smaller now that Sam was here. It wasn't just that he was tall, although he was at least 6'1 and towered over her own 5'6.

It was something else she couldn't really put a name to. He filled the room. As simply as that. For the first time since she'd opened her closet door, she felt safe.

She'd always thought he was good looking. He wore his dark brown hair a bit long, much like Daemon, and it curled slightly, onto the collar of his white shirt. He could do that because CID detectives didn't have to have the shorter hair of the regular police.

His eyes were a clear hazel brown and usually had a bit of a twinkle. He was a good-natured flirt and had an almost endearing way of lifting the left side of his mouth when he grinned. It made him look a bit rakish in a Cornish pirate sort of a way.

But she knew he had a boarding school and Oxford background and had belonged to the rowing team and equestrian teams in university. Unless pirates used rowing team sculls once in a while, the image didn't fit.

Beth looked down at his lean-fingered hand as it held hers and felt enormous relief that he was here. His strong frame and police experience were a buffer against what had recently happened. And she had to remind herself that was all he could be. She'd worked so hard to keep her growing feelings for him tucked away…Miranda…she had to remind herself that another woman was part of his life.

"Miss Duncan, I suggest for tonight you close up the cottage and stay in St. Ives. Until we run a background check on the deceased."

The deceased.

It sounded so ugly. So trite. Sort of like the murder mysteries she liked to read and watch on television. But now that she'd seen a 'deceased' up close, the word meant something else quite different.

"I wish I could. But I have to stay here. I'm expecting my architect to come and it has to be tonight. He's leaving for another job tomorrow."

Sam, gaze narrowed, considering, turned to the policeman.

"What kind of danger do you think there might be if she stays here tonight?"

The officer gathered up his papers and pushed back the chair to get up. He looked at Beth and then Sam.

"Don't really know yet. Until we do, we can't guarantee there isn't a level of danger for her. We've ruled her out as a suspect because she has a solid alibi. We checked and there are any number of witnesses who put her at the gallery about the time the coroner estimates this man died."

Beth sucked in a surprised breath. She hadn't realized she'd been a suspect. She'd thought they were only covering all the bases when they'd asked where she'd been.

All of a sudden, she had the most inappropriate urge to laugh. Completely inappropriate given the situation and the way her heart was aching for the man who had died. But it came out of nowhere. Probably the way her body was reacting to stress and horror.

She managed to choke it down but replayed the moment she'd first seen the body. Would it have been a plausible alibi to say she couldn't have killed someone and left them to bleed all over the most expensive shoes she'd ever owned?

She'd loved the size 7 Manolo Blahnik black satin slides the minute she'd seen them. She'd bought them the last time she'd been home in Carmel, even though she'd winced at the price tag.

She concentrated on staying calm and turned to the policeman.

"So, why would I be in danger if the man who was killed here doesn't have anything to do with me?"

The officer peered at her over his glasses.

"Miss Duncan, we don't know why he was killed. We don't know why he was even in your house. We don't know who killed him. We don't know if he's hidden something here and whoever killed him needs to come back to look for it."

"Can't be that."

Both men swung their heads around to look at her.

"That would be too coincidental. My friend Ashley has already gone through this. Crooks put a package in her bag and both the bad guys and the police chased her all over Ireland. These things can't reasonably happen all the time. There has to be another answer for this."

Her black eyebrows rose, punctuation marks in her tense face. Their color matched the black eyelashes that looked so incongruous and startling with her white-blonde hair. Her coloring had been a gift from her Swedish grandmother and made Beth a stunning runway model during university when she'd modeled for a Los Angeles fashion house to earn extra tuition money.

"So it has to be something else. Obviously, the body was here. Maybe the killers chased him into the house. Maybe that's all. Maybe they killed him somewhere else and put his body here to hide it. I don't think there's anything more to it."

She looked at Sam, watching to see if he would agree to this most simple of possibilities.

"She's probably right," he said. "But…"

Beth waited for the rest of the 'but'.

"But?"

"But I agree with the officer there's always an off-chance they might come back and they would want to come back right away."

The officer nodded his head.

"So, I'll stay here with you tonight."

***

Sam let go of Beth's hand and got to his feet, ignoring the fact that he had left her with her mouth wide open.

He walked to the door with the constable and waited until the forensics team cleared away all of their equipment and the coroner picked up his black bag.

"Does Miss Duncan need to avoid any parts of the house tonight? I see you still have some crime scene tape up."

"We have all the prints we need. We're taking the shoes in because we'll have to do further checks on them. She might want to stay out of her bedroom until we send in a team to clean up all the blood. There's quite a mess in there."

Beth nodded her head and watched her shoes go out the door in a clear plastic bag.

"I don't think I want to be in that room tonight, Sam. It's going to take a long time before I'll be able to get that image out of my head. I can use the spare bedroom. You don't have to stay, I'll really be okay."

He was expecting that. She was fiercely independent and determined to do things on her own. She'd thrown caution to the wind when she'd decided to leave her former California surfer girl and model life behind to join Ashley halfway around the world.

"I'll stay anyway, if you don't mind. The sofa looks long enough and I've got the day off tomorrow."

***

When the police cars and van pulled away and wound up the driveway to the road, the cottage seemed even more isolated and lonely than ever and Sam was left wondering what it had been that she'd found so appealing about being so far away from her neighbors.

"Sam, I bought this place because it was out of town. It was on a beach and the isolation was perfect. It's close enough to St. Ives to dash in for groceries or go to the gallery and it's peaceful here and I loved it."

Her voice caught a little.

"Or, at least I did."

Sam watched Beth as she stood up and put the phone back on its charger. She was such a fascinating mix of fragility and strength. He hadn't been surprised when Daemon had told him about her modeling background. She had a natural poise and grace that was apparent no matter what she was wearing or what she was doing. And the breathtakingly beautiful paintings that both Beth and Ashley created left him without words.

But it had amazed him to learn that Beth, who barely came up to his chin, routinely rode the Cornish surf on the short, pink surfboard she'd brought from California.

Now 28, Beth could still look 16 when she was up on her board, her long, poker straight hair wet and streaming behind her. Sam sometimes felt like Methuselah at his own advanced age of 36. But then working as a detective added emotional age too…and some days he felt worn out and closer to 80. Seeing how happy Daemon was with the change in his life since he'd resigned from the Force, Sam was mulling his choices.

"Okay then, we need to go back to my apartment to pick up a change of clothes for me and some groceries for dinner tonight. I will cook."

Beth grinned. "You've given me a reason to smile, thank goodness. You're famous for your cooking. I love it when you barbeque at Daemon and Ashley's when I'm there. But you've never cooked here and I can't wait."

In fact, he hadn't been here a lot at all. Today he'd needed to drop off the legal papers for the architect. He'd been careful not to be around when it was only Beth. Too many issues in his life right now to let himself act on the way he was feeling about her.

"Could you do me a huge favor?"

Sam stopped as he bent over to pick up his jacket and looked her way. Kiss her? Wrap his arms around her again?

Pick her up and carry her to the rumpled bed in that room with the closet?

'Anything'.

***

Beth's heart did a strange skip when she saw something in his eyes that hadn't been there before and she was suddenly short of breath.

"I was getting a sweater when I found that body. I don't think I can go in my bedroom again today with all that blood. If I stand at the door and tell you where to look, could you go?"

His smile turned into a gentle grin... the lopsided one she'd always liked so much. All Beth had expected from him this past three years was to be a friend, a big brother, and her heart had needed to keep some distance.

But as she watched him navigate around the crime scene tape, with her sweater dangling off his fingers, she wondered at the sudden shift in the way her heart was behaving. It surprised her to realize it had been coming on for a long, long time.

They crunched out to his car and Beth got in, her nose sniffing the 'new car smell' of the leather seats in Sam's new blue BMW convertible.

"I like it. I'm glad you got it. I didn't think CID detectives could afford something like this though."

***

Sam got in his side and waited until Beth did up her seatbelt, watching as the metal clasp slid over her inky blue silk dress. The material showed a lot of leg when she was sitting down. She'd somehow managed to get some of the dead man's blood on her nylons and had tried to scrub it off. The dried rusty stain made him feel sick.

Once they were both in the car, Sam realized he'd never been this close to Beth before. Sure, he'd given her quick pecks on the cheek at get-togethers at the O'Hare's Stud farm and had put a brotherly arm around her shoulder when she'd come into Daemon's law office. That's all.

His senses were in overdrive all of a sudden. Had he never noticed that light smell of vanilla before? Her perfume was unusual, a soft ocean smell, like the flowers in a tropical place somewhere.

He leaned over to playfully sniff her hair, trying to lift her mood, distract her from the horrors of the afternoon.

"Vanilla?"

"It's a vanilla-based perfume from Tahiti. I went with Ashley a few years ago and we stayed in Bora Bora. It was gorgeous and we had a chance to swim with sharks. Everywhere I went I smelled vanilla. It's so much stronger in the heat and humidity of a tropical island but every time I use it now, I remember how much fun I had there. Ashley got some perfume that smells like peaches."

"Today's been bad, hasn't it?" Sam heard her sigh and shot her a quick glance as he drove the car back up the road.

Beth put her head on the headrest and closed her eyes for a second and he could almost see her willing her thoughts away from blood and bullet holes.

"Awful."

"How about we talk cars then...maybe if I tell you all about the technical and mechanical things going on in the motor compartment of this car you'll be distracted and think about something else. Or we could talk about the fact that you know I have money from my ridiculously huge trust fund and can afford this car and will be keeping it in St. Ives to drive in my secret life as a non-detective?"

He won a small smile from her and they drove in silence for the next few minutes, Beth looking out the window at the cascading surf that crashed in on the long white sand beaches that reminded her so much of home in Carmel.

"The trees are different here Sam, and it's the Atlantic Ocean, not the Pacific, but I've been so surprised to find how comfortable I've been. Except for bodies and blood."

The road wound along the coast road and into St. Ives as Sam's car passed the tiny granite cottages that lined the road on the outskirts of town. Then he turned to drive up the narrow, cobbled lane that led to his apartment.

Everywhere along the lane there were gardens; a profusion of flowers scenting the air. He noticed that Beth looked away from the red poppies. When he asked why, she said they looked too much like blood.

By the time they got to his front door she was shivering again and he waited until he got the key in the lock and then held his arms open for her. She walked straight into them and he rested his chin on the top of her head and simply stood, holding her until the shaking stopped.

He wondered what had happened that felt so different. Sam had admired her poise and sweet personality and had been interested from the start. But Ashley had taken him aside and told him about the fiancé who had given Beth such a hard time not so long ago. Ashley said it had been ugly and Beth wasn't ready to be in a relationship yet.

And Sam was still trying to decide what to do about Miranda. He'd been busy either being with her or breaking up with her so many times over the past few years that he needed to figure that out too.

So being friends and only friends had been, if not perfect, then on the edge of okay.

Until today scared him to death.

Standing here with her in his arms was incredibly painful. There was nothing 'just friends' about the way he was feeling.

He stepped back and looked at her as she rested her cheek against his shirt.

"All right now?" He could feel her smile.

"I think so. Thanks. What do you need to get? Toothbrush? Pyjamas? Ice cream?"

"Ice cream?"

"Chocolate. We have to get chocolate ice cream. Lots of it. Whenever I've had anything bad happen in my life, I've eaten chocolate ice cream until I feel better."

Sam laughed and watched the first real smile he'd seen on Beth's face since he'd driven up to her door over two hours ago.

His apartment was the whole top floor of a converted 16th Century coach house and the building had been modernized over the past few years. It still had its traditional high-beamed ceiling and bay windows and felt open and airy during the summer. But there was a gas fireplace now, central heating and a modern kitchen and bathroom.

Beth wandered over to the main window and looked out. Sam was only a five minutes walk from the surfing beach and the harbor and could go to the shops and restaurants if he wanted. But he preferred to cook at home.

"Is there anything I can do to help?"

He popped his head out of the bedroom and threw her a small duffle bag.

"Nope. If you could put this by the door and I'll be out in a second. You could make us both a quick cup of tea if you like. Are you still cold?"

***

Beth wandered into the small kitchen and put a kettle on the stove. It didn't take long and she found the act of doing something normal helped her to relax. She held out her hands and let the warmth from the stove seep into her bones. She transferred the heat to her face, putting her hands on her eyes and cheekbones. By the time Sam came out into the kitchen the tea was ready, steaming in two cups on the small galley table.

He had changed, his hair all ruffled from pulling a grey turtleneck sweater over his head. He'd put on well-washed blue jeans and sneakers and was ready to go.

They stopped at a market before they turned back along the road out of town.

The thought of being back in her cottage made Beth cold again.

"I don't even know if my back door locks now. Should I be getting someone in to fix it?"

"Let's see what the police say tomorrow. We can do something for tonight and then go from there. Or come back into town when you're finished with the architect tonight. You could stay at a hotel or…"

Beth looked at him, noticing the way his eyebrows rose as he waited for her response. He'd put on a pair of sunglasses against the bright early-evening glare and she couldn't see his eyes.

"Or?"

"Or you could stay with me. I have a spare bedroom too."

"I am really okay. If you can stay tonight, I'll be able to get back to normal tomorrow. Tonight, I keep getting flashes of finding that body. How have you and Daemon managed to work with all the dead bodies in your jobs? Does it ever get easier? Ashley says Daemon still has restless nights sometimes, thinking about really ugly cases he's had.

Especially with children."

He was quiet for the longest time and then, taking a breath, shook his head.

"Our job has a high burn-out rate. Those dead bodies pile up in our nightmares and they can come back and haunt us any time. It never gets easier."

The endless line of great rolling breakers they passed on the coast road went on as far as the eye could see. It sounded kind of ridiculous, but suddenly the idea of running away from everything and getting out on her surfboard tomorrow was really appealing. The simple act of getting up on a board and putting all of your concentration on simply staying upright on the wave was one of the best ways in the world of forgetting everything. It wouldn't get rid of the image of that perfect round bullet hole. But it might help the terrible new pain in her stomach.

Growing up, Beth had spent every spare second at the beach, learning to ride the waves, learning to read the ocean. Every summer she'd go with Ashley to Malibu or to the other coast beaches. Ashley to swim, Beth to surf.

"Sam. You said you had tomorrow off. You said once you'd never seen me surf. I know this is bizarre but some sea air would make me feel normal. And nothing is normal right now. Want to learn to surf?"

Sam sighed and took his eyes off the road long enough to give her a mock look of terror.

"I swim, I row, I sail. I will definitely come and watch you wear a tiny bikini. But…"

He wiggled his eyebrows at her, making her smile in spite of herself.

"But I will not stand on one of those small bouncing boards and risk death out there."

It was Beth's turn to grin. "It' fun to imagine you trying to balance on a tiny board. All 6' whatever of you. I would have so much fun teaching you." But her grin faded.

"Sam? Do you have any idea why that man was in my house? Really. Do you think he was already there and someone found him? Was he looking for something hidden away in my closet? I know I told the policeman it couldn't be that I was having the same thing happen that Ashley went through. But could it be?"

Sam slowed to take the turn down Beth's driveway. Her question had suddenly brought them back to the stark reality of the afternoon. Someone had been murdered in her house. This house. The one they were going into right now.

"I don't know. I guess that's what the police are going to try to find out. Whatever it was, we'll have to grit our teeth and wait."

"What if I can't?"

Sam stopped the car and sat, looking at her over the top of his sunglasses.

"You can't?"

"I can't shake the feeling that I'm connected now to whatever this was. Someone picked my house. He ran in here for a reason and someone chased him or caught him here and killed him. I need to find out what happened."

***

There was a subtle change in her voice. Sam heard the stubborn, adventure-loving Beth taking charge again. Spunky.

It chilled him to think of the trouble she could get herself into if she decided to get involved in detective work on her own.

Spunk helped a lot when Beth decided she needed to go into her bedroom to get changed. She always dressed up to go into the gallery. Both that area of St. Ives and her job were upscale and she said she felt more professional in her 'city clothes'. She loved fashion anyway and her modeling days had taught her style and elegance, both of which she had in abundance.

So, he watched as she stared at the closed bedroom door, took a deep breath and opened it to go inside.

"Well-done, medium or rare? How do you like your steak?" Sam yelled into the house a while later, and he held a long barbeque fork in his hand and an oven mitt in the other, he came into the kitchen and looked at her closed bedroom door.

He knocked and then opened it, a crack.

"Beth?"

He could see her legs…long, clad in jeans now. Her feet, nails manicured bright pink, were bare. She was sitting on the bed, her eyes fixed on the open closet. The forensics team had cleaned up most of the blood and were coming back tomorrow to do the rest of the crime scene cleanup.

But there was still a wide stain of red that had already started to turn brown.

There were smudged footprints everywhere and a piece of yellow police tape was still attached to one side of the closet door. Sam watched as it blew back and forth in the slight breeze that was coming in from the window that Beth had opened to try and air out the room.

She was deathly still; her face serious and strangely absent. She had put on a wheat-colored pullover sweater and it emphasized the stark white of her face.

“Beth. What’s happening? Talk to me, sweetheart.”

Sam didn’t know where that word came from. He’d never called Miranda ‘sweetheart’ It hadn’t fit her at all. But Beth…this was different.

Beth pointed, her finger trembling a little.

“He was lying right over there. There was this tiny hole in his head. It was probably really big on the other side of his head but I didn’t see that. And he bled all over my shoes.”

She looked up at Sam, her gaze serious.

“It’s more important to find out what happened to him than I thought. He died in my house, Sam. I’m going to find out what happened. It’s like that Chinese saying about what happens if you save someone’s life. You know the one?”

Sam’s voice was gentle. “If you save someone’s life, they belong to you?”

She nodded her head. “If you get killed in my house it’s my mystery to solve. I owe it to that man to find out who killed him. If the police do that, then I’m happy. If they don’t….”

Sam felt chilled. She wasn’t kidding He looked at her silvery, blonde hair and the way it framed her heart-shaped face. She reminded him of a dandelion puff. But there was steel inside.

Something made him fear for the murderer. He put a hand on either side of her face and turned it so that she was looking right at him.

"…If they don't, I feel sorry for the person who did this. But Beth…let me work with the police. I've got some Scotland Yard friends I'll call in. We'll all take this on. It's too dangerous for you to start looking on your own. Promise?"

Her mouth lifted in a part-grin that had him watchful and worried.

"Maybe."

***

Beth wondered why she'd never noticed before, that in spite of the goofy, endearing grin and the on and off girlfriend and the laughter, Sam had always steadily been there.

But she had never been ready.

Maybe now she was.

ABOUT THE AUTHOR

Laurel Gurnsey has always been curious about life…soaking up adventures like swimming with sharks in Bora Bora, riding camels in the Australian Outback, racing around the track at Le Mans in a vintage Lagonda, or sharing her passion for traveling, history, and the environment with her students during her teaching career.

Her romantic suspense novels are enriched by those adventures and they often add personal experiences to the 75+ historical/social articles she has written for the Classic Car Club of America (Pacific Northwest Region) magazine.

Laurel and her husband, Colin, live in British Columbia, Canada with their Sheltie, Keira and have been on the organizing committees of several major events.

Laurel would love to hear from readers. Contact her at:

LaurelG.author7@gmail.com

Also check out her website at **www.laurelgurnsey-author.com**

Manufactured by Amazon.ca
Bolton, ON